THE NICOMACHEAN ETHICS

ARISTOTLE (384–322 BC), with Plato one of the two greatest philosophers of antiquity, and in the view of many the greatest philosopher of all time, lived and taught in Athens for most of his career. He began as a pupil of Plato, and for some time acted as tutor to Alexander the Great. He left writings on a prodigious variety of subjects, covering the whole field of knowledge from biology and astronomy to rhetoric and literary criticism, from political theory to the most abstract reaches of philosophy. He wrote two treatises on ethics, called *Eudemian* and *Nicomachean* after their first editors, his pupil Eudemus and his son Nicomachus. *The Nicomachean Ethics* was probably written later, in Aristotle's fifties and sixties, when he was head of the Lyceum, the school he founded in Athens.

SIR DAVID ROSS (1877–1971) was Provost of Oriel College and Deputy Professor of Moral Philosophy at Oxford. He was the author of important editions of many of Aristotle's works, and acted as General Editor of the complete Oxford Translation of Aristotle, for which the present translation was first written.

LESLEY BROWN is Centenary Fellow and Tutor at Somerville College, Oxford, and a University Lecturer in the Philosophy Faculty, University of Oxford.

OXFORD WORLD'S CLASSICS

*For over 100 years Oxford World's Classics have brought
readers closer to the world's great literature. Now with over 700
titles—from the 4,000-year-old myths of Mesopotamia to the
twentieth century's greatest novels—the series makes available
lesser-known as well as celebrated writing.*

*The pocket-sized hardbacks of the early years contained
introductions by Virginia Woolf, T. S. Eliot, Graham Greene,
and other literary figures which enriched the experience of reading.
Today the series is recognized for its fine scholarship and
reliability in texts that span world literature, drama and poetry,
religion, philosophy, and politics. Each edition includes perceptive
commentary and essential background information to meet the
changing needs of readers.*

OXFORD WORLD'S CLASSICS

ARISTOTLE

The Nicomachean Ethics

Translated by
DAVID ROSS

Revised with an Introduction and Notes by
LESLEY BROWN

OXFORD
UNIVERSITY PRESS

OXFORD
UNIVERSITY PRESS

Great Clarendon Street, Oxford OX2 6DP

Oxford University Press is a department of the University of Oxford.
It furthers the University's objective of excellence in research, scholarship,
and education by publishing worldwide in

Oxford New York

Auckland Cape Town Dar es Salaam Hong Kong Karachi
Kuala Lumpur Madrid Melbourne Mexico City Nairobi
New Delhi Shanghai Taipei Toronto

With offices in

Argentina Austria Brazil Chile Czech Republic France Greece
Guatemala Hungary Italy Japan Poland Portugal Singapore
South Korea Switzerland Thailand Turkey Ukraine Vietnam

Oxford is a registered trade mark of Oxford University Press
in the UK and in certain other countries

Published in the United States
by Oxford University Press Inc., New York

Editorial material © Lesley Brown 2009

The moral rights of the author have been asserted
Database right Oxford University Press (maker)

First published as a World's Classics paperback 1980
This edition first published as an Oxford World's Classics paperback 2009

British Library Cataloguing in Publication Data
Data available

Library of Congress Cataloging-in-Publication Data
Aristotle.
[Nicomachean Ethics. English]
The Nicomachean Ethics/Aristotle; translated by David Ross; revised with an
introduction and notes by Lesley Brown.
p. cm.
Includes bibliographical references and index.
ISBN 978-0-19-921361-0
1. Ethics. I. Ross, W. D. (William David), 1877–1971. II. Brown, Lesley, 1944–
III. Title. B430.A5R67 2009
171'.3—dc22
2009005379

Typeset by Cepha Imaging Private Ltd., Bangalore, India
Printed in Great Britain
on acid-free paper by
Clays Ltd., Elcograf S.p.A.

ISBN 978-0-19-921361-0

20

CONTENTS

CONTENTS

INTRODUCTION

ARISTOTLE was the first Western thinker to divide philosophy into
branches which are still recognizable today: logic, metaphysics, natural philosophy, philosophy of mind, ethics and politics, rhetoric; he
made major contributions in all these fields. He was born in Stagira,
a city of northern Greece, in 384 BC. His father Nicomachus was a
doctor at the court of Amyntas of Macedon, who preceded Philip,
the conqueror of much of Greece. Aristotle later served as tutor to
Philip's remarkable son, Alexander the Great.

As a young man Aristotle went to Athens in 367 to study with Plato
at his Academy, remaining there until Plato's death in 347. This was a
period in which Plato wrote works such as *Timaeus*, *Sophist*, *Statesman*,
and *Philebus*, as well as his *Laws*, and it is intriguing to ask how much
these owe to the challenges from his brilliant pupil Aristotle. After
a period in Asia Minor (where he may have pursued research for
his biological works) and then back in Macedon as tutor, Aristotle
returned to Athens and founded his own philosophical school, the
Lyceum: some of its remains have been recently discovered in modern
Athens. He died in 322 BC, a year after he had to leave Athens in the
wake of the death of his former pupil, the emperor Alexander.

Apart from a few fragments of more popular works, the writings
that have come down to us are academic treatises, some more, some
less polished. They were not published, in any modern sense, and
Aristotle may have continued to revise them. The breadth and character of the teaching at the Lyceum can be gauged from the surviving
treatises, which cover an immense range, and are always cast in a
questioning, argumentative, and non-dogmatic style. It may be that
the works as they survive are lecture-notes, and this would indeed
account for some of the rougher features. The fact is that we know
little about their original form and purpose, the order in which they
were written or how they were edited.

Three works on ethics have come down under his name: *Nicomachean
Ethics* (*NE*) in ten 'books', *Eudemian Ethics* (*EE*) in eight 'books', and
the so-called *Magna Moralia* or 'great ethics'.[1] The last is probably

---

[1] A short work, also ascribed to Aristotle, called 'On Virtues and Vices' is undoubtedly
by a later author.

not by Aristotle but may be a pupil's record of a lecture course. The titles of the other two are thought to derive from their editors after Aristotle's death: Nicomachus was Aristotle's son, while Eudemus was a pupil. The two works cover many of the same topics, and the relation between them is controversial, with an added puzzle that three books are common to both works: Books V–VII of the *NE* correspond to Books IV–VI of the *EE*. The more common scholarly opinion is that the *Nicomachean Ethics* is the later work, and it has been regarded as Aristotle's major and definitive work on ethics at least since the first or second century AD.[2] Some parts are more polished than others, and in one of the common books (Book V, on justice) some material seems out of place. Aristotle's writing has a certain terse elegance, and it is ideally suited to the presentation of arguments, in which his philosophy abounds. The work opens with a discussion of happiness, then moves to the moral virtues—the virtues of character—including justice; and to the virtues of the intellect; it discusses pleasure and friendship and its role in the best life, returning to a further discussion of happiness, then a final transition to political theory. Aristotle regards ethics as a branch of politics, and his work *Politics* was designed as a sequel.

Plato, and his teacher Socrates, set the scene for much of Aristotle's philosophizing. Condemned to death in 399 BC, Socrates left no written philosophy and we have to discern his views from Plato's dialogues, as well as from works by Xenophon. Aristotle, who first studied with Plato some forty years after the death of Socrates, credits Socrates with exclusive interest in ethical questions, and attributes some key theses to him: that all the virtues are kinds of knowledge (VI. 13) and that no one acts contrary to what they know (or judge) to be best (VII. 2). The ethical questions discussed by Socrates, and by Plato after him, concern how one should live; what the virtues are, whether they can be taught, and most of all, why they are worth choosing. 'The unexamined life is not worth living,' declares Socrates in his *Apology*—the speech Plato wrote purporting to be his defence at his trial. In it Socrates describes his lifestyle of questioning so-called experts to see if they can defend their beliefs.

Much of Aristotle's philosophy is a reflection on and a response to writings by his predecessors, and he is keen to distance himself from

[2] Anthony Kenny discusses the issues in *The Aristotelian Ethics* (Oxford 1978), and *Aristotle on the Perfect Life* (Oxford 1992).

their views on metaphysics, natural philosophy, and philosophy of mind. But on the major ethical questions, Socrates, Plato, and Aristotle are in agreement—though Aristotle never admits this in so many words. All three agree that the highest good for human beings is happiness, and that a rational choice of life will be one directed to one's own happiness. Only a life in which one cultivates the traditional virtues (justice, temperance, courage, and practical wisdom) will be a happy life. Plato's dialogues had featured Socrates facing some immoralist challenges to the traditional virtues,[3] but treatment of sceptical attacks on morality is largely absent from Aristotle's work. His major contributions include an in-depth study of what happiness is, of how the virtues relate to happiness, and of what the different types of virtue—moral and intellectual—are. He questions the prominence Socrates gives to knowledge in the account of moral virtue, but his own considered view gives a key role in moral virtue to *phronēsis*, practical wisdom, and he agrees with Socrates in holding that the moral virtues are essentially united (VI.13). Aristotle challenges his teacher Plato in a famous chapter discussing Plato's Form of the Good (I.6), while admitting that 'the inquiry is an uphill one, since the Forms have been admitted by friends of our own'. Insisting that different subjects of inquiry have different starting points and require different kinds of approach, Aristotle dismisses a so-called universal good, or 'Form' or 'Idea' of good, introduced in Plato's *Republic* as the foundation of the goodness and even of the being of all else. He regards it both as an impossible concept and as anyway irrelevant to ethics, which is a study of the *human* good.

Plato, as well as other predecessors, had explored at length the relation of pleasure to goodness. In one dialogue, *Protagoras*, Plato depicts Socrates defending hedonism, the thesis that pleasure is the good, against the more conventional morality of Protagoras. Aristotle's contribution to the debate was to go much deeper into the question of how we should think of pleasure, and what it is, as well as asking how it is related to the good.[4] On the question of the place of pleasure in the good life his answer is similar to Plato's in *Republic* and *Philebus*: while pleasure is not the good, the best life will necessarily

---

[3] From Callicles in *Gorgias*, and from Thrasymachus in *Republic* I, discussed below.

[4] Two treatments of pleasure are found in *NE*, one in VII and one in X. As mentioned above, Book VII is one of the books common to *NE* and *EE*. There are good reasons for thinking that the 'common books' were written originally for the *EE*; this would partly explain the presence in *NE* of two, not fully consistent, discussions of pleasure.

also be the most pleasant, involving those pleasures suited to our nature as rational beings. Similarly Aristotle probes in great depth other concepts central to ethics such as voluntariness, choice, deliberation, and practical reasoning; some of these are discussed in more detail below.

Aristotle's Ethical Theory: Its Key Elements

The Human Good: Happiness

For Aristotle, ethics is the inquiry into the human good. What is the highest of all goods attainable by action? Among everyone—educated and lowly, healthy and sick—(he writes) there is verbal agreement: it is happiness, *eudaimonia* (I.4). And they all equate this with doing well or faring well. But what happiness is is a matter of long-standing dispute, we learn, with three 'lives' in contention: those of sensual enjoyment, of political achievement, and of intellectual contemplation (I.5). Aristotle adds, but swiftly dismisses, a fourth contender for the best life: the pursuit of wealth. To dismiss it he need only point out that wealth is sought *for something else*. The highest good must be wanted *for itself*; it must consist in *activity* (rather than some *state* a person is in) and must be self-sufficient and lacking in nothing. All this offers confirmation that happiness, which satisfies these conditions, is indeed the highest good. But to get a more informative answer, he invokes the idea that human beings have a function—rational activity—and concludes that happiness is excellent rational activity: in his words, *rational activity in accordance with virtue* (I.7). 'Function' translates *ergon*, literally 'task' or 'work'. We return below to the 'function argument', and to excellence and virtue.

Already we have found much to surprise a modern reader. Why should ethics be the study of happiness, and not—perhaps—of what I owe to others, or of the criterion of right action? We return to this question below. Defining happiness as outstanding rational activity may seem puzzling to those who assume happiness is a mental state, a state of subjective well-being. To ease the problem, some have suggested that *eudaimonia* should instead be translated 'flourishing' or 'fulfilment'. Clearly by 'happiness' Aristotle is not speaking of any kind of mental state, still less of one where subjects' self-reports are invited and treated as definitive.

In his investigation of happiness, i.e. of the best life for human beings, Aristotle makes various assumptions. The answer will not vary according to an individual's preferences; and people's assessment of their own happiness may be incorrect. Happiness is not to be equated with pleasure, but, for all that, he will (in Book X) solve the ancient question of the relation between pleasure and the highest good by finding that the truly happy life will indeed be the most pleasant, even though the source of its being the highest good is not its pleasantness. Happiness is available only to those whose age, gender, and civic status allow them to pursue a life of the excellent activities that make it up. Children can be called happy only in the sense that their lives promise happiness; the life of slaves precludes happiness, and so—we may perhaps infer—does that of women, though this is left unsaid. Most striking of all, perhaps, is his use of the famous 'function argument'.

Happiness and Human Function: Rational Activity

The 'function argument' is used to find the human good via the human function (I.7). It gets off to a bad start, with examples of function-bearers—flute-players, eyes, hands, or feet—that seem irrelevant. Flute-players are, by their very title, persons whose role it is to play the flute, and nothing seems to follow about a role for human beings, as such. And though we can readily agree that the eye's function is to see, this is because that's the role it plays *in the whole organism*. These parallels will not convince us that human beings have a function. Rather, Aristotle is drawing on a key assumption from his philosophy of nature. There is a way human beings ought to be and ought to live. This is not because god created them for a purpose—something Aristotle did not hold—but simply because they are a certain kind of living being, and every living species has its own work or function. Human beings have many capacities—Aristotle calls them capacities of soul, but by soul he just means that in virtue of which a thing is alive. Some are shared with lower animals; reason is the capacity that sets man apart. So, since the function of a kind of being is what is special, not what is shared, reason is the key to the best human life.

Before investigating rational capacities further, let's pause for some objections. First, why infer what it's *best* that men should do from what they alone *can* do? There are plenty of things only humans, with their rational capacities, can do. Take cheating at cards, devising weapons of mass destruction, or grooming children for sex-abuse: we don't want to make these part of the best human life. Or again, why exclude from the best life any activities we share with other animals, such as rearing offspring? (This we can answer easily, by recognizing that doing so *using reason* may count as different from merely doing so as an animal does.) Most seriously of all, why insist on a function of human beings *in general*? Surely what is special about human beings is that individuals differ so markedly in their abilities, preferences, and goals.

Some raise a different objection: why should the *good for* a human being consist in doing what a *good person* typically does? They charge Aristotle with conflating the good in the sense of the beneficial (i.e. what's good for humans), with a different, perhaps moral good (i.e. what a good person does), when he declares that the good for an F (a flute-player, a human being) will be what the good F does. But this isn't a real difficulty. In searching for the human good, Aristotle is searching for the good as far as human beings are concerned, not for something *good for* human beings, in the way in which food and water are good for them. And when he speaks of a good human being, he hasn't illicitly smuggled in the notion of a morally good person. A good person, so far, is just a good specimen of a human being, akin to a good oak tree or a good elephant. But then what about moral goodness and the virtues: how do they get into the picture?

Excellent Rational Activity and the Virtues

So far an immoralist such as Thrasymachus in Plato's *Republic* could agree with Aristotle's definition of happiness as a life of rational activity in accordance with excellence or virtue (*aretē*). Thrasymachus, in praising a life of injustice, i.e. of exploiting and getting the better of others, called it a virtue and praised it as rational and sensible. So the key questions are: what are reason and rationality, and what counts as exercising them in a way that manifests excellence or virtue? Here we encounter a problem for translation. *Aretē*, usually translated virtue, means excellence of any kind, and can be applied to pruning-hooks as well as to persons. As just noted, Plato's character Thrasymachus can deny justice is a virtue, simply because he does not regard it as an excellent quality to possess. So how does Aristotle justify his selection of virtues—of excellent rational activities?

Reason, as we learn in I.13, features in different ways in the human soul. (When he speaks of the soul, as we saw, Aristotle means simply the capacities of a living thing in so far as it is alive.) One soul-part, the intellect, has reason in the full sense, but the part that has appetites is rational in a secondary way. That is, the appetites are *responsive to reason*, though they are not themselves rational. We may label them semi-rational, though Aristotle doesn't put it this way. As there are two soul-parts, rational in their different ways, so there are two kinds of virtue, the virtues of character—whose locus is the appetites, and virtues of intellect. The moral virtues, or virtues of character, will have the lion's share of the discussion (II–V), while VI discusses those of the intellect, among them the vital link with the moral virtues, practical wisdom. In the account of virtues of character, we find that the traditional virtues of courage, temperance, and justice have soon entered the discussion, although—as we saw—the notion of a morally good person was not already implicit in the definition of happiness. What we look for in vain is an argument that to exercise one's rationality in the best possible way, 'in accordance with excellence', is to have and exercise the traditional moral virtues. Perhaps Aristotle held that such a proof was not possible; and since his audience were to be well-brought-up young men (but not too young!), it wasn't necessary either.

What, in Aristotle's account, is valuable about the virtues, whether they be the virtues of the intellect or the moral virtues, whether self-regarding ones such as temperance, or other-regarding ones such as justice? In his system, what makes them virtues is simply that, by having and exercising them, one is living a life that is the best life for a human being. They contribute intrinsically to a person's *eudaimonia*. (He allows that certain external goods are necessary conditions for *eudaimonia* also, attacking a view—perhaps he took it to be Plato's—that virtue is sufficient.) Contrast this with a consequentialist view whereby human virtues are valuable for *the results* they bring about, for society or one's neighbours or even oneself. I return to this contrast below.

How Moral Virtues are Acquired and How they 'Lie in a Mean'

Aristotle insists that habituation, not teaching, is the route to moral virtue (II.1). We must *practise doing* good actions, not just read about virtue. Though importantly true, this oversimplifies, and soon it becomes clear that reason too has a role. While the moral virtues are the excellences of the semi-rational soul part containing appetites (including emotions), to be virtues proper, responsiveness to reason is required. In tandem with responsiveness to reason, a virtuous person comes to enjoy doing good actions (II.3), and develops the right feelings (of fear, anger, etc.).

Now we come to Aristotle's famous doctrine that moral virtue is a sort of mean. To have a moral virtue is to be disposed to feel and act 'in an intermediate way'; virtues are 'mean' or 'intermediate' states. We should not think of this as a doctrine of 'moderation in everything'. Rather, it requires having feelings (e.g. of anger) and responses that are 'intermediate' in the sense of *appropriate* or proportional. Although Aristotle characterizes this as avoiding excess and defect, too much and too little, in truth that idea is somewhat misleading, because not every way of going wrong involves too much or too little. More helpful is the characterization of the intermediate as what is *best*, and as doing and feeling 'at the right times, with reference to the right objects, towards the right people, with the right motive, and in the right way' (II.6). His eventual definition of a moral virtue is that it is 'a state of character concerned with choice, lying in a mean, i.e. the mean relative to us, this being determined by reason, and by that reason by which the man of practical wisdom would determine it (II.6)'. So far he has outlined the roles of feelings and actions, and identified moral virtue as an acquired state of character disposing us to feel and to choose to act appropriately. As the last clause of the definition reveals, this leaves a gap in his account, to be filled once he comes to discuss the virtues of intellect, of which practical wisdom (*phronēsis*) is one of the most prominent.

Virtue Proper and Continence

Imagine two soldiers. One is reasonably fearless without being a dare-devil, has developed a proper sense of what dangers ought to be faced, and is able to face them feeling just the appropriate degree of fear. His comrade-in-arms is different; plagued by terrors he nonetheless manages to hold his post and play the part in battle he knows is expected of him. The first, but not the second, soldier is to be credited with the moral virtue of courage, according to Aristotle. Or again, imagine three citizens, with access to the pleasures a city can offer: good food and wine, opportunities for sex. Citizen A desires and enjoys these in the appropriate measures, with due reflection but without any feeling of conflict. B indulges to no greater an extent than A, but often has to rein in his over-strong appetites for physical pleasures, while C is aware that he should do so, but at times succumbs and indulges more than he knows he should. Of these, A has the virtue of temperance, while B is merely 'continent' or self-controlled (*enkratēs*), and C is 'incontinent', in other words lacking in self-control though not yet vicious, since he realizes he shouldn't indulge in the ways he does. Aristotle's verdict, that A and not B is the morally virtuous one, has seemed perverse, and indeed shocking, to an ethical outlook deriving from Christianity that values overcoming temptation. But we must recall that moral virtue, i.e. excellence of character, is the best state of character a person can possess. If, by wishing, you could bring it about that your godson becomes one of these, you would surely wish him to be the first, not the second soldier, and again, like A, to be free of unruly or over-powerful appetites, rather than the one who has to curb them. We find no extended discussion of continence, but its opposite—incontinence—receives lengthy discussion, because of the apparent problem it poses in Aristotle's moral psychology (discussed below).

The Virtues of Intellect and Practical Wisdom

The account of happiness requires a discussion (Book VI) of the virtues of intellect, for two reasons. First, as virtues, they are needed for the best life: to be happy one must employ these virtues in thinking and reasoning. Second, as we saw, the definition of moral virtue contained an essential reference to reason, namely, the reason the *phronimos* (the person of practical wisdom) uses to determine what the virtuous act is in any given instance. (For brevity, I use henceforth the Greek term, the *phronimos*.) So we need in particular a discussion of *phronēsis*, practical wisdom.

Highlighting the distinction between theoretical and practical thinking, Aristotle aligns it (VI.1) with a distinction between necessary truths, such as those of mathematics, and contingent truths such as whether there will be a sea-battle tomorrow. On the theoretical side he finds two virtues, scientific knowledge and intuitive reason, which together constitute wisdom (*sophia*) (VI.7). Since scientific knowledge requires proof, and any proof has to start from unproven assumptions, intuitive reason (*nous*) is needed as the grasp of these starting points for the deductive reasoning he takes scientific knowledge to require. On the practical side (dealing with matters that can be otherwise, hence are suitable for deliberation) he draws an important distinction between 'making'—the province of art (i.e. expertise in producing some outcome)—and 'doing', where no outcome beyond the doing itself is aimed at (VI.5). Practical wisdom (*phronēsis*) is the intellectual virtue concerned with doing.

The complex discussion reveals some tensions in his account: does the *phronimos* need general principles, or is it enough to be right in particular cases? To what extent does he deliberate and reason, or is *phronēsis* more a matter of 'seeing' the salient features in any situation calling for action? The latter is certainly a key feature of *phronēsis*. In the last two chapters of VI further important points are made, reinforcing the close connection between *phronēsis* and moral virtue. 'Virtue makes the goal correct and practical wisdom makes what leads to it correct': at first sight this suggests there is a problematic division of labour, and that the role of practical wisdom is nothing more than means–end reasoning. But this cannot be the full picture Aristotle wishes to paint. For, unless reason guides someone's emotional development, they will not possess moral virtue in the first place. By the end of Book VI, we find that the initial division of virtues into the moral and the intellectual was somewhat misleading. *Phronēsis*, though it is an intellectual virtue, cannot develop independently of the moral virtues, while they in turn, though virtues of the non-rational (or, as we called it, semi-rational) part of a person, can only reach their perfection under the guidance of reason.[5]

The Final Account of Happiness: Contemplation

Returning, in Book X, to the initial question, Aristotle writes: 'If happiness is activity in accordance with virtue, it is reasonable that it should be in accordance with the highest virtue; and this will be that of the best thing in us.' As he goes on to argue, the best thing in us is one aspect of reason, not reason in general. It is the aspect that studies unchanging objects and necessary truths; the highest activity is contemplation, and its virtue is wisdom (*sophia*), in that special

[5] An excellent treatment of many issues arising from Book VI may be found in C. C. W. Taylor, 'Aristotle's Epistemology', in S. Everson (ed.), *Companions to Ancient Thought*, i. *Epistemology* (Cambridge 1990).

sense confining it to excellence in *theoretical*, i.e. philosophical, thinking. Invoking once again the criteria he laid down in I.7 for the best good, he tries to show that the contemplative life is most end-like and most self-sufficient, and surpasses the life of moral virtue in both those respects (and others). Does this betoken a change of emphasis, or did Aristotle even in Book I lay the ground for his eventual declaration that the contemplative life is happiest, with the life of moral virtue only happiest in a secondary way?

This is a matter of intense scholarly dispute, and hard to resolve. One school of interpretation finds Aristotle firmly advocating an *inclusive* account of happiness in I.7, such that the best life will include the best *combination* of those goods we desire for themselves. Only thus can it 'not be made more desirable by the addition' of other goods. But, if Aristotle favoured such an inclusive account in Book I, this seems to clash with selecting just *one* kind of activity, contemplation, as best, and relegating the practice of moral virtue (with its consort, *practical* wisdom) to second place. The other line of interpretation notes that, alongside indications that happiness is an inclusive end, Book I already hinted that happiness would be identified with *the best of* the best activities (1099a30). Nonetheless, most of the work has focused on the moral virtues and on related issues in the philosophy of action, such as voluntariness, choice, and deliberation. That being so, the reader is likely to find surprising the final paean to the life of contemplation (X.7 and 8), and the downplaying of the value of morally virtuous action.

Aristotle's focus on practical matters, however, returns in the final chapter. True to his initial statement that ethics is a branch of politics, he asks how morally good behaviour, and the dispositions (the moral virtues) that prompt it, can best be developed. Besides the ordinary upbringing by parents, good laws are essential for a number of reasons. Laws ordain certain aspects of child-rearing; they set standards for good behaviour, and people respond better when laws, rather than despots, seek to impose standards. So a full study of ethics will need to include the discussions of law and of the best type of constitution that he will proceed to give in his *Politics*.

Aristotle's Ethics and Alternative Approaches

Those who read Aristotle and are familiar with some other important approaches in ethics are bound to ask how the theories compare.

Some even claim that Aristotle isn't really discussing *morality* as we now understand it at all. I touch briefly on two more recent, and famous, ethical theories, and then look at a newer approach, so-called neo-Aristotelian Virtue Theory.

Kant

Kant's moral theory is adumbrated in *The Groundwork of the Metaphysic of Morals*. (A later work, the *Metaphysic of Morals*, develops and in some ways mitigates the positions taken up in the *Groundwork*.) Its key tenets include the idea that 'good will' is the only unconditionally good thing and that to have moral worth actions must be done from the motive of duty. Emotions, feelings, and inclinations, even benevolent ones, contribute nothing to the moral worth of an action. Neither actual nor intended consequences can give an action any moral worth, but only its being done for the sake of duty. Famously he writes: 'I ought never to act except in such a way that I can also will that my maxim should become a universal law.' In a different formulation, he insists that one must always treat humanity never solely as means but always also an end in itself.

Even from this very brief sketch some seemingly sharp contrasts with Aristotle's theory are evident. For Kant 'good will' is the unconditionally good thing, for Aristotle happiness. While Aristotle assumes that one's own happiness is the end it is rational to aim at, and is what the *phronimos* is concerned with, Kant goes so far as to deny that one's own happiness should be any proper concern of what he calls 'pure practical reason'. This is no doubt in part because Kant differed from Aristotle in his understanding of happiness. For Aristotle the virtuous man is one who enjoys his good actions and who has the appropriate feelings as well as acting correctly. By contrast, Kant—in effect—accords moral worth to the person Aristotle calls merely 'continent', since what matters (on Kant's account) is whether the agent is motivated by duty, not what their feelings are. Kant cannot allow that moral worth could depend in any way on non-rational appetites or inclinations. And though both thinkers lay important stress on the role of reason in the ethical life, it takes a rather different form in each. Universality is the hallmark of the morality of a maxim for Kant. Aristotle, however, in his account of practical wisdom, lays more emphasis on the particularity of the circumstances, and the need for the *phronimos* to 'see' the ethically salient features in each case.

Consequentialism

Consequentialist theories, of which utilitarianism is the most famous version, take a very different form. Jeremy Bentham and J. S. Mill—a close reader of Aristotle—are the most famous advocates of utilitarianism. As we saw, Kant's theory emphasized the motive of duty and denied any role to consequences—for this reason it is classed as a deontological theory. Consequentialism, as its name suggests, regards the consequences of actions as the only feature relevant to their rightness. For utilitarianism, what makes an action right is that it is the one (of all those available to an agent) that maximizes the general happiness. In so far as it holds that happiness is the sole intrinsically valuable thing, it seems closer to Aristotle's theory. But there are at least two major differences in this regard. First, Mill equates happiness with a mental state, pleasure (though admitting quality as well as quantity in the evaluation of pleasure). More important still, utilitarianism insists that it is the happiness of all—including sentient non-humans—and not just the agent's happiness, that is the criterion of right action. Mill writes, 'between his own happiness and that of others utilitarianism requires him to be as strictly impartial as a disinterested and benevolent spectator' (*Utilitarianism*, ch. 2). And while a consequentialist theory does value many of the virtues and encourage their cultivation, it regards them as only *instrumentally* valuable. That is, they are valuable for the consequences they help bring about, since the virtues are propensities to do right actions, i.e. ones that maximize the general happiness.

Despite their enormous differences, Kantian and consequentialist ethical theories share some features. Both are primarily concerned with what makes actions right (or, in Kant's terms, what gives actions moral worth). Both seem to require impartiality, a certain disinterestedness, and a detachment from one's own concerns. That is not to say that for these theories morality is simply a matter of one's relations to others: Kant holds that one has duties to oneself, and, in consequentialism, the agent's own happiness is no less, but also no more, important than that of anyone else. But both theories lay an emphasis on disinterestedness and impartiality that contrasts sharply with what we might call the agent-centred approach of Aristotle. While his theory is by no means narrowly egoistic, it is certainly ego-centred.

Neo-Aristotelian Virtue Theories

Since the mid-twentieth century several writers have attempted to forge theories that avoid some of the perceived objectionable features of both the Kantian and consequentialist approaches, and in doing so have appealed to what they take to be essentially Aristotelian themes.[6] There are two ways to approach this task, both of which make the notion of the best kind of human life prominent. One approach is to abandon the idea that an ethical theory has to offer its own criterion of right action. It should stress instead the questions of what sort of person one should be, and how one should live, taking into account human nature and perhaps the nature of the community in which one lives. A second way[7] is to develop a theory that (like the first) gives a central role to human flourishing and the virtues, but that also claims to offer a criterion of right action, of a very different kind from that offered by each of the rivals discussed above.

Central tenets of this second version of 'Virtue Ethics' are: (1) What makes a virtuous action virtuous is that it is what a virtuous agent would do in the relevant circumstances; (2) A virtuous agent is one who possesses the virtues; (3) Virtues are those character-traits that enable a human being to flourish, i.e. to live the best life. Now the Aristotelian provenance of (2) and (3) are clear, and (3) is a highly controversial claim, in so far as it assumes that the virtues necessarily benefit the person who possesses them. Not that they do so in the way medicine benefits a sick person—because being healthy can be attained without medicine, while, on the theory in question, flourishing (*eudaimonia*) without the virtues is not possible; they are intrinsically, not instrumentally beneficial to the possessor. But should we credit Aristotle with (1) also?

The answer 'yes' may be suggested by a remark in II.4: 'Actions, then, are called just and temperate when they are such as the just or the temperate man would do.' But arguably the point of this remark is different, as the context indicates. The purpose of this chapter is to establish Aristotle's claim that you can do a just act without yet being a just person; he needs that for his important view that we

---

[6] The revival of interest in the virtues is often credited to G. E. M. Anscombe's article 'Modern Moral Philosophy', in *Philosophy* (1958), repr. in R. Crisp and M. Slote (eds.), *Virtue Ethics* (Oxford 1990). See also Philippa Foot, *Natural Goodness*, and A. MacIntyre, *After Virtue*.

[7] Taken by R. Hursthouse, *On Virtue Ethics* (Oxford 1999).

become just by doing just acts. In the above quotation he may simply be driving the point home, as indeed the sequel to that quotation suggests. If he is not committed to (1) above, and if that is thought to be a key tenet for Virtue Ethics[8]—the so-called explanatory priority of the virtues over right or virtuous actions—then to that extent modern Virtue Ethics goes beyond what Aristotle intended.

But if we deny that Aristotle held (1), then the question arises again: what, for Aristotle, makes a given action a just or a temperate action? We have already seen that his theory of the moral virtues makes essential appeal to the idea that a virtuous action is one where an agent feels and does what is appropriate ('intermediate' or 'mean') in a given situation. But, as Aristotle himself acknowledges (VI.1), this is no more helpful than saying to someone who wants to be healthy, 'do what medical science would prescribe'. Another important claim Aristotle often makes is that a virtuous person chooses certain actions 'because of the noble' (*kalon*). Again, this hardly clarifies matters. What is it to act 'for the sake of the noble'? Must an agent act *from the thought that* his action is noble? (Probably not, but at least the man with the virtue of 'pride' will do so, IV.3.) And what characteristics of a way of acting qualify it as noble? There are no clear answers to these questions in our text, and no systematic discussion of 'the noble'.

But Aristotle would, I think, simply reject outright the demand for a criterion of right action. He expects a well-brought-up person to have a pretty good idea of what features and considerations are relevant to acting well in any given situation, and these considerations will be of many and various kinds. What consequences the action has, especially for the common good, will be one factor; the relationship in which the agent stands to the other parties involved will also be crucial. For the so-called self-regarding virtues, such as temperance, he will take it to be obvious that some kinds of indulgence simply are not appropriate to a good human life, not just because of their effect in impairing one's activities, but also in themselves. In some cases, particularly justice, he is able to say much more about what makes an action just, but in that respect, as he admits himself (V.5), justice is somewhat different from the other virtues. We return to justice and friendship below, after a discussion of Aristotle's method of ethical theorizing.

[8] As Hursthouse suggests, ibid. 39.

Aristotle's Method and Meta-ethical Assumptions

Method

Early in the work (I.3) Aristotle says a little of his method: he will examine those of the many opinions that are the most prevalent, and are arguable, i.e. plausible. In a famous passage introducing his discussion of incontinence and related 'affections' (VII.1) he writes:

We must, as in all other cases, set the apparent facts before us and, after first discussing the difficulties, go on to prove, if possible, the truth of all the common opinions about these affections of the mind, or, failing this, of the greater number and the most authoritative; for if we both resolve the difficulties and leave the common opinions undisturbed, we shall have proved the case sufficiently.

But this important feature of his method—its dialectical character—raises a lot of questions. We know that he tries to *explain* common opinions and why they conflict, if they do. But what kind of theory does that leave? Is it just common sense morality regimented and rendered consistent? Might not a hard look at everyday moral opinions serve to undermine them—in the manner of the immoralist critiques offered by some of Plato's main speakers such as Thrasymachus? Aristotle never seems to envisage that as an outcome to his dialectical inquiry. In any case, he has more tools at his disposal than simply common opinions, important though these are. He will also draw on some theses from his other philosophical works. We have already discussed his appeal to human nature and human function (I.7). Prominent also is the thesis that activity or actuality is superior to potentiality or capacity: that explains why happiness (an activity) cannot be virtue (a state, i.e. a kind of potentiality). Views about the parts of the soul (I.13 and VI.1) and the nature of the gods (X.7 and 8) are important too.

Meta-ethical Assumptions

Despite according a lot of weight to common opinions, Aristotle is not at all tempted to adopt a relativist or subjectivist view of ethics. That is, he neither holds that right and wrong can only be relative to a given society, nor that right and wrong are simply a matter of what someone or some group believes to be so.

He had come across views such as these, and alludes to them early on (I.3):

'Now noble and just actions, which political science investigates, exhibit much variety and fluctuation, so that they may be thought to exist only by convention, and not by nature.'

Some thinkers did indeed draw the conclusion that the just and the noble (*kalon*) exist only by convention. The variety and fluctuation he has in mind is twofold: the variety of views about what is just, and the fact that what is just fluctuates according to circumstance. These facts explain why some have concluded that all morality is a matter of convention (*nomos*), i.e. is a matter of what people believe, or have enshrined in law, and that nothing is right or wrong 'by nature'. In V.7 he returns to the subject, this time discussing the question whether justice is simply a matter of *nomos*, law or convention, or whether some things are just or unjust by nature. Again he remarks that what prompts the view that all justice is a matter of convention is the recognition of the variability of justice.

In response, Aristotle adopts a position that has a lot of merit, and exposes a mistake that is still commonly found in modern discussions of ethics. To put it in modern terms, he insists on moral objectivity, while denying universality. The view he opposes thinks that, without universally true moral judgements, there are no objectively true moral judgements. And this, he rightly points out, is an error. Judgements about right or wrong, just or unjust, may be objectively true or false; their truth is more than a matter of someone's believing them to be true. It does not follow, he insists, that ethical truths must take the form 'it is always unjust to withhold payment of a debt' or 'you should always defer to the authority of your father'. Even if these are usually correct, there may be exceptions, which the *phronimos*, the person with trained moral understanding, will recognize. You don't have to insist that X-ing is always or universally wrong, to hold that it is objectively true that X-ing on this occasion would be wrong. The point is developed in his discussion (V.10) of equity. This virtue involves recognizing where legal justice needs modifying to suit the particular case.

What the basis of these objective moral truths is is a difficult matter, and, as we saw above, not one Aristotle gives a clear answer to. In this he fares no worse—arguably—than any other moral philosopher. But nailing the mistake just described was a signal achievement.[9]

[9] See R. Heinaman (ed.), *Aristotle and Moral Realism* (London 1995), for a series of essays discussing these issues.

Other-Regarding and Self-Regarding Concerns

As we have seen, Aristotle holds that it is rational to make my own happiness the end at which I aim. His ethics is the study of what happiness is and how it is to be achieved, and his account of the virtues assumes that the virtues—both moral and intellectual—are, essentially, states that benefit their possessor. Does this not miss the point of morality, some will ask? What room does he leave for concern for others, for the need to recognize the claims they have on me, and, at times, to give them priority over myself and my own happiness?

While a full answer to these questions cannot be given in this brief introduction, consideration of two so-far undiscussed topics will help: justice and friendship.

Justice (Book V)

'Justice is another's good' declared Thrasymachus (Plato, *Republic* 1), and so he declares it to be not worth having. Aristotle agrees with the first, but still holds it to be a virtue. As a virtue it must be good for the agent as well as for others, though Aristotle does not spell out how this is so. Instead, he draws some important distinctions, some of which have dominated accounts of justice ever since. First he distinguishes what he calls 'universal' justice and injustice from 'particular' justice and injustice. Universal justice, he says, is the whole of virtue in its other-regarding aspect. Particular justice is one specific kind of virtue, which in turn has important subdivisions.

'The whole of virtue in its other-regarding aspect' is an interesting concept, suggesting that in some way all branches of moral virtue, even those we think of as self-regarding, such as temperance, involve our relations to others. But Aristotle does not develop this intriguing idea further. Instead he goes into 'particular justice', distinguishing distributive—the variety that deals with the fair distribution of goods and burdens—from what he calls rectificatory justice. In the first he makes the crucial observation that sharing goods fairly means taking into account the relevant merits of the parties concerned, and sharing out the goods in proportion to those merits. But he doesn't attempt to discuss what is the *right* basis to take account of. As such he gives a formal but not a substantive account of fair distribution. As for the second—rectificatory justice—instead of discussing just punishment, as we might expect, he focuses on making things right for the victim—hence the label 'rectificatory'. The conceptual distinctions he draws in these chapters (with the 'help' of some mathematical illustrations) are important. But we look in vain for a defence of acting justly, of a kind that would answer the sceptic's worry that acting justly benefits another *and not oneself*.

Friendship

One-fifth of the whole work (Books VIII and IX) is devoted to friendship, a mark of its importance for Aristotle. In these books we find further exploration of the role of other-regarding concerns in ethics. But it takes a very different shape from that found in moralities that stress impartiality. In his account, the people we can consider our friends can extend as widely as fellow citizens but some *relation to the agent* is crucial. (The term 'friends' includes loved ones such as relatives, business associates, and others.) The idea that we might have obligations to others simply as such is completely absent from Aristotle, and from all moralities he would have been familiar with. The best kind of friendship, he maintains, is friendship with those to whom we wish well and with whom we can spend time in shared valuable activities, all *because of their virtue*. Friendships based on pleasure and utility also exist, he allows, but only the first kind is perfect friendship.

On the one hand we may be puzzled by this restriction, and may protest that true friendship can exist between those who are not virtuous people. On the other, we may feel that Aristotle still has too egocentric an approach when he argues that our relation to our friends is in some way derivative from our relation to ourselves (IX.3). In an important chapter on self-love (IX.8) we find him recognizing, and not fully resolving, the tension between his egocentric approach and his correct insistence that in friendship one wishes another good for that other's sake.

In the books on friendship, contrasting aspects of Aristotle's writings are very evident. His more theoretical discussions can seem obscure and strained, for instance his convoluted proof in IX.9 showing why the happy person will need virtuous friends. But at many points, for instance in the chapters (VIII.13–IX.3) discussing specific issues—the casuistry of friendship—and in his insightful remarks about the love of mothers for their children, we find Aristotle displaying a sure touch and a more plausible grasp of the nature and value of friendship.

Aristotle's Moral Psychology

Voluntary and Involuntary

Students of virtue and legislators alike need to know about the basis of voluntariness (III.1). The main outlines Aristotle gives have stood the test of time. Lack of knowledge and lack of power (i.e. being 'forced'), the chief excusing conditions in today's law, are the criteria he identified for an act not being voluntary. He draws an important distinction between force proper and cases where people claim they were compelled, but where external force is not involved. The latter are 'the things that are done from fear of greater evils or for some noble object (e.g. if a tyrant were to order one to do something base, having one's parents and children in his power, and if one did the action they were to be saved, but otherwise would be put to death)': since one *did* them to avoid something worse, the actions are not forced, nor involuntary. Labelling them 'mixed, but more like voluntary' he adds a vital point: even though it's your act, and so not involuntary, it doesn't follow that you should be blamed for doing it. Praise (if you saved the crew by jettisoning the cargo) or pardon (if you did a wrongful act under terrible pressure) may be appropriate.

The discussion of when ignorance makes an act involuntary is complex, but contains an important distinction. The excuse 'I didn't know' is not sufficient to exculpate; what matters is whether the ignorance was your fault or not (III.5). Hence acts done *in* ignorance but *by reason of* drunkenness or anger don't count as involuntary, and are liable to blame. In III.5 Aristotle tries to show (against the sceptics) that we are responsible for our good and bad characters as well as for our good and bad actions. This is the closest he comes to a discussion of the modern problem of the basis of moral responsibility. He puts the sceptics' arguments strongly, and, though he dismisses them, he perhaps concedes something to them when formulating his conclusion: 'we are somehow part-causes of our states of character'.

Choice

What matters in a law-court, and for praise or blame, is whether the act was voluntary. But what matters for questions of virtue and vice is whether your acts are not merely voluntary but also chosen. Choice, *prohairesis*, is an important but also puzzling concept. It is narrower than our everyday notion of choice (and indeed Aristotle also has a concept nearer to that, *hairesis*.) A child cannot manifest choice (in this technical sense), and when I act in anger, or in an incontinent manner, my acts are voluntary—so can be praised or blamed—but are not chosen. Only an adult with a settled and reasoned state of character can make choices, in Aristotle's sense. He discusses choice (III.2–3), and concludes that it is 'deliberate desire of things in our power'. Virtue was defined (II.6) as a state of character concerned with choice, in other words, issuing in choices, and vice is the same (except of course that the choices of the one are good and of the other bad). So, as Aristotle admits (V.9), it's quite hard to be unjust! Plenty of people do virtuous acts without yet being virtuous—for instance all those who are still learning to be virtuous (II.1, 4). Their acts may be praised, even though they cannot yet be credited with possessing a virtue. And plenty of people do bad acts without being vicious; their bad acts are voluntary, and deserve blame, but are not choices. Signal examples of this are incontinent actions.

Incontinence

Can someone know what is best, but act contrary to that knowledge, being overcome by pleasure or pain or anger or some such passion? Yes, say 'the many', i.e. most people; no, counters Socrates in Plato's dialogue *Protagoras*. Socrates' theses that virtue is knowledge and that the person who knows what is best will always do it, are ones Aristotle touches on at several points (VI.13, VII.1–3). Already in II.4 he argued that, to possess virtue, knowing was not as important as reliably choosing, for their own sakes, the virtuous actions. So we expect him to side with the many against Socrates, and accept the common opinion that 'the incontinent man, knowing that what he does is bad, does it as a result of passion' (VII.I). He certainly affirms that incontinent actions are voluntary and blameworthy. But instead of robustly insisting that the incontinent person acts in full knowledge that what he does is bad, he develops a set of distinctions between different ways of knowing, and different parts (premisses) of a piece of practical reasoning. At one point—apparently siding with Socrates—he likens an incontinent person to those asleep, mad, or drunk. This is apparently because, under the influence of the strong passion—say, desire for another drink—the incontinent person's knowledge (say, that this is one too many) is temporarily inaccessible. Does Aristotle at any point allow (with 'the many') that when acting incontinently a person's knowledge and reasoning can be unimpaired? There are very diverse interpretations of this difficult chapter (VII.3), and different answers. One thing is clear: Aristotle is keen to distance himself from any view (of Plato or Socrates) that equates all vice with incontinence or lack of self-control. Unlike the vicious person, the incontinent has the right overall standards and choices, and, to that extent at least, knows that what he is now doing is bad, even if, in some other way, at the very moment of acting, he does not do so in full knowledge.

Concluding Remarks

Can work in ethics have relevance and even truth in all historical periods? Some writers in a broadly Aristotelian tradition—such as A. MacIntyre[10]—disown such an ambition, holding that any conception of the best life and of what the virtues are is necessarily grounded in a given historical period and community. Aristotle shows no such qualms; he seems concerned to present a theory that is more universal in its scope, based on an account of human nature as such. But, two and a half millennia later and in the light of developments in morality and in moral theory, today's readers may be struck, and even appalled, by some of his assumptions and values. Aristotle accepts slavery, and a lowly status for women, without question, though his remarks on women's love for their children are telling and sympathetic. The translation makes no attempt to avoid the frequent use of 'man'—as in 'the truthful man', 'the boastful man', 'the good-tempered man', and so forth. For the virtues and vices described are those of males, and his assumption from the start is that the best life can be lived only by well-born, well-educated male citizens with no need to earn their own living. Only these can develop those virtues (intellectual and/or moral) in whose practice the life of happiness consists.

And in the list of virtues and vices we find some surprising inclusions, and likewise omissions. We have already seen that impartiality was no kind of ideal for Aristotle, though to what extent it should be reckoned a value today is a controversial matter. Likewise the idea that we should try to alleviate suffering and help our fellow men no matter how remote from us is quite foreign to Aristotle and indeed to all at his time. Neither kindness nor cruelty get a mention, despite the proximity Aristotle had had to the ruthless conqueror Alexander.

[10] A. MacIntyre, *After Virtue* (London 1981).

For Aristotle the virtue of truthfulness is a matter of being appropriately open about *your own merits*, not of truth-telling in general. The two grand-scale virtues are perhaps at first sight the most foreign: magnificence—making large-scale public donations appropriately (IV.2), and *megalopsuchia*, literally 'greatness of soul' but here translated as 'pride' (IV.3). The properly proud man is and knows himself to be worthy of great honour. He acts appropriately; he is a man of few deeds but great and noble ones, with a slow step, a deep voice, and a level utterance. But here too modern readers find some admirable features: the proud man overlooks wrongs done to him; speaks his mind freely; maintains his dignity among equals but is unassuming with those of lower social status; does not gossip or harbour grudges.

For many readers the most alien aspect of Aristotle's ethics may be its ultimate elevation (X.7, 8) of the life of philosophical contemplation above any other life, including that of the active citizen who develops and manifests the moral virtues. We have already noted the scholarly dispute over this perhaps surprising development at the end of the work. However, many traditions, both Western and Eastern, accord highest place to a life in which man transcends his more human nature and the need for the human virtues. From a different perspective, we might be surprised that Aristotle never considers, as a candidate for the best life, that of the poet or dramatist, artist or sculptor. The reason, I think, is to be found in a metaphysical assumption: any activity that has an end beyond itself is for that reason less valuable than activities that are ends in themselves. At one blow all forms of creativity are demoted, including, perhaps, Aristotle's own productive investigations into all matters philosophical. Yet, despite his strange claim that those who know pass their time more pleasantly than those who inquire (X.7), we may be thankful for Aristotle's life of inquiry.

NOTE ON THE TEXT AND TRANSLATION

THE translation is that of the noted Aristotle scholar, W. D. Ross. It was first published in 1925 in volume ix of *The Works of Aristotle translated into English* (Oxford University Press). It is based on the Oxford Classical Text of the *Nicomachean Ethics* (ed. Bywater) from which, wrote Ross, he departed only occasionally, where there seemed to be a good deal to be gained by doing so. The translation was revised by J. O. Urmson in 1973, and published in World's Classics in 1980 with further revisions by J. L. Ackrill.

For the present edition a very few further changes have been made. Like the previous revisers, the current editor has left unchanged Ross's translation of the central terminology, with a very few exceptions. For example, *logos*, which Ross usually translated as 'rational principle' or 'rule', I have rendered with 'reason' at almost all points; and I have translated *orthos logos* as 'correct reason'. In III.1 'force' and cognates are now used consistently for *bia*, 'compelled'/'compulsion' for cognates of *anagkē*. I have substituted 'for the sake of the noble' where Ross often had 'for honour's sake' when the Greek uses *kalon*. In V.5 the literal translation 'need' now replaces 'demand' for *chreia*. In a handful of places a now almost obsolete term has been replaced (e.g. 'drink' for 'draught', 'perfume' for 'unguent'). Written over eighty years ago, the translation is still justly admired, and has required little further adjustment.

The numbering system, with references such as 1098b10, is that used by all modern editors, translators, and commentators. The numbers (Bekker numbers) derive from the 1831 Berlin edition of Aristotle's works. The marginal numbers correspond to those of the Greek text; this means that occasionally in the translation the correspondence is not exact. For those using secondary literature, having the Bekker line numbers is nonetheless an invaluable help. Where a passage in the translation is enclosed by square brackets, the corresponding Greek words are regarded by the editor of the Oxford Classical Text as a marginal gloss.

The reference II.4, for example, is to Book II chapter 4. The division into books goes back to antiquity, while that into chapters is more recent. Occasionally the chapter breaks come at an illogical point.

The headings and summaries used, as well as the occasional numbers in the body of the translation, are (apart from a few that I have revised) those introduced by Ross. The footnoted cross-references were also supplied in Ross's original translation. As with the Introduction, the explanatory endnotes are newly written for this edition. They are much fuller than the previous notes, but very occasionally I have quoted *verbatim*, with acknowledgement, Ross's original note. Endnotes are indicated by an asterisk in the text.

I should like to acknowledge my debt to the writings (and also the lectures) of J. L. Ackrill, and to the work of S. Broadie and C. Rowe, and of T. H. Irwin, in their respective translations with notes, as well as the commentary by C. C. W. Taylor on Books II–IV.

The *Nicomachean Ethics* has been the subject of innumerable commentaries since antiquity, not least by St Thomas Aquinas; about one commentary a decade has appeared since the Middle Ages, according to one estimate.[1] All who venture to comment on the work owe a profound debt to the labours of their predecessors.

[1] A. Kenny, *The Aristotelian Ethics* (Oxford 1978), 1.

SELECT BIBLIOGRAPHY

Brief works on Aristotle

Ackrill, J. L., *Aristotle the Philosopher* (Oxford 1981).
Barnes, J., *Aristotle* (Oxford 1982).
Ross, W. D., *Aristotle* (London and New York 1964; 1st pub. 1923).
Shields, C., *Aristotle* (London 2007).

Translations

Broadie, S., and Rowe, C., *Aristotle, Nicomachean Ethics*, trans., introd.,
   and comm. (Oxford 2002) with full bibliography.
Crisp, R., *Aristotle, Nicomachean Ethics* (Cambridge 2000).
Gauthier, R., and Jolif, J., *L'Éthique à Nicomaque*, 4 vols. (Louvain 1970),
   trans. and full comm. in French.
Irwin, T. H., *Aristotle, Nicomachean Ethics*, trans. with introd., notes, and
   full glossary (Indianapolis 1999); cited as Irwin.

Older Commentaries

Aquinas, St Thomas, *In decem libros Ethicorum Aristotelis ad Nicomachum
   Expositio*, ed. R. M. Spiazzi (Turin 1964).
Aspasius (2nd cent. AD), *Aspasii in Ethica Nicomachorum Commentaria*, ed.
   G. Heylbut (Berlin 1889).
Stewart, J. A., *Notes on the Nicomachean Ethics of Aristotle*, 2 vols. (Oxford
   1892, and repr.).

Recent Commentaries

Broadie, S., and Rowe, C., *Aristotle, Nicomachean Ethics*, trans., introd.,
   and comm. (Oxford 2002), with full bibliography.
Gauthier, R., and Jolif, J., *L'Éthique à Nicomaque*, 4 vols. (Louvain 1970),
   trans. and full comm. in French.
Irwin, T. H., *Aristotle, Nicomachean Ethics*, trans. with introd., notes, and
   full glossary (Indianapolis 1999); cited as Irwin.

Commentaries on selected books

Pakaluk, M., *Aristotle: Nicomachean Ethics, Books VIII and IX* (Oxford
   1998) (cited as Pakaluk).
Taylor, C. C. W., *Aristotle: Nicomachean Ethics, Books II–IV* (Oxford
   2006).

Books on the Whole Work

Bostock, D., *Aristotle's Ethics* (Oxford 2000).
Broadie, S., *Ethics With Aristotle* (Oxford 1991): a longer, more advanced discussion.
Hardie, W., *Aristotle's Ethical Theory*, 2nd edn. (Oxford 1980).
Hughes, G. J., *Aristotle on Ethics* (London 2001): introductory work.
Urmson, J., *Aristotle's Ethics* (Oxford 1988): a good basic introduction.

On the relation with the Eudemian Ethics

Kenny, A., *The Aristotelian Ethics* (Oxford 1978).
—— *Aristotle on the Perfect Life* (Oxford 1992).
Rowe, C. J., *The Eudemian and Nicomachean Ethics* (Cambridge 1971).

Collections of Essays

1. Exclusively on Aristotle's ethics

Heinaman, R. (ed.), *Aristotle and Moral Realism* (London 1995).
Kraut, R. (ed.), *The Blackwell Guide to Aristotle's Nicomachean Ethics* (Oxford 2006).
Rorty, A. (ed.), *Essays on Aristotle's Ethics* (Berkeley and Los Angeles 1980).

2. In part on Aristotle's ethics

Ackrill, J. L., *Essays on Plato and Aristotle* (Oxford 1997).
Cooper, J., *Reason and Emotion* (Princeton 1999).
Crisp, R. (ed.), *How Should One Live? Essays on the Virtues* (Oxford 1996).
—— and Slote, M. (eds.), *Virtue Ethics* (Oxford 1990).
Engstrom, S., and Whiting, J. (eds.), *Aristotle, Kant and the Stoics* (Cambridge 1996).

Other books

Annas, J., *The Morality of Happiness* (New York 1993).
Charles, D., *Aristotle's Philosophy of Action* (London 1984).
Davidson, J. N., *The Greeks and Greek Love* (London 2007).
Dover, K. J., *Greek Popular Morality in the time of Plato and Aristotle* (Berkeley 1974).
—— *Greek Homosexuality* (London 1978).
Foot, P. R., *Natural Goodness* (Oxford 2000).
Gosling, J., and Taylor, C., *The Greeks on Pleasure* (Oxford 1982).
Hursthouse, R., *On Virtue Ethics* (Oxford 1999).
Irwin, T. H., *The Development of Ethics* (Oxford 2007), i.
Kraut, R., *Aristotle on the Human Good* (Princeton 1989).
MacIntyre, A., *After Virtue* (London 1981; 3rd edn. 2007).

Nussbaum, M., *The Fragility of Goodness* (Cambridge 1986).

Price, A., *Love and Friendship in Plato and Aristotle* (Oxford 1979).

Selected list of articles

Ackrill, J. L., 'Aristotle on Eudaimonia', in his *Essays on Plato and Aristotle* (Oxford 1997); repr. in A. Rorty (ed.), *Essays on Aristotle's Ethics* (Berkeley and Los Angeles 1980).

—— 'Aristotle on Good and the Categories', in id., *Essays on Plato and Aristotle* (Oxford 1997).

Brown, L., 'What is the "Mean Relative to Us" in Aristotle's Ethics?', in *Phronesis* 42 (1997), 77–93.

Burnyeat, M., 'Aristotle on Learning to be Good', in A. Rorty (ed.), *Essays on Aristotle's Ethics* (Berkeley and Los Angeles 1980).

Cooper, J., 'Aristotle on Friendship', in A. Rorty (ed.), *Essays on Aristotle's Ethics* (Berkeley and Los Angeles 1980).

—— 'Aristotle on the Forms of Friendship', in id. (Princeton 1999).

—— 'Contemplation and Happiness, a Reconsideration', in id. (Princeton 1999).

Davidson, D., 'How is Weakness of the Will Possible?', in his *Essays on Actions and Events* (Oxford 1980).

Hursthouse, R., 'A False Doctrine of the Mean', in *Proceedings of the Aristotelian Society* 81 (1980–1), 57–72.

Irwin, T. H., 'Ethics as an Inexact Science', in B. Hooker and M. Little (eds.), *Moral Particularism* (Oxford 2000).

—— 'Reason and Responsibility in Aristotle', in A. Rorty (ed.), *Essays on Aristotle's Ethics* (Berkeley and Los Angeles 1980).

—— 'The Virtues: Theory and Common Sense in Greek Philosophy', in R. Crisp (ed.), *How Should One Live? Essays on the Virtues* (Oxford 1996).

Judson, R. L., 'Aristotle on Fair Exchange', *Oxford Studies in Ancient Philosophy* 15 (1997), 147–75.

McDowell, J., 'The Role of Eudaimonia in Aristotle's Ethics', in A. Rorty (ed.), *Essays on Aristotle's Ethics* (Berkeley and Los Angeles 1980).

—— 'Virtue and Reason', in *Monist* 62 (1979), 331–51.

Meyer, S. Sauvé, 'Aristotle on the Voluntary', in R. Kraut (ed.), *The Blackwell Guide to Aristotle's Nicomachean Ethics* (Oxford 2006).

Taylor, C. C. W., 'Aristotle's Epistemology', in S. Everson (ed.), *Companions to Ancient Thought, i. Epistemology* (Cambridge 1990).

Wilkes, K., 'The Good Man and the Good for Man in Aristotle's Ethics', in A. Rorty (ed.), *Essays on Aristotle's Ethics* (Berkeley and Los Angeles 1980).

Williams, B., 'Justice as a Virtue', in A. Rorty (ed.), *Essays on Aristotle's Ethics* (Berkeley and Los Angeles 1980).

Further Reading in Oxford World's Classics

Aristotle, *Physics*, trans. Robin Waterfield, ed. David Bostock.
—— *Politics*, trans. Ernest Barker, rev. and ed. R. F. Stalley.
Plato, *Protagoras*, trans. C. C. W. Taylor.
—— *Republic*, trans. Robin Waterfield.

A CHRONOLOGY OF ARISTOTLE

(All dates are BC)

399 Trial and death of Socrates in Athens; Plato was around 30 at the time.

384 Aristotle born in Stagira, northern Greece. His father is doctor at the court of Macedon.

367 Aristotle goes to study in Athens; joins Plato's Academy.

347 Death of Plato, whose nephew Speusippus succeeds him as head of the Academy. Aristotle leaves Athens. He travels to Asia Minor and marries Pythias, the daughter of Hermias who hosts him in Assos, Asia Minor.

342 Aristotle becomes tutor to Alexander, later 'the Great', son of Philip II of Macedon.

338 Battle of Chaironeia, at which Philip II defeats Thebes and Athens, and becomes master of the Greek world.

336 Death of Philip; he is succeeded by his son Alexander.

335 Aristotle returns to Athens and founds his own 'school', the Lyceum. After the death of his wife, he lives with a slave-mistress, Herpyllis, by whom he has a son, Nicomachus.

323 Death of Alexander; anti-Macedonian feeling prompts Aristotle to leave Athens.

322 Death of Aristotle at Chalcis in Euboia.

Information about the life of Aristotle, as well as a report of his will, may be found in *Lives of the Famous Philosophers* (5.1), by the ancient writer Diogenes Laertius (probably 3rd century AD).

OUTLINE OF *THE NICOMACHEAN ETHICS*

BOOK I. THE HUMAN GOOD

BOOK II. MORAL VIRTUE

BOOK III. MORAL VIRTUE (*cont.*)

BOOK VII. CONTINENCE AND INCONTINENCE: PLEASURE

BOOK VIII. FRIENDSHIP

THE NICOMACHEAN ETHICS

BOOK I · THE HUMAN GOOD

SUBJECT OF OUR INQUIRY

All human activities aim at some good: some goods subordinate to others

1. EVERY art and every inquiry, and similarly every action and choice, is thought to aim at some good; and for this reason the good has rightly been declared to be that at which all things aim.* But a certain difference is found among ends; some are activities, others are products apart from the activities that produce them. Where there are ends apart from the actions, it is the nature of the products to be better than the activities. Now, as there are many actions, arts, and sciences, their ends also are many; the end of the medical art is health, that of shipbuilding a vessel, that of strategy victory, that of economics wealth. But where such arts fall under a single capacity—as bridle-making and the other arts concerned with the equipment of horses fall under the art of riding, and this and every military action under strategy, in the same way other arts fall under yet others—in all of these the ends of the master arts are to be preferred to all the subordinate ends; for it is for the sake of the former that the latter are pursued. It makes no difference whether the activities themselves are the ends of the actions, or something else apart from the activities, as in the case of the sciences just mentioned.

The science of the human good is politics

2. If, then, there is some end of the things we do, which we desire for its own sake (everything else being desired for the sake of this), and if we do not choose everything for the sake of something else (for at that rate the process would go on to infinity, so that our desire would be empty and vain), clearly this must be the good and the chief good.* Will not the knowledge of it, then, have a great influence on life? Shall we not, like archers who have a mark to aim at, be more likely to hit upon what is right? If so, we must try, in outline at least, to determine what it is, and of which of the sciences or capacities it is the object. It would seem to belong to the most authoritative art and that which is most truly the master art. And politics

appears to be of this nature;* for it is this that ordains which of the
1094b sciences should be studied in a state, and which each class of citizens should learn and up to what point they should learn them; and
we see even the most highly esteemed of capacities to fall under this,
e.g. strategy, economics, rhetoric; now, since politics uses the rest of
5 the sciences, and since, again, it legislates as to what we are to do and
what we are to abstain from, the end of this science must include
those of the others, so that this end must be the human good. For
even if the end is the same for a single man and for a state, that of the
state seems at all events something greater and more complete
whether to attain or to preserve; though it is worth while to attain the
10 end merely for one man, it is finer and more godlike to attain it for
a nation or for city-states. These, then, are the ends at which our
inquiry aims, since it is political science, in one sense of that term.

NATURE OF THE SCIENCE

*We must not expect more precision than the subject-matter admits
of. The student should have reached years of discretion*

3. Our discussion will be adequate if it has as much clearness as the
subject-matter admits of, for precision is not to be sought for alike
in all discussions, any more than in all the products of the crafts.
15 Now noble and just actions, which political science investigates,
exhibit much variety and fluctuation, so that they may be thought
to exist only by convention, and not by nature.* But goods exhibit
a similar fluctuation because they bring harm to many people; for
before now men have been undone by reason of their wealth, and
others by reason of their courage. We must be content, then, in
20 speaking of such subjects and with such premises to indicate the
truth roughly and in outline, and in speaking about things which
are only for the most part true, and with premises of the same kind,
to reach conclusions that are no better. In the same spirit, therefore,
should each type of statement be *received*; for it is the mark of an
educated man to look for precision in each class of things just so far
25 as the nature of the subject admits; it is evidently equally foolish to
accept probable reasoning from a mathematician and to demand
from a rhetorician demonstrative proofs.

Now each man judges well the things he knows, and of these he
is a good judge. And so the man who has been educated in a subject

is a good judge of that subject, and the man who has received an 1095a
all-round education is a good judge in general. Hence a young man
is not a proper hearer of lectures on political science;* for he is
inexperienced in the actions that occur in life, but its discussions
start from these and are about these; and, further, since he tends to
follow his passions, his study will be vain and unprofitable, because 5
the end aimed at is not knowledge but action. And it makes no
difference whether he is young in years or youthful in character; the
defect does not depend on time, but on his living, and pursuing
each successive object, as passion directs. For to such persons, as
to the incontinent, knowledge brings no profit; but to those who 10
desire and act in accordance with reason, knowledge about such
matters will be of great benefit.

These remarks about the student, the sort of treatment to be
expected, and the purpose of the inquiry, may be taken as our preface.

WHAT IS THE HUMAN GOOD?

*It is generally agreed to be happiness, but there are various views as to
what happiness is. What is required at the start is an unreasoned
conviction about the facts, such as is produced by a good upbringing*

4. Let us resume our inquiry and state, in view of the fact that all
knowledge and every pursuit aims at some good, what it is that we 15
say political science aims at and what is the highest of all goods
achievable by action. Verbally there is very general agreement; for
both the general run of men and people of superior refinement say
that it is happiness,* and identify living well and faring well with
being happy; but with regard to what happiness is they differ, and 20
the many do not give the same account as the wise. For the former
think it is some plain and obvious thing, like pleasure, wealth, or
honour; they differ, however, from one another—and often even
the same man identifies it with different things, with health when
he is ill, with wealth when he is poor; but, conscious of their ignor- 25
ance, they admire those who proclaim some great thing that is
above their comprehension. Now some thought that apart from
these many goods there is another which is good in itself* and
causes the goodness of all these as well. To examine all the opinions
that have been held were perhaps somewhat fruitless; enough to
examine those that are most prevalent or that seem to be arguable.

30   Let us not fail to notice, however, that there is a difference between
arguments from and those to the first principles. For Plato, too, was
right in raising this question and asking, as he used to do, 'Are we
on the way from or to the first principles?' There is a difference,
1095b as there is in a racecourse between the course from the judges to
the turning-point and the way back. For, while we must begin with
what is evident, things are evident in two ways—some to us, some
without qualification. Presumably, then, *we* must begin with things
evident to *us*. Hence anyone who is to listen intelligently to lectures
about what is noble and just and, generally, about the subjects of
5   political science must have been brought up in good habits. For the
fact is a starting-point,* and if this is sufficiently plain to him, he will
not need the reason as well; and the man who has been well brought
up has or can easily get starting-points. And as for him who neither
has nor can get them, let him hear the words of Hesiod:

10   Far best is he who knows all things himself;
             Good, he that hearkens when men counsel right;
             But he who neither knows, nor lays to heart
             Another's wisdom, is a useless wight.

*Discussion of the popular views that the good is pleasure, honour,
    wealth; a fourth kind of life, that of contemplation, deferred
    for future discussion*

5. Let us, however, resume our discussion from the point at which
15   we digressed.[1] To judge from the lives that men lead, most men,
and men of the most vulgar type, seem (not without some ground)
to identify the good, or happiness, with pleasure; which is the reason why they love the life of enjoyment. For there are, we may say,
three prominent types of life—that just mentioned, the political,
and thirdly the contemplative life.* Now the mass of mankind are
20   evidently quite slavish in their tastes, preferring a life suitable to
beasts, but they get some ground for their view from the fact that
many of those in high places share the tastes of Sardanapallus.*
A consideration of the prominent types of life shows that people of
superior refinement and of active disposition identify happiness
with honour; for this is, roughly speaking, the end of the political
life. But it seems too superficial to be what we are looking for, since

[1] a30.

it is thought to depend on those who bestow honour rather than on 25
him who receives it, but the good we divine to be something of
one's own and not easily taken from one. Further, men seem to
pursue honour in order that they may be assured of their merit; at
least it is by men of practical wisdom that they seek to be honoured,
and among those who know them, and on the ground of their virtue; clearly, then, according to them, at any rate, virtue is better.
And perhaps one might even suppose this to be, rather than hon- 30
our, the end of the political life. But even this appears somewhat
incomplete;* for possession of virtue seems actually compatible
with being asleep, or with lifelong inactivity, and, further, with the
greatest sufferings and misfortunes; but a man who was living so 1096a
no one would call happy, unless he were maintaining a thesis at all
costs. But enough of this; for the subject has been sufficiently
treated even in the popular discussions. Third comes the contemplative life, which we shall consider later.[1]

The life of money-making is one undertaken under compulsion, 5
and wealth is evidently not the good we are seeking; for it is merely
useful and for the sake of something else. And so one might rather
take the aforenamed objects to be ends; for they are loved for themselves. But it is evident that not even these are the end; yet many
arguments have been wasted on the support of them. Let us leave 10
this subject, then.

Discussion of the philosophical view that there is a Form of good

6. We had perhaps better consider the universal good and discuss
thoroughly what is meant by it, although such an inquiry is made
an uphill one by the fact that the Forms have been introduced by
friends of our own.* Yet it would perhaps be thought to be better,
indeed to be our duty, for the sake of maintaining the truth even to 15
destroy what touches us closely, especially as we are philosophers
or lovers of wisdom; for, while both are dear, piety requires us to
honour truth above our friends.

The men who introduced this doctrine did not posit Ideas of
classes within which they recognized priority and posteriority (which
is the reason why they did not maintain the existence of an Idea
embracing all numbers); but the term 'good' is used both in the 20
category of substance and in that of quality and in that of relation,

[1] 1177a12–1178a8, 1178a22–1179a32.

and that which is *per se*, i.e. substance, is prior in nature to the relative (for the latter is like an offshoot and accident of being); so that there could not be a common Idea set over all these goods. Further, since 'good' has as many senses as 'being'* (for it is predi-
25 cated both in the category of substance, as of god and of reason, and in quality, i.e. of the virtues, and in quantity, i.e. of that which is moderate, and in relation, i.e. of the useful, and in time, i.e. of the right opportunity, and in place, i.e. of the right locality and the like), clearly it cannot be something universally present in all cases and single; for then it could not have been predicated in all the categories, but in one only. Further, since of the things answering
30 to one Idea there is one science, there would have been one science of all the goods; but as it is there are many sciences even of the things that fall under one category, e.g. of opportunity, for opportunity in war is studied by strategics and in disease by medicine, and the moderate in food is studied by medicine and in exercise by the science of gymnastics. And one might ask the question, what in the world they *mean* by 'a thing itself', if (as is the case) in 'man
35 himself' and in a particular man the account of man is one and the
1096b same. For in so far as they are men, they will in no respect differ; and if this is so, neither will 'good itself' and particular goods, in so far as they are good. But again it will not be good any the more for being eternal, since that which lasts long is no whiter than that which
5 perishes in a day.* The Pythagoreans seem to give a more plausible account of the good, when they place the One in the column of goods; and it is they that Speusippus seems to have followed.*

But let us discuss these matters elsewhere;[1] an objection to what we have said, however, may be discerned in the fact that the Platonists have not been speaking about *all* goods, and that the goods that are pursued and loved for themselves are called good
10 by reference to a single Form, while those which tend to produce or to preserve these somehow or to prevent their contraries are called good by reason of these, and in a different way. Clearly, then, goods must be spoken of in two ways, and some must be good in themselves, the others by reason of these. Let us separate, then,
15 things good in themselves from useful things, and consider whether the former are called good by reference to a single Idea. What sort of goods would one call good in themselves? Is it those

[1] Cf. *Met.* 986a22–6, 1028b21–4, 1072b30–1073a3, 1091a29–b3, b13–1092a17.

that are pursued even when isolated from others, such as intelligence, sight, and certain pleasures and honours? Certainly, if we pursue these also for the sake of something else, yet one would place them among things good in themselves. Or is nothing other than the Idea of good good in itself? In that case the Form will be 20 empty. But if the things we have named are also things good in themselves, the account of the good will have to appear as something identical in them all, as that of whiteness is identical in snow and in white lead. But of honour, wisdom, and pleasure, just in respect of their goodness, the accounts are distinct and diverse.* The good, therefore, is not something common answering to one 25 Idea.

But what then do we mean by the good? It is surely not like the things that only chance to have the same name.* Are goods one, then, by being derived from one good or by all contributing to one good, or are they rather one by analogy? Certainly, as sight is in the body, so is reason in the soul, and so on in other cases. But perhaps 30 these subjects had better be dismissed for the present; for perfect precision about them would be more appropriate to another branch of philosophy. And similarly with regard to the Idea; even if there is some one good which is universally predicable of goods, or is capable of separate and independent existence, clearly it could not be achieved or attained by man; but we are now seeking something attainable.* Perhaps, however, someone might think it worth while 35 to have knowledge of it with a view to the goods that *are* attainable and achievable; or, having this as a sort of pattern, we shall know 1097a better the goods that are good for us, and if we know them shall attain them. This argument has some plausibility, but seems to clash with the procedure of the sciences; for all of these, though they aim at some good and seek to supply the deficiency of it, leave on one 5 side the knowledge of *the* good. Yet that all the exponents of the arts should be ignorant of, and should not even seek, so great an aid is not probable. It is hard, too, to see how a weaver or a carpenter will be benefited in regard to his own craft by knowing this 'good itself', or how the man who has viewed the Idea itself will be a better 10 doctor or general thereby. For a doctor seems not even to study health in this way, but the health of man, or perhaps rather the health of a particular man; it is individuals that he is healing. But enough of these topics.

The good must be something final and self-sufficient. Definition of
  happiness reached by considering the characteristic function of man

15 7. Let us again return to the good we are seeking, and ask what it
can be. It seems different in different actions and arts; it is different
in medicine, in strategy, and in the other arts likewise. What then
is the good of each? Surely that for whose sake everything else is
done. In medicine this is health, in strategy victory, in architecture
20 a house, in any other sphere something else, and in every action and
pursuit the end; for it is for the sake of this that all men do whatever
else they do. Therefore, if there is an end for all that we do, this will
be the good achievable by action, and if there are more than one,
these will be the goods achievable by action.

So the argument has by a different course reached the same
25 point; but we must try to state this even more clearly. Since there
are evidently more than one end, and we choose some of these (e.g.
wealth, flutes, and in general instruments) for the sake of something
else, clearly not all ends are final ends; but the chief good is evidently something final.* Therefore, if there is only one final end,
this will be what we are seeking, and if there are more than one, the
30 most final of these will be what we are seeking. Now we call that
which is in itself worthy of pursuit more final than that which is
worthy of pursuit for the sake of something else, and that which is
never desirable for the sake of something else more final than the
things that are desirable both in themselves and for the sake of that
other thing, and therefore we call final without qualification that
which is always desirable in itself and never for the sake of something else.

1097b   Now such a thing happiness, above all else, is held to be; for this
we choose always for itself and never for the sake of something else,
but honour, pleasure, reason, and every virtue we choose indeed for
themselves (for if nothing resulted from them we should still choose
each of them), but we choose them also for the sake of happiness,
5 judging that through them we shall be happy. Happiness, on the
other hand, no one chooses for the sake of these, nor, in general, for
anything other than itself.

From the point of view of self-sufficiency the same result seems
to follow; for the final good is thought to be self-sufficient. Now by
self-sufficient we do not mean that which is sufficient for a man by

himself, for one who lives a solitary life, but also for parents, children,   10
wife, and in general for his friends and fellow citizens, since man is
born for citizenship.* But some limit must be set to this; for if we
extend our requirement to ancestors and descendants and friends'
friends we are in for an infinite series. Let us examine this question,
however, on another occasion;[1] the self-sufficient we now define as   15
that which when isolated makes life desirable and lacking in nothing; and such we think happiness to be;* and further we think it
most desirable of all things, not a thing counted as one good thing
among others*—if it were so counted it would clearly be made more
desirable by the addition of even the least of goods; for that which
is added becomes an excess of goods, and of goods the greater is
always more desirable. Happiness, then, is something final and self-   20
sufficient, and is the end of action.

Presumably, however, to say that happiness is the chief good
seems a platitude, and a clearer account of what it is is still desired.
This might perhaps be given, if we could first ascertain the function
of man. For just as for a flute-player, a sculptor, or any artist, and,   25
in general, for all things that have a function or activity, the good
and the 'well' is thought to reside in the function, so would it seem
to be for man, if he has a function. Have the carpenter, then, and
the tanner certain functions or activities, and has man none? Is he
born without a function? Or as eye, hand, foot, and in general each   30
of the parts evidently has a function, may one lay it down that man
similarly has a function apart from all these?* What then can this
be? Life seems to belong even to plants, but we are seeking what is
peculiar to man. Let us exclude, therefore, the life of nutrition and
growth. Next there would be a life of perception, but *it* also seems   1098a
to be shared even by the horse, the ox, and every animal. There
remains, then, an active life of the element that has reason; of this,
one part has it in the sense of being obedient to reason, the other in
the sense of possessing reason and exercising thought.* And, as 'life
of the rational element' also has two meanings,* we must state that   5
life in the sense of activity is what we mean; for this seems to be the
more proper sense of the term. Now if the function of man is an
activity of soul which follows or implies reason, and if we say 'a so-
and-so' and 'a good so-and-so' have a function which is the same in
kind, e.g. a lyre-player and a good lyre-player, and so without

[1] i. 10, 11, ix. 10.

10 qualification in all cases, eminence in respect of goodness being added to the name of the function (for the function of a lyre-player is to play the lyre, and that of a good lyre-player is to do so well): if this is the case [and we state the function of man to be a certain kind of life, and this to be an activity or actions of the soul implying a rational principle, and the function of a good man to be the good and noble performance of these, and if any action is well performed
15 when it is performed in accordance with the appropriate virtue: if this is the case], human good turns out to be activity of soul exhibiting virtue,* and if there are more than one virtue, in accordance with the best and most complete.*

But we must add 'in a complete life'. For one swallow does not make a summer, nor does one day; and so too one day, or a short time, does not make a man blessed and happy.

20   Let this serve as an outline of the good; for we must presumably first sketch it roughly, and then later fill in the details. But it would seem that any one is capable of carrying on and articulating what has once been well outlined, and that time is a good discoverer or partner in such a work; to which facts the advances of the arts are
25 due; for any one can add what is lacking. And we must also remember what has been said before,[1] and not look for precision in all things alike, but in each class of things such precision as accords with the subject-matter, and so much as is appropriate to the inquiry. For a carpenter and a geometer investigate the right angle
30 in different ways; the former does so in so far as the right angle is useful for his work, while the latter inquires what it is or what sort of thing it is; for he is a spectator of the truth. We must act in the same way, then, in all other matters as well, that our main task may not be subordinated to minor questions. Nor must we demand the
1098b cause in all matters alike; it is enough in some cases that the *fact* be well established, as in the case of the first principles; the fact is a primary thing and first principle. Now of first principles we see some by induction, some by perception, some by a certain habituation, and others too in other ways. But each set of principles we must try
5 to investigate in the natural way, and we must take pains to determine them correctly, since they have a great influence on what follows. For the beginning is thought to be more than half of the whole, and many of the questions we ask are cleared up by it.

[1] 1094b11–27.

Our definition is confirmed by current beliefs about happiness

8. But we must consider happiness in the light not only of our conclusion and our premisses, but also of what is commonly said about it; for with a true view all the data harmonize, but with a false one the facts soon clash. Now goods have been divided into three classes,* and some are described as external, others as relating to soul or to body; we call those that relate to soul most properly and truly goods, and psychical actions and activities we class as relating to soul. Therefore our account must be sound, at least according to this view, which is an old one and agreed on by philosophers. It is correct also in that we identify the end with certain actions and activities; for thus it falls among goods of the soul and not among external goods. Another belief which harmonizes with our account is that the happy man lives well and fares well; for we have practically defined happiness as a sort of living and faring well. The characteristics that are looked for in happiness seem also, all of them, to belong to what we have defined happiness as being. For some identify happiness with virtue, some with practical wisdom, others with a kind of philosophic wisdom, others with these, or one of these, accompanied by pleasure or not without pleasure; while others include also external prosperity. Now some of these views have been held by many men and men of old, others by a few eminent persons; and it is not probable that either of these should be entirely mistaken, but rather that they should be right in at least some one respect, or even in most respects.

With those who identify happiness with virtue or some one virtue our account is in harmony;* for to virtue belongs virtuous activity. But it makes, perhaps, no small difference whether we place the chief good in possession or in use, in state of mind or in activity. For the state of mind may exist without producing any good result, as in a man who is asleep or in some other way quite inactive, but the activity cannot; for one who has the activity will of necessity be acting, and acting well. And as in the Olympic Games it is not the most beautiful and the strongest that are crowned but those who compete (for it is some of these that are victorious), so those who act win, and rightly win, the noble and good things in life.

Their life is also in itself pleasant. For pleasure is a state of *soul*, and to each man that which he is said to be a lover of is pleasant;

e.g. not only is a horse pleasant to the lover of horses, and a spec-
10 tacle to the lover of sights, but also in the same way just acts are
pleasant to the lover of justice and in general virtuous acts to the
lover of virtue. Now for most men their pleasures are in conflict
with one another because these are not by nature pleasant, but
the lovers of what is noble find pleasant the things that are by
nature pleasant; and virtuous actions are such, so that these are
15 pleasant for such men as well as in their own nature. Their life,
therefore, has no further need of pleasure as a sort of adventitious
charm, but has its pleasure in itself. For, besides what we have said,
the man who does not rejoice in noble actions is not even good;
since no one would call a man just who did not enjoy acting justly,
20 nor any man liberal who did not enjoy liberal actions; and similarly
in all other cases.* If this is so, virtuous actions must be in themselves pleasant. But they are also *good* and *noble*, and have each of
these attributes in the highest degree, since the good man judges
well about these attributes; his judgement is such as we have
described. Happiness then is the best, noblest, and most pleasant
25 thing in the world, and these attributes are not severed as in the
inscription at Delos—

> Most noble is that which is justest, and best is health; But most
> pleasant it is to win what we love.

For all these properties belong to the best activities; and these, or
30 one—the best—of these, we identify with happiness.

Yet evidently, as we said,[1] it needs the external goods as well; for
it is impossible, or not easy, to do noble acts without the proper
1099b equipment. In many actions we use friends and riches and political
power as instruments; and there are some things the lack of which
takes the lustre from happiness—good birth, goodly children,
beauty;* for the man who is very ugly in appearance or ill-born or
solitary and childless is not very likely to be happy, and perhaps a
5 man would be still less likely if he had thoroughly bad children or
friends or had lost good children or friends by death. As we said,[2]
then, happiness seems to need this sort of prosperity in addition;
for which reason some identify happiness with good fortune,
though others identify it with virtue.

---

[1] 1098b26–9.   [2] ibid.

Is happiness acquired by learning or habituation, or sent by god or by chance?

9. For this reason also the question is asked, whether happiness is to be acquired by learning or by habituation or some other sort of training, or comes in virtue of some divine providence or again by 10 chance. Now if there is *any* gift of the gods to men, it is reasonable that happiness should be god-given* and most surely god-given of all human things inasmuch as it is the best. But this question would perhaps be more appropriate to another inquiry; happiness seems, however, even if it is not god-sent but comes as a result of virtue and 15 some process of learning or training, to be among the most godlike things; for that which is the prize and end of virtue seems to be the best thing in the world, and something godlike and blessed.

It will also on this view be very generally shared; for all who are not maimed as regards their potentiality for virtue may win it by a certain kind of study and care. But if it is better to be happy thus 20 than by chance, it is reasonable that the facts should be so, since everything that depends on the action of nature is by nature as good as it can be, and similarly everything that depends on art or any rational cause, and especially if it depends on the best of all causes. To entrust to chance what is greatest and most noble would be a very defective arrangement.

The answer to the question we are asking is plain also from the 25 definition of happiness;* for it has been said to be a virtuous activity of soul, of a certain kind. Of the remaining goods, some must necessarily pre-exist as conditions of happiness, and others are naturally co-operative and useful as instruments. And this will be found to agree with what we said at the outset;[1] for we stated the end of political science to be the best end, and political science spends 30 most of its pains on making the citizens to be of a certain character, namely, good and capable of noble acts.

It is natural, then, that we call neither ox nor horse nor any other of the animals happy; for none of them is capable of sharing in such activity. For this reason also a boy is not happy; for he is not yet 1100a capable of such acts, owing to his age; and boys who are called happy are being congratulated by reason of the hopes we have for them. For there is required, as we said,[2] not only complete virtue

---

[1] 1094a27.   [2] 1098a18–20.

but also a complete life, since many changes occur in life, and all manner of chances, and the most prosperous may fall into great misfortunes in old age, as is told of Priam in the Trojan Cycle;* and one who has experienced such chances and has ended wretchedly no one calls happy.

Should no man be called happy while he lives?

10 **10.** Must no one at all, then, be called happy while he lives; must we, as Solon* says, see the end? Even if we are to lay down this doctrine, is it also the case that a man *is* happy when he is *dead*? Or is not this quite absurd, especially for us who say that happiness is an activity? But if we do not call the dead man happy, and if Solon
15 does not mean this, but that one can then safely *call* a man blessed, as being at last beyond evils and misfortunes, this also affords matter for discussion; for both evil and good are thought to exist for a dead man, as much as for one who is alive but not aware of them;* e.g.
20 honours and dishonours and the good or bad fortunes of children, and in general of descendants. And this also presents a problem; for though a man has lived blessedly until old age and has had a death worthy of his life, many reverses may befall his descendants—some of them may be good and attain the life they deserve, while with
25 others the opposite may be the case; and clearly too the degrees of relationship between them and their ancestors may vary indefinitely. It would be odd, then, if the dead man were to share in these changes and become at one time happy, at another wretched; while it would also be odd if the fortunes of the descendants did not for
30 *some* time have *some* effect on the happiness of their ancestors.

But we must return to our first difficulty;* for perhaps by a consideration of it our present problem might be solved. Now if we must see the end and only then call a man blessed, not as being blessed but as having been so before, surely this is a paradox, that when he is happy the attribute that belongs to him is not to be truly
35 predicated of him because we do not wish to call living men happy,
1100b on account of the changes that may befall them, and because we have assumed happiness to be something permanent and by no means easily changed, while a single man may suffer many turns of fortune's wheel. For clearly if we were to follow his fortunes, we
5 should often call the same man happy and again wretched, making the happy man out to be 'a chameleon, and insecurely based'. Or is

this following his fortunes quite wrong? Success or failure in life does not depend on these, but human life, as we said,[1] needs these as well, while virtuous activities or their opposites are what determine happiness or the reverse.

The question we have now discussed confirms our definition. For no function of man has so much permanence as virtuous activities (these are thought to be more durable even than knowledge of the sciences), and of these themselves the most valuable are more durable because those who are blessed spend their life most readily and most continuously in these; for this seems to be the reason why we do not forget them. The attribute in question, then, will belong to the happy man, and he will be happy throughout his life; for always, or by preference to everything else, he will do and contemplate what is excellent, and he will bear the chances of life most nobly and altogether decorously, if he is 'truly good' and 'foursquare beyond reproach'.

Now many events happen by chance, and events differing in importance; small pieces of good fortune or of its opposite clearly do not weigh down the scales of life one way or the other, but a multitude of great events if they turn out well will make life more blessed (for not only are they themselves such as to add beauty to life, but the way a man deals with them may be noble and good), while if they turn out ill they crush and maim blessedness; for they both bring pain with them and hinder many activities. Yet even in these nobility shines through, when a man bears with resignation many great misfortunes, not through insensibility to pain but through nobility and greatness of soul.

If activities are, as we said, what determines the character of life, no blessed man can become miserable; for he will never do the acts that are hateful and mean. For the man who is truly good and wise, we think, bears all the chances of life becomingly and always makes the best of circumstances, as a good general makes the best military use of the army at his command, and a good shoemaker makes the best shoes out of the hides that are given him; and so with all other craftsmen. And if this is the case, the happy man can never become miserable—though he will not reach *blessedness*, if he meet with fortunes like those of Priam.*

---

[1] 1099a31–b7.

Nor, again, is he many-coloured and changeable; for neither will
he be moved from his happy state easily or by any ordinary misad-
10 ventures, but only by many great ones, nor, if he has had many great
misadventures, will he recover his happiness in a short time, but if
at all, only in a long and complete one in which he has attained
many splendid successes.

Why then should we not say that he is happy who is active in
accordance with complete virtue and is sufficiently equipped with
15 external goods, not for some chance period but throughout a complete
life? Or must we add 'and who is destined to live thus and die as befits
his life'?* Certainly the future is obscure to us, while happiness, we
claim, is an end and something in every way final. If so, we shall call
20 blessed those among living men in whom these conditions are, and are
to be, fulfilled—but blessed *men*. So much for these questions.

Do the fortunes of the living affect the dead?

11. That the fortunes of descendants and of all a man's friends
should not affect his happiness at all seems a very unfriendly doctrine, and one opposed to the opinions men hold; but since the
events that happen are numerous and admit of all sorts of differ-
25 ence, and some come more near to us and others less so, it seems a
long—nay, an infinite—task to discuss each in detail; a general
outline will perhaps suffice. If, then, as some of a man's own misadventures have a certain weight and influence on life while others
are, as it were, lighter, so too there are differences among the mis-
30 adventures of our friends taken as a whole, and it makes a difference
whether the various sufferings befall the living or the dead (much
more even than whether lawless and terrible deeds are presupposed
in a tragedy or done on the stage*), this difference also must be
taken into account; or rather, perhaps, the fact that doubt is felt
1101b whether the dead share in any good or evil. For it seems, from these
considerations, that even if anything whether good or evil pene-
trates to them, it must be something weak and negligible,* either in
itself or for them, or if not, at least it must be such in degree and
kind as not to make happy those who are not happy nor to take away
5 their blessedness from those who are. The good or bad fortunes of
friends, then, seem to have some effects on the dead, but effects of
such a kind and degree as neither to make the happy not happy nor
to produce any other change of the kind.

Virtue is praiseworthy, but happiness is above praise

12. These questions having been definitely answered, let us consider 10 whether happiness is among the things that are praised or rather among the things that are prized;* for clearly it is not to be placed among *potentialities*. Everything that is praised seems to be praised because it is of a certain kind and is related somehow to something else; for we praise the just or brave man, and in general both the good man and virtue itself, because of the actions and functions involved, 15 and we praise the strong man, the good runner, and so on, because he is of a certain kind and is related in a certain way to something good and important. This is clear also from the praise given to the gods; it seems absurd that the gods should be measured by our standard,* but we do so measure them, since praise involves a reference, as we said, 20 to something else. But if praise is for things such as we have described, clearly what applies to the best things is not praise, but something greater and better, as is indeed obvious; for what we do to the gods and the most godlike of men is to call them blessed and happy. And so too 25 with good *things*; no one praises happiness as he does justice, but rather calls it blessed, as being something more divine and better.

Eudoxus* also seems to have been right in his method of advocating the supremacy of pleasure; he thought that the fact that, though a good, it is not praised indicated it to be better than the things that are praised, and that this is what god and the good are; for by refer- 30 ence to these all other things are judged. *Praise* is appropriate to virtue, for as a result of virtue men tend to do noble deeds; but *encomia* are bestowed on acts, whether of the body or of the soul. But perhaps nicety in these matters is more proper to those who have made a study of encomia; to us it is clear from what has been said that happiness is among the things that are prized and perfect. It 35 seems to be so also from the fact that it is a first principle; for it is for 1102a the sake of this that we all do everything else,* and the first principle and cause of goods is, we claim, something prized and divine.

KINDS OF VIRTUE

Division of the soul, and resultant division of virtue into intellectual and moral

13. Since happiness is an activity of soul in accordance with perfect 5 virtue, we must consider the nature of virtue;* for perhaps we shall

thus see better the nature of happiness. The true student of politics,
too, is thought to have studied virtue above all things; for he wishes
to make his fellow citizens good and obedient to the laws. As an
10 example of this we have the lawgivers of the Cretans and the
Spartans,* and any others of the kind that there may have been.
And if this inquiry belongs to political science, clearly the pursuit
of it will be in accordance with our original plan.* But clearly the
virtue we must study is human virtue; for the good we were seeking
15 was human good and the happiness human happiness. By human
virtue we mean not that of the body but that of the soul; and
happiness also we call an activity of soul. But if this is so, clearly the
student of politics must know somehow the facts about the soul, as
the man who is to heal the eyes must know about the whole body
20 also; and all the more since political science is more prized and better
than medical; but even among doctors the best educated spend much
labour on acquiring knowledge of the body. The student of politics,
then, must study the soul, and must study it with these objects in
view, and do so just to the extent which is sufficient for the ques-
25 tions we are discussing; for further precision would perhaps involve
more labour than our purposes require.

Some things are said about it, adequately enough, even in the
discussions outside our school, and we must use these; e.g. that one
element in the soul is irrational and one has reason.* Whether these
30 are separated as the parts of the body or of anything divisible are,
or are distinct by definition but by nature inseparable, like convex
and concave in the circumference of a circle, does not affect the
present question.

Of the irrational element one division seems to be widely distributed, and vegetative in its nature, I mean that which causes nutrition and growth;* for it is this kind of power of the soul that one
1102b must assign to all nurslings and to embryos, and this same power to
full-grown creatures; this is more reasonable than to assign some
different power to them. Now the excellence of this seems to be
common to all species and not specifically human; for this part or
faculty seems to function most in sleep, while goodness and badness
5 are least manifest in sleep (whence comes the saying that the happy
are no better off than the wretched for half their lives; and this
happens naturally enough, since sleep is an inactivity of the soul in
that respect in which it is called good or bad), unless perhaps to a

small extent some of the movements actually penetrate to the soul, and in this respect the dreams of good men are better than those of ordinary people. Enough of this subject, however; let us leave the nutritive faculty alone, since it has by its nature no share in human excellence.

There seems to be also another irrational element in the soul— one which in a sense, however, shares in reason.* For we praise the reason of the continent man and of the incontinent, and the part of their soul that has reason, since it urges them aright and towards the best objects; but there is found in them also another natural element beside reason, which fights against and resists it. For exactly as paralysed limbs, when we intend to move them to the right, turn on the contrary to the left, so is it with the soul; the impulses of incontinent people move in contrary directions. But while in the body we see that which moves astray, in the soul we do not. No doubt, however, we must none the less suppose that in the soul too there is something beside reason, resisting and opposing it. In what sense it is distinct from the other elements does not concern us. Now even this seems to have a share in reason, as we said; at any rate in the continent man it obeys reason*—and presumably in the temperate and brave man it is still more obedient; for in him it speaks, on all matters, with the same voice as reason.

Therefore the irrational element also appears to be twofold. For the vegetative element in no way shares in reason, but the appetitive and in general the desiring element* in a sense shares in it, in so far as it listens to and obeys it; this is the sense in which we speak of 'taking account' of one's father or one's friends, not that in which we speak of 'accounting' for a mathematical property.* That the irrational element is in some sense persuaded by a rational principle is indicated also by the giving of advice and by all reproof and exhortation. And if this element also must be said to have a rational principle, that which has a rational principle (as well as that which has not) will be twofold, one subdivision having it in the strict sense and in itself, and the other having a tendency to obey as one does one's father.

Virtue too is distinguished into kinds in accordance with this difference;* for we say that some of the virtues are intellectual and others moral, philosophic wisdom and understanding and practical wisdom being intellectual, liberality and temperance moral. For in

speaking about a man's character* we do not say that he is wise or
has understanding, but that he is good-tempered or temperate; yet
we praise the wise man also with respect to his state of mind; and
10 of states of mind we call those which merit praise virtues.

BOOK II · MORAL VIRTUE

MORAL VIRTUE, HOW IT IS ACQUIRED

Moral virtue, like the arts, is acquired by repetition of the corresponding acts

1. VIRTUE, then, being of two kinds, intellectual and moral, intellectual virtue in the main owes both its birth and its growth to teaching (for which reason it requires experience and time), while moral virtue comes about as a result of habit, whence also its name (*ēthikē*) is one that is formed by a slight variation from the word *ethos* (habit). From this it is also plain that none of the moral virtues arises in us by nature; for nothing that exists by nature can form a habit contrary to its nature. For instance the stone which by nature moves downwards cannot be habituated to move upwards, not even if one tries to train it by throwing it up ten thousand times; nor can fire be habituated to move downwards, nor can anything else that by nature behaves in one way be trained to behave in another. Neither by nature, then, nor contrary to nature do the virtues arise in us; rather we are adapted by nature to receive them, and are made perfect by habit.*

Again, of all the things that come to us by nature we first acquire the potentiality and later exhibit the activity (this is plain in the case of the senses;* for it was not by often seeing or often hearing that we got these senses, but on the contrary we had them before we used them, and did not come to have them by using them); but the virtues we get by first exercising them, as also happens in the case of the arts as well. For the things we have to learn before we can do them, we learn by doing them, e.g. men become builders by building and lyre-players by playing the lyre; so too we become just by doing just acts, temperate by doing temperate acts, brave by doing brave acts.

This is confirmed by what happens in states; for legislators make the citizens good by forming habits in them, and this is the wish of every legislator, and those who do not effect it miss their mark, and it is in this that a good constitution differs from a bad one.

Again, it is from the same causes and by the same means that every virtue is both produced and destroyed, and similarly every art; for

it is from playing the lyre that both good and bad lyre-players are
10 produced. And the corresponding statement is true of builders and
of all the rest; men will be good or bad builders as a result of building well or badly. For if this were not so, there would have been no
need of a teacher, but all men would have been born good or bad at
their craft. This, then, is the case with the virtues also; by doing the
15 acts that we do in our transactions with other men we become just
or unjust, and by doing the acts that we do in the presence of danger, and by being habituated to feel fear or confidence, we become
brave or cowardly.* The same is true of appetites and feelings of
anger; some men become temperate and good-tempered, others
20 self-indulgent and irascible, by behaving in one way or the other in
the appropriate circumstances. Thus, in one word, states of character arise out of like activities. This is why the activities we exhibit
must be of a certain kind; it is because the states of character correspond to the differences between these. It makes no small difference, then, whether we form habits of one kind or of another from
25 our very youth; it makes a very great difference, or rather *all* the
difference.

*These acts cannot be prescribed exactly, but must avoid excess and
defect*

2. Since, then, the present inquiry does not aim at theoretical
knowledge like the others (for we are inquiring not in order to know
what virtue is, but in order to become good,* since otherwise our
inquiry would have been of no use), we must examine the nature of
30 actions, namely how we ought to do them; for these determine also
the nature of the states of character that are produced, as we have
said.[1] Now, that we must act in accordance with correct reason is a
common principle and must be assumed—it will be discussed later,[2]
i.e. both what correct reason is, and how it is related to the other
1104a virtues. But this must be agreed upon beforehand, that the whole
account of matters of conduct must be given in outline and not precisely, as we said at the very beginning[3] that the accounts we demand
must be in accordance with the subject-matter; matters concerned
with conduct and questions of what is good for us have no fixity, any
5 more than matters of health.* The general account being of this

----

[1] a31–b25.   [2] Book VI.   [3] 1094b11–27.

nature, the account of particular cases is yet more lacking in exactness; for they do not fall under any art or precept, but the agents themselves must in each case consider what is appropriate to the occasion, as happens also in the art of medicine or of navigation.*

But though our present account is of this nature we must give what help we can. First, then, let us consider this, that it is the nature of such things to be destroyed by defect and excess, as we see in the case of strength and of health (for to gain light on things imperceptible we must use the evidence of sensible things); exercise either excessive or defective destroys the strength, and similarly drink or food which is above or below a certain amount destroys the health, while that which is proportionate both produces and increases and preserves it. So too is it, then, in the case of temperance and courage and the other virtues. For the man who flies from and fears everything and does not stand his ground against anything becomes a coward, and the man who fears nothing at all but goes to meet every danger becomes rash; and similarly the man who indulges in every pleasure and abstains from none becomes self-indulgent, while the man who shuns every pleasure, as boors do, becomes in a way insensible;* temperance and courage, then, are destroyed by excess and defect, and preserved by the mean.*

But not only are the sources and causes of their origination and growth the same as those of their destruction, but also the sphere of their actualization will be the same; for this is also true of the things which are more evident to sense, e.g. of strength; it is produced by taking much food and undergoing much exertion, and it is the strong man that will be most able to do these things. So too is it with the virtues; by abstaining from pleasures we become temperate,* and it is when we have become so that we are most able to abstain from them; and similarly too in the case of courage; for by being habituated to despise things that are fearful and to stand our ground against them we become brave, and it is when we have become so that we shall be most able to stand our ground against them.

Pleasure in doing virtuous acts is a sign that the virtuous disposition has been acquired: a variety of considerations show the essential connection of moral virtue with pleasure and pain

3. We must take as a sign of states of character the pleasure or pain that supervenes upon acts; for the man who abstains from bodily

pleasures and delights in this very fact is temperate, while the man who is annoyed at it is self-indulgent, and he who stands his ground against things that are terrible and delights in this or at least is not pained is brave, while the man who is pained is a coward.* For moral virtue is concerned with pleasures and pains; it is on account

10 of the pleasure that we do bad things, and on account of the pain that we abstain from noble ones. Hence we ought to have been brought up in a particular way from our very youth, as Plato says,[1] so as both to delight in and to be pained by the things that we ought; this is the right education.

Again, if the virtues are concerned with actions and passions,* and every passion and every action is accompanied by pleasure and

15 pain, for this reason also virtue will be concerned with pleasures and pains. This is indicated also by the fact that punishment is inflicted by these means; for it is a kind of cure, and it is the nature of cures to be effected by contraries.*

Again, as we said but lately, every state of soul has a nature relative to and concerned with the kind of things by which it tends to

20 be made worse or better; but it is by reason of pleasures and pains that men become bad, by pursuing and avoiding these—either the pleasures and pains they ought not or when they ought not or as they ought not, or by going wrong in one of the other similar ways that may be distinguished. Hence men even define the virtues as

25 certain states of impassivity and tranquillity;* not well, however, because they speak absolutely, and do not say 'as one ought' and 'as one ought not' and 'when one ought or ought not', and the other things that may be added. We assume, then, that this kind of virtue tends to do what is best with regard to pleasures and pains, and vice does the contrary.

The following facts also may show us that virtue and vice are

30 concerned with these same things. There being three objects of choice and three of avoidance, the noble, the advantageous, the pleasant, and their contraries, the base, the injurious, the painful, about all of these the good man tends to go right and the bad man to go wrong, and especially about pleasure; for this is common to the animals,

35 and also it accompanies all objects of choice; for even the noble and
1105a the advantageous appear pleasant.

---

[1] *Laws*, 653 A ff., *Rep.* 401 E–402 A.

Again, it has grown up with us all from our infancy; this is why it is difficult to rub off this passion, engrained as it is in our life. And we measure even our actions, some of us more and others less, by the rule of pleasure and pain. For this reason, then, our whole inquiry 5 must be about these; for to feel delight and pain rightly or wrongly has no small effect on our actions.

Again, it is harder to fight against pleasure than anger, to use Heraclitus' phrase,* but both art and virtue are always concerned with what is harder; for even the good is better when it is harder. 10 Therefore for this reason also the whole concern both of virtue and of political science is with pleasures and pains; for the man who uses these well will be good, he who uses them badly bad.

That virtue, then, is concerned with pleasures and pains, and that by the acts from which it arises it is both increased and, if they are 15 done differently, destroyed, and that the acts from which it arose are those in which it actualizes itself—let this be taken as said.

An objection to the view that one acquires virtues by doing virtuous acts; and a reply: the conditions needed to possess virtue and act from it

4. The question might be asked, what we mean by saying[1] that we must become just by doing just acts, and temperate by doing temperate acts; for if men do just and temperate acts, they are already 20 just and temperate, exactly as, if they do what is grammatical or musical, they are grammarians and musicians.

Or is this not true even of the arts?* It is possible to do something grammatical, either by chance or under the guidance of another. A man will be a grammarian, then, only when he has both done something grammatical and done it grammatically; and this means doing 25 it in accordance with the grammatical knowledge in himself.

Again, the case of the arts and that of the virtues are not similar; for the products of the arts have their goodness in themselves, so that it is enough that they should have a certain character, but if the acts that are in accordance with the virtues have themselves a certain character it does not follow that they are done justly or temperately.* The agent also must be in a certain condition when 30 he does them; in the first place he must have knowledge, secondly he must choose the acts, and choose them for their own sakes, and

[1] 1103a31–b25, 1104a27–b3.

thirdly his action must proceed from a firm and unchangeable character. These are not reckoned in as conditions of the possession of
1105b the arts, except the bare knowledge; but as a condition of the possession of the virtues knowledge has little or no weight,* while the
other conditions count not for a little but for everything, i.e. the
very conditions which result from often doing just and temperate
acts.

5   Actions, then, are called just and temperate when they are such
as the just or the temperate man would do;* but it is not the man
who does these that is just and temperate, but the man who also
does them *as* just and temperate men do them. It is well said, then,
that it is by doing just acts that the just man is produced, and by
10 doing temperate acts the temperate man; without doing these no
one would have even a prospect of becoming good.

But most people do not do these, but take refuge in theory and
think they are being philosophers and will become good in this
15 way, behaving somewhat like patients who listen attentively to their
doctors, but do none of the things they are ordered to do. As the
latter will not be made well in body by such a course of treatment, the
former will not be made well in soul by such a course of philosophy.

DEFINITION OF MORAL VIRTUE

*The genus of moral virtue: it is a state of character, not a passion,
nor a capacity*

5. Next we must consider what virtue is. Since things that are
20 found in the soul are of three kinds—passions, capacities, states of
character—virtue must be one of these.* By passions I mean appetite, anger, fear, confidence, envy, joy, friendly feeling, hatred, long-
ing, emulation, pity, and in general the feelings that are accompanied
by pleasure or pain; by capacities the things in virtue of which we
are said to be capable of feeling these, e.g. of becoming angry or
25 being pained or feeling pity; by states of character the things in
virtue of which we stand well or badly with reference to the passions,
e.g. with reference to anger we stand badly if we feel it violently or
too weakly, and well if we feel it in an intermediate way;* and
similarly with reference to the other passions.

Now neither the virtues nor the vices are *passions*, because we are
30 not called good or bad on the ground of our passions, but are so

called on the ground of our virtues and our vices, and because we
are neither praised nor blamed for our passions (for the man who
feels fear or anger is not praised, nor is the man who simply feels
anger blamed, but the man who feels it in a certain way), but for our   1106a
virtues and our vices we *are* praised or blamed.

Again, we feel anger and fear without choice, but the virtues
are modes of choice or involve choice.* Further, in respect of the
passions we are said to be moved, but in respect of the virtues and   5
the vices we are said not to be moved but to be disposed in a particular way.

For these reasons also they are not *capacities*; for we are neither
called good or bad, nor praised or blamed, for the simple capacity
of feeling the passions; again, we have the capacities by nature, but
we are not made good or bad by nature; we have spoken of this   10
before.[1]

If, then, the virtues are neither passions nor capacities, all that
remains is that they should be *states of character*.*

Thus we have stated what virtue is in respect of its genus.

*The differentia of moral virtue: it is a disposition to choose the
'intermediate'. Two kinds of intermediate distinguished*

6. We must, however, not only describe virtue as a state of character, but also say what sort of state it is. We may remark, then, that   15
every virtue or excellence* both brings into good condition the
thing of which it is the excellence and makes the work of that thing
be done well; e.g. the excellence of the eye makes both the eye and
its work good; for it is by the excellence of the eye that we see well.
Similarly the excellence of the horse makes a horse both good in
itself and good at running and at carrying its rider and at awaiting   20
the attack of the enemy. Therefore, if this is true in every case, the
virtue of man also will be the state of character which makes a man
good and which makes him do his own work well.

How this is to happen we have stated already,[2] but it will be made
plain also by the following consideration of the specific nature of   25
virtue. In everything that is continuous and divisible it is possible
to take more, less, or an equal amount, and that either in terms of
the thing itself or relatively to us; and the equal is an intermediate

---

[1] 1103a18–b2.   [2] 1104a11–27.

between excess and defect. By the intermediate in the object I mean
30 that which is equidistant from each of the extremes, which is one
and the same for all; by the intermediate relatively to us that which
is neither too much nor too little*—and this is not one, nor the
same for all.* For instance, if ten is many and two is few, six is the
intermediate, taken in terms of the object; for it exceeds and is
exceeded by an equal amount; this is intermediate according to
35 arithmetical proportion. But the intermediate relatively to us is not
to be taken so; if ten pounds is too much for a particular person to
1106b eat and two too little, it does not follow that the trainer will order
six pounds; for this also is perhaps too much for the person who is
to take it, or too little—too little for Milo, too much for the beginner
in athletic exercises.* The same is true of running and wrestling.
5 Thus a master of any art avoids excess and defect, but seeks the
intermediate and chooses this—the intermediate not in the object
but relatively to us.*

If it is thus, then, that every art does its work well— by looking
to the intermediate and judging its works by this standard (so
10 that we often say of good works of art that it is not possible either
to take away or to add anything, implying that excess and defect
destroy the goodness of works of art, while the mean preserves
it;* and good artists, as we say, look to this in their work), and if,
further, virtue is more exact and better than any art, as nature also
15 is, then virtue must have the quality of aiming at the intermediate.
I mean moral virtue; for it is this that is concerned with passions
and actions, and in these there is excess, defect, and the intermediate. For instance, both fear and confidence and appetite and anger
and pity and in general pleasure and pain may be felt both too
20 much and too little, and in both cases not well; but to feel them at
the right times, with reference to the right objects, towards the
right people, with the right motive, and in the right way, is what is
both intermediate and best, and this is characteristic of virtue.*
Similarly with regard to actions also there is excess, defect, and the
25 intermediate. Now virtue is concerned with passions and actions,
in which excess is a form of failure, and so is defect, while the
intermediate is praised and is a form of success; and being praised
and being successful are both characteristics of virtue. Therefore
virtue is a kind of mean, since, as we have seen, it aims at what is
intermediate.

Again, it is possible to fail in many ways (for evil belongs to the class of the unlimited, as the Pythagoreans conjectured, and good to that of the limited), while to succeed is possible only in one way (for which reason also one is easy and the other difficult—to miss the mark easy, to hit it difficult); for these reasons also, then, excess and defect are characteristic of vice, and the mean of virtue;

For men are good in but one way, but bad in many.

Virtue, then, is a state of character concerned with choice, lying in a mean, i.e. the mean relative to us, this being determined by reason, and by that reason by which the man of practical wisdom would determine it.* Now it is a mean between two vices, that which depends on excess and that which depends on defect; and again it is a mean because the vices respectively fall short of or exceed what is right in both passions and actions, while virtue both finds and chooses that which is intermediate. Hence in respect of what it is, i.e. the definition which states its essence, virtue is a mean, with regard to what is best and right an extreme.

But not every action nor every passion admits of a mean; for some have names that already imply badness, e.g. spite, shamelessness, envy, and in the case of actions adultery, theft, murder; for all of these and suchlike things imply by their names that they are themselves bad,* and not the excesses or deficiencies of them. It is not possible, then, ever to be right with regard to them; one must always be wrong. Nor does goodness or badness with regard to such things depend on committing adultery with the right woman, at the right time, and in the right way, but simply to do any of them is to go wrong. It would be equally absurd, then, to expect that in unjust, cowardly, and self-indulgent action there should be a mean, an excess, and a deficiency; for at that rate there would be a mean of excess and of deficiency, an excess of excess, and a deficiency of deficiency. But as there is no excess and deficiency of temperance and courage* because what is intermediate is in a sense an extreme, so too of the actions we have mentioned there is no mean nor any excess and deficiency, but however they are done they are wrong; for in general there is neither a mean of excess and deficiency, nor excess and deficiency of a mean.

The above proposition illustrated by reference to particular virtues

7. We must, however, not only make this general statement, but also apply it to the individual facts. For among statements about conduct those which are general apply more widely, but those which are particular are more true, since conduct has to do with individual cases, and our statements must harmonize with the facts in these cases. We may take these cases from our table.* With regard to feelings of fear and confidence courage is the mean; of the people who exceed, he who exceeds in fearlessness has no name (many of the states have no name), while the man who exceeds in confidence is rash, and he who exceeds in fear and falls short in confidence is a coward. With regard to pleasures and pains—not all of them, and not so much with regard to the pains—the mean is temperance, the excess self-indulgence. Persons deficient with regard to the pleasures are not often found; hence such persons also have received no name. But let us call them 'insensible'.*

With regard to giving and taking of money the mean is liberality, the excess and the defect prodigality and meanness. In these actions people exceed and fall short in contrary ways; the prodigal exceeds in spending and falls short in taking, while the mean man exceeds in taking and falls short in spending. (At present we are giving a mere outline or summary, and are satisfied with this; later these states will be more exactly determined.)[1] With regard to money there are also other dispositions—a mean, magnificence (for the magnificent man differs from the liberal man; the former deals with large sums, the latter with small ones), an excess, tastelessness and vulgarity, and a deficiency, niggardliness; these differ from the states opposed to liberality, and the mode of their difference will be stated later.[2]

With regard to honour and dishonour the mean is proper pride, the excess is known as a sort of 'empty vanity', and the deficiency is undue humility; and as we said liberality was related to magnificence, differing from it by dealing with small sums, so there is a state similarly related to proper pride, being concerned with small honours while that is concerned with great. For it is possible to desire honour as one ought, and more than one ought, and less, and the man who exceeds in his desires is called ambitious, the man

---

[1] IV. 1.   [2] 1122a20–29, b10–18.

who falls short unambitious, while the intermediate person has no name. The dispositions also are nameless, except that that of the ambitious man is called ambition. Hence the people who are at the extremes lay claim to the middle place; and we ourselves sometimes call the intermediate person ambitious and sometimes unambitious, and sometimes praise the ambitious man and sometimes the unambitious. The reason of our doing this will be stated in what follows;[1] but now let us speak of the remaining states according to the method which has been indicated.

With regard to anger also there is an excess, a deficiency, and a mean. Although they can scarcely be said to have names, yet since we call the intermediate person good-tempered let us call the mean good temper; of the persons at the extremes let the one who exceeds be called irascible, and his vice irascibility, and the man who falls short an unirascible sort of person, and the deficiency unirascibility.

There are also three other means, which have a certain likeness to one another, but differ from one another: for they are all concerned with intercourse in words and actions, but differ in that one is concerned with truth in this sphere, the other two with pleasantness; and of this one kind is exhibited in giving amusement, the other in all the circumstances of life. We must therefore speak of these too, that we may the better see that in all things the mean is praiseworthy, and the extremes neither praiseworthy nor right, but worthy of blame. Now most of these states also have no names, but we must try, as in the other cases, to invent names ourselves so that we may be clear and easy to follow. With regard to truth, then, the intermediate is a truthful sort of person and the mean may be called truthfulness, while the pretence which exaggerates is boastfulness and the person characterized by it a boaster, and that which understates is mock modesty and the person characterized by it mock-modest.* With regard to pleasantness in the giving of amusement the intermediate person is ready-witted and the disposition ready wit, the excess is buffoonery and the person characterized by it a buffoon, while the man who falls short is a sort of boor and his state is boorishness. With regard to the remaining kind of pleasantness, that which is exhibited in life in general, the man who is pleasant in the right way is friendly and the mean is friendliness, while the man who exceeds is an obsequious person if he has no end in view, a flatterer

[1] b11–26, 1125b14–18.

if he is aiming at his own advantage, and the man who falls short
30 and is unpleasant in all circumstances is a quarrelsome and surly
sort of person.

There are also means in the passions and concerned with the
passions; since shame is not a virtue, and yet praise is extended to
the modest man. For even in these matters one man is said to be
intermediate, and another to exceed, as for instance the bashful
man who is ashamed of everything; while he who falls short or is
35 not ashamed of anything at all is shameless, and the intermediate
person is modest. Righteous indignation is a mean between envy
1108b and spite, and these states are concerned with the pain and pleasure
that are felt at the fortunes of our neighbours; the man who is characterized by righteous indignation is pained at undeserved good
fortune, the envious man, going beyond him, is pained at all good
5 fortune, and the spiteful man falls so far short of being pained that
he even rejoices.* But these states there will be an opportunity of
describing elsewhere; with regard to justice, since it has not one
simple meaning, we shall, after describing the other states, distinguish its two kinds and say how each of them is a mean;[1] and similarly
10 we shall treat also of the rational virtues.[2]

CHARACTERISTICS OF THE EXTREME AND MEAN
STATES: PRACTICAL COROLLARIES

The extremes are opposed to each other and to the mean

8. There are three kinds of disposition, then, two of them vices,
involving excess and deficiency respectively, and one a virtue,
namely, the mean, and all are in a sense opposed to all; for the
extreme states are contrary both to the intermediate state and to
15 each other, and the intermediate to the extremes; as the equal is
greater relatively to the less, less relatively to the greater, so the
middle states are excessive relatively to the deficiencies, deficient
relatively to the excesses, both in passions and in actions. For the
brave man appears rash relatively to the coward, and cowardly rela-
20 tively to the rash man; and similarly the temperate man appears
self-indulgent relatively to the insensible man, insensible relatively
to the self-indulgent, and the liberal man prodigal relatively to the

---

[1] 1129a26–b1, 1130a14–b5, 1131b9–15, 1132a24–30, 1133b30–1134a1
[2] Bk. VI.

mean man, mean relatively to the prodigal. Hence also the people
at the extremes push the intermediate man each over to the other,
and the brave man is called rash by the coward, cowardly by the   25
rash man, and correspondingly in the other cases.

These states being thus opposed to one another, the greatest
contrariety is that of the extremes to each other, rather than to the
intermediate; for these are further from each other than from the
intermediate, as the great is further from the small and the small
from the great than both are from the equal. Again, to the inter-   30
mediate some extremes show a certain likeness, as that of rashness
to courage and that of prodigality to liberality; but the extremes
show the greatest unlikeness to each other; now contraries are
defined as the things that are furthest from each other, so that
things that are further apart are more contrary.

To the intermediate in some cases the deficiency, in some the   1109a
excess, is more opposed;* e.g. it is not rashness, which is an excess,
but cowardice, which is a deficiency, that is more opposed to courage,
and not insensibility, which is a deficiency, but self-indulgence, which
is an excess, that is more opposed to temperance. This happens from
two reasons, one being drawn from the thing itself; for because one   5
extreme is nearer and liker to the intermediate, we oppose not this
but rather its contrary to the intermediate. For example, since rashness is thought more like and nearer to courage, and cowardice
more unlike, we oppose rather the latter to courage; for things that   10
are further from the intermediate are thought more contrary to it.
This, then, is one cause, drawn from the thing itself; another is
drawn from ourselves; for the things to which we ourselves more
naturally tend seem more contrary to the intermediate. For instance,
we ourselves tend more naturally to pleasures, and hence are more   15
easily carried away towards self-indulgence than towards propriety.
We describe as contrary to the mean, then, rather the directions
in which we more often go to great lengths; and therefore self-
indulgence, which is an excess, is the more contrary to temperance.

*The mean is hard to attain, and is grasped by perception, not by
  reasoning*

9. That moral virtue is a mean, then, and in what sense it is so, and   20
that it is a mean between two vices, the one involving excess, the
other deficiency, and that it is such because its character is to aim

at what is intermediate in passions and in actions, has been sufficiently stated. Hence also it is no easy task to be good. For in every-
25 thing it is no easy task to find the middle, e.g. to find the middle of
a circle is not for everyone but for him who knows; so, too, anyone
can get angry—that is easy—or give or spend money; but to do this
to the right person, to the right extent, at the right time, with the
right motive, and in the right way, *that* is not for everyone, nor is it
easy; wherefore goodness is both rare and laudable and noble.

30   Hence he who aims at the intermediate must first depart from
what is the more contrary to it, as Calypso advises—

Hold the ship out beyond that surf and spray.*

For of the extremes one is more erroneous, one less so; therefore,
since to hit the intermediate is hard in the extreme, we must as a
35 second best, as people say, take the least of the evils; and this will
1109b be done best in the way we describe.

But we must consider the things towards which we ourselves also
are easily carried away; for some of us tend to one thing, some to
another;* and this will be recognizable from the pleasure and the
pain we feel. We must drag ourselves away to the contrary extreme;
5 for we shall get into the intermediate state by drawing well away
from error, as people do in straightening sticks that are bent.

Now in everything the pleasant or pleasure is most to be guarded
against; for we do not judge it impartially. We ought, then, to feel
towards pleasure as the elders of the people felt towards Helen, and
10 in all circumstances repeat their saying;[1] for if we dismiss pleasure
thus we are less likely to go astray. It is by doing this, then, (to sum
the matter up) that we shall best be able to hit the intermediate.

But this is no doubt difficult, and especially in individual cases;
15 for it is not easy to determine both how and with whom and on what
provocation and how long one should be angry; for we too sometimes praise those who fall short and call them good-tempered, but
sometimes we praise those who get angry and call them manly.

The man, however, who deviates little from goodness is not
blamed, whether he do so in the direction of the more or of the less,
but only the man who deviates more widely; for *he* does not fail to
20 be noticed. But up to what point and to what extent a man must
deviate before he becomes blameworthy it is not easy to determine

---

[1] *Iliad* iii.156–60.

by reasoning, any more than anything else that is perceived by the senses; such things depend on particular facts, and the decision rests with perception.* So much, then, is plain, that the intermediate state is in all things to be praised, but that we must incline sometimes towards the excess, sometimes towards the deficiency; 25 for so shall we most easily hit the intermediate and what is right.

VOLUNTARY AND INVOLUNTARY ACTIONS, CHOICE, RESPONSIBILITY

Praise and blame attach to voluntary actions, i.e. actions done
(1) not by force, and (2) with knowledge of the circumstances

30 1. SINCE virtue is concerned with passions and actions, and on voluntary ones praise and blame are bestowed, on those that are involuntary pardon, and sometimes also pity, to distinguish the voluntary and the involuntary is presumably necessary for those who are studying the nature of virtue, and useful also for legislators with a view to the assigning both of honours and of punishments.*

35 Those things, then, are thought involuntary, which take place by
1110a force or by reason of ignorance;* and that is forced of which the moving principle is outside, being a principle in which nothing is contributed by the person who acts—or, rather, is acted upon, e.g. if he were to be carried somewhere by a wind, or by men who had him in their power.

But with regard to the things that are done from fear of greater
5 evils or for some noble object (e.g. if a tyrant were to order one to do something base, having one's parents and children in his power, and if one did the action they were to be saved, but otherwise would be put to death), it may be debated whether such actions are involuntary or voluntary.* Something of the sort happens also with regard to the throwing of goods overboard in a storm; for in the abstract no one
10 throws goods away voluntarily, but on condition of its securing the safety of himself and his crew any sensible man does so. Such actions, then, are mixed, but are more like voluntary actions; for they are chosen at the time when they are done, and the end of an action is relative to the occasion.* Both the terms, then, 'voluntary' and 'invol- untary', must be used with reference to the moment of action. Now
15 the man acts voluntarily; for the principle that moves the instrumen- tal parts of the body in such actions is in him, and the things of which the moving principle is in a man himself are in his power to do or not to do. Such actions, therefore, are voluntary, but in the abstract per- haps involuntary; for no one would choose any such act in itself.*

For such actions men are sometimes even praised, when they 20
endure something base or painful in return for great and noble
objects gained; in the opposite case they are blamed, since to endure
the greatest indignities for no noble end or for a trifling end is the
mark of an inferior person.* On some actions praise indeed is not
bestowed, but pardon is, when one does a wrongful act under pressure which overstrains human nature and which no one could 25
withstand. But some acts, perhaps, we cannot be compelled to do,
but ought rather to face death after the most fearful sufferings; for
the things that 'compelled' Euripides' Alcmaeon to slay his mother
seem absurd.* It is difficult sometimes to determine what should be
chosen at what cost, and what should be endured in return for what 30
gain, and yet more difficult to abide by our decisions; for as a rule
what is expected is painful, and what we are compelled to do is
base, whence praise and blame are bestowed on those who have
been compelled or have not.

What sort of acts, then, should be called forced? We answer that 1110b
without qualification actions are so when the cause is in the external
circumstances and the agent contributes nothing. But the things
that in themselves are involuntary, but now and in return for these
gains are chosen, and whose moving principle is in the agent, are in
themselves involuntary, but now and in return for these gains vol- 5
untary.* They are more like voluntary acts; for actions are in the
class of particulars, and the particular acts here are voluntary. What
sort of things are to be chosen, and in return for what, it is not easy
to state; for there are many differences in the particular cases.

But if someone were to say that pleasant and noble objects have
a forcing power, compelling us from without, all acts would be for 10
him forced; for it is for these objects that all men do everything they
do. And those who act by force and unwillingly act with pain, but
those who do acts for their pleasantness or nobility do them with
pleasure; it is absurd to make external circumstances responsible, and
not oneself, as being easily caught by such attractions, and to make 15
oneself responsible for noble acts but the pleasant objects responsible for base acts. The forced, then, seems to be that whose moving
principle is outside, the person forced contributing nothing.

Everything that is done by reason of ignorance is *not* voluntary;
it is only what produces pain and regret that is *in*voluntary.* For
the man who has done something by reason of ignorance, and feels 20

not the least vexation at his action, has not acted voluntarily, since
he did not know what he was doing, nor yet involuntarily, since he
is not pained. Of people, then, who act by reason of ignorance he
who regrets is thought an involuntary agent, and the man who does
not regret may, since he is different, be called a not voluntary agent;
for, since he differs from the other, it is better that he should have
a name of his own.

25 Acting by reason of ignorance seems also to be different from
acting *in* ignorance; for the man who is drunk or in a rage is thought
to act as a result not of ignorance but of one of the causes mentioned, yet not knowingly but in ignorance.

Now every wicked man is ignorant of what he ought to do and
what he ought to abstain from, and error of this kind makes men
30 unjust and in general bad; but the term 'involuntary' tends to be
used not if a man is ignorant of what is to his advantage—for it is
not mistaken purpose that makes an action involuntary (*it* makes
men *wicked*), nor ignorance of the universal (for *that* men are
blamed), but ignorance of particulars, i.e. of the circumstances of
1111a the action and the objects with which it is concerned.* For it is on
these that both pity and pardon depend, since the person who is
ignorant of any of these acts involuntarily.

Perhaps it is just as well, therefore, to determine their nature
and number. A man may be ignorant, then, of who he is, what he is
doing, what or whom he is acting on, and sometimes also what (e.g.
what instrument) he is doing it with, and to what end (e.g. he may
5 think his act will conduce to someone's safety), and how he is doing
it (e.g. whether gently or violently). Now of all of these no one could
be ignorant unless he were mad, and evidently also he could not be
ignorant of the agent; for how could he not know himself? But of
what he is doing a man might be ignorant, as for instance people say
'it slipped out of their mouths as they were speaking', or 'they did
10 not know it was a secret', as Aeschylus said of the mysteries, or a
man might say he 'let it go off when he merely wanted to show its
working', as the man did with the catapult. Again, one might think
one's son was an enemy, as Merope did, or that a pointed spear had
a button on it, or that a stone was pumice-stone; or one might give
a man a draught to save him, and really kill him; or one might want
to touch a man, as people do in sparring, and really wound him.
15 The ignorance may relate, then, to any of these things, and the man

who was ignorant of any of these is thought to have acted involuntarily, and especially if he was ignorant on the most important points; and these are thought to be the circumstances of the action and its end. Further, the doing of an act that is called involuntary in virtue of ignorance of this sort must be painful and involve regret.   20

Since that which is done by force or by reason of ignorance is involuntary, the voluntary would seem to be that of which the moving principle is in the agent himself, he being aware of the particular circumstances of the action.* Presumably acts done by reason of anger or appetite are not rightly called involuntary. For in the first   25 place, on that showing none of the other animals will act voluntarily, nor will children; and secondly, is it meant that we do not do voluntarily *any* of the acts that are due to appetite or anger, or that we do the noble acts voluntarily and the base acts involuntarily? Is not this absurd, when one and the same thing is the cause? But it would surely be odd to describe as involuntary the things one ought   30 to desire; and we ought both to be angry at certain things and to have an appetite for certain things, e.g. for health and for learning. Also what is involuntary is thought to be painful, but what is in accordance with appetite is thought to be pleasant. Again, what is the difference in respect of involuntariness between errors committed upon calculation and those committed in anger? Both are to be avoided, but the irrational passions are thought not less human than   1111b reason is, and therefore also the actions which proceed from anger or appetite are the man's actions. It would be odd, then, to treat them as involuntary.*

Choice distinguished from the voluntary: the object of choice is the result of previous deliberation

2. Both the voluntary and the involuntary having been delimited, we must next discuss choice; for it is thought to be most closely bound up   5 with virtue, and to discriminate characters better than actions do.

Choice, then, seems to be voluntary, but not the same thing as the voluntary; the latter extends more widely. For both children and the lower animals share in voluntary action, but not in choice, and acts done on the spur of the moment we describe as voluntary, but not as chosen.*   10

Those who say it is appetite or anger or wish or a kind of opinion do not seem to be right. For choice is not common to irrational

creatures as well, but appetite and anger are. Again, the incontinent
man acts with appetite, but not with choice; while the continent
15 man on the contrary acts with choice, but not with appetite.* Again,
appetite is contrary to choice, but not appetite to appetite. Again,
appetite relates to the pleasant and the painful, choice neither to the
painful nor to the pleasant.

Still less is it anger; for acts due to anger are thought to be less
than any others objects of choice.

20   But neither is it wish, though it seems near to it; for choice cannot
relate to impossibles, and if any one said he chose them he would
be thought silly; but there may be a wish even for impossibles, e.g.
for immortality. And wish may relate to things that could in no way
be brought about by one's own efforts, e.g. that a particular actor or
25 athlete should win in a competition; but no one chooses such
things, but only the things that he thinks could be brought about by
his own efforts.* Again, wish relates rather to the end, choice to the
means; for instance, we wish to be healthy, but we choose the acts
which will make us healthy, and we wish to be happy and say we
do, but we cannot well say we choose to be so; for, in general, choice
30 seems to relate to the things that are in our own power.*

For this reason, too, it cannot be opinion; for opinion is thought
to relate to all kinds of things, no less to eternal things and impossible things than to things in our own power; and it is distinguished
by its falsity or truth, not by its badness or goodness, while choice
is distinguished rather by these.

Now with opinion in general perhaps no one even says it is
1112a identical. But it is not identical even with any kind of opinion; for
by choosing what is good or bad we are men of a certain character,
which we are not by holding certain opinions. And we choose to get
or avoid something good or bad, but we have opinions about what
a thing is or whom it is good for or how it is good for him; we can
5 hardly be said to opine to get or avoid anything. And choice is
praised for being related to the right object or for being *right*, opinion for being true.* And we choose what we best know to be good,
but we opine what we do not in the least know to be good; and it is
not the same people that are thought to make the best choices and
to have the best opinions, but some are thought to have fairly good
10 opinions, but by reason of vice to choose what they should not. If
opinion precedes choice or accompanies it, that makes no difference;

for it is not this that we are considering, but whether choice is *identical* with some kind of opinion.

What, then, or what kind of thing is it, since it is none of the things we have mentioned? It seems to be voluntary, but not all that is voluntary to be an object of choice. Is it, then, what has been decided by earlier deliberation? At any rate choice involves reason and thought. Even the name seems to suggest that it is what is chosen before other things.*

The nature of deliberation and its objects: choice is deliberate desire of things in our own power

3. Do we deliberate about everything, and is everything a possible subject of deliberation, or is deliberation impossible about some things? We ought presumably to call not what a fool or a madman would deliberate about, but what a sensible man would deliberate about, a subject of deliberation. Now about eternal things no one deliberates, e.g. about the material universe or the incommensurability of the diagonal and the side of a square.* But no more do we deliberate about the things that involve movement but always happen in the same way, whether of necessity or by nature or from any other cause, e.g. the solstices and the risings of the stars; nor about things that happen now in one way, now in another, e.g. droughts and rains; nor about chance events, like the finding of treasure. But we do not deliberate even about all human affairs; for instance, no Spartan deliberates about the best constitution for the Scythians. For none of these things can be brought about by our own efforts.

We deliberate about things that are in our power and can be done; and these are in fact what is left. For nature, necessity, and chance are thought to be causes, and also reason and everything that depends on man. Now every class of men deliberates about the things that can be done by their own efforts. And in the case of exact and self-contained sciences there is no deliberation, e.g. about the letters of the alphabet (for we have no doubt how they should be written); but the things that are brought about by our own efforts, but not always in the same way, are the things about which we deliberate, e.g. questions of medical treatment or of money-making. And we do so more in the case of the art of navigation than in that of gymnastics, inasmuch as it has been less exactly worked out, and again about other things in the same ratio, and more also

in the case of the arts than in that of the sciences; for we have more
doubt about the former. Deliberation is concerned with things that
happen in a certain way for the most part, but in which the outcome
is obscure, and with things in which it is indeterminate. We call in
10 others to aid us in deliberation on important questions, distrusting
ourselves as not being equal to deciding.

We deliberate not about ends but about means.* For a doctor
does not deliberate whether he shall heal, nor an orator whether he
shall convince, nor a statesman whether he shall produce law and
15 order, nor does any one else deliberate about his end. Having set
the end, they consider how and by what means it is to be attained;
and if it seems to be produced by several means they consider by
which it is most easily and best produced, while if it is achieved by
one only they consider how it will be achieved by this and by what
means *this* will be achieved, till they come to the first cause, which
20 in the order of discovery is last. For the person who deliberates
seems to inquire and analyse in the way described as though he
were analysing a geometrical construction (not all inquiry appears
to be deliberation—for instance mathematical inquiries—but all
deliberation is inquiry), and what is last in the order of analysis
seems to be first in the order of becoming.* And if we come on an
25 impossibility, we give up the search, e.g. if we need money and this
cannot be got; but if a thing appears possible we try to do it. By
'possible' things I mean things that might be brought about by our
own efforts; and these in a sense include things that can be brought
about by the efforts of our friends, since the moving principle is
in ourselves. The subject of investigation is sometimes the instruments, sometimes the use of them; and similarly in the other cases—
30 sometimes the means, sometimes the mode of using it or the means
of bringing it about. It seems, then, as has been said, that man is a
moving principle of actions; now deliberation is about the things to
be done by the agent himself, and actions are for the sake of things
other than themselves. For the end cannot be a subject of deliberation, but only the means; nor indeed can the particular facts be a
subject of it, e.g. whether this is bread or has been baked as it
1113a should; for these are matters of perception. If we are to be always
deliberating, we shall have to go on to infinity.

The same thing is deliberated upon and is chosen, except that
the object of choice is already determinate, since it is that which has

been decided upon as a result of deliberation that is the object of choice. For everyone ceases to inquire how he is to act when he has 5 brought the moving principle back to himself and to the ruling part of himself; for this is what chooses. This is plain also from the ancient constitutions, which Homer represented; for the kings announced their choices to the people.* The object of choice being one of the things in our own power which is desired after deliberation, choice will be deliberate desire of things in our own power; for when we 10 have reached a judgement as a result of deliberation, we desire in accordance with our deliberation.

We may take it, then, that we have described choice in outline; we have stated the nature of its objects and the fact that it is concerned with means.

The object of rational wish is the end, i.e. the good or apparent good

4. That *wish* is for the end has already been stated;[1] some think it 15 is for the good, others for the apparent good. Now those who say that the good is the object of wish must admit in consequence that that which the man who does not choose aright wishes for is not an object of wish (for if it is to be so, it must also be good; but it may well have been bad); while those who say the apparent good is the 20 object of wish must admit that there is no natural object of wish, but only what seems good to each man.* Now different things appear good to different people, and, if it so happens, even contrary things.

If these consequences are unpleasing, are we to say that absolutely and in truth the good is the object of wish, but for each person the apparent good; that that which is in truth an object of wish 25 is an object of wish to the good man, while any chance thing may be so to the bad man, as in the case of bodies also the things that are in truth wholesome are wholesome for bodies which are in good condition, while for those that are diseased other things are wholesome—or bitter or sweet or hot or heavy, and so on; since the good man judges each class of things rightly, and in each the truth 30 appears to him?* For each state of character has its own ideas of the noble and the pleasant, and perhaps the good man differs from others most by seeing the truth in each class of things, being as it were the norm and measure of them.* In most things the error seems

---

[1] 1111b26.

1113b to be due to pleasure; for this appears a good when it is not. We
therefore choose the pleasant as a good and avoid pain as an evil.

Virtue and vice are in our power

5. The end, then, being what we wish for, the means what we deliberate about and choose, actions concerning means must be according
5 to choice and voluntary. Now the exercise of the virtues is concerned with means. Therefore virtue also is in our own power, and
so too vice. For where it is in our power to act it is also in our power
not to act, and *vice versa*; so that, if to act, where this is noble, is in
our power, not to act, which will be base, will also be in our power,
10 and if not to act, where this is noble, is in our power, to act, which
will be base, will also be in our power. Now if it is in our power to
do noble or base acts, and likewise in our power not to do them, and
this was what being good or bad meant, then it is in our power to
be virtuous or vicious.*

The saying that 'no one is voluntarily wicked nor involuntarily
15 happy' seems to be partly false and partly true; for no one is involuntarily happy, but wickedness *is* voluntary. Or else we shall have
to dispute what has just been said, at any rate, and deny that man
is a moving principle or begetter of his actions, as of children.

But if these facts are evident and we cannot refer actions to mov-
20 ing principles other than those in ourselves, the acts whose moving
principles are in us must themselves also be in our power and
voluntary.*

Witness seems to be borne to this both by individuals in their
private capacity and by legislators themselves; for these punish and
take vengeance on those who do wicked acts (unless they have acted
under compulsion or as a result of ignorance for which they are not
25 themselves responsible*), while they honour those who do noble
acts, as though they meant to encourage the latter and deter the
former. But no one is encouraged to do the things that are neither
in our power nor voluntary; it is assumed that there is no gain in
being persuaded not to be hot or in pain or hungry or the like, since
we shall experience these feelings none the less. Indeed, we punish
30 a man for his very ignorance, if he is thought responsible for the
ignorance, as when penalties are doubled in the case of drunkenness;* for the moving principle is in the man himself, since he had
the power of not getting drunk and his getting drunk was the cause

of his ignorance. And we punish those who are ignorant of anything in the laws that they ought to know and that is not difficult, and so 1114a too in the case of anything else that they are thought to be ignorant of through carelessness; we assume that it is in their power not to be ignorant, since they have the power of taking care.*

But perhaps a man is the kind of man not to take care. Still they are themselves by their slack lives responsible for becoming men of 5 that kind, and men are themselves responsible for being unjust or self-indulgent, in that they cheat or spend their time in drinking-bouts and the like; for it is activities exercised on particular objects that make the corresponding character. This is plain from the case of people training for any contest or action; they practise the activity the whole time. Now not to know that it is from the exercise of activities on particular objects that states of character are produced 10 is the mark of a thoroughly senseless person. Again, it is irrational to suppose that a man who acts unjustly does not wish to be unjust or a man who acts self-indulgently to be self-indulgent.* But if *without* being ignorant a man does the things which will make him unjust, he will be unjust voluntarily. Yet it does not follow that if he wishes he will cease to be unjust and will be just. For neither does the man who is ill become well on those terms. We may suppose a case in which he is ill voluntarily, through living incontinently and 15 disobeying his doctors. In that case it was *then* open to him not to be ill, but not now, when he has thrown away his chance, just as when you have let a stone go it is too late to recover it; but yet it was in your power to throw it, since the moving principle was in you. So, too, to the unjust and to the self-indulgent man it was open at 20 the beginning not to become men of this kind, and so they are unjust and self-indulgent voluntarily; but now that they have become so it is not possible for them not to be so.*

But not only are the vices of the soul voluntary, but those of the body also for some men, whom we accordingly blame; while no one blames those who are ugly by nature, we blame those who are so owing to want of exercise and care. So it is, too, with respect to 25 weakness and infirmity; no one would reproach a man blind from birth or by disease or from a blow, but rather pity him, while every one would blame a man who was blind from drunkenness or some other form of self-indulgence. Of vices of the body, then, those in our own power are blamed, those not in our power are not. And if

30 this be so, in the other cases also the vices that are blamed must be in our own power.

Now someone may say that all men aim at the apparent good, but have no control over the appearance, but the end appears to each
1114b man in a form answering to his character. We reply that if each man is somehow responsible for his state of character, he will also be himself somehow responsible for the appearance; but if not, no one is responsible for his own evildoing, but everyone does evil acts through ignorance of the end, thinking that by these he will get
5 what is best, and the aiming at the end is not self-chosen but one must be born with an eye, as it were, by which to judge rightly and choose what is truly good, and he is well endowed by nature who is well endowed with this. For it is what is greatest and most noble, and what we cannot get or learn from another, but must have just
10 such as it was when given us at birth, and to be well and nobly endowed with this will be perfect and true excellence of natural endowment. If this is true, then, how will virtue be more voluntary than vice? To both men alike, the good and the bad, the end appears and is fixed by nature or however it may be, and it is by referring
15 everything else to this that men do whatever they do.*

Whether, then, it is not by nature that the end appears to each man such as it does appear, but something also depends on him, or the end is natural but because the good man adopts the means voluntarily virtue is voluntary, vice also will be none the less volun-
20 tary; for in the case of the bad man there is equally present that which depends on himself in his actions even if not in his end. If, then, as is asserted, the virtues are voluntary (for we are ourselves somehow part-causes of our states of character,* and it is by being persons of a certain kind that we set the end to be so and so), the
25 vices also will be voluntary; for the same is true of them.

With regard to the virtues *in general* we have stated their genus in outline, namely, that they are means and that they are states of character, and that they tend, and by their own nature, to the doing of the acts by which they are produced, and that they are in our
30 power and voluntary, and act as reason prescribes. But actions and states of character are not voluntary in the same way; for we are masters of our actions from the beginning right to the end, if we know the particular facts, but though we control the beginning of
1115a our states of character the gradual progress is not obvious, any more

than it is in illnesses; because it was in our power, however, to act in this way or not in this way, therefore the states are voluntary.

Let us take up the several virtues, however, and say which they are and what sort of things they are concerned with and how they are concerned with them; at the same time it will become plain how 5 many they are. And first let us speak of courage.

COURAGE

Courage concerned with the feelings of fear and confidence—
strictly speaking, with the fear of death in battle

6. That it is a mean with regard to feelings of fear and confidence has already been made evident;* and plainly the things we fear are fearful things, and these are, to speak without qualification, evils; for which reason people even define fear as expectation of evil.* Now we fear all evils, e.g. disgrace, poverty, disease, friendlessness, 10 death, but the brave man is not thought to be concerned with all; for to fear some things is even right and noble, and it is base not to fear them—e.g. disgrace; he who fears this is good and modest, and he who does not is shameless. He is, however, by some people called brave, by a transference of the word to a new meaning; for he 15 has in him something which is like the brave man, since the brave man also is a fearless person.* Poverty and disease we perhaps ought not to fear, nor in general the things that do not proceed from vice and are not due to a man himself. But not even the man who is fearless of these is brave. Yet we apply the word to him also in virtue of a similarity; for some who in the dangers of war are cowards 20 are liberal and are confident in face of the loss of money. Nor is a man a coward if he fears insult to his wife and children or envy or anything of the kind; nor brave if he is confident when he is about to be flogged. With what sort of fearful things, then, is the brave man concerned? Surely with the greatest; for no one is more likely 25 than he to stand his ground against what is awe-inspiring. Now death is the most fearful of all things; for it is the end, and nothing is thought to be any longer either good or bad for the dead. But the brave man would not seem to be concerned even with death in *all* circumstances, e.g. at sea or in disease.* In what circumstances, then? Surely in the noblest. Now such deaths are those in battle; for 30 these take place in the greatest and noblest danger. And these are

correspondingly honoured in city-states and at the courts of mon-
archs. Properly, then, he will be called brave who is fearless in face
of a noble death, and of all emergencies that involve death; and the
35 emergencies of war are in the highest degree of this kind. Yet at sea
1115b also, and in disease, the brave man is fearless, but not in the same
way as the seamen; for he has given up hope of safety, and is dislik-
ing the thought of death in this shape, while they are hopeful
because of their experience. At the same time, we show courage in
situations where there is the opportunity of showing prowess or
5 where death is noble; but in these forms of death neither of these
conditions is fulfilled.

The motive of courage is the noble: characteristics of the opposite vices, cowardice and rashness

7. What is fearful is not the same for all men; but we say there are
things fearful even beyond human strength. These, then, are fearful
to everyone—at least to every sensible man; but the fearful things
10 that are *not* beyond human strength differ in magnitude and degree,
and so too do the things that inspire confidence. Now the brave man
is as dauntless as man may be. Therefore, while he will fear even
the things that are not beyond human strength, he will face them as
he ought and as reason directs, for the sake of the noble;* for this is
the end of virtue. But it is possible to fear these more, or less, and
again to fear things that are not fearful as if they were. Of the faults
15 that are committed, one consists in fearing what we should not,
another in fearing as we should not, another in fearing when we
should not, and so on; and so too with respect to the things that
inspire confidence. The man, then, who faces and who fears the
right things and from the right motive, in the right way and at the
right time, and who feels confidence under the corresponding conditions, is brave; for the brave man feels and acts according to the
20 merits of the case and in whatever way reason directs.* Now the
end of every activity is conformity to the corresponding state of
character. This is true, therefore, of the brave man as well as of
others. But courage is noble. Therefore the end also is noble; for
each thing is defined by its end. Therefore it is for a noble end that
the brave man endures and acts as courage directs.

Of those who go to excess he who exceeds in fearlessness has no
25 name (we have said previously that many states of character have

no names[1]), but he would be a sort of madman or insensitive to pain if he feared nothing, neither earthquakes nor the waves, as they say the Celts* do not; while the man who exceeds in confidence about what really is fearful is rash. The rash man, however, is also thought to be boastful and only a pretender to courage; at all events, as the brave man *is* with regard to what is fearful, so the rash man wishes to *appear*; and so he imitates him in situations where he can. Hence also most of them are a mixture of rashness and cowardice; for, while in these situations they display confidence, they do not hold their ground against what is really fearful. The man who exceeds in fear is a coward; for he fears both what he ought not and as he ought not, and all the similar characterizations attach to him. He is lacking also in confidence; but he is more conspicuous for his excess of fear in painful situations. The coward, then, is a despairing sort of person; for he fears everything. The brave man, on the other hand, has the opposite disposition; for confidence is the mark of a hopeful disposition. The coward, the rash man, and the brave man, then, are concerned with the same objects but are differently disposed towards them; for the first two exceed and fall short, while the third holds the middle, which is the right, position; and rash men are precipitate, and wish for dangers beforehand but draw back when they are in them, while brave men are excited in the moment of action, but collected beforehand.

As we have said, then, courage is a mean with respect to things that inspire confidence or fear, in the circumstances that have been stated;[2] and it chooses or endures things because it is noble to do so, or because it is base not to do so.[3] But to die to escape from poverty or love or anything painful is not the mark of a brave man, but rather of a coward; for it is softness to fly from what is troublesome, and such a man endures death not because it is noble but to fly from evil.

Five kinds of courage improperly so called

8. Courage, then, is something of this sort, but the name is also applied to five other kinds. (1) First comes the courage of the citizen-soldier; for this is most like true courage. Citizen-soldiers seem to face dangers because of the penalties imposed by the laws and the

---

[1] 1107b2, cf. 1107b29, 1108a5.   [2] Ch. 6.   [3] 1115b11–24.

reproaches they would otherwise incur, and because of the honours
they win by such action; and therefore those peoples seem to be
20 bravest among whom cowards are held in dishonour and brave men
in honour. This is the kind of courage that Homer depicts, e.g. in
Diomede and in Hector:

> First will Polydamas be to heap reproach on me then;

and

25 For Hector one day 'mid the Trojans shall utter his vaunting harangue:
'Afraid was Tydeides, and fled from my face.'*

This kind of courage is most like to that which we described earlier,
because it is due to virtue; for it is due to shame and to desire of
a noble object (i.e. honour) and avoidance of disgrace, which is
ignoble.* One might rank in the same class even those who are
30 compelled by their rulers; but they are inferior, inasmuch as they
do what they do not from shame but from fear, and to avoid not
what is disgraceful but what is painful; for their masters compel
them, as Hector does:

> But if I shall spy any dastard that cowers far from the fight,
35   Vainly will such an one hope to escape from the dogs.*

And those who give them their posts, and beat them if they retreat,
do the same, and so do those who draw them up with trenches or
1116b something of the sort behind them; all of these apply compulsion.
But one ought to be brave not under compulsion but because it is
noble to be so.

(2) Experience with regard to particular facts is also thought to
5 be courage; this is indeed the reason why Socrates thought courage
was knowledge.* Other people exhibit this quality in other dangers,
and professional soldiers exhibit it in the dangers of war; for there
seem to be many empty alarms in war, of which these have had the
most comprehensive experience; therefore they seem brave, because
the others do not know the nature of the facts. Again, their experience makes them most capable in attack and in defence, since they
10 can use their arms and have the kind that are likely to be best both
for attack and for defence; therefore they fight like armed men
against unarmed or like trained athletes against amateurs; for in
such contests too it is not the bravest men that fight best, but those
15 who are strongest and have their bodies in the best condition.

Professional soldiers turn cowards, however, when the danger puts
too great a strain on them and they are inferior in numbers and
equipment; for they are the first to fly, while citizen-forces die at
their posts, as in fact happened at the temple of Hermes.* For to
the latter flight is disgraceful and death is preferable to safety on   20
those terms; while the former from the very beginning faced the
danger on the assumption that they were stronger, and when they
know the facts they fly, fearing death more than disgrace; but the
brave man is not that sort of person.

(3) Passion also is sometimes reckoned as courage; those who act
from passion, like wild beasts rushing at those who have wounded   25
them, are thought to be brave, because brave men also are passionate;
for passion above all things is eager to rush on danger, and hence
Homer's 'put strength into his passion' and 'aroused their spirit
and passion' and 'hard he breathed panting' and 'his blood boiled'.*
For all such expressions seem to indicate the stirring and onset of   30
passion. Now brave men act for the sake of the noble, but passion aids
them; while wild beasts act under the influence of pain; for they
attack because they have been wounded or because they are afraid,
since if they are in a forest they do not come near one. Thus they are
not brave because, driven by pain and passion, they rush on danger   35
without foreseeing any of the perils, since at that rate even asses
would be brave when they are hungry; for blows will not drive them
from their food; and lust also makes adulterers do many daring   1117a
things. Those creatures are not brave, then, which are driven on to
danger by pain or passion. The 'courage' that is due to passion
seems to be the most natural, and to be courage if choice and motive
be added.*   5

Men, then, as well as beasts, suffer pain when they are angry, and
are pleased when they exact their revenge; those who fight for these
reasons, however, are pugnacious but not brave; for they do not act
for the sake of the noble nor as reason directs, but from strength of
feeling; they have, however, something akin to courage.

(4) Nor are sanguine people brave; for they are confident in dan-   10
ger only because they have conquered often and against many foes.
Yet they closely resemble brave men, because both are confident;
but brave men are confident for the reasons stated earlier,[1] while
these are so because they think they are the strongest and can suffer

[1] 1115b11–24.

nothing. (Drunken men also behave in this way; they become
15 sanguine.) When their adventures do not succeed, however, they
run away; but it was the mark of a brave man to face things that are,
and seem, terrible for a man, because it is noble to do so and disgraceful not to do so. Hence also it is thought the mark of a braver
man to be fearless and undisturbed in sudden alarms than to be so
in those that are foreseen; for it must have proceeded more from a
20 state of character, because less from preparation; acts that are foreseen may be chosen by calculation and reason, but sudden actions
must be in accordance with one's state of character.*

(5) People who are ignorant of the danger also appear brave, and
they are not far removed from those of a sanguine temper, but are
inferior inasmuch as they have no self-reliance while these have.
Hence also the sanguine hold their ground for a time; but those
25 who have been deceived about the facts fly if they know or suspect
that these are different from what they supposed, as happened to
the Argives when they fell in with the Spartans and took them for
Sicyonians.*

We have, then, described the character both of brave men and of
those who are thought to be brave.

Relation of courage to pain and pleasure

9. Though courage is concerned with confidence and fear, it is not
concerned with both alike, but more with the things that inspire
30 fear; for he who is undisturbed in face of these and bears himself as
he should towards these is more truly brave than the man who does
so towards the things that inspire confidence. It is for facing what
is painful, then, as has been said,[1] that men are called brave. Hence
also courage involves pain, and is justly praised; for it is harder to
face what is painful than to abstain from what is pleasant. Yet the
35 end which courage sets before itself would seem to be pleasant, but
1117b to be concealed by the attending circumstances, as happens also in
athletic contests; for the end at which boxers aim is pleasant—the
crown and the honours—but the blows they take are distressing to
5 flesh and blood, and painful, and so is their whole exertion; and
because the blows and the exertions are many the end, which is but
small, appears to have nothing pleasant in it. And so, if the case of
courage is similar, death and wounds will be painful to the brave

---

[1] 1115b7–13.

man and against his will, but he will face them because it is noble
to do so or because it is base not to do so. And the more he is possessed of virtue in its entirety and the happier he is, the more he   10
will be pained at the thought of death; for life is best worth living
for such a man, and he is knowingly losing the greatest goods, and
this is painful. But he is none the less brave, and perhaps all the
more so, because he chooses noble deeds of war at that cost. It is not
the case, then, with all the virtues that the exercise of them is pleas-   15
ant, except in so far as it attains its end.* But it is quite possible that
the best soldiers may be not men of this sort but those who are less
brave but have no other good; for these are ready to face danger,
and they sell their life for trifling gains.   20

So much, then, for courage; it is not difficult to grasp its nature
in outline, at any rate, from what has been said.

TEMPERANCE

Temperance is limited to certain pleasures of touch

10. After courage let us speak of temperance; for these seem to be
the virtues of the irrational parts. We have said[1] that temperance is
a mean with regard to pleasures (for it is less, and not in the same   25
way, concerned with pains); self-indulgence also is manifested in
the same sphere. Now, therefore, let us determine with what sort of
pleasures they are concerned. We may assume the distinction
between bodily pleasures and those of the soul, such as love of honour and love of learning; for the lover of each of these delights in
that of which he is a lover, the body being in no way affected, but   30
rather the mind; but men who are concerned with such pleasures
are called neither temperate nor self-indulgent. Nor, again, are those
who are concerned with the other pleasures that are not bodily; for
those who are fond of hearing and telling stories and who spend their
days on anything that turns up are gossips, but not self-indulgent,   35
nor are those who are pained at the loss of money or of friends.   1118a

Temperance must be concerned with bodily pleasures, but not
all even of these; for those who delight in objects of vision, such as
colours and shapes and painting, are called neither temperate nor
self-indulgent; yet it would seem possible to delight even in these   5
either as one should or to excess or to a deficient degree.

[1] 1107b4–6.

And so too is it with objects of hearing; no one calls those who delight extravagantly in music or acting self-indulgent, nor those who do so as they ought temperate.

Nor do we apply these names to those who delight in odour, unless it be incidentally; we do not call those self-indulgent who
10 delight in the odour of apples or roses or incense, but rather those who delight in the odour of perfumes or of dainty dishes; for self-indulgent people delight in these because these remind them of the objects of their appetite.* And one may see even other people, when they are hungry, delighting in the smell of food; but to delight in
15 this kind of thing is the mark of the self-indulgent man; for these are objects of appetite to him.

Nor is there in animals other than man any pleasure connected with these senses, except incidentally. For dogs do not delight in the scent of hares, but in the eating of them, but the scent told them
20 the hares were there; nor does the lion delight in the lowing of the ox, but in eating it; but he perceived by the lowing that it was near, and therefore appears to delight in the lowing; and similarly he does not delight because he sees 'a stag or a wild goat',[1] but because he is going to make a meal of it.* Temperance and self-indulgence, however, are concerned with the kind of pleasures that the other
25 animals share in, which therefore appear slavish and brutish; these are touch and taste. But even of taste they appear to make little or no use; for the business of taste is the discriminating of flavours, which is done by wine-tasters and people who season dishes; but they hardly take pleasure in making these discriminations, or at
30 least self-indulgent people do not, but in the actual enjoyment, which in all cases comes through touch, both in the case of food and in that of drink and in that of sexual intercourse. This is why a certain gourmand prayed that his throat might become longer than a crane's, implying that it was the contact that he took pleasure in.
1118b Thus the sense with which self-indulgence is connected is the most widely shared of the senses; and self-indulgence would seem to be justly a matter of reproach, because it attaches to us not as men but as animals. To delight in such things, then, and to love them above all others, is brutish. For even of the pleasures of touch the most
5 refined have been eliminated, e.g. those produced in the gymnasium by rubbing and by the consequent heat; for the contact characteristic

---

[1] *Iliad.* iii.24.

of the self-indulgent man does not affect the whole body but only
certain parts.*

*Characteristics of temperance and its opposites, self-indulgence
    and 'insensibility'*

11. Of the appetites some seem to be common, others to be peculiar to individuals and acquired; e.g. the appetite for food is natural,
since everyone who is without it craves for food or drink, and some-   10
times for both, and for 'bed' also (as Homer says)[1] if he is young and
lusty; but not everyone craves for this or that kind of these, nor for
the same things. Hence such craving appears to be our very own.
Yet it has of course something natural about it; for different things
are pleasant to different kinds of people, and some things are more
pleasant to everyone than chance objects. Now in the natural appe-   15
tites few go wrong, and only in one direction, that of excess; for to
eat or drink whatever offers itself till one is surfeited is to exceed the
natural amount, since natural appetite is the replenishment of one's
deficiency. Hence these people are called belly-gods, this implying
that they fill their belly beyond what is right. It is people of entirely   20
slavish character that become like this. But with regard to the pleasures peculiar to individuals many people go wrong and in many
ways. For while the people who are 'fond of so-and-so' are so called
because they delight either in the wrong things, or more than most
people do, or in the wrong way, the self-indulgent exceed in all
three ways; they both delight in some things that they ought not to   25
delight in (since they are hateful), and if one ought to delight in
some of the things they delight in, they do so more than one ought
and than most men do.

Plainly, then, excess with regard to pleasures is self-indulgence
and is culpable; with regard to pains one is not, as in the case of
courage, called temperate for facing them or self-indulgent for not
doing so, but the self-indulgent man is so called because he is   30
pained more than he ought at not getting pleasant things (even his
pain being caused by pleasure), and the temperate man is so called
because he is not pained at the absence of what is pleasant and at his
abstinence from it.

The self-indulgent man, then, craves for all pleasant things or   1119a
those that are most pleasant, and is led by his appetite to go for

[1] Ibid. xxiv.130.

these at the cost of everything else; hence he is pained both when he fails to get them and when he is merely craving for them (for appetite involves pain); but it seems absurd to be pained because of

5 pleasure. People who fall short with regard to pleasures and delight in them less than they should are hardly found; for such insensibility is not human. Even the other animals distinguish different kinds of food and enjoy some and not others; and if there is anyone who finds nothing pleasant and nothing more attractive than anything else, he must be something quite different from a man; this sort of

10 person has not received a name because he hardly occurs. The temperate man occupies a middle position with regard to these objects. For he neither enjoys the things that the self-indulgent man enjoys most—but rather dislikes them—nor in general the things that he should not, nor anything of this sort to excess, nor does he feel pain or craving when they are absent, or does so only to a moderate

15 degree, and not more than he should, nor when he should not, and so on; but the things that, being pleasant, make for health or for good condition, he will desire moderately and as he should, and also other pleasant things if they are not hindrances to these ends, or contrary to what is noble, or beyond his means. For he who neglects these conditions loves such pleasures more than they are worth, but the temperate man is not that sort of person, but the sort of person

20 that correct reason prescribes.

*Self-indulgence more voluntary than cowardice: comparison of
    the self-indulgent man to the spoilt child*

12. Self-indulgence is more like a voluntary state than cowardice. For the former is actuated by pleasure, the latter by pain, of which the one is to be chosen and the other to be avoided; and pain upsets and destroys the nature of the person who feels it, while pleasure does nothing of the sort. Therefore self-indulgence is more voluntary.

25 Hence also it is more a matter of reproach; for it is easier to become accustomed to its objects, since there are many things of this sort in life, and the process of habituation to them is free from danger, while with terrible objects the reverse is the case. But cowardice would seem to be voluntary in a different degree from its particular manifestations; for it is itself painless, but in these we are upset by

30 pain, so that we even throw down our arms and disgrace ourselves in other ways; hence our acts are even thought to be done under

compulsion. For the self-indulgent man, on the other hand, the particular acts are voluntary (for he does them with craving and desire),
but the whole state is less so; for no one craves to be self-indulgent.

The name self-indulgence is applied also to childish faults; for
they bear a certain resemblance to what we have been considering. 3
Which is called after which, makes no difference to our present 1119b
purpose; plainly, however, the later is called after the earlier.* The
transference of the name seems not a bad one; for that which desires
what is base and which develops quickly ought to be kept in a chastened condition, and these characteristics belong above all to appetite and to the child, since children in fact live at the beck and call 5
of appetite, and it is in them that the desire for what is pleasant is
strongest. If, then, it is not going to be obedient and subject to the
ruling principle, it will go to great lengths; for in an irrational being
the desire for pleasure is insatiable even if it tries every source of
gratification, and the exercise of appetite increases its innate force,
and if appetites are strong and violent they even expel the power of 10
calculation. Hence they should be moderate and few, and should in
no way oppose the rational principle—and this is what we call an
obedient and chastened state—and as the child should live according to the direction of his tutor,* so the appetitive element should
live according to reason. Hence the appetitive element in a temper- 15
ate man should harmonize with reason; for the noble is the mark at
which both aim, and the temperate man craves for the things he
ought, as he ought, and when he ought; and this is what reason
directs.

Here we conclude our account of temperance.

BOOK IV · MORAL VIRTUE (cont.)

VIRTUES CONCERNED WITH MONEY

Liberality

1. LET us speak next of liberality.* It seems to be the mean with regard to wealth; for the liberal man is praised not in respect of military matters, nor of those in respect of which the temperate man is praised, nor of judicial decisions, but with regard to the 25 giving and taking of wealth, and especially in respect of giving. Now by 'wealth' we mean all the things whose value is measured by money. Further, prodigality and meanness are excesses and defects with regard to wealth; and meanness we always impute to those who care more than they ought for wealth, but we sometimes apply 30 the word 'prodigality' in a complex sense; for we call those men prodigals who are incontinent and spend money on self-indulgence. Hence also they are thought the poorest characters; for they combine more vices than one. Therefore the application of the word to them is not its proper use; for a 'prodigal' means a man who has a 1120a single evil quality, that of wasting his substance; since a prodigal is one who is being ruined by his own fault,* and the wasting of substance is thought to be a sort of ruining of oneself, life being held to depend on possession of substance.

This, then, is the sense in which we take the word 'prodigality'. Now the things that have a use may be used either well or badly; 5 and riches are a useful thing; and everything is used best by the man who has the virtue concerned with it; riches, therefore, will be used best by the man who has the virtue concerned with wealth; and this is the liberal man. Now spending and giving seem to be the using of wealth; taking and keeping rather the possession of it. 10 Hence it is more the mark of the liberal man to give to the right people than to take from the right sources and not to take from the wrong. For it is more characteristic of virtue to do good than to have good done to one, and more characteristic to do what is noble than not to do what is base; and it is not hard to see that giving implies doing good and doing what is noble, and taking implies 15 having good done to one or not acting basely. And gratitude is felt towards him who gives, not towards him who does not take, and praise also is bestowed more on him. It is easier, also, not to take than to give; for men are apter to give away their own too little than to take what is another's. Givers, too, are called liberal; but those who do not take are not praised for liberality but rather for justice; 20 while those who take are hardly praised at all. And the liberal are almost the most loved of all virtuous characters, since they are useful; and this depends on their giving.

Now virtuous actions are noble and done for the sake of the noble. Therefore the liberal man, like other virtuous men, will give for the sake of the noble, and rightly; for he will give to the right 25 people, the right amounts, and at the right time, with all the other qualifications that accompany right giving; and that too with pleasure or without pain; for that which is virtuous is pleasant or free from pain—least of all will it be painful. But he who gives to the 15 wrong people or not for the sake of the noble but for some other cause, will be called not liberal but by some other name. Nor is he liberal who gives with pain; for he would prefer the wealth to the 30 noble act, and this is not characteristic of a liberal man. But no more will the liberal man take from wrong sources; for such taking is not characteristic of the man who sets no store by wealth. Nor will he be a ready asker; for it is not characteristic of a man who confers benefits to accept them lightly. But he will take from the right sources, e.g. from his own possessions, not as something noble but 1120b as a necessity, that he may have something to give. Nor will he neglect his own property, since he wishes by means of this to help others. And he will refrain from giving to anybody and everybody, that he may have something to give to the right people, at the right time, and where it is noble to do so. It is highly characteristic of a liberal man also to go to excess in giving, so that he leaves too little 5 for himself; for it is the nature of a liberal man not to look to himself. The term 'liberality' is used relatively to a man's substance; for liberality resides not in the multitude of the gifts but in the state of character of the giver, and this is relative to the giver's substance. There is therefore nothing to prevent the man who gives less from being the more liberal man, if he has less to give. Those are thought 10 to be more liberal who have not made their wealth but inherited it; for in the first place they have no experience of want, and secondly all men are fonder of their own productions, as are parents and

poets. It is not easy for the liberal man to be rich, since he is not apt
15 either at taking or at keeping, but at giving away, and does not value
wealth for its own sake but as a means to giving. Hence comes the
charge that is brought against fortune, that those who deserve
riches most get them least. But it is not unreasonable that it should
turn out so; for he cannot have wealth, any more than anything else,
20 if he does not take pains to have it. Yet he will not give to the wrong
people nor at the wrong time, and so on; for he would no longer be
acting in accordance with liberality, and if he spent on these objects
he would have nothing to spend on the right objects. For, as has
been said, he is liberal who spends according to his substance and
25 on the right objects; and he who exceeds is prodigal. Hence we do
not call despots prodigal; for it is thought not easy for them to give
and spend beyond the amount of their possessions. Liberality, then,
being a mean with regard to giving and taking of wealth, the liberal
man will both give and spend the right amounts and on the right
30 objects, alike in small things and in great, and that with pleasure;
he will also take the right amounts and from the right sources. For,
the virtue being a mean with regard to both, he will do both as he
ought; since this sort of taking accompanies proper giving, and that
which is not of this sort is contrary to it, and accordingly the giving
and taking that accompany each other are present together in the
1121a same man, while the contrary kinds evidently are not. But if he
happens to spend in a manner contrary to what is right and noble,
he will be pained, but moderately and as he ought; for it is the mark
of virtue both to be pleased and to be pained at the right objects and
in the right way. Further, the liberal man is easy to deal with in
5 money matters; for he can be got the better of, since he sets no store
by money, and is more annoyed if he has not spent something that
he ought than pained if he has spent something that he ought not,
and does not agree with the saying of Simonides.*

The prodigal errs in these respects also; for he is neither pleased
nor pained at the right things or in the right way; this will be more
10 evident as we go on. We have said[1] that prodigality and meanness
are excesses and deficiencies, and in two things, in giving and
taking; for we include spending under giving. Now prodigality
exceeds in giving and not taking, and falls short in taking, while

[1] 1119b27.

meanness falls short in giving, and exceeds in taking, but only in 15
small things.

The characteristics of prodigality are not often combined; for it
is not easy to give to all if you take from none; private persons soon
exhaust their substance with giving, and it is to these that the name
of prodigals is applied—though a man of this sort would seem to
be in no small degree better than a mean man. For he is easily cured 20
both by age and by poverty, and thus he may move towards the
middle state. For he has the characteristics of the liberal man, since
he both gives and refrains from taking, though he does neither of
these in the right manner or well. Therefore if he were brought to
do so by habituation or in some other way, he would be liberal; for
he will then give to the right people, and will not take from the
wrong sources. This is why he is thought to have not a bad charac- 25
ter; it is not the mark of a wicked or ignoble man to go to excess in
giving and not taking, but only of a foolish one. The man who is
prodigal in this way is thought much better than the mean man
both for the aforesaid reasons and because he benefits many while
the other benefits no one, not even himself.

But most prodigal people, as has been said,[1] also take from the 30
wrong sources, and are in this respect mean. They become apt to
take because they wish to spend and cannot do this easily; for their
possessions soon run short. Thus they are forced to provide means
from some other source. At the same time, because they care noth- 1121b
ing for the noble, they take recklessly and from any source; for they
have an appetite for giving, and they do not mind how or from what
source. Hence also their giving is not liberal; for it is not noble, nor
does it aim at nobility, nor is it done in the right way; sometimes
they make rich those who should be poor, and will give nothing to 5
people of respectable character, and much to flatterers or those who
provide them with some other pleasure. Hence also most of them
are self-indulgent; for they spend lightly and waste money on their
indulgences, and incline towards pleasures because they do not live
with a view to what is noble. 10

The prodigal man, then, turns into what we have described if he
is left untutored, but if he is treated with care he will arrive at the
intermediate and right state. But meanness is both incurable (for
old age and every disability is thought to make men mean) and

[1] ll. 16–19.

15 more innate in men than prodigality; for most men are fonder of
getting money than of giving. It also extends widely, and is multi-
form, since there seem to be many kinds of meanness.

For it consists in two things, deficiency in giving and excess in
taking, and is not found complete in all men but is sometimes
20 divided; some men go to excess in taking, others fall short in giving.
Those who are called by such names as 'miserly', 'close', 'stingy',
all fall short in giving, but do not covet the possessions of others nor
wish to get them. In some this is due to a sort of honesty and avoidance of what is disgraceful (for some seem, or at least profess, to
25 hoard their money for this reason, that they may not some day be
forced to do something disgraceful; to this class belong the cheese-
parer and everyone of the sort; he is so called from his excess of
unwillingness to give anything); while others again keep their hands
off the property of others from fear, on the ground that it is not
30 easy, if one takes the property of others oneself, to avoid having
one's own taken by them; they are therefore content neither to take
nor to give.

Others again exceed in respect of taking by taking anything and
20 from any source, e.g. those who ply sordid trades, pimps and all such
people, and those who lend small sums and at high rates. For all of
1122a these take more than they ought and from wrong sources. What is
common to them is evidently sordid love of gain; they all put up with
a bad name for the sake of gain, and little gain at that. For those who
make great gains but from wrong sources, and not the right gains, e.g.
5 despots when they sack cities and spoil temples, we do not call mean
but rather wicked, impious, and unjust. But the gambler and the
footpad [and the highwayman] belong to the class of the mean, since
they have a sordid love of gain. For it is for gain that both of them ply
their craft and endure the disgrace of it, and the one faces the greatest
10 dangers for the sake of the booty, while the other makes gain from his
friends, to whom he ought to be giving. Both, then, since they are
willing to make gain from wrong sources, are sordid lovers of gain;
therefore all such forms of taking are mean.

And it is natural that meanness is described as the contrary of
15 liberality; for not only is it a greater evil than prodigality, but men
err more often in this direction than in the way of prodigality as we
have described it.

So much, then, for liberality and the opposed vices.

Magnificence

2. It would seem proper to discuss magnificence next. For this also seems to be a virtue concerned with wealth; but it does not, like liberality, extend to all the actions that are concerned with wealth, 20 but only to those that involve expenditure; and in these it surpasses liberality in scale. For, as the name itself suggests, it is a fitting expenditure involving largeness of scale. But the scale is relative; for the expense of equipping a trireme is not the same as that of heading a sacred embassy. It is what is fitting, then, in relation to 25 the agent, and to the circumstances and the object. The man who in small or middling things spends according to the merits of the case is not called magnificent (e.g. the man who can say 'Many a gift I gave the wanderer'[1]), but only the man who does so in great things.* For the magnificent man is liberal, but the liberal man is not necessarily magnificent. The deficiency of this state of character 30 is called niggardliness, the excess vulgarity, lack of taste, and the like, which do not go to excess in the amount spent on right objects, but by showy expenditure in the wrong circumstances and the wrong manner; we shall speak of these vices later.[2]

The magnificent man is like an artist; for he can see what is 35 fitting and spend large sums tastefully. For, as we said at the beginning,[3] a state of character is determined by its activities and by its 1122b objects. Now the expenses of the magnificent man are large and fitting. Such, therefore, are also his results; for thus there will be a great expenditure and one that is fitting to its result. Therefore the result should be worthy of the expense, and the expense should be 5 worthy of the result, or should even exceed it. And the magnificent man will spend such sums for the sake of the noble; for this is common to the virtues. And further he will do so gladly and lavishly; for precise calculation is a niggardly thing. And he will consider how the result can be made most beautiful and most becoming rather than for how much it can be produced and how it can be produced most cheaply. It is necessary, then, that the magnificent man be also 10 liberal. For the liberal man also will spend what he ought and as he ought; and it is in these matters that the greatness implied in the name of the magnificent man—his bigness, as it were—is manifested,

---

[1] *Odyssey* xvii.420.
[2] 1123a19–33.
[3] Not in so many words, but cf. 1103b21–3, 1104a27–9.

since liberality is concerned with these matters; and at an equal expense he will produce a more magnificent work of art. For a possession and a work of art have not the same excellence. The most
15 valuable possession is that which is worth most, e.g. gold, but the most valuable work of art is that which is great and beautiful (for the contemplation of such a work inspires admiration, and so does magnificence); and a work has an excellence—namely, magnificence—which involves magnitude. Magnificence is an attribute of expenditures of the kind which we call honourable, e.g. those con-
20 nected with the gods —votive offerings, buildings, and sacrifices— and similarly with any form of religious worship, and all those that are proper objects of public-spirited ambition, as when people think they ought to equip a chorus or a trireme, or entertain the city, in a brilliant way.* But in all cases, as has been said, we have
25 regard to the agent as well and ask who he is and what means he has; for the expenditure should be worthy of his means, and suit not only the result but also the producer. Hence a poor man cannot be magnificent, since he has not the means with which to spend large sums fittingly; and he who tries is a fool, since he spends beyond what can be expected of him and what is proper, but it is *right* expenditure that is virtuous. But great expenditure is becom-
30 ing to those who have suitable means to start with, acquired by their own efforts or from ancestors or connections, and to people of high birth or reputation, and so on; for all these things bring with them greatness and prestige. Primarily, then, the magnificent man is of this sort, and magnificence is shown in expenditures of this
35 sort, as has been said;[1] for these are the greatest and most honourable. Of *private* occasions of expenditure the most suitable are those
1123a that take place once for all, e.g. a wedding or anything of the kind, or anything that interests the whole city or the people of position in it, and also the receiving of foreign guests and the sending of them on their way, and gifts and counter-gifts; for the magnificent man spends not on himself but on public objects, and gifts bear some
5 resemblance to votive offerings. A magnificent man will also furnish his house suitably to his wealth (for even a house is a sort of public ornament), and will spend by preference on those works that are lasting (for these are the most beautiful), and on every class of things he will spend what is becoming; for the same things are not

[1] ll. 19–23.

suitable for gods and for men, nor in a temple and in a tomb. And 10
since each expenditure may be great of its kind, and what is most
magnificent absolutely is great expenditure on a great object, but
what is magnificent *here* is what is great in *these* circumstances, and
greatness in the work differs from greatness in the expense (for the
most beautiful ball or bottle is magnificent as a gift to a child, but 15
the price of it is small and mean)—therefore it is characteristic of
the magnificent man, whatever kind of result he is producing, to
produce it magnificently (for such a result is not easily surpassed)
and to make it worthy of the expenditure. Such, then, is the magnificent man; the man who goes to excess and is vulgar exceeds, 20
as has been said,[1] by spending beyond what is right. For on small
objects of expenditure he spends much and displays a tasteless
showiness; e.g. he gives a club dinner on the scale of a wedding
banquet, and when he provides the chorus for a comedy he brings
them on to the stage in purple, as they do at Megara. And all such
things he will do not for the sake of the noble but to show off his 25
wealth, and because he thinks he is admired for these things, and
where he ought to spend much he spends little and where little,
much. The niggardly man on the other hand will fall short in
everything, and after spending the greatest sums will spoil the
beauty of the result for a trifle, and whatever he is doing he will
hesitate and consider how he may spend least, and lament even that, 30
and think he is doing everything on a bigger scale than he ought.

These states of character, then, are vices; yet they do not bring
disgrace because they are neither harmful to one's neighbour nor
very unseemly.

VIRTUES CONCERNED WITH HONOUR

Pride

3. Pride seems even from its name to be concerned with great
things; what sort of great things, is the first question we must try to
answer.* It makes no difference whether we consider the state of 1123b
character or the man characterized by it. Now the man is thought
to be proud who thinks himself worthy of great things and *is*
worthy of them; for he who does so beyond his deserts is a fool, but
no virtuous man is foolish or silly. The proud man, then, is the man

[1] 1122a31–3.

5 we have described. For he who is worthy of little and thinks himself worthy of little is temperate, but not proud; for pride implies greatness, as beauty implies a good-sized body, and little people may be neat and well-proportioned but cannot be beautiful. On the other hand, he who thinks himself worthy of great things, being unworthy of them, is vain; though not every one who thinks himself worthy of more than he really is worthy of is vain. The man who thinks
10 himself worthy of less than he is really worthy of is unduly humble, whether his deserts be great or moderate, or his deserts be small but his claims yet smaller. And the man whose deserts are great would seem *most* unduly humble; for what would he have done if they had been less? The proud man, then, is an extreme in respect of the greatness of his claims, but intermediate in respect of the rightness of them; for he claims what is in accordance with his merits, while the others go to excess or fall short.

15   If, then, he deserves and claims great things, and above all the greatest things, he will be concerned with one thing in particular.* Desert is relative to external goods; and the greatest of these, we should say, is that which we render to the gods, and which people of position most aim at, and which is the prize appointed for the
20 noblest deeds; and this is honour; that is surely the greatest of external goods. Honours and dishonours, therefore, are the objects with respect to which the proud man is as he should be. And even apart from argument it is evident that proud men are concerned with honour; for it is honour that they chiefly claim, but in accordance with their deserts. The unduly humble man falls short both in
25 comparison with his own merits and in comparison with the proud man's claims. The vain man goes to excess in comparison with his own merits, but does not exceed the proud man's claims.

    Now the proud man, since he deserves most, must be good in the highest degree; for the better man always deserves more, and the best man most. Therefore the truly proud man must be good. And great-
30 ness in every virtue would seem to be characteristic of a proud man.

    And it would be most unbecoming for a proud man to fly from danger, swinging his arms by his sides, or to wrong another; for to what end should he do disgraceful acts, he to whom nothing is great? If we consider him point by point we shall see the utter absurdity of a proud man who is not good. Nor, again, would he be
35 worthy of honour if he were bad; for honour is the prize of virtue,

and it is to the good that it is rendered. Pride, then, seems to be a   1124a
sort of crown of the virtues;* for it makes them greater, and it is not
found without them. Therefore it is hard to be truly proud; for it is
impossible without nobility and goodness of character. It is chiefly
with honours and dishonours, then, that the proud man is con-   5
cerned; and at honours that are great and conferred by good men he
will be moderately pleased, thinking that he is coming by his own
or even less than his own; for there can be no honour that is worthy
of perfect virtue, yet he will at any rate accept it since they have
nothing greater to bestow on him; but honour from casual people   10
and on trifling grounds he will utterly despise, since it is not this
that he deserves, and dishonour too, since in his case it cannot be just.
In the first place, then, as has been said,[1] the proud man is concerned with honours; yet he will also bear himself with moderation
towards wealth and power and all good or evil fortune, whatever   15
may befall him, and will be neither overjoyed by good fortune nor
over-pained by evil. For not even towards honour does he bear
himself as if it were a very great thing. Power and wealth are desirable for the sake of honour (at least those who have them wish to
get honour by means of them); and for him to whom even honour
is a little thing the others must be so too.* Hence proud men are   20
thought to be disdainful.

The goods of fortune also are thought to contribute towards
pride. For men who are well-born are thought worthy of honour,
and so are those who enjoy power or wealth; for they are in a superior position, and everything that has a superiority in something
good is held in greater honour. Hence even such things make men
prouder; for they are honoured by some for having them; but in
truth the good man alone is to be honoured; he, however, who has   25
both advantages is thought the more worthy of honour. But those
who without virtue have such goods are neither justified in making
great claims nor entitled to the name of 'proud'; for these things
imply perfect virtue. Disdainful and insolent, however, even those
who have such goods become. For without virtue it is not easy to bear   30
gracefully the goods of fortune; and, being unable to bear them, and
thinking themselves superior to others, they despise others and   1124b
themselves do what they please. They imitate the proud man without being like him, and this they do where they can; so they do not

[1] 1123b15–22.

5 act virtuously, but they do despise others. For the proud man despises
justly (since he thinks truly), but the many do so at random.

He does not run into trifling dangers, nor is he fond of danger,
because he honours few things; but he will face great dangers, and
when he is in danger he is unsparing of his life, knowing that there
are conditions on which life is not worth having. And he is the sort
of man to confer benefits, but he is ashamed of receiving them;
10 for the one is the mark of a superior, the other of an inferior. And
he is apt to confer greater benefits in return; for thus the original
benefactor besides being paid will incur a debt to him, and will be
the gainer by the transaction. They seem also to remember any
service they have done, but not those they have received (for he
who receives a service is inferior to him who has done it, but the
proud man wishes to be superior), and to hear of the former with
15 pleasure, of the latter with displeasure; this, it seems, is why Thetis
did not mention to Zeus the services she had done him, and why
the Spartans did not recount their services to the Athenians, but
those they had received.* It is a mark of the proud man also to ask
for nothing or scarcely anything, but to give help readily, and to be
dignified towards people who enjoy high position and good fortune,
but unassuming towards those of the middle class; for it is a difficult
20 and lofty thing to be superior to the former, but easy to be so to the
latter, and a lofty bearing over the former is no mark of ill-breeding,
but among humble people it is as vulgar as a display of strength
against the weak. Again, it is characteristic of the proud man not to
aim at the things commonly held in honour, or the things in which
others excel; to be sluggish and to hold back except where great
honour or a great work is at stake, and to be a man of few deeds, but
25 of great and notable ones. He must also be open in his hate and in
his love (for to conceal one's feelings, i.e. to care less for truth than
for what people will think, is a coward's part), and must speak and
act openly; for he is free of speech because he is contemptuous, and
30 he is given to telling the truth, except when he speaks in irony to
the vulgar.* He must be unable to make his life revolve round
1125a another, unless it be a friend; for this is slavish, and for this reason all
flatterers are servile and people lacking in self-respect are flatterers.
Nor is he given to admiration; for nothing to him is great. Nor is he
mindful of wrongs; for it is not the part of a proud man to have a
long memory, especially for wrongs, but rather to overlook them.

Nor is he a gossip; for he will speak neither about himself nor about 5
another, since he cares not to be praised nor for others to be blamed;
nor again is he given to praise; and for the same reason he is not an
evil-speaker, even about his enemies, except from haughtiness. With
regard to necessary or small matters he is least of all men given to
lamentation or the asking of favours; for it is the part of one who 10
takes such matters seriously to behave so with respect to them. He
is one who will possess beautiful and profitless things rather than
profitable and useful ones; for this is more proper to a character that
suffices to itself.

Further, a slow step is thought proper to the proud man, a deep
voice, and a level utterance; for the man who takes few things seriously is not likely to be hurried, nor the man who thinks nothing 15
great to be excited, while a shrill voice and a rapid gait are the
results of hurry and excitement.

Such, then, is the proud man; the man who falls short of him is
unduly humble, and the man who goes beyond him is vain. Now
these too are not thought to be bad (for they are not evildoers), but
only mistaken. For the unduly humble man, being worthy of good
things, robs himself of what he deserves, and seems to have some- 20
thing bad about him from the fact that he does not think himself
worthy of good things, and seems also not to know himself; else he
would have desired the things he was worthy of, since these were
good. Yet such people are not thought to be fools, but rather
unduly retiring. Such an estimate, however, seems actually to make
them worse; for each class of people aims at what corresponds to its 25
worth, and these people stand back even from noble actions and
undertakings, deeming themselves unworthy, and from external
goods no less. Vain people, on the other hand, are fools and ignorant of themselves, and that manifestly; for, not being worthy of
them, they attempt honourable undertakings, and then are found
out; and they adorn themselves with clothing and outward show 30
and such things, and wish their strokes of good fortune to be made
public, and speak about them as if they would be honoured for
them. But undue humility is more opposed to pride than vanity is;
for it is both commoner and worse.*

Pride, then, is concerned with honour on the grand scale, as has
been said.[1]   35

[1] 1107b26, 1123a34–b22.

The virtue intermediate between ambition and unambitiousness

1125b 4. There seems to be in the sphere of honour also, as was said in our first remarks on the subject,[1] a virtue which would appear to be related to pride as liberality is to magnificence. For neither of these has anything to do with the grand scale, but both dispose us as is 5 right with regard to middling and unimportant objects; as in getting and giving of wealth there is a mean and an excess and defect, so too honour may be desired more than is right, or less, or from the right sources and in the right way. We blame both the ambitious man as aiming at honour more than is right and from wrong sources, and 10 the unambitious man as not willing to be honoured even for noble reasons. But sometimes we praise the ambitious man as being manly and a lover of what is noble, and the unambitious man as being moderate and self-controlled, as we said in our first treatment of the subject.[2] Evidently, since 'fond of such and such an object' has more than one meaning, we do not assign the term 'ambition' or 15 'love of honour' always to the same thing, but when we praise the quality we think of the man who loves honour more than most people, and when we blame it we think of him who loves it more than is right.* The mean being without a name, the extremes seem to dispute for its place as though that were vacant by default. But where there is excess and defect, there is also an intermediate; now 20 men desire honour both more than they should and less; therefore it is possible also to do so as one should; at all events this is the state of character that is praised, being an unnamed mean in respect of honour. Relatively to ambition it seems to be unambitiousness, and relatively to unambitiousness it seems to be ambition, while relatively to both severally it seems in a sense to be both together. This appears to be true of the other virtues also. But in this case the extremes seem to be contradictories because the intermediate has 25 not received a name.

THE VIRTUE CONCERNED WITH ANGER

Good temper

5. Good temper is a mean with respect to anger; the middle state being unnamed, and the extremes almost without a name as well,

---

[1] Ibid. 24–7.   [2] 1107b33.

we place good temper in the middle position, though it inclines towards the deficiency, which is without a name. The excess might be called a sort of 'irascibility'. For the passion is anger, while its causes are many and diverse.

The man who is angry at the right things and with the right people, and, further, as he ought, when he ought, and as long as he ought, is praised. This will be the good-tempered man, then, since good temper is praised. For the good-tempered man tends to be unperturbed and not to be led by passion, but to be angry in the manner, at the things, and for the length of time, that reason dictates; but he is thought to err rather in the direction of deficiency; for the good-tempered man is not revengeful, but rather tends to make allowances.

The deficiency, whether it is a sort of 'unirascibility' or whatever it is, is blamed. For those who are not angry at the things they should be angry at are thought to be fools, and so are those who are not angry in the right way, at the right time, or with the right persons; for such a man is thought not to feel things nor to be pained by them, and, since he does not get angry, he is thought unlikely to defend himself; and to endure being insulted and put up with insult to one's friends is slavish.

The excess can be manifested in all the points that have been named (for one can be angry with the wrong persons, at the wrong things, more than is right, too quickly, or too long); yet *all* are not found in the same person. Indeed they could not; for evil destroys even itself, and if it is complete becomes unbearable. Now *hot-tempered* people get angry quickly and with the wrong persons and at the wrong things and more than is right, but their anger ceases quickly—which is the best point about them. This happens to them because they do not restrain their anger but retaliate openly owing to their quickness of temper, and then their anger ceases. By reason of excess *choleric* people are quick-tempered and ready to be angry with everything and on every occasion; whence their name. *Sulky* people are hard to appease, and retain their anger long; for they repress their passion. But it ceases when they retaliate; for revenge relieves them of their anger, producing in them pleasure instead of pain. If this does not happen they retain their burden; for owing to its not being obvious no one even reasons with them, and to digest one's anger in oneself takes time. Such people are most troublesome to themselves and to their dearest friends. We call *bad-tempered* those who are angry at the wrong things, more than is right, and longer, and cannot be appeased until they inflict vengeance or punishment.

30 To good temper we oppose the excess rather than the defect; for not only is it commoner (since revenge is the more human), but bad-tempered people are worse to live with.

What we have said in our earlier treatment of the subject[1] is plain also from what we are now saying; namely, that it is not easy to define how, with whom, at what, and how long one should be angry, and at what point right action ceases and wrong begins. For the man 35 who strays a little from the path, either towards the more or towards the less, is not blamed; since sometimes we praise those who exhibit 1126b the deficiency, and call them good-tempered, and sometimes we call angry people manly, as being capable of ruling. How far, therefore, and how a man must stray before he becomes blameworthy, it is not easy to state in words; for the decision depends on the particular facts and on perception.* But so much at least is plain, 5 that the middle state is praiseworthy—that in virtue of which we are angry with the right people, at the right things, in the right way, and so on, while the excesses and defects are blameworthy—slightly so if they are present in a low degree, more if in a higher degree, and very much if in a high degree. Evidently, then, we must cling 10 to the middle state. Enough of the states relative to anger.

VIRTUES OF SOCIAL INTERCOURSE

Friendliness

6. In gatherings of men, in social life and the interchange of words and deeds, some men are thought to be obsequious, namely, those who to give pleasure praise everything and never oppose, but think it their duty 'to give no pain to the people they meet'; while those 15 who, on the contrary, oppose everything and care not a whit about giving pain are called churlish and contentious. That the states we have named are culpable is plain enough, and that the middle state is laudable—that in virtue of which a man will put up with, and will resent, the right things and in the right way; but no name has been 20 assigned to it, though it most resembles friendship.* For the man

---

[1] 1109b14–26.

who corresponds to this middle state is very much what, with affection added, we call a good friend. But the state in question differs
from friendship in that it implies no passion or affection for one's
associates; since it is not by reason of loving or hating that such a
man takes everything in the right way, but by being a man of a
certain kind. For he will behave so alike towards those he knows   25
and those he does not know, towards intimates and those who are
not so, except that in each of these cases he will behave as is befitting; for it is not proper to have the same care for intimates and for
strangers, nor again is it the same conditions that make it right to
give pain to them. Now we have said generally that he will associate
with people in the right way; but it is by reference to what is honourable and expedient that he will aim at not giving pain or at
contributing pleasure. For he seems to be concerned with the pleas-   30
ures and pains of social life; and wherever it is not honourable, or is
harmful, for him to contribute pleasure, he will refuse, and will
choose rather to give pain; also if his acquiescence in another's
action would bring disgrace, and that in a high degree, or injury,
on that other, while his opposition brings a little pain, he will not
acquiesce but will decline. He will associate differently with people   35
in high station and with ordinary people, with closer and more
distant acquaintances, and so too with regard to all other differ-   1127a
ences, rendering to each class what is befitting, and while for its
own sake he chooses to contribute pleasure, and avoids the giving
of pain, he will be guided by the consequences, if these are greater,
i.e. honour and expediency. For the sake of a great future pleasure,   5
too, he will inflict small pains.

The man who attains the intermediate, then, is such as we have
described, but has not received a name; of those who contribute
pleasure, the man who aims at being pleasant with no ulterior
object is obsequious, but the man who does so in order that he may
get some advantage in the direction of money or the things that
money buys is a flatterer; while the man who quarrels with every-   10
thing is, as has been said,[1] churlish and contentious. And the extremes
seem to be contradictory to each other because the intermediate is
without a name.

----

[1] 1125b14–16.

Truthfulness

7. The mean opposed to boastfulness is found in almost the same sphere; and this also is without a name.* It will be no bad plan to
15 describe these states as well; for we shall know the facts about character better if we go through them in detail, and we shall be convinced that the virtues are means if we see this to be so in all cases. In the field of social life those who make the giving of pleasure or pain their object in associating with others have been described;[1] let us now describe those who pursue truth or falsehood alike in words
20 and deeds and in the claims they put forward. The boastful man, then, is thought to be apt to claim the things that bring glory, when he has not got them, or to claim more of them than he has, and the mock-modest man on the other hand to disclaim what he has or belittle it, while the man who observes the mean is one who calls a thing by its own name, being truthful both in life and in word, own-
25 ing to what he has, neither to more nor to less. Now each of these courses may be adopted either with or without an object. But each man speaks and acts and lives in accordance with his character, if he is *not* acting for some ulterior object. And falsehood is *in itself* mean and culpable, and truth noble and worthy of praise. Thus the
30 truthful man is another case of a man who, being intermediate, is worthy of praise, and both forms of untruthful man are culpable, and particularly the boastful man.

Let us discuss them both, but first of all the truthful man. We are not speaking of the man who keeps faith in his agreements,* i.e. in the things that pertain to justice or injustice (for this would belong
1127b to another virtue), but the man who in the matters in which nothing of this sort is at stake is true both in word and in life because his character is such. But such a man would seem to be as a matter of fact equitable. For the man who loves truth, and is truthful where nothing is at stake, will still more be truthful where something is at
5 stake; he will avoid falsehood as something base, seeing that he avoided it even for its own sake; and such a man is worthy of praise. He inclines rather to understate the truth; for this seems in better taste because exaggerations are wearisome.

He who claims more than he has with no ulterior object is a con-
10 temptible sort of fellow (otherwise he would not have delighted in

---

[1] Ch. 6.

falsehood), but seems futile rather than bad; but if he does it for an object, he who does it for the sake of reputation or honour is (for a boaster) not very much to be blamed, but he who does it for money, or the things that lead to money, is an uglier character (it is not the capacity that makes the boaster, but the purpose; for it is in virtue of his state of character and by being a man of a certain kind that he is a boaster); as one man is a liar because he enjoys the lie itself, and 15 another because he desires reputation or gain. Now those who boast for the sake of reputation claim such qualities as win praise or congratulation, but those whose object is gain claim qualities which are of value to one's neighbours and one's lack of which is not easily detected, e.g. the powers of a seer, a sage, or a physician. For this 20 reason it is such things as these that most people claim and boast about; for in them the above-mentioned qualities are found.

Mock-modest people, who understate things, seem more attractive in character; for they are thought to speak not for gain but to avoid parade; and here too it is qualities which bring reputation that 25 they disclaim, as Socrates used to do.* Those who disclaim trifling and obvious qualities are called humbugs and are more contemptible; and sometimes this seems to be boastfulness, like the Spartan dress;* for both excess and great deficiency are boastful. But those who use understatement with moderation and understate about 30 matters that do not very much force themselves on our notice seem attractive. And it is the boaster that seems to be opposed to the truthful man; for he is the worse character.

Ready wit

8. Since life includes rest as well as activity, and in this is included leisure and amusement, there seems here also to be a kind of intercourse which is tasteful; there is such a thing as saying—and again 1128a listening to—what one should and as one should. The kind of people one is speaking or listening to will also make a difference. Evidently here also there is both an excess and a deficiency as compared with the mean. Those who carry humour to excess are thought to be vulgar buffoons, striving after humour at all costs, and aiming 5 rather at raising a laugh than at saying what is becoming and at avoiding pain to the object of their fun; while those who can neither make a joke themselves nor put up with those who do are thought to be boorish and unpolished.* But those who joke in a tasteful way 10

are called ready-witted, which implies a sort of readiness to turn
this way and that; for such sallies are thought to be movements of
the character, and as bodies are discriminated by their movements,
so too are characters. The ridiculous side of things is not far to seek,
however, and most people delight more than they should in amuse-
15 ment and in jesting, and so even buffoons are called ready-witted
because they are found attractive; but that they differ from the
ready-witted man, and to no small extent, is clear from what has
been said.

To the middle state belongs also tact; it is the mark of a tactful
man to say and listen to such things as befit a good and well-bred
man; for there are some things that it befits such a man to say and
20 to hear by way of jest, and the well-bred man's jesting differs from
that of a vulgar man, and the joking of an educated man from that
of an uneducated. One may see this even from the old and the new
comedies;* to the authors of the former indecency of language was
amusing, to those of the latter innuendo is more so; and these differ
25 in no small degree in respect of propriety. Now should we define
the man who jokes well by his saying what is not unbecoming to a
well-bred man, or by his not giving pain, or even giving delight, to
the hearer? Or is the latter definition, at any rate, itself indefinite,
since different things are hateful or pleasant to different people?
The kind of jokes he will listen to will be the same; for the kind he
can put up with are also the kind he seems to make. There are, then,
30 jokes he will not make; for the jest is a sort of abuse, and there are
things that lawgivers forbid us to abuse; and they should, perhaps,
have forbidden us even to make a jest of such. The refined and well-
bred man, therefore, will be as we have described, being as it were
a law to himself.*

Such, then, is the intermediate man, whether he be called tactful
or ready-witted. The buffoon, on the other hand, is the slave of his
35 sense of humour, and spares neither himself nor others if he can raise
a laugh, and says things none of which a man of refinement would
1128b say, and to some of which he would not even listen. The boor,
again, is useless for such social intercourse; for he contributes nothing and finds fault with everything. But relaxation and amusement
are thought to be a necessary element in life.

The means in life that have been described, then, are three in
5 number,* and are all concerned with an interchange of words and

deeds of some kind. They differ, however, in that one is concerned with truth, and the other two with pleasantness. Of those concerned with pleasure, one is displayed in jests, the other in the general social intercourse of life.

A QUASI-VIRTUE

Shame

9. Shame should not be described as a virtue; for it is more like a 10 passion than a state of character. It is defined, at any rate, as a kind of fear of dishonour,* and produces an effect similar to that produced by fear of danger; for people who feel disgraced blush, and those who fear death turn pale. Both, therefore, seem to be in a sense bodily conditions, which is thought to be characteristic of passion rather than of a state of character.   15

The passion is not becoming to every age, but only to youth. For we think young people should be prone to shame because they live by passion and therefore commit many errors, but are restrained by shame; and we praise young people who are prone to this passion, but an older person no one would praise for being prone to the 20 sense of disgrace, since we think he should not do anything that need cause this sense. For the sense of disgrace is not even characteristic of a good man, since it is consequent on bad actions (for such actions should not be done; and if some actions are disgraceful in very truth and others only according to common opinion, this makes no difference; for neither class of actions should be done, so that no disgrace should be felt); and it is a mark of a bad man even 25 to be such as to do any disgraceful action.* To be so constituted as to feel disgraced if one does such an action, and for this reason to think oneself good, is absurd; for it is for voluntary actions that shame is felt, and the good man will never voluntarily do bad actions. But shame may be said to be conditionally a good thing; *if* 30 a good man does such actions, he will feel disgraced; but the virtues are not subject to such a qualification. And if shamelessness—not to be ashamed of doing base actions—is bad, that does not make it good to be ashamed of doing such actions. Continence too is not virtue, but a mixed sort of state; this will be shown later.[1] Now, 35 however, let us discuss justice.

[1] VII.1-10.

BOOK V · JUSTICE

JUSTICE: ITS SPHERE AND OUTER NATURE: IN WHAT SENSE IT IS A MEAN

The just as the lawful (universal justice) and the just as the fair and equal (particular justice): the former considered

1129a **1.** WITH regard to justice and injustice we must consider what kind
of actions they are concerned with, what sort of mean justice is, and
5 between what extremes the just act is intermediate. Our investigation shall follow the same course as the preceding discussions.*

We see that all men mean by justice that kind of state of character which makes people disposed to do what is just and makes them
act justly and wish for what is just; and similarly by injustice that
10 state which makes them act unjustly and wish for what is unjust.*
Let us too, then, lay this down as a general basis. For the same is
not true of the sciences and the faculties as of states of character. A
faculty or a science which is one and the same is held to relate to
contrary objects, but a state which is one of two contraries does *not*
produce the contrary results; e.g. as a result of health we do not do
15 what is the opposite of healthy, but only what is healthy; for we say
a man walks healthily, when he walks as a healthy man would.*

Now often one contrary state is recognized from its contrary, and
often states are recognized from the subjects that exhibit them; for
if good condition is known, bad condition also becomes known, and
20 good condition is known from the things that are in good condition,
and they from it. If good condition is firmness of flesh, it is necessary both that bad condition should be flabbiness of flesh and that
the wholesome should be that which causes firmness in flesh. And
it follows for the most part that if one contrary is ambiguous the
25 other also will be ambiguous; e.g. that if 'just' is so, 'unjust' will be
so too.

Now 'justice' and 'injustice' seem to be ambiguous, but because
their different meanings approach near to one another the ambiguity escapes notice and is not obvious as it is, comparatively, when
the meanings are far apart, e.g. (for here the difference in outward
30 form is great) as the ambiguity in the use of *kleis* for the collar-bone

of an animal and for that with which we lock a door. Let us take as a starting-point, then, the various meanings of 'an unjust man'. Both the lawless man and the grasping and unfair man are thought to be unjust, so that evidently both the law-abiding and the fair man will be just. The just, then, is the lawful and the fair, the unjust the unlawful and the unfair.*

Since the unjust man is grasping, he must be concerned with 1129b goods—not all goods, but those with which prosperity and adversity have to do, which taken absolutely are always good, but for a particular person are not always good. Now men pray for and pursue these things; but they should not, but should pray that the things 5 that are good absolutely may also be good for them, and should choose the things that *are* good for them. The unjust man does not always choose the greater, but also the less—in the case of things bad absolutely; but because the lesser evil is itself thought to be in a sense good, and graspingness is directed at the good, therefore he is thought to be grasping.* And he is unfair; for this contains and is 10 common to both.

Since the lawless man was seen to be unjust and the law-abiding man just, evidently all lawful acts are in a sense just acts; for the acts laid down by the legislative art are lawful, and each of these, we say, is just.* Now the laws in their enactments on all subjects aim at the common advantage either of all or of the best or of those who hold 15 power, or something of the sort; so that in one sense we call those acts just that tend to produce and preserve happiness and its components for the political society. And the law bids us do both the acts of a brave man (e.g. not to desert our post nor take to flight nor 20 throw away our arms), and those of a temperate man (e.g. not to commit adultery nor to gratify one's lust), and those of a good-tempered man (e.g. not to strike another nor to speak evil), and similarly with regard to the other virtues and forms of wickedness, commanding some acts and forbidding others; and the rightly-framed law does this rightly, and the hastily conceived one less 25 well.

This form of justice, then, is complete virtue, although not without qualification, but in relation to another.* And therefore justice is often thought to be the greatest of virtues, and 'neither evening nor morning star' is so wonderful; and proverbially 'in justice is every virtue comprehended'.* And it is complete virtue in its fullest 30 sense because it is the actual exercise of complete virtue. It is complete because he who possesses it can exercise his virtue not only in himself but towards another also; for many men can exercise virtue in their own affairs, but not in their relations to others. This is why the saying of Bias is thought to be true, that 'rule will show the man'; for a ruler is necessarily in relation to other men, and a member of a society. For this same reason justice, alone of the virtues, is thought to be 'another's good',* because it is related to another; for it does what is advantageous to another, either a ruler or a co-partner. Now the worst man is he who exercises his wickedness both towards himself and towards his friends, and the best man is not he who exercises his virtue towards himself but he who exercises it towards another; for this is a difficult task. Justice in this sense, then, is not part of virtue but the whole of virtue, nor is the contrary injustice a part of vice but the whole of vice. What the difference is between virtue and justice in this sense is plain from what we have said; they are the same but their essence is not the same; what, as a relation to another, is justice is, as a certain kind of state without qualification, virtue.*

The just as the fair and equal: divided into distributive and rectificatory justice

2. But at all events what we are investigating is the justice which is a *part* of virtue; for there is a justice of this kind, as we maintain. Similarly it is with injustice in the particular sense that we are concerned.

That there is such a thing is indicated by the fact that while the man who exhibits in action the other forms of wickedness acts wrongly indeed, but not graspingly (e.g. the man who throws away his shield through cowardice or speaks harshly through bad temper or fails to help a friend with money through meanness), when a man acts graspingly he often exhibits none of these vices—no, nor all together, but certainly wickedness of some kind (for we blame him) and injustice. There is, then, another kind of injustice which is a part of injustice in the wide sense, and a use of the word 'unjust' which answers to a part of what is unjust in the wide sense of 'contrary to the law'. Again, if one man commits adultery for the sake of gain and makes money by it, while another does so at the bidding of appetite though he loses money and is penalized for it, the latter would be held to be self-indulgent rather than grasping, but the former is unjust, but not self-indulgent; evidently, therefore, he is unjust by reason of his making gain by his act. Again, all other unjust acts are ascribed invariably to some particular kind of wickedness, e.g. adultery to self-indulgence, the desertion of a comrade 30 in battle to cowardice, physical violence to anger; but if a man makes gain, his action is ascribed to no form of wickedness but injustice.* Evidently, therefore, there is apart from injustice in the wide sense another, 'particular', injustice which shares the name and nature of the first, because its definition falls within the same genus; for the significance of both consists in a relation to another, 1130b but the one is concerned with honour or money or safety*—or that which includes all these, if we had a single name for it—and its motive is the pleasure that arises from gain; while the other is concerned with all the objects with which the good man is concerned. 5

It is clear, then, that there is more than one kind of justice, and that there is one which is distinct from the whole of virtue; we must try to grasp what it is and what sort of thing it is.

The unjust has been divided into the unlawful and the unfair, and the just into the lawful and the fair. To the unlawful answers the aforementioned sense of injustice. But since the unfair and the 10 unlawful are not the same, but are different as a part is from its whole (for all that is unfair is unlawful, but not all that is unlawful is unfair), the unjust and injustice in the sense of the unfair are not the same as but different from the former kind, as part from whole; for injustice in this sense is a part of injustice in the wide sense, and similarly justice in the one sense is a part of justice in the other. 15 Therefore we must speak also about particular justice and particular injustice, and similarly about the just and the unjust. The justice, then, which answers to the whole of virtue, and the corresponding injustice, one being the exercise of virtue as a whole, and the other that of vice as a whole, towards another, we may leave on one side. 20 And how the meanings of 'just' and 'unjust' which answer to these are to be distinguished is evident; for practically the majority of the acts commanded by the law are those which are prescribed from the point of view of virtue taken as a whole; for the law bids us practise every virtue and forbids us to practise any vice. And the things that tend to produce virtue taken as a whole are those of the 25 acts prescribed by the law which have been prescribed with a view to education for the common good. But with regard to the education of the individual as such, which makes him without qualification a good *man*, we must determine later[1] whether this is the function of the political art or of another; for perhaps it is not the same to be a good man and a good citizen of any state taken at random.

30   Of particular justice and that which is just in the corresponding sense, (A) one kind is that which is manifested in distributions of honour or money or the other things that fall to be divided among those who have a share in the constitution (for in these it is possible for one man to have a share either unequal or equal to that of another), and (B) one is that which plays a rectifying part in transac-
1131a tions between man and man.* Of this there are two divisions; of transactions (1) some are voluntary and (2) others involuntary— voluntary such transactions as sale, purchase, loan for consumption, pledging, loan for use, depositing, letting (they are called voluntary
5   because the *origin* of these transactions is voluntary*), while of the involuntary (*a*) some are clandestine, such as theft, adultery, poisoning, procuring, enticement of slaves, assassination, false witness, and (*b*) others involve force, such as assault, imprisonment, murder, robbery with violence, mutilation, abuse, insult.

Distributive justice, in accordance with geometrical proportion

10   3. (A) We have shown that both the unjust man and the unjust act are unfair or unequal;* now it is clear that there is also an intermediate between the two unequals involved in either case. And this is the equal; for in any kind of action in which there is a more and a less there is also what is equal.* If, then, the unjust is unequal, the just is equal, as all men suppose it to be, even apart from argument. And since the equal is intermediate, the just will be an intermediate.
15   Now equality implies at least two things. The just, then, must be both intermediate and equal and relative (i.e. for certain persons). And *qua* intermediate it must be between certain things (which are respectively greater and less*); *qua* equal, it involves *two* things; *qua* just, it is for certain people. The just, therefore, involves at least four terms; for the persons for whom it is in fact just are two, and the
20   things in which it is manifested, the objects distributed, are two. And the same equality will exist between the persons and between

---

[1] 1179b20–1181b12. *Pol.* 1276b16–1277b32, 1278a40–b5, 1288a32–b2, 1333a11–16, 1337a11–14.

the things concerned; for as the latter—the things concerned—are related, so are the former; if they are not equal, they will not have what is equal,* but this is the origin of quarrels and complaints—when either equals have and are awarded unequal shares, or un-equals equal shares. Further, this is plain from the fact that awards should be 'according to merit'; for all men agree that what is just in 25 distribution must be according to merit in some sense, though they do not all specify the same sort of merit, but democrats identify it with the status of freeman, supporters of oligarchy with wealth (or with noble birth), and supporters of aristocracy with virtue.*

The just, then, is a species of the proportionate (proportion being not a property only of the kind of number which consists of 30 abstract units, but of number in general). For proportion is equality of ratios, and involves four terms at least (that discrete proportion involves four terms is plain, but so does continuous proportion, for it uses one term as two and mentions it twice; e.g. 'as the line A is 1131b to the line B, so is the line B to the line C'; the line B, then, has been mentioned twice, so that if the line B be assumed twice, the propor-tional terms will be four); and the just, too, involves at least four terms, and the ratio between one pair is the same as that between the other pair; for there is a similar distinction between the persons and between the things.* As the term A, then, is to B, so will C be 5 to D, and therefore, *alternando*, as A is to C, B will be to D. Therefore also the whole is in the same ratio to the whole;* and the distribution pairs them in this way, and if they are so combined, pairs them justly. The conjunction, then, of the term A with C and of B with D is what is just in distribution, and this species of the 10 just is intermediate, and the unjust is what violates the proportion; for the proportional is intermediate, and the just is proportional.* (Mathematicians call this kind of proportion geometrical;* for it is in geometrical proportion that it follows that the whole is to the whole as either part is to the corresponding part.) This proportion is not continuous; for we cannot get a single term standing for a 15 person and a thing.

This, then, is what the just is—the proportional; the unjust is what violates the proportion. Hence one term becomes too great, the other too small, as indeed happens in practice; for the man who acts unjustly has too much, and the man who is unjustly treated too little, of what is good.* In the case of evil the reverse is true; for the 20 lesser evil is reckoned a good in comparison with the greater evil, since the lesser evil is rather to be chosen than the greater,* and what is worthy of choice is good, and what is worthier of choice a greater good.

This, then, is one species of the just.

Rectificatory justice, in accordance with arithmetical proportion

25 4. (B) The remaining one is the rectificatory,* which arises in connection with transactions both voluntary and involuntary. This form of the just has a different specific character from the former. For the justice which distributes common possessions is always in accordance with the kind of proportion mentioned above (for in the case also in which the distribution is made from the common funds
30 of a partnership it will be according to the same ratio which the funds put into the business by the partners bear to one another); and the injustice opposed to this kind of justice is that which violates the proportion.* But the justice in transactions between man and man is a sort of equality indeed, and the injustice a sort of
1132a inequality; not according to that kind of proportion, however, but according to arithmetical proportion. For it makes no difference whether a good man has defrauded a bad man or a bad man a good one, nor whether it is a good or a bad man that has committed adultery; the law looks only to the distinctive character of the
5 injury, and treats the parties as equal, if one is in the wrong and the other is being wronged, and if one inflicted injury and the other has received it. Therefore, this kind of injustice being an inequality, the judge tries to equalize it; for in the case also in which one has received and the other has inflicted a wound, or one has slain and the other been slain, the suffering and the action have been unequally distributed; but the judge tries to equalize things by means
10 of the penalty, taking away from the gain of the assailant.* For the term 'gain' is applied generally to such cases—even if it be not a term appropriate to certain cases, e.g. to the person who inflicts a wound—and 'loss' to the sufferer; at all events when the suffering has been estimated, the one is called loss and the other gain. Therefore the equal is intermediate between the greater and the
15 less, but the gain and the loss are respectively greater and less in contrary ways; more of the good and less of the evil are gain, and the contrary is loss; intermediate between them is, as we saw, the

equal, which we say is just; therefore the just in rectification will be the intermediate between loss and gain.* This is why, when people dispute, they take refuge in the judge; and to go to the judge is to go to justice; for the nature of the judge is to be a sort of animate justice; and they seek the judge as an intermediate, and in some states they call judges mediators, on the assumption that if they get what is intermediate they will get what is just. The just, then, is an intermediate, since the judge is so. Now the judge restores equality; it is as though there were a line divided into unequal parts, and he took away that by which the greater segment exceeds the half, and added it to the smaller segment. And when the whole has been equally divided, then they say they have 'their own'—i.e. when they have got what is equal.* The equal is intermediate between the greater and the lesser line according to arithmetical proportion. It is for this reason also that it is called just (*dikaion*), because it is a division into two equal parts (*dikha*), just as if one were to call it *dikhaion*; and the judge (*dikastēs*) is one who bisects (*dikhastēs*). For when something is subtracted from one of two equals and added to the other, the other is in excess by these two; since if what was taken from the one had not been added to the other, the latter would have been in excess by one only. It therefore exceeds the intermediate by one, and the intermediate exceeds by one that from which something was taken. By this, then, we shall recognize both what we must subtract from that which has more, and what we must add to that which has less; we must add to the latter that by which the intermediate exceeds it, and subtract from the greatest that by which it exceeds the intermediate.* Let the lines AA′, BB′, CC′ be equal to one another; from the line AA′ let the segment AE have been subtracted, and to the line CC′ let the segment CD have been added, so that the whole line DCC′ exceeds the line EA′ by the segment CD and the segment CF; therefore it exceeds the line BB′ by the segment CD.*

These names, both loss and gain, have come from voluntary exchange; for to have more than one's own is called gaining, and to have less than one's original share is called losing, e.g. in buying and selling and in all other matters in which the law has left people free to make their own terms; but when they get neither more nor less but just what belongs to themselves, they say that they have their own and that they neither lose nor gain.

Therefore the just is intermediate between a sort of gain and a sort of loss, namely, those which are involuntary; it consists in
20 having an equal amount before and after the transaction.*

Justice in exchange, reciprocity

5. Some think that *reciprocity* is without qualification just, as the Pythagoreans said; for they defined justice without qualification as reciprocity. Now 'reciprocity' fits neither distributive nor rectifica-
25 tory justice*—yet people *want* even the justice of Rhadamanthus to mean this:

Should a man suffer what he did, right justice would be done*

—for in many cases reciprocity and rectificatory justice are not in accord; e.g. (1) if an official has inflicted a wound, he should not be wounded in return, and if someone has wounded an official, he
30 ought not to be wounded only but punished in addition.* Further (2) there is a great difference between a voluntary and an involuntary act. But in associations for exchange this sort of justice does hold men together—reciprocity in accordance with a proportion and not on the basis of precisely equal return. For it is by proportionate requital that the city holds together. Men seek to return either evil for evil—and if they cannot do so, think their position
1133a mere slavery—or good for good—and if they cannot do so there is no exchange, but it is by exchange that they hold together. This is why they give a prominent place to the temple of the Graces—to promote the requital of services; for this is characteristic of grace—we should serve in return one who has shown grace to us,
5 and should another time take the initiative in showing it.*

Now proportionate return is secured by cross-conjunction. Let A be a builder, B a shoemaker, C a house, D a shoe.* The builder, then, must get from the shoemaker the latter's work, and must
10 himself give him in return his own. If, then, first there is proportionate equality of goods, and then reciprocal action takes place, the result we mention will be effected.* If not, the bargain is not equal, and does not hold; for there is nothing to prevent the work of the one being better than that of the other; they must therefore be equated.* (And this is true of the other arts also; for they would
15 have been destroyed if what the patient suffered had not been just what the agent did, and of the same amount and kind.) For it is not

two doctors that associate for exchange, but a doctor and a farmer, or in general people who are different and unequal; but these must be equated. This is why all things that are exchanged must be somehow comparable. It is for this end that money has been introduced, and it becomes in a sense an intermediate; for it measures all things, and therefore the excess and the defect—how many shoes are equal to a house or to a given amount of food. The number of shoes exchanged for a house [or for a given amount of food] must therefore correspond to the ratio of builder to shoemaker. For if this be not so, there will be no exchange and no intercourse. And this proportion will not be effected unless the goods are somehow equal. All goods must therefore be measured by some one thing, as we said before. Now this unit is in truth need, which holds all things together (for if men did not need one another's goods at all, or did not need them equally, there would be either no exchange or not the same exchange); but money has become by convention a sort of representative of need;* and this is why it has the name 'money' (*nomisma*)—because it exists not by nature but by law (*nomos*) and it is in our power to change it and make it useless. There will, then, be reciprocity when the terms have been equated so that as farmer is to shoemaker, the amount of the shoemaker's work is to that of the farmer's work for which it exchanges.* But we must not bring them into a figure of proportion when they have already exchanged (otherwise one extreme will have both excesses), but when they still have their own goods.* Thus they are equals and associates just because this equality can be effected in their case. Let A be a farmer, C food, B a shoemaker, D his product equated to C. If it had not been possible for reciprocity to be thus effected, there would have been no association of the parties. That need holds things together as a single unit is shown by the fact that when men do not need one another, i.e. when neither needs the other or one does not need the other, they do not exchange, as we do when someone wants what one has oneself, e.g. when people permit the exportation of corn in exchange for wine. This equation therefore must be established. And for the future exchange—that if we do not need a thing now we shall have it if ever we do need it—money is as it were our surety; for it must be possible for us to get what we want by bringing the money. Now the same thing happens to money itself as to goods—it is not always worth the same; yet it tends to be steadier.

This is why all goods must have a price set on them; for then there
15 will always be exchange, and if so, association of man with man.
Money, then, acting as a measure, makes goods commensurate and
equates them; for neither would there have been association if there
were not exchange, nor exchange if there were not equality, nor
equality if there were not commensurability. Now in truth it is
impossible that things differing so much should become commen-
20 surate, but with reference to need they may become so sufficiently.
There must, then, be a unit, and that fixed by agreement (for which
reason it is called money); for it is this that makes all things commensurate, since all things are measured by money. Let A be a house,
B ten minae, C a bed. A is half of B, if the house is worth five minae
or equal to them; the bed, C, is a tenth of B; it is plain, then, how
25 many beds are equal to a house, namely, five. That exchange took
place thus before there was money is plain; for it makes no difference whether it is five beds that exchange for a house, or the money
value of five beds.*

We have now defined the unjust and the just.* These having
been marked off from each other, it is plain that just action is inter-
30 mediate between acting unjustly and being unjustly treated; for
the one is to have too much and the other to have too little. Justice
is a kind of mean, but not in the same way as the other virtues,*
but because it relates to an intermediate amount, while injustice
1134a relates to the extremes. And justice is that in virtue of which the
just man is said to be a doer, by choice, of that which is just, and
one who will distribute either between himself and another or
between two others not so as to give more of what is desirable to
5 himself and less to the other (and conversely with what is harmful),
but so as to give what is equal in accordance with proportion; and
similarly in distributing between two other persons. Injustice on
the other hand is similarly related to the unjust, which is excess
and defect, contrary to proportion, of the useful or hurtful. For
which reason injustice is excess and defect, namely, because it is
10 productive of excess and defect—in one's own case excess of what
is in its own nature useful and defect of what is hurtful, while in the
case of others it is as a whole like what it is in one's own case, but
proportion may be violated in either direction. In the unjust act to
have too little is to be unjustly treated; to have too much is to act
unjustly.*

Let this be taken as our account of the nature of justice and injus- 15
tice, and similarly of the just and the unjust in general.

Political justice and analogous kinds of justice

6. Since acting unjustly does not necessarily imply being unjust,
we must ask what sort of unjust acts imply that the doer is unjust
with respect to each type of injustice, e.g. a thief, an adulterer, or a
brigand. Surely the answer does not turn on the difference between
these types. For a man might even lie with a woman knowing who 20
she was, but the origin of his act might be not deliberate choice but
passion. He acts unjustly, then, but is not unjust; e.g. a man is not
a thief, yet he stole, nor an adulterer, yet he committed adultery;
and similarly in all other cases.*

Now we have previously stated how the reciprocal is related
to the just;[1] but we must not forget that what we are looking for is 25
not only what is just without qualification but also political justice.
This is found among men who share their life with a view to self-
sufficiency, men who are free and either proportionately or arithmetically equal,* so that between those who do not fulfil this
condition there is no political justice but justice in a special sense
and by analogy. For justice exists only between men whose mutual 30
relations are governed by law; and law exists for men between
whom there is injustice; for legal justice is the discrimination of the
just and the unjust. And between men between whom injustice is
done there is also unjust action (though there is not injustice
between all between whom there is unjust action),* and this is
assigning too much to oneself of things good in themselves and
too little of things evil in themselves. This is why we do not allow 35
a *man* to rule, but *rational principle*, because a man behaves thus
in his own interests and becomes a tyrant. The magistrate on the 1134b
other hand is the guardian of justice, and, if of justice, then of
equality also. And since he is assumed to have no more than his
share, if he is just (for he does not assign to himself more of what is
good in itself, unless such a share is proportional to his merits—
so that it is for others that he labours, and it is for this reason that
men, as we stated previously,[2] say that justice is 'another's good'), 5
therefore a reward must be given him, and this is honour and

---

[1] 1132b21–1133b28.   [2] 1130a3.

privilege; but those for whom such things are not enough become
tyrants.

   The justice of a master and that of a father are not the same as
the justice of citizens, though they are like it; for there can be no
injustice in the unqualified sense towards things that are one's own,
10 but a man's chattel,* and his child until it reaches a certain age and
sets up for itself, are as it were part of himself, and no one chooses
to hurt himself (for which reason there can be no injustice towards
oneself). Therefore the justice or injustice of citizens is not manifested in these relations; for it was as we saw according to law, and
between people naturally subject to law, and these as we saw are
15 people who have an equal share in ruling and being ruled.* Hence
justice can more truly be manifested towards a wife than towards
children and chattels, for the former is household justice; but even
this is different from political justice.

Natural and legal justice

7. Of political justice part is natural, part legal,*—natural, that
which everywhere has the same force and does not exist by people's
20 thinking this or that; legal, that which is originally indifferent, but
when it has been laid down is not indifferent, e.g. that a prisoner's
ransom shall be a mina, or that a goat and not two sheep shall be
sacrificed, and again all the laws that are passed for particular cases,
e.g. that sacrifice shall be made in honour of Brasidas, and the pro-
visions of decrees. Now some think that all justice is of this sort,
25 because that which is by nature is unchangeable and has everywhere the same force (as fire burns both here and in Persia), while
they see change in the things recognized as just.* This, however, is
not true in this unqualified way, but is true in a sense; or rather,
with the gods it is perhaps not true at all, while with us there is
something that is just even by nature, yet all of it is changeable;*
30 but still some is by nature, some not by nature. It is evident which
sort of thing, among things capable of being otherwise, is by nature;
and which is not but is legal and conventional, given that both are
equally changeable. And in all other things the same distinction will
apply; by nature the right hand is stronger, yet it is possible that all
35 men should come to be ambidextrous. The things which are just by
1135a virtue of convention and expediency are like measures; for wine and
corn measures are not everywhere equal, but larger in wholesale

and smaller in retail markets. Similarly, the things which are just
not by nature but by human enactment are not everywhere the
same, since constitutions also are not the same, though there is but 5
one which is everywhere by nature the best.*

Of things just and lawful each is related as the universal to its
particulars; for the things that are done are many, but each type is
one, since it is universal.*

There is a difference between the act of injustice and what is
unjust, and between the act of justice and what is just; for a thing is
unjust by nature or by enactment; and this very thing, when it has 10
been done, is an act of injustice, but before it is done is not yet that
but is unjust. So, too, with an act of justice (though the general
term is rather 'just action', and 'act of justice' is applied to the
correction of the act of injustice).

Each of these must later[1] be examined separately with regard to
the nature and number of its species and the nature of the things
with which it is concerned.

JUSTICE: ITS INNER NATURE AS INVOLVING CHOICE

The scale of degrees of wrongdoing

8. Acts just and unjust being as we have described them, a man acts 15
unjustly or justly whenever he does such acts voluntarily; when
involuntarily, he acts neither unjustly nor justly except in an incidental way; for he does things which happen to be just or unjust.*
Whether an act is or is not one of injustice (or of justice) is determined by its voluntariness or involuntariness; for when it is volun- 20
tary it is blamed, and at the same time is then an act of injustice; so
that there will be things that are unjust but not yet acts of injustice,
if voluntariness be not present as well. By the voluntary I mean, as
has been said before,[2] any of the things in a man's own power which
he does with knowledge, i.e. not in ignorance either of the person 25
acted on or of the instrument used or of the end that will be attained
(e.g. whom he is striking, with what, and to what end), each such
act being not done incidentally nor forced (e.g. if A takes B's hand
and therewith strikes C, B does not act voluntarily; for the act was
not in his own power*). The person struck may be the striker's

---

[1] Possibly a reference to an intended (or now lost) book of the *Politics* on laws.
[2] 1109b35–1111a24.

father, and the striker may know that it is a man or one of the
30 persons present, but not know that it is his father; a similar distinction may be made in the case of the end, and with regard to the whole
action.* Therefore that which is done in ignorance, or though not
done in ignorance is not in the agent's power, or is forced, is involuntary (for many natural processes too, we knowingly perform or
1135b undergo, none of which is either voluntary or involuntary; e.g.
growing old or dying*). But in the case of unjust and just acts alike
the injustice or justice may be only incidental; for a man might
return a deposit unwillingly and from fear, and then he must not be
5 said either to do what is just or to act justly, except in an incidental
way. Similarly the man who under compulsion and unwillingly fails
to return the deposit must be said to act unjustly, and to do what is
unjust, only incidentally. Of voluntary acts we do some by choice,
10 others not by choice; by choice those which we do after deliberation,
not by choice those which we do without previous deliberation.*
Thus there are three kinds of injury in transactions between man
and man;* those involving ignorance are mistakes when the person
acted on, the act, the instrument, or the end that will be attained is
other than the agent supposed; the agent thought either that he was
not hitting anyone or that he was not hitting with this missile or not
hitting this person or to this end, but a result followed other than
that which he thought likely (e.g. he threw not with intent to
15 wound but only to prick), or the person hit or the missile was other
than he supposed. Now when the injury takes place contrary to
reasonable expectation, it is a *misadventure*. When it is not contrary
to reasonable expectation, but does not imply vice, it is a *mistake*
(for a man makes a mistake when the fault originates in him, but is
the victim of misfortune when the origin lies outside him*). When
20 he acts with knowledge but not after deliberation, it is an *act of
injustice*—e.g. the acts due to anger or to other passions necessary
or natural to man; for when men do such harmful and mistaken acts
they act unjustly, and the acts are acts of injustice, but this does not
imply that the doers are unjust or wicked; for the injury is not due
25 to vice.* But when a man acts from choice, he is an *unjust man* and
a vicious man.*

Hence acts proceeding from anger are rightly judged not to be
done of malice aforethought; for it is not the man who acts in anger
but he who enraged him that starts the mischief. Again, the matter

in dispute is not whether the thing happened or not, but its justice; for it is apparent injustice that occasions rage. For they do not 30 dispute about the occurrence of the act—as in commercial transactions where one of the two parties *must* be vicious unless there is forgetfulness; but, agreeing about the fact, they dispute on which side justice lies (whereas a man who has deliberately injured another cannot help knowing that he has done so), so that the one thinks he is being treated unjustly and the other disagrees.

But if a man harms another by choice, he acts unjustly; and *these* 1136a are the acts of injustice which imply that the doer is an unjust man, provided that the act violates proportion or equality. Similarly, a man *is just* when he acts justly by choice; but he *acts justly* if he merely acts voluntarily.

Of involuntary acts some are excusable, others not. For the mis- 5 takes which men make not only in ignorance but also by reason of ignorance are excusable, while those which men do not by reason of ignorance but (though they do them *in* ignorance) owing to a passion which is neither natural nor such as man is liable to, are not excusable.*

Can a man be voluntarily treated unjustly? Is it the distributor or the recipient that is guilty of injustice in distribution? Justice not so easy as it might seem, because it is not a way of acting but an inner disposition

9. Assuming that we have sufficiently defined the suffering and 10 doing of injustice, it may be asked (1) whether the truth is expressed in Euripides' paradoxical words:

> 'I slew my mother, that's my tale in brief.'
> 'Were you both willing, or unwilling both?'

Is it truly possible to be willingly treated unjustly, or is all suffering 15 of injustice on the contrary involuntary, as all unjust action is voluntary?* And is suffering of injustice all of one kind or all of the other, or is it sometimes voluntary, sometimes involuntary? So, too, with the case of being justly treated; all just action is voluntary, so that it is reasonable that there should be a similar opposition in 20 either case—that both being unjustly and being justly treated should be either alike voluntary or alike involuntary. But it would be thought paradoxical even in the case of being justly treated, if it

were always voluntary; for some are unwillingly treated justly.*
(2) One might raise this question also, whether everyone who has
suffered what is unjust is being unjustly treated, or on the other
25 hand it is with suffering as with acting. In action and in passivity
alike it is possible for justice to be done incidentally, and similarly (it
is plain) injustice; for to do what is unjust is not the same as to act
unjustly, nor to suffer what is unjust as to be treated unjustly, and
similarly in the case of acting justly and being justly treated; for it
30 is impossible to be unjustly treated if the other does not act unjustly,
or justly treated unless he acts justly. Now if to act unjustly is simply
to harm someone voluntarily, and 'voluntarily' means 'knowing the
person acted on, the instrument, and the manner of one's acting',
and the incontinent man voluntarily harms himself, not only will he
voluntarily be unjustly treated but it will be possible to treat oneself
unjustly. (This also is one of the questions in doubt, whether a man
1136b can treat himself unjustly.) Again, a man may voluntarily, owing to
incontinence, be harmed by another who acts voluntarily, so that it
would be possible to be voluntarily treated unjustly. Or is our definition incorrect; must we to 'harming another, with knowledge
both of the person acted on, of the instrument, and of the manner'
add 'contrary to the wish of the person acted on'?* Then a man may
5 be voluntarily harmed and voluntarily suffer what is unjust, but no
one is voluntarily treated unjustly; for no one wishes to be unjustly
treated, not even the incontinent man. He acts contrary to his wish;
for no one *wishes* for what he does not think to be good, but the
incontinent man does *do* things that he does not think he ought to
do. Again, one who gives what is his own, as Homer says Glaucus
10 gave Diomede

Armour of gold for brazen, the price of a hundred oxen for nine,*

is not unjustly treated; for though to give is in his power, to be unjustly
treated is not, but there must be someone to treat him unjustly. It
is plain, then, that being unjustly treated is not voluntary.

15   Of the questions we intended to discuss two still remain for
discussion; (3) whether it is the man who has assigned to another
more than his share that acts unjustly, or he who has the excessive
share, and (4) whether it is possible to treat oneself unjustly. The
questions are connected; for if the former alternative is possible and
the distributor acts unjustly and not the man who has the excessive

share, then if a man assigns more to another than to himself, knowingly and voluntarily, he treats himself unjustly; which is what
modest people seem to do, since the virtuous man tends to take less   20
than his share. Or does this statement too need qualification? For
(a) he perhaps gets more than his share of some other good, e.g. of
reputation or of intrinsic nobility,* (b) The question is solved by
applying the distinction we applied to unjust action; for he suffers
nothing contrary to his own wish, so that he is not unjustly treated
so far as this goes, but at most only suffers harm.   25

   It is plain too that the distributor acts unjustly, but not always
the man who has the excessive share; for it is not he to whom injustice is done that acts unjustly, but he to whom it appertains to do
the unjust act voluntarily, i.e. the person in whom lies the origin of
the action, and this lies in the distributor, not in the receiver. Again,
since the word 'do' is ambiguous, and there is a sense in which lifeless things, or a hand, or a servant who obeys an order, may be said   30
to slay, he who gets an excessive share does not act unjustly, though
he 'does' what is unjust.

   Again, if the distributor gave his judgement in ignorance, he
does not act unjustly in respect of legal justice, and his judgement
is not unjust in this sense, but in a sense it *is* unjust (for what is just
by law, and in the primary way, are different); but if with knowledge
he judged unjustly, he is himself aiming at an excessive share either   1137a
of gratitude or of revenge.* As much, then, as if he were to share in
the plunder, the man who has judged unjustly for these reasons has
got too much; the fact that what he gets is different from what he
distributes makes no difference, for even if he awards land with a
view to sharing in the plunder he gets not land but money.

   Men think that acting unjustly is in their power, and therefore   5
that being just is easy. But it is not; to lie with one's neighbour's
wife, to wound another, to deliver a bribe, is easy and in our power,
but to do these things as a result of a certain state of character is
neither easy nor in our power.* Similarly to know what is just and
what is unjust requires, men think, no great wisdom, because it is   10
not hard to understand the matters dealt with by the laws (though
these are not the things that are just, except incidentally); but how
actions must be done and distributions effected in order to be just,
to know *this* is a greater achievement than knowing what is good for
the health; though even there, while it is easy to know that honey,

15 wine, hellebore, cautery, and the use of the knife are so, to know how,
to whom, and when these should be applied with a view to producing health, is no less an achievement than that of being a physician.
Again, for this very reason men think that acting unjustly is characteristic of the just man no less than of the unjust, because he would
be not less but even more capable of doing each of these unjust acts;
20 for he could lie with a woman or wound a neighbour; and the brave
man could throw away his shield and turn to flight in this direction
or in that.* But to play the coward or to act unjustly consists not in
doing these things, except incidentally, but in doing them as the
result of a certain state of character, just as to practise medicine and
healing consists not in applying or not applying the knife, in using
25 or not using medicines, but in doing so in a certain way.

Just acts occur between people who participate in things good in
themselves and can have too much or too little of them; for some
beings (e.g. presumably the gods) cannot have too much of them,
and to others, those who are incurably bad, not even the smallest
share in them is beneficial but all such goods are harmful, while to
others they are beneficial up to a point; therefore justice is essentially
30 something human.*

Equity, a corrective of legal justice

10. Our next subject is equity and the equitable, and their respective
relations to justice and the just.* For on examination they appear to
be neither absolutely the same nor generically different; and while
35 we sometimes praise what is equitable and the equitable man (so
that we apply the name by way of praise even to instances of the
1137b other virtues, instead of 'good', meaning by 'more equitable' that
a thing is better), at other times, when we reason it out, it seems
strange if the equitable, being something different from the just, is
yet praiseworthy; for either the just or the equitable is not good, if
6 they are different; or, if both are good, they are the same.

These, then, are pretty much the considerations that give rise to
the problem about the equitable; they are all in a sense correct and
not opposed to one another; for the equitable, though it is better
than one kind of justice, yet is just, and it is not as being a different
class of thing that it is better than the just. The same thing, then, is
10 just and equitable, and while both are good the equitable is superior. What creates the problem is that the equitable is just, but not

the legally just but a correction of legal justice.* The reason is that all law is universal but about some things it is not possible to make a universal statement which shall be correct. In those cases, then, in which it is necessary to speak universally, but not possible to do so 15 correctly, the law takes the usual case, though it is not ignorant of the possibility of error. And it is none the less correct; for the error is not in the law nor in the legislator but in the nature of the thing, since the matter of practical affairs is of this kind from the start. When the law speaks universally, then, and a case arises on it which 20 is not covered by the universal statement, then it is right, where the legislator fails us and has erred by over-simplicity, to correct the omission—to say what the legislator himself would have said had be been present, and would have put into his law if he had known. Hence the equitable is just, and better than one kind of justice—not better than absolute justice, but better than the error that arises 25 from the absoluteness of the statement. And this is the nature of the equitable, a correction of law where it is defective owing to its universality. In fact this is the reason why all things are not determined by law, namely, that about some things it is impossible to lay down a law, so that a decree is needed. For when the thing is indefinite the rule also is indefinite, like the leaden rule used in making the Lesbian moulding; the rule adapts itself to the shape of the stone 30 and is not rigid,* and so too the decree is adapted to the facts.

It is plain, then, what the equitable is, and that it is just and is better than one kind of justice. It is evident also from this who the equitable man is; the man who chooses and does such acts, and is 35 no stickler for his rights in a bad sense* but tends to take less than his share though he has the law on his side, is equitable, and this 1138a state of character is equity, which is a sort of justice and not a different state of character.

Can a man treat himself unjustly?

11. Whether a man can treat himself unjustly or not, is evident from what has been said.* For (a) one class of just acts is those acts 5 that accord with any virtue and that are prescribed by the law; e.g. the law does not expressly permit suicide, and what it does not expressly permit it forbids.* Again, when a man in violation of the law harms another (otherwise than in retaliation) voluntarily, he acts unjustly, and a voluntary agent is one who knows both the person

he is affecting by his action and the instrument he is using; and he
10 who through anger voluntarily stabs himself does this contrary to
the right rule of life, and this the law does not allow; therefore he is
acting unjustly. But towards whom? Surely towards the state, not
towards himself. For he suffers voluntarily, but no one is voluntarily
treated unjustly. This is also the reason why the state punishes; a
certain loss of civil rights attaches to the man who destroys himself,
on the ground that he is treating the state unjustly.*

Further, (b) in that sense of 'acting unjustly' in which the man
15 who 'acts unjustly' is unjust only and not bad all round, it is not
possible to treat oneself unjustly (this is different from the former
sense; the unjust man in one sense of the term is wicked in a par-
ticularized way just as the coward is, not in the sense of being
wicked all round, so that his 'unjust act' does not manifest wickedness in general). For (i) that would imply the possibility of the same
thing's having been subtracted from and added to the same thing at
the same time; but this is impossible—the just and the unjust
20 always involve more than one person. Further, (ii) unjust action is
voluntary and done by choice, and *takes the initiative* (for the man
who because he has suffered does the same in return is not thought
to act unjustly); but if a man harms himself he suffers and does the
same things *at the same time*. Further, (iii) if a man could treat himself
unjustly, he could be voluntarily treated unjustly.* Besides, (iv) no
one acts unjustly without committing particular acts of injustice;
25 but no one can commit adultery with his own wife or housebreak-
ing on his own house or theft on his own property.

In general, the question 'Can a man treat himself unjustly?' is
solved also by the distinction we applied to the question 'Can a man
be voluntarily treated unjustly?'[1]

(It is evident too that both are bad, being unjustly treated and
30 acting unjustly; for the one means having less and the other having
more than the intermediate amount, which plays the part here that
the healthy does in the medical art, and that good condition does in
the art of bodily training. But still acting unjustly is the worse, for
it involves vice and is blameworthy—involves vice which is either
of the complete and unqualified kind or almost so (we must admit
the latter alternative, because not all voluntary unjust action implies
injustice as a state of character), while being unjustly treated does

---

[1] Cf. 1136a31–b5.

not involve vice and injustice in oneself. In itself, then, being 35
unjustly treated is less bad, but there is nothing to prevent its being 1138b
incidentally a greater evil. But theory cares nothing for this;* it calls
pleurisy a more serious mischief than a stumble; yet the latter may
become incidentally the more serious, if the fall due to it leads to
your being taken prisoner or put to death by the enemy.)

Metaphorically and in virtue of a certain resemblance there is a 5
justice, not indeed between a man and himself, but between certain
parts of him; yet not every kind of justice but that of master and
servant or that of husband and wife.[1] For these are the ratios in
which the part of the soul that has a rational principle stands to the
irrational part; and it is with a view to these parts that people also 10
think a man can be unjust to himself, namely, because these parts
are liable to suffer something contrary to their respective desires;
there is therefore thought to be a mutual justice between them as
between ruler and ruled.

Let this be taken as our account of justice and the other, i.e. the
other moral, virtues.

[1] Cf. 1134b15–17.

BOOK VI · INTELLECTUAL VIRTUE

INTRODUCTION

Reasons for studying intellectual virtue: intellect divided into the contemplative and the calculative

1. SINCE we have previously said that one ought to choose that which is intermediate, not the excess nor the defect,[1] and that the 20 intermediate is determined by reason,[2] let us discuss this.* In all the states of character we have mentioned,[3] as in all other matters, there is a mark to which the man who has reason looks, and heightens or relaxes his activity accordingly, and there is a standard which determines the mean states which we say are intermediate between excess and defect, being in accordance with correct reason. But such 25 a statement, though true, is by no means clear; for not only here but in all other pursuits which are objects of knowledge it is indeed true to say that we must not exert ourselves nor relax our efforts too much or too little, but to an intermediate extent and as correct reason dictates; but if a man had only this knowledge he would be none the 30 wiser—e.g. we should not know what sort of medicines to apply to our body if someone were to say 'all those which the medical art prescribes, and which agree with the practice of one who possesses the art'. Hence it is necessary with regard to the states of the soul also, not only that this true statement should be made, but also that it should be determined what correct reason is and what is the standard that fixes it.*

We divided the virtues of the soul and said that some are moral 1139a virtues and others virtues of intellect.[4] Now we have discussed in detail the moral virtues;[5] with regard to the others let us express our view as follows, beginning with some remarks about the soul. We said before[6] that there are two parts of the soul—that which grasps a rational principle, and the non-rational; let us now draw 5 a similar distinction within the part which grasps a rational principle. And let it be assumed that there are two parts which grasp

---

[1] 1104a11–27, 1106a26–1107a27.
[2] 1107a1, cf. 1103b31, 1114b29.
[3] In iii. 6–v. 11.

[4] 1103a3–7.
[5] In iii. 6–v. 11.
[6] 1102a26–8.

a rational principle—one by which we contemplate the kind of things whose originative causes are invariable, and one by which we contemplate variable things; for where objects differ in kind the part of the soul answering to each of the two is different in kind, 10 since it is in virtue of a certain likeness and kinship with their objects that they have the knowledge they have.* Let one of these parts be called the scientific and the other the calculative; for to deliberate and to calculate are the same thing, but no one deliberates about the invariable. Therefore the calculative is one part of the faculty which grasps a rational principle. We must, then, learn 15 what is the best state of each of these two parts; for this is the virtue of each.

The object of contemplation is truth; that of calculation is truth corresponding with right desire

2. The virtue of a thing is relative to its proper work. Now there are three things in the soul which control action and truth—perception, reason, desire.

Of these perception originates no action; this is plain from the fact that the lower animals have perception but no share in action.* 20

What affirmation and negation are in thinking, pursuit and avoidance are in desire; so that since moral virtue is a state of character concerned with choice, and choice is deliberate desire, therefore both the reasoning must be true and the desire right, if the choice is to be good, and the latter must pursue just what the 25 former asserts. Now this kind of intellect and of truth is practical; of the intellect which is contemplative, not practical nor productive, the good and the bad state are truth and falsity respectively (for this is the work of everything intellectual); while of the part which is practical and intellectual the good state is truth in agree- 30 ment with right desire.*

The origin of action—its efficient, not its final cause*—is choice, and that of choice is desire and reasoning with a view to an end. This is why choice cannot exist either without reason and intellect or without a moral state; for good action and its opposite cannot exist without a combination of intellect and character. Intellect 35 itself, however, moves nothing, but only the intellect which aims at an end and is practical;* for this rules the productive intellect as 1139b well, since everyone who makes makes for an end, and that which

is made is not an end in the unqualified sense (but only an end in a particular relation, and the end of a particular operation)—only that which is *done* is that;* for good action is an end, and desire aims at this.* Hence choice is either desiderative reason or ratiocinative
5 desire, and such an origin of action is a man. (It is to be noted that nothing that is past is an object of choice, e.g. no one chooses to have sacked Troy; for no one *deliberates* about the past, but about what is future and capable of being otherwise, while what is past is not capable of not having taken place; hence Agathon is right in saying:

10   For this alone is lacking even to god,
            To make undone things that have once been done.*)

The work of both the intellectual parts, then, is truth. Therefore the states that are most strictly those in respect of which each of
15 these parts will reach truth are the virtues of the two parts.

THE CHIEF INTELLECTUAL VIRTUES

Scientific knowledge—demonstrative knowledge of the necessary and eternal

3. Let us begin, then, from the beginning, and discuss these states
15 once more. Let it be assumed that the states by virtue of which the soul possesses truth by way of affirmation or denial are five in number, i.e. art, scientific knowledge, practical wisdom, philosophic wisdom, intuitive reason; we do not include judgement and opinion because in these we may be mistaken.*

Now what *scientific knowledge* is, if we are to speak exactly and not follow mere similarities, is plain from what follows. We all suppose
20 that what we know is not even capable of being otherwise; of things capable of being otherwise we do not know, when they have passed outside our observation, whether they exist or not. Therefore the object of scientific knowledge is of necessity.* Therefore it is eternal; for things that are of necessity in the unqualified sense are all eternal; and things that are eternal are ungenerated and imperishable. Again, every science is thought to be capable of being
25 taught, and its object of being learnt. And all teaching starts from what is already known, as we maintain in the *Analytics* also;* for it proceeds sometimes through induction and sometimes by deduction.

Now induction is the starting-point which knowledge even of the universal presupposes, while deduction proceeds *from* universals. There are therefore starting-points from which deduction proceeds, 30 which are not reached by deduction; it is therefore by induction that they are acquired.* Scientific knowledge is, then, a state of capacity to demonstrate, and has the other limiting characteristics which we specify in the *Analytics*;* for it is when a man believes in a certain way and the starting-points are known to him that he has scientific knowledge, since if they are not better known to him than the conclusion, he will have his knowledge only incidentally.   35

Let this, then, be taken as our account of scientific knowledge.

Art—knowledge of how to make things

4. In the variable are included both things made and things done; 1140a making and acting are different (for their nature we treat even the discussions outside our school as reliable); so that the reasoned state of capacity to act is different from the reasoned state of capacity to make.* Hence too they are not included one in the other; for neither 5 is acting making nor is making acting. Now since architecture is an art and is essentially a reasoned state of capacity to make, and there is neither any art that is not such a state nor any such state that is not an art, *art* is identical with a state of capacity to make, involving 10 true reasoning.* All art is concerned with coming into being, i.e. with contriving and considering how something may come into being which is capable of either being or not being, and whose origin is in the maker and not in the thing made; for art is concerned neither with things that are, or come into being, by necessity, nor 15 with things that do so in accordance with nature (since these have their origin in themselves). Making and acting being different, art must be a matter of making, not of acting. And in a sense chance and art are concerned with the same objects; as Agathon says, 'Art loves chance and chance loves art.'* Art, then, as has been said, is a 20 state concerned with making, involving true reasoning, and lack of art on the contrary is a state concerned with making, involving a false course of reasoning; both are concerned with the variable.

Practical wisdom—knowledge of how to secure the ends of human life

5. Regarding *practical wisdom* we shall get at the truth by considering who are the persons we credit with it. Now it is thought to be a 25

mark of a man of practical wisdom to be able to deliberate well
about what is good and expedient for himself, not in some particular
respect, e.g. about what sorts of thing conduce to health or to
strength, but about what sorts of thing conduce to the good life in
general.* This is shown by the fact that we credit men with practical wisdom in some particular respect when they have calculated
well with a view to some good end which is one of those that are not
30 the object of any art. It follows that in the general sense also the
man who is capable of deliberating has practical wisdom. Now no
one deliberates about things that are invariable, or about things that
it is impossible for him to do. Therefore, since scientific knowledge
involves demonstration, but there is no demonstration of things
35 whose first principles are variable (for all such things might actually
be otherwise), and since it is impossible to deliberate about things
1140b that are of necessity, practical wisdom cannot be scientific knowledge or art; not science because that which can be done is capable
of being otherwise, not art because action and making are different
kinds of thing.* The remaining alternative, then, is that it is a true
5 and reasoned state of capacity to act with regard to the things that
are good or bad for man.* For while making has an end other than
itself, action cannot; for good action itself is its end. It is for this
reason that we think Pericles and men like him have practical wisdom,
namely, because they can see what is good for themselves and what
is good for men in general; we consider that those can do this who
10 are good at managing households or states. (This is why we call
temperance (sōphrosunē) by this name; we imply that it preserves
one's practical wisdom (sōzousa tēn phronēsin). Now what it preserves is a judgement of the kind we have described. For it is not
any and every judgement that pleasant and painful objects destroy
and pervert, e.g. the judgement that the triangle has or has not its
15 angles equal to two right angles, but only judgements about what is
to be done. For the originating causes of the things that are done
consist in the end at which they are aimed; but the man who has
been ruined by pleasure or pain forthwith fails to see any such
originating cause—to see that for the sake of this or because of this
he ought to choose and do whatever he chooses and does; for vice
is destructive of the originating cause of action.*)
20   Practical wisdom, then, must be a reasoned and true state of
capacity to act with regard to human goods. But further, while

there is such a thing as excellence in art, there is no such thing as excellence in practical wisdom; and in art he who errs willingly is preferable, but in practical wisdom, as in the virtues, he is the reverse.* Plainly, then, practical wisdom is a virtue and not an art. There being two parts of the soul that can follow a course of reason- 25 ing, it must be a virtue of one of the two, i.e. of that part which forms opinions; for opinion is about the variable and so is practical wisdom. But yet it is not only a reasoned state; this is shown by the fact that a state of that sort may be forgotten but practical wisdom cannot.* 30

Intuitive reason—knowledge of the principles from which science proceeds

6. Scientific knowledge is judgement about things that are universal and necessary; and the conclusions of demonstration, and all scien- tific knowledge, follow from first principles (for scientific knowledge involves demonstration*). This being so, the first principle from which what is scientifically known follows cannot be an object of scientific knowledge, of art, or of practical wisdom; for that which can be scientifically known can be demonstrated, and art and prac- 35 tical wisdom deal with things that are variable. Nor are these first 1141a principles the objects of philosophic wisdom, for it is a mark of the philosopher to have *demonstration* about some things. If, then, the states of mind by which we have truth and are never deceived about things invariable or even variable are scientific knowledge, practical 5 wisdom, philosophic wisdom, and intuitive reason, and it cannot be any of the three (i.e. practical wisdom, scientific knowledge, or philosophic wisdom), the remaining alternative is that it is *intuitive reason* that grasps the first principles.*

Philosophic wisdom—the union of intuitive reason and science

7. *Wisdom* (1) in the arts we ascribe to their most finished exponents, e.g. to Phidias as a sculptor and to Polyclitus as a maker of portrait- 10 statues, and here we mean nothing by wisdom except excellence in art; but (2) we think that some people are wise in general, not in some particular field or in any other limited respect, as Homer says in the *Margites*,

> Him did the gods make neither a digger nor yet a ploughman   15
> Nor wise in anything else.*

Therefore wisdom must plainly be the most finished of the forms of knowledge. It follows that the wise man must not only know what follows from the first principles, but must also possess truth about the first principles. Therefore wisdom must be intuitive reason combined with scientific knowledge*—scientific knowledge
20 of the highest objects which has received as it were its proper completion.

Of the highest objects, we say; for it would be strange to think that the art of politics, or practical wisdom, is the best knowledge, since man is not the best thing in the world. Now if what is healthy or good is different for men and for fishes, but what is white or straight is always the same, anyone would say that what is wise is the same but what is practically wise is different; for it is to that
25 which considers well the various matters concerning itself that one ascribes practical wisdom, and it is to this that one will entrust such matters. This is why we say that some even of the lower animals have practical wisdom, namely, those which are found to have a power of foresight with regard to their own life. It is evident also that philosophic wisdom and the art of politics cannot be the same; for if the state of mind concerned with a man's own interests
30 is to be called philosophic wisdom, there will be many philosophic wisdoms; there will not be one concerned with the good of all animals (any more than there is one art of medicine for all existing things), but a different philosophic wisdom about the good of each species.

But if the argument be that man is the best of the animals, this makes no difference; for there are other things much more divine in
1141b their nature even than man, e.g., most conspicuously, the bodies of which the heavens are framed.* From what has been said it is plain, then, that philosophic wisdom is scientific knowledge, combined with intuitive reason, of the things that are highest by nature. This is why we say Anaxagoras, Thales, and men like them have philo-
5 sophic but not practical wisdom, when we see them ignorant of what is to their own advantage, and why we say that they know things that are remarkable, admirable, difficult, and divine, but useless;* namely, because it is not human goods that they seek.

Practical wisdom on the other hand is concerned with things human and things about which it is possible to deliberate; for we
10 say this is above all the work of the man of practical wisdom, to

deliberate well, but no one deliberates about things invariable, or about things which have not an end which is a good that can be brought about by action. The man who is without qualification good at deliberating is the man who is capable of aiming in accordance with calculation at the best for man of things attainable by action. Nor is practical wisdom concerned with universals only—it 15 must also recognize the particulars; for it is practical, and practice is concerned with particulars.* This is why some who do not know, and especially those who have experience, are more practical than others who know; for if a man knew that light meats are digestible and wholesome, but did not know which sorts of meat are light, he 20 would not produce health, but the man who knows that chicken is wholesome is more likely to produce health.*

Now practical wisdom is concerned with action; therefore one should have both forms of it, or the latter in preference to the former.* But here, too, there must be a controlling kind.*

Relations between practical wisdom and political science

8. Political wisdom and practical wisdom are the same state of mind, but their essence is not the same. Of the wisdom concerned with the city, the practical wisdom which plays a controlling part is legislative wisdom, while that which is related to this as particulars 25 to their universal is known by the general name 'political wisdom'; this has to do with action and deliberation, for a decree is a thing to be carried out in the form of an individual act. This is why the exponents of this art are alone said to 'take part in politics'; for these alone 'do things' as manual labourers 'do things'.*

Practical wisdom also is identified especially with that form of it which is concerned with a man himself—with the individual; and 30 this is known by the general name 'practical wisdom'; of the other kinds one is called household management, another legislation, the third politics, and of the latter one part is called deliberative and the other judicial. Now knowing what is good for oneself will be one kind of knowledge, but it is very different from the other kinds; and 1142a the man who knows and concerns himself with his own interests is thought to have practical wisdom, while politicians are thought to be busybodies; hence the words of Euripides:*

> But how could I be wise, who might at ease,
> Numbered among the army's multitude,

5   Have had an equal share?. . .
         For those who aim too high and do too much . . .

Those who think thus seek their own good, and consider that one
ought to do so. From this opinion, then, has come the view that such
men have practical wisdom; yet perhaps one's own good cannot exist
without household management, nor without a form of government.
10 Further, how one should order one's own affairs is not clear and
needs inquiry.

What has been said is confirmed by the fact that while young
men become geometricians and mathematicians and wise in matters
like these, it is thought that a young man of practical wisdom
cannot be found. The cause is that such wisdom is concerned not
only with universals but with particulars, which become familiar
15 from experience, but a young man has no experience, for it is length
of time that gives experience; indeed one might ask this question
too, why a boy may become a mathematician, but not a philosopher
or a physicist. Is it because the objects of mathematics exist by
abstraction, while the first principles of these other subjects come
from experience, and because young men have no conviction about
20 the latter but merely use the proper language, while the essence of
mathematical objects is plain enough to them?

Further, error in deliberation may be either about the universal
or about the particular; we may fail to know either that all water
that weighs heavy is bad, or that this particular water weighs
heavy.*

That practical wisdom is not scientific knowledge is evident; for
it is, as has been said,[1] concerned with the ultimate particular fact,
25 since the thing to be done is of this nature. It is opposed, then, to
intuitive reason;* for intuitive reason is of the limiting premisses,
for which no reason can be given, while practical wisdom is concerned
with the ultimate particular, which is the object not of scientific
knowledge but of perception—not the perception of qualities peculiar to one sense but a perception akin to that by which we perceive
that the particular figure before us is a triangle; for in that direction
as well there will be a limit. But this is rather perception than prac-
30 tical wisdom, though it is another kind of perception than that of
the qualities peculiar to each sense.*

[1] 1141b14–22.

MINOR INTELLECTUAL VIRTUES
CONCERNED WITH CONDUCT

Goodness in deliberation, how related to practical wisdom

9. There is a difference between inquiry and deliberation; for deliberation is a particular kind of inquiry. We must grasp the nature of excellence in deliberation* as well—whether it is a form of scientific knowledge, or opinion, or skill in conjecture, or some other kind of thing. *Scientific knowledge* it is not; for men do not inquire about the things they know about, but good deliberation is a kind 1142b of deliberation, and he who deliberates inquires and calculates. Nor is it *skill in conjecture*; for this both involves no reasoning and is something that is quick in its operation, while men deliberate a long time, and they say that one should carry out quickly the conclusions of one's deliberation, but should deliberate slowly. Again, *readiness* 5 *of mind* is different from excellence in deliberation; it is a sort of skill in conjecture. Nor again is excellence in deliberation *opinion* of any sort. But since the man who deliberates badly makes a mistake, while he who deliberates well does so correctly, excellence in deliberation is clearly a kind of correctness, but neither of knowledge nor of opinion; for there is no such thing as correctness of knowledge 10 (since there is no such thing as error of knowledge), and correctness of opinion is truth; and at the same time everything that is an object of opinion is already determined.* But again excellence in deliberation involves reasoning. The remaining alternative, then, is that it is *correctness of thinking*; for this is not yet assertion, since, while even opinion is not inquiry but has reached the stage of assertion, the man who is deliberating, whether he does so well or ill, is 15 searching for something and calculating.

But excellence in deliberation is a certain correctness of deliberation; hence we must first inquire what deliberation is and what it is about. And, there being more than one kind of correctness, plainly excellence in deliberation is not any and every kind; for (1) the incontinent man and the bad man, if he is clever, will reach as a result of his calculation what he sets before himself, so that he will have deliberated correctly, but he will have got for himself a great 20 evil. Now to have deliberated well is thought to be a good thing; for it is this kind of correctness of deliberation that is excellence in deliberation, namely, that which tends to attain what is good.*

But (2) it is possible to attain even good by a false syllogism, and to attain what one ought to do but not by the right means, the middle
25 term being false; so that this too is not yet excellence in deliberation—this state in virtue of which one attains what one ought but not by the right means. Again (3) it is possible to attain it by long deliberation while another man attains it quickly. Therefore in the former case we have not yet got excellence in deliberation, which is rightness with regard to the expedient—rightness in respect both of the end, the manner, and the time. (4) Further, it is possible to have deliberated well either in the unqualified sense or with reference to a particular end. Excellence in deliberation in the unquali-
30 fied sense, then, is that which succeeds with reference to what is the end in the unqualified sense, and excellence in deliberation in a particular sense is that which succeeds relatively to a particular end. If, then, it is characteristic of men of practical wisdom to have deliberated well, excellence in deliberation will be correctness with regard to what conduces to the end which practical wisdom apprehends truly.*

Understanding—the critical quality answering to the imperative quality practical wisdom

10. Understanding, also, and goodness of understanding, in virtue of which men are said to be men of understanding or of good
1143a understanding, are neither entirely the same as opinion or scientific knowledge (for at that rate all men would have been men of understanding), nor are they one of the particular sciences, such as medicine, the science of things connected with health, or geometry, the science of spatial magnitudes. For understanding is neither about
5 things that are always and are unchangeable, nor about any and every one of the things that come into being, but about things which may become subjects of questioning and deliberation. Hence it is about the same objects as practical wisdom; but understanding and practical wisdom are not the same. For practical wisdom issues commands, since its end is what ought to be done or not to be done; but under-
10 standing only judges.* (Understanding is identical with goodness of understanding, men of understanding with men of good understanding.) Now understanding is neither the having nor the acquiring of practical wisdom; but as learning is called understanding when it means the exercise of the faculty of knowledge,* so 'understanding'

is applicable to the exercise of the faculty of opinion for the purpose of judging of what someone else says about matters with which practical wisdom is concerned—and of judging soundly; for 'well' and 'soundly' are the same thing. And from this has come the use of the name 'understanding' in virtue of which men are said to be 'of good understanding', namely, from the application of the word to the grasping of scientific truth; for we often call such grasping understanding.

Judgement—right discrimination of the equitable: the place of intuition in morals

11. What is called judgement, in virtue of which men are said to 'be sympathetic judges' and to 'have judgement', is the right discrimination of the equitable.* This is shown by the fact that we say the equitable man is above all others a man of sympathetic judgement, and identify equity with sympathetic judgement about certain facts. And sympathetic judgement is judgement which discriminates what is equitable and does so correctly; and correct judgement is that which judges what is true.

Now all the states we have considered converge, as might be expected, to the same point; for when we speak of judgement and understanding and practical wisdom and intuitive reason we credit the same people with possessing judgement and having reached years of reason and with having practical wisdom and understanding.* For all these faculties deal with ultimates, i.e. with particulars; and being a man of understanding and of good or sympathetic judgement consists in being able to judge about the things with which practical wisdom is concerned; for what is equitable is the common concern of all good men in their dealings with others. Now all things which have to be done are included among particulars or ultimates; for not only must the man of practical wisdom know particular facts, but understanding and judgement are also concerned with things to be done, and these are ultimates. And intuitive reason is concerned with the ultimates in both directions; for both the first terms and the last are objects of intuitive reason and not of a rational account, and the intuitive reason which is presupposed by demonstrations grasps the unchangeable and first terms, while the intuitive reason involved in practical reasonings grasps the last and variable fact, i.e. the minor premiss.* For these variable

facts are the starting-points for the apprehension of the end, since
the universals are reached from the particulars; of these therefore
5 we must have perception, and this perception is intuitive reason.*

This is why these states are thought to be natural endowments—
why, while no one is thought to be a philosopher by nature, people
are thought to have by nature judgement, understanding, and
intuitive reason. This is shown by the fact that we think our powers
correspond to our time of life, and that a particular age brings with
it intuitive reason and judgement; this implies that nature is the
cause. [Hence intuitive reason is both beginning and end; for dem-
10 onstrations are from these and about these.] Therefore we ought to
attend to the undemonstrated sayings and opinions of experienced
and older people or of people of practical wisdom not less than to
demonstrations; for because experience has given them an eye they
see aright.*

We have stated, then, what practical and philosophic wisdom
15 are, and with what each of them is concerned, and we have said that
each is the virtue of a different part of the soul.*

RELATION OF PHILOSOPHIC TO PRACTICAL WISDOM

*What is the use of philosophic and of practical wisdom? Puzzles,
and some solutions*

12. Difficulties might be raised as to the utility of these qualities of
mind.* For (1) philosophic wisdom will contemplate none of the
20 things that will make a man happy (for it is not concerned with any
coming into being), and though practical wisdom has *this* merit, for
what purpose do we need it? Practical wisdom is the quality of
mind concerned with things just and noble and good for man, but
these are the things which it is the mark of a *good* man to do, and
we are none the more able to act for *knowing* them if the virtues
25 are states of *character*, just as we are none the better able to act for
knowing the things that are healthy and sound, in the sense not of
producing but of issuing from the state of health; for we are none
the more able to act for having the art of medicine or of gymnastics.* But (2) if we are to say that a man should have practical wisdom not for the sake of knowing moral truths but for the sake of
becoming good, practical wisdom will be of no use to those who *are*
30 good; but again it is of no use to those who have *not* virtue;* for it

will make no difference whether they have practical wisdom themselves or obey others who have it, and it would be enough for us to
do what we do in the case of health; though we wish to become
healthy, yet we do not learn the art of medicine. (3) Besides this, it
would be thought strange if practical wisdom, being inferior to
philosophic wisdom, is to be put in authority over it, as seems to be
implied by the fact that the art which produces anything rules and
issues commands about that thing.*   35

These, then, are the questions we must discuss; so far we have
only stated the difficulties.

Now first let us say that in themselves these states must be   1144a
worthy of choice because they are the virtues of the two parts of the
soul respectively,* even if neither of them produces anything.

Secondly, they do produce something, not as the art of medicine
produces health, however, but as health produces health;* so does
philosophic wisdom produce happiness; for, being a part of virtue   5
entire, by being possessed and by actualizing itself it makes a man
happy.

Again, the work of man is achieved only in accordance with practical wisdom as well as with moral virtue; for virtue makes the goal
correct, and practical wisdom makes what leads to it correct.* (Of
the fourth part of the soul—the nutritive—there is no such virtue;
for there is nothing which it is in its power to do or not to do.)   10

With regard to our being none the more able to do because of our
practical wisdom what is noble and just, let us begin a little further
back, starting with the following principle. As we say that some
people who do just acts are not necessarily just, i.e. those who do the
acts ordained by the laws either unwillingly or owing to ignorance or   15
for some other reason and not for the sake of the acts themselves
(though, to be sure, they do what they should and all the things that
the good man ought), so is it, it seems, that in order to be good one
must be in a certain state when one does the several acts, i.e. one
must do them as a result of choice and for the sake of the acts themselves.* Now virtue makes the choice right, but the question of the   20
things which should naturally be done to carry out our choice belongs
not to virtue but to another faculty. We must devote our attention
to these matters and give a clearer statement about them. There is
a faculty which is called cleverness; and this is such as to be able
to do the things that tend towards the mark we have set before   25

ourselves, and to hit it. Now if the mark be noble, the cleverness is
laudable, but if the mark be bad, the cleverness is mere smartness;
hence we call even men of practical wisdom clever or smart.*
Practical wisdom is not the faculty, but it does not exist without
30 this faculty. And this eye of the soul acquires its formed state not
without the aid of virtue, as has been said and is plain; for the
syllogisms which deal with acts to be done are things which involve
a starting-point, namely, 'since the end, i.e. what is best, is of such
and such a nature', whatever it may be (let it for the sake of argument be what we please); and this is not evident except to the good
35 man;* for wickedness perverts us and causes us to be deceived
about the starting-points of action. Therefore it is evident that it is
impossible to be practically wise without being good.*

Relation of practical wisdom to natural virtue, moral virtue, and
correct reason

1144b 13. We must therefore consider virtue also once more; for virtue
too is similarly related; as practical wisdom is to cleverness—not
the same, but like it—so is natural virtue to virtue in the strict
sense.* For all men think that each type of character belongs to its
5 possessors in some sense by nature; for from the very moment of
birth we are just or fitted for self-control or brave or have the other
moral qualities; but yet we seek something else as that which is
good in the strict sense—we seek for the presence of such qualities
in another way. For both children and brutes have the natural dispositions to these qualities, but without reason these are evidently
hurtful.* Only we seem to see this much, that, while one may be led
10 astray by them, as a strong body which moves without sight may
stumble badly because of its lack of sight, still, if a man once acquires
reason, that makes a difference in action; and his state, while still
like what it was, will then be virtue in the strict sense. Therefore,
as in the part of us which forms opinions there are two types, clev-
15 erness and practical wisdom, so too in the moral part there are two
types, natural virtue and virtue in the strict sense, and of these the
latter involves practical wisdom. This is why some say that all the
virtues are forms of practical wisdom, and why Socrates in one
respect was on the right track while in another he went astray; in
thinking that all the virtues were forms of practical wisdom he was
20 wrong, but in saying they implied practical wisdom he was right.*

This is confirmed by the fact that even now all men, when they define virtue, after naming the state of character and its objects add 'that (state) which is in accordance with correct reason'; now correct reason is that which is in accordance with practical wisdom. All men, then, seem somehow to divine that this kind of state is virtue, namely, that which is in accordance with practical wisdom. But we must go a little further. For it is not merely the state in accordance with correct reason, but the state that implies the *presence* of correct 25 reason, that is virtue; and practical wisdom is correct reason about such matters.* Socrates, then, thought the virtues were instances of reason (for he thought they were, all of them, forms of scientific knowledge), while we think they *involve* reason.*

It is clear, then, from what has been said, that it is not possible to 30 be good in the strict sense without practical wisdom, or practically wise without moral virtue. But in this way we may also refute the dialectical argument whereby it might be contended that the virtues exist in separation from each other; the same man, it might be said, is not best equipped by nature for all the virtues, so that he will have already acquired one when he has not yet acquired another. 35 This is possible in respect of the natural virtues, but not in respect of those in respect of which a man is called without qualification good;* for with the presence of the one quality, practical wisdom, 1145a will be given all the virtues. And it is plain that, even if it were of no practical value, we should have needed it because it is the virtue of the part of us in question; plain too that the choice will not be right without practical wisdom any more than without virtue; for the one determines the end and the other makes us do the things 5 that lead to the end.

But again it is not *supreme* over philosophic wisdom, i.e. over the superior part of us, any more than the art of medicine is over health; for it does not use it but provides for its coming into being; it issues orders, then, for its sake, but not to it. Further, to maintain its supremacy would be like saying that the art of politics rules the 10 gods because it issues orders about all the affairs of the state.*

BOOK VII · CONTINENCE AND INCONTINENCE: PLEASURE

CONTINENCE AND INCONTINENCE

Six varieties of character: method of treatment: current opinions

15 1. LET us now make a fresh beginning and point out that of moral states to be avoided there are three kinds—vice, incontinence, brutishness. The contraries of two of these are evident—one we call virtue, the other continence; to brutishness it would be most fitting to oppose superhuman virtue, a heroic and divine kind of virtue, as
20 Homer has represented Priam saying of Hector that he was very good.

> For he seemed not, he,
> The child of a mortal man, but as one that of god's seed came.[1]

Therefore if, as they say, men become gods by excess of virtue, of this kind must evidently be the state opposed to the brutish state:
25 for as a brute has no vice or virtue, so neither has a god; his state is higher than virtue, and that of a brute is a different kind of state from vice.

Now, since it is rarely that a godlike man is found—to use the epithet of the Spartans, who when they admire anyone highly call him a 'godlike man'—so too the brutish type is rarely found among
30 men; it is found chiefly among barbarians, but some brutish qualities are also produced by disease or deformity; and we also call by this evil name those who surpass ordinary men in vice. Of this kind of disposition, however, we must later make some mention,[2] while we have discussed vice before;[3] we must now discuss incontinence
35 and softness (or effeminacy), and continence and endurance; for we
1145b must treat each of the two neither as identical with virtue or wickedness, nor as a different genus.* We must, as in all other cases, set the apparent facts before us and, after first discussing the difficulties, go on to prove, if possible, the truth of all the common opinions
5 about these affections of the mind, or, failing this, of the greater

---

[1] *Iliad* xxiv.258–9.   [2] Ch. 5.   [3] Bks. II–V.

number and the most authoritative; for if we both resolve the difficulties and leave the common opinions undisturbed, we shall have
proved the case sufficiently.*

Now (1) both continence and endurance are thought to be
included among things good and praiseworthy, and both incontinence and softness among things bad and blameworthy; and the 10
same man is thought to be continent and ready to abide by the result
of his calculations, or incontinent and ready to abandon them.
And (2) the incontinent man, knowing that what he does is bad,
does it as a result of passion, while the continent man, knowing that
his appetites are bad, refuses on account of his rational principle to
follow them. (3) The temperate man all men call continent and
disposed to endurance, while the continent man some maintain to 15
be always temperate but others do not; and some call the self-
indulgent man incontinent and the incontinent man self-indulgent
indiscriminately, while others distinguish them. (4) The man of
practical wisdom, they sometimes say, cannot be incontinent, while
sometimes they say that some who are practically wise and clever
are incontinent. Again, (5) men are said to be incontinent even with
respect to anger, honour, and gain.—These, then, are the things 20
that are said.

Discussion of the current opinions

2. Now we may ask (1) what kind of right judgement has the
man who behaves incontinently.* That he should behave so when
he has knowledge, some say is impossible; for it would be strange—
so Socrates thought—if when knowledge was in a man something
else could master it and drag it about like a slave. For Socrates was 25
entirely opposed to the view in question, holding that there is no
such thing as incontinence; no one, he said, when he judges acts
against what he judges best—people act so only by reason of ignorance.* Now this view plainly contradicts the apparent facts, and we
must inquire about what happens to such a man; if he acts by reason
of ignorance, what is the manner of his ignorance?* For that the
man who behaves incontinently does not, before he gets into this 30
state, *think* he ought to act so, is evident. But there are *some* who
concede certain of Socrates' contentions but not others; that nothing is stronger than knowledge they admit, but not that no one acts
contrary to what has seemed to him the better course, and therefore

they say that the incontinent man has not knowledge when he is
35 mastered by his pleasures, but opinion.* But *if it* is opinion and not
knowledge, if it is not a strong conviction that resists but a weak
1146a one, as in men who hesitate, we sympathize with their failure to
stand by such convictions against strong appetites; but we do not
sympathize with wickedness, nor with any of the other blameworthy states. Is it then *practical wisdom* whose resistance is mas-
5 tered? That is the strongest of all states. But this is absurd; the same
man will be at once practically wise and incontinent, but *no one*
would say that it is the part of a practically wise man to do willingly
the basest acts. Besides, it has been shown before that the man of
practical wisdom is one who will *act* (for he is a man concerned with
the individual facts)[1] and who has the other virtues.*

10   (2) Further, if continence involves having strong and bad appetites, the temperate man will not be continent nor the continent
man temperate; for a temperate man will have neither excessive nor
bad appetites. But the continent man *must*; for if the appetites are
good, the state of character that restrains us from following them is
bad, so that not all continence will be good; while if they are weak
15 and not bad, there is nothing admirable in resisting them, and if they
are weak and bad, there is nothing great in resisting these either.

(3) Further, if continence makes a man ready to stand by any and
every opinion, it is bad, i.e. if it makes him stand even by a false
opinion; and if incontinence makes a man apt to abandon any and
every opinion, there will be a good incontinence, of which Sophocles'
20 Neoptolemus in the *Philoctetes* will be an instance; for he is to be
praised for not standing by what Odysseus persuaded him to do,
because he is pained at telling a lie.*

(4) Further, the sophistic argument presents a difficulty; the
syllogism arising from men's wish to expose paradoxical results
arising from an opponent's view, in order that they may be admired
25 when they succeed, is one that puts us in a difficulty (for thought is
bound fast when it will not rest because the conclusion does not
satisfy it, and cannot advance because it cannot refute the argument). There is an argument from which it follows that folly coupled
with incontinence is virtue; a man does the opposite of what he
thinks right, owing to incontinence, but thinks what is good to be

---

[1] 1141b16, 1142a24.

evil and something that he should not do, and in consequence he 30
will do what is good and not what is evil.*

(5) Further, he who on conviction does and pursues and chooses
what is pleasant would be thought to be better than one who does
so as a result not of calculation but of incontinence; for he is easier
to cure since he may be persuaded to change his mind. But to the
incontinent man may be applied the proverb 'When water chokes,
what is one to wash it down with?' If he had been persuaded of the 35
rightness of what he does, he would have desisted when he was
persuaded to change his mind; but now he acts in spite of his being 1146b
persuaded of something quite different.*

(6) Further, if incontinence and continence are concerned with
any and every kind of object, who is it that is incontinent in the
unqualified sense? No one has all the forms of incontinence, but we
say some people are incontinent without qualification. 5

Solution to the problem about the incontinent man's knowledge

3. Of some such kind are the difficulties that arise; some of these
points must be refuted and the others left in possession of the field;
for the solution of the difficulty is the discovery of the truth. (1) We
must consider first, then, whether incontinent people act knowingly or not, and with what sort of knowledge; then (2) with what
sorts of object the incontinent and the continent man may be said 10
to be concerned (i.e. whether with any and every pleasure and pain
or with certain determinate kinds), and whether the continent man
and the man of endurance are the same or different; and similarly with
regard to the other matters germane to this inquiry. The starting-
point of our investigation is (a) the question whether the continent 15
man and the incontinent are differentiated by their objects or by their
attitude, i.e. whether the incontinent man is incontinent simply by
being concerned with such-and-such objects, or, instead, by his attitude, or, instead of that, by both these things; (b) the second question is whether incontinence and continence are concerned with
any and every object or not. The man who is incontinent in the
unqualified sense neither is concerned with any and every object,
but with precisely those with which the self-indulgent man is 20
concerned, nor is he characterized by being simply related to these
(for then his state would be the same as self-indulgence), but by
being related to them in a certain way. For the one is led on in

accordance with his own choice, thinking that he should always pursue the present pleasure; while the other does not think so, but yet pursues it.

25 (1) As for the suggestion that it is true opinion and not knowledge against which we act incontinently, that makes no difference to the argument; for some people when in a state of opinion do not hesitate, but think they know exactly. If, then, the notion is that owing to their weak conviction those who have opinion are more likely to act against their judgement than those who know, we answer that there need be no difference between knowledge and opinion in this respect; for some men are no less convinced of what 30 they think than others of what they know; as is shown by the case of Heraclitus.* But (a), since we use the word 'know' in two senses (for both the man who has knowledge but is not using it and he who is using it are said to know), it *will* make a difference whether, when a man does what he should not, he has the knowledge but is not 35 exercising it, or *is* exercising it;* for the latter seems strange, but not the former.

1147a   (b) Further, since there are two kinds of premiss, there is nothing to prevent a man's having both premisses and acting against his knowledge, provided that he is using only the universal premiss and not the particular; for it is particular acts that have to be done. And there are also two kinds of universal term; one is predicable of 5 the agent, the other of the object; e.g. 'dry food is good for every man', and 'I am a man', or 'such-and-such food is dry'; but whether 'this food is such-and-such', of this a man either has not or is not exercising the knowledge.* There will, then, be, firstly, an enormous difference between these manners of knowing, so that to know in one way would not seem anything strange, while to know in the other way would be extraordinary.*

10   And further (c) the possession of knowledge in another sense than those just named is something that happens to men; for within the case of having knowledge but not using it we see a difference of state, admitting of the possibility of having knowledge in a sense and yet not having it, as in the instance of a man asleep, mad, or drunk.* But now this is just the condition of men under the influ- 15 ence of passions; for outbursts of anger and sexual appetites and some other such passions, it is evident, actually alter our bodily condition, and in some men even produce fits of madness. It is

plain, then, that incontinent people must be said to be in a similar condition to men asleep, mad, or drunk.

The fact that men use the language that flows from knowledge proves nothing; for even men under the influence of these passions utter scientific proofs and verses of Empedocles, and those who have just begun to learn a science can string together its phrases, but do not yet know it; for it has to become part of themselves, and that takes time; so that we must suppose that the use of language by men in an incontinent state means no more than its utterance by actors on the stage.*

(d) Again, we may also view the cause as follows in the way a student of nature would.* The one opinion is universal, the other is concerned with the particular facts, and here we come to something within the sphere of perception; when a single opinion results from the two, the soul must in one type of case affirm the conclusion, while in the case of opinions concerned with production it must immediately act* (e.g. if 'everything sweet ought to be tasted', and 'this is sweet', in the sense of being one of the particular sweet things, the man who can act and is not restrained must at the same time actually act accordingly). When, then, the universal opinion is present in us restraining us from tasting, and there is also the opinion that 'everything sweet is pleasant', and that 'this is sweet' (now this is the opinion that is active), and when appetite happens to be present in us, the one opinion bids us avoid this, but appetite leads us towards it (for it can move each of our bodily parts);* so that it turns out that a man behaves incontinently under the influence (in a sense) of reason and an opinion, and of one not contrary in itself, but only incidentally—for the appetite is contrary, not the opinion—to correct reason. It also follows that this is the reason why the lower animals are not incontinent, namely, because they have no universal judgement but only imagination and memory of particulars.

The explanation of how the ignorance is dissolved and the incontinent man regains his knowledge, is the same as in the case of the man drunk or asleep and is not peculiar to this condition; we must go to the students of natural science for it. Now, the last premiss being an opinion about a perceptible object, and being also what determines our actions, this a man either has not when he is in the state of passion, or has it in the sense in which having knowledge

did not mean knowing but only talking, as a drunken man may mutter the verses of Empedocles.[1] And because the last term is not universal nor equally an object of scientific knowledge with the
15 universal term, the position that Socrates sought to establish[2] actually seems to result; for it is not in the presence of what is thought to be knowledge proper that the passion occurs (nor is it this that is 'dragged about' as a result of the passion), but in that of perceptual knowledge.*

This must suffice as our answer to the question of whether an incontinent man acts knowingly or not, and with what sort of knowledge it is possible to be incontinent.

Solution to the problem, what is the sphere of incontinence: its proper and its extended sense distinguished

20 4. (2) We must next discuss whether there is anyone who is incontinent without qualification, or all men who are incontinent are so in a particular sense, and if there is, with what sort of objects he is concerned. That both continent persons and persons of endurance, and incontinent and soft persons, are concerned with pleasures and pains, is evident.

Now of the things that produce pleasure some are necessary,
25 while others are worthy of choice in themselves but admit of excess, the bodily causes of pleasure being necessary (by such I mean both those concerned with food and those concerned with sexual intercourse, i.e. the bodily matters with which we defined self-indulgence and temperance as being concerned), while the others are not necessary but worthy of choice in themselves (e.g. victory, honour,
30 wealth, and good and pleasant things of this sort). This being so, (a) those who go to excess with reference to the latter, contrary to correct reason which is in themselves, are not called incontinent simply, but incontinent with the qualification 'in respect of money, gain, honour, or anger'—not simply incontinent, on the ground that they are different from incontinent people and are called incontin-
35 ent by reason of a resemblance.* (Compare the case of Anthropos,* who won a contest at the Olympic games; in his case the general
1148a definition of man differed little from the definition peculiar to *him*, but yet it *was* different.) This is shown by the fact that incontinence either without qualification or in respect of some particular bodily

---
[1] Cf. a10–24.   [2] 1145b22–4.

pleasure is blamed not only as a fault but as a kind of vice, while none of the people who are incontinent in these other respects is so blamed.

But (*b*) of the people who are incontinent with respect to bodily 5 enjoyments, with which we say the temperate and the self-indulgent man are concerned, he who pursues the excesses of things pleasant—and shuns those of things painful, of hunger and thirst and heat and cold and all the objects of touch and taste—not by choice but contrary to his choice and his judgement, is called incontinent, not with the qualification 'in respect of this or that', e.g. of 10 anger, but just simply. This is confirmed by the fact that men are called 'soft' with regard to these pleasures, but not with regard to any of the others. And for this reason we group together the incontinent and the self-indulgent, the continent and the temperate man—but not any of these other types—because they are concerned 15 somehow with the same pleasures and pains; but though these are concerned with the same objects, they are not similarly related to them, but some of them make a deliberate choice while the others do not.*

This is why we should describe as self-indulgent rather the man who without appetite or with but a slight appetite pursues the excesses of pleasure and avoids moderate pains, than the man who does so because of his strong appetites; for what would the former 20 do, if he had in addition a vigorous appetite, and a violent pain at the lack of the 'necessary' objects?

Now of appetites and pleasures some belong to the class of things generically noble and good—for some pleasant things are by nature worthy of choice, while others are contrary to these, and others are intermediate, to adopt our previous distinction*—e.g. wealth, gain, 25 victory, honour. And with reference to all objects whether of this or of the intermediate kind men are not blamed for being affected by them, for desiring and loving them, but for doing so in a certain way, i.e. for going to excess. (This is why all those who contrary to reason either are mastered by or pursue one of the objects which are naturally noble and good, e.g. those who busy themselves more 30 than they ought about honour or about children and parents, ⟨are not wicked⟩; for these too are goods, and those who busy themselves about them are praised; but yet there is an excess even in them—if like Niobe one were to fight even against the gods, or were to be as

much devoted to one's father as Satyrus* nicknamed 'the filial', who
1148b was thought to be very silly on this point.) There is no wickedness,
then, with regard to these objects, for the reason named, namely,
because each of them is by nature a thing worthy of choice for its
own sake; yet excesses in respect of them are bad and to be avoided.*
Similarly there is no incontinence with regard to them; for incontin-
5 ence is not only to be avoided but is also a thing worthy of blame;
but owing to a similarity in the state of feeling people apply the name
incontinence, adding in each case what it is in respect of, as we may
describe as a bad doctor or a bad actor one whom we should not call
bad, simply. As, then, in this case we do not apply the term without
qualification because each of these conditions is not badness but only
10 analogous to it, so it is clear that in the other case also that alone
must be taken to be incontinence and continence which is concerned
with the same objects as temperance and self-indulgence, but we
apply the term to anger by virtue of a resemblance; and this is why
we say with a qualification 'incontinent in respect of anger' as we say
'incontinent in respect of honour, or of gain'.

*Incontinence in its extended sense includes a brutish and a morbid
form*

15 **5.** Some things are pleasant by nature, and of these some are so
without qualification, and others are so with reference to particular
classes either of animals or of men; while others are not pleasant
by nature, but some of them become so by reason of injuries to the
system, and others by reason of acquired habits, and others by reason
of originally bad natures. This being so, it is possible with regard to
each of the latter kinds to discover similar states of character to those
recognized with regard to the former; I mean the brutish states, as
20 in the case of the female who, they say, rips open pregnant women
and devours the infants, or of the things in which some of the tribes
about the Black Sea that have gone savage are said to delight—in
raw meat or in human flesh, or in lending their children to one
another to feast upon—or of the story told of Phalaris.*
These states are brutish, but others arise as a result of disease (or,
25 in some cases, of madness, as with the man who sacrificed and ate
his mother, or with the slave who ate the liver of his fellow), and
others are morbid states resulting from custom, e.g. the habit of
plucking out the hair or of gnawing the nails, or even coals or earth,

and in addition to these paederasty; for these arise in some by
nature and in others, as in those who have been the victims of lust   30
from childhood, from habit.

Now those in whom nature is the cause of such a state no one
would call incontinent, any more than one would apply the epithet
to women, because of the passive part they play in copulation; nor
would one apply it to those who are in a morbid condition as a
result of habit. To have these various types of habit is beyond the
limits of vice, as brutishness is too; for a man who has them to   1149a
master or be mastered by them is not simple ⟨continence or⟩ incontinence but that which is so by analogy, as the man who is in this
condition in respect of fits of anger is to be called incontinent in
respect of that feeling, but not incontinent simply.*

For every excessive state whether of folly, of cowardice, of self-   5
indulgence, or of bad temper, is either brutish or morbid; the man
who is by nature apt to fear everything, even the squeak of a mouse, is
cowardly with a brutish cowardice, while the man who feared a weasel
did so in consequence of disease; and of foolish people those who by
nature are thoughtless and live by their senses alone are brutish, like   10
some races of the distant barbarians, while those who are so as a result
of disease (e.g. of epilepsy) or of madness are morbid. Of these characteristics it is possible to have some only at times, and not to be
mastered by them, e.g. Phalaris may have restrained a desire to eat the
flesh of a child or an appetite for unnatural sexual pleasure; but it is   15
also possible to be mastered, not merely to have the feelings. Thus, as
the wickedness which is on the human level is called wickedness simply, while that which is not is called wickedness not simply but with
the qualification 'brutish' or 'morbid', in the same way it is plain that
some incontinence is brutish and some morbid, while only that which
corresponds to *human* self-indulgence is incontinence simply.   20

That incontinence and continence, then, are concerned only with
the same objects as self-indulgence and temperance, and that what
is concerned with other objects is a type distinct from incontinence,
and called incontinence by a metaphor and not simply, is plain.

*Incontinence in respect of anger is less disgraceful than
    incontinence proper*

6. That incontinence in respect of anger is less disgraceful than
that in respect of the appetites is what we will now proceed to see.   25

(1) Anger seems to listen to reason to some extent, but to mishear it, as do hasty servants who run out before they have heard the whole of what one says, and then muddle the order, or as dogs bark if there is but a knock at the door, before looking to see if it is a
30 friend; so anger by reason of the warmth and hastiness of its nature, though it hears, does not hear an order, and springs to take revenge. For reason or appearance informs us that we have been insulted or slighted, and anger, reasoning as it were that anything like this must be fought against, boils up straightway; while appetite, if reason or
35 perception merely says that an object is pleasant, springs to the
1149b enjoyment of it.* Therefore anger obeys reason in a sense, but appetite does not. It is therefore more disgraceful; for the man who is incontinent in respect of anger is in a sense conquered by reason, while the other is conquered by appetite and not by reason.

(2) Further, we pardon people more easily for following natural
5 desires, since we pardon them more easily for following such appetites as are common to all men, and in so far as they are common; now anger and bad temper are more natural than the appetites for excess, i.e. for unnecessary objects. Take for instance the man who defended himself on the charge of striking his father by saying 'Yes,
10 but *he* struck *his* father, and *he* struck *his*, and' (pointing to his child) 'this boy will strike *me* when he is a man; it runs in the family'; or the man who when he was being dragged along by his son bade him stop at the doorway, since he himself had dragged his father only as far as that.*

(3) Further, those who are more given to plotting against others are more criminal.* Now an angry man is not given to plotting, nor
15 is anger itself—it is open; but the nature of appetite is illustrated by what the poets call Aphrodite, 'guile-weaving daughter of Cyprus', and by Homer's words about her 'embroidered girdle':

> And the whisper of wooing is there, Whose subtlety
> stealeth the wits of the wise, how prudent soe'er.[1]

Therefore if this form of incontinence is more criminal and disgraceful than that in respect of anger, it is both incontinence without qualification and in a sense vice.*

20 (4) Further, no one commits wanton outrage* with a feeling of pain, but everyone who acts in anger acts with pain, while the man

---

[1] *Iliad* xiv.214, 217.

who commits outrage acts with pleasure. If, then, those acts at which it is most just to be angry are more criminal than others, the incontinence which is due to appetite is the more criminal; for there is no wanton outrage involved in anger.

Plainly, then, the incontinence concerned with appetite is more disgraceful than that concerned with anger, and continence and incontinence are concerned with bodily appetites and pleasures; but we must grasp the differences among the latter themselves. For, as has been said at the beginning,[1] some are human and natural both in kind and in magnitude, others are brutish, and others are due to organic injuries and diseases. Only with the first of these are temperance and self-indulgence concerned; this is why we call the lower animals neither temperate nor self-indulgent, except by a metaphor, and only if some one race of animals exceeds another as a whole in wantonness, destructiveness, and omnivorous greed; these have no power of choice or calculation, but they *are* departures from the natural norm, as, among men, madmen are.* Now brutishness is a less evil than vice, though more alarming; for it is not that the better part has been perverted, as in man—they *have* no better part. Thus it is like comparing a lifeless thing with a living in respect of badness; for the badness of that which has no originative source of movement is always less hurtful, and reason is an originative source. Thus it is like comparing injustice in the abstract with an unjust man. Each is in some sense worse; for a bad man will do ten thousand times as much evil as a brute.*

Softness and endurance: two forms of incontinence—weakness and impetuosity

7. With regard to the pleasures and pains and appetites and aversions arising through touch and taste, to which both self-indulgence and temperance were formerly narrowed down,[2] it is possible to be in such a state as to be defeated even by those of them which most people master, or to master even those by which most people are defeated; among these possibilities, those relating to pleasures are incontinence and continence, those relating to pains softness and endurance. The state of most people is intermediate, even if they lean more towards the worse states.

---

[1] 1148b15–31.   [2] III. 10.

Now, since some pleasures are necessary while others are not, and are necessary up to a point while the excesses of them are not, nor the deficiencies, and this is equally true of appetites and pains, the man who pursues the excesses of things pleasant, or pursues to
20 excess necessary objects, and does so by choice, for their own sake and not at all for the sake of any result distinct from them, is self-indulgent; for such a man is of necessity without regrets, and therefore incurable, since a man without regrets cannot be cured.* The man who is deficient in his pursuit of them is the opposite of self-indulgent; the man who is intermediate is temperate. Similarly, there is the man who avoids bodily pains not because he is defeated
25 by them but by choice. (Of those who do not *choose* such acts, one kind of man is led to them as a result of the pleasure involved, another because he avoids the pain arising from the appetite, so that these types differ from one another. Now any one would think worse of a man if with no appetite or with weak appetite he were to do something disgraceful, than if he did it under the influence of powerful appetite, and worse of him if he struck a blow not in anger than if he did it in anger; for what would he have done if he *had*
20 been strongly affected? This is why the self-indulgent man is worse than the incontinent.) Of the states named, then, the latter is rather a kind of softness;* the former is self-indulgence. While to the incontinent man is opposed the continent, to the soft is opposed the man of endurance; for endurance consists in resisting, while contin-
35 ence consists in conquering, and resisting and conquering are different, as not being beaten is different from winning; this is why
1150b continence is also more worthy of choice than endurance. Now the man who is defective in respect of resistance to the things which most men both resist and resist successfully is soft and effeminate; for effeminacy too is a kind of softness; such a man trails his cloak to avoid the pain of lifting it, and plays the invalid without thinking
5 himself wretched, though the man he imitates is a wretched man.

The case is similar with regard to continence and incontinence. For if a man is defeated by violent and excessive pleasures or pains, there is nothing wonderful in that; indeed we are ready to pardon him if he has resisted, as Theodectes' Philoctetes does when bitten
10 by the snake, or Carcinus' Cercyon in the *Alope*, and as people who try to restrain their laughter burst out in a guffaw, as happened to Xenophantus.* But it is surprising if a man is defeated by and

cannot resist pleasures or pains which most men can hold out against, when this is not due to heredity or disease, like the softness that is hereditary with the kings of the Scythians, or that which distinguishes the female sex from the male.

The lover of amusement, too, is thought to be self-indulgent, but is really soft. For amusement is a relaxation, since it is a rest from work; and the lover of amusement is one of the people who go to excess in this.

Of incontinence one kind is impetuosity, another weakness. For some men after deliberating fail, owing to their emotion, to stand by the conclusions of their deliberation, others because they have not deliberated are led by their emotion;* since some men (just as people who first tickle others are not tickled themselves), if they have first perceived and seen what is coming and have first roused themselves and their calculative faculty, are not defeated by their emotion, whether it be pleasant or painful. It is keen and excitable people that suffer especially from the impetuous form of incontinence; for the former by reason of their quickness and the latter by reason of the violence of their passions do not await the argument, because they are apt to follow appearance.

Self-indulgence worse than incontinence

8. The self-indulgent man, as was said, has no regrets; for he stands by his choice; but any incontinent man is subject to regrets. This is why the position is not as it was expressed in the formulation of the problem,* but the self-indulgent man is incurable and the incontinent man curable; for wickedness is like a disease such as dropsy or consumption, while incontinence is like epilepsy; the former is a permanent, the latter an intermittent badness. And generally incontinence and vice are different in kind; vice is unconscious of itself, incontinence is not* (of incontinent men themselves, those who become temporarily beside themselves are better than those who have reason but do not abide by it, since the latter are defeated by a weaker passion, and do not act without previous deliberation like the others); for the incontinent man is like the people who get drunk quickly and on little wine, i.e. on less than most people.

Evidently, then, incontinence is not vice (though perhaps it is so in a qualified sense); for incontinence is contrary to choice while vice is in accordance with choice; not but what they are similar in

respect of the actions they lead to; as in the saying of Demodocus
about the Milesians, 'The Milesians are not without sense, but they
10 do the things that senseless people do,' so too incontinent people
are not criminal, but they will do criminal acts.

Now, since the incontinent man is apt to pursue, not on conviction,
bodily pleasures that are excessive and contrary to correct reason,
while the self-indulgent man is convinced because he is the sort of
man to pursue them, it is on the contrary the former that is easily
persuaded to change his mind, while the latter is not.* For virtue
15 and vice respectively preserve and destroy the first principle, and in
actions the final cause is the first principle, as the hypotheses are in
mathematics; neither in that case is it reason that teaches the first
principles, nor is it so here—virtue either natural or produced by
habituation is what teaches right opinion about the first principle.*
Such a man as this, then, is temperate; the contrary type is the self-
indulgent.

20   But there is a sort of man who is carried away as a result of passion
and contrary to correct reason—a man whom passion masters so
that he does not act according to correct reason, but does not master
to the extent of making him ready to believe that he should pursue
such pleasures without reserve; this is the incontinent man, who is
better than the self-indulgent man, and not bad without qualifica-
25 tion; for the best thing in him, the first principle, is preserved.*
And contrary to him is another kind of man, he who abides by his
convictions and is not carried away, at least as a result of passion. It
is evident from these considerations that the latter is a good state
and the former a bad one.

*Relation of continence to obstinacy, incontinence, 'insensibility',
temperance*

9. Is the man continent who abides by any and every reasoning and
30 any and every choice, or the man who abides by the right choice,
and is he incontinent who abandons any and every choice and any
and every reasoning, or he who abandons the reasoning that is not
false and the choice that is right; this is how we put it before in our
statement of the problem.[1] Or is it incidentally any and every choice
but *per se* the true reasoning and the right choice by which the one
35 abides and the other does not? If anyone chooses or pursues this for

---

[1] 1146a16–31.

the sake of that, *per se* he pursues and chooses the latter, but inci-   1151b
dentally the former. But when we speak without qualification we
mean what is *per se*. Therefore in a sense the one abides by, and the
other abandons, any and every opinion; but without qualification,
the true opinion.

There are some who are apt to abide by their opinion, who are   5
called obstinate, namely, those who are hard to persuade in the first
instance and are not easily persuaded to change; these have some
likeness to the continent man, as the prodigal is in a way like the
liberal man and the rash man like the confident man; but they are
different in many respects. For it is to passion and appetite that the
one will not yield, since on occasion the continent man *will* yield to   10
reason; but it is to reason that the others refuse to yield, for they do
form appetites and many of them are led by their pleasures. Now
the people who are obstinate are the opinionated, the ignorant, and
the boorish—the opinionated being influenced by pleasure and
pain; for they delight in the victory they gain if they are not per-   15
suaded to change, and are pained if their decisions become null and
void as decrees sometimes do; so that they resemble the incontinent
rather than the continent man.

But there are some who fail to abide by their resolutions, not as
a result of incontinence, e.g. Neoptolemus in Sophocles' *Philoctetes*;
yet it was for the sake of pleasure that he did not stand fast—but a
noble pleasure; for telling the truth was noble to him, but he had
been persuaded by Odysseus to tell a lie.* For not everyone who   20
does anything for the sake of pleasure is either self-indulgent or bad
or incontinent, but he who does it for a disgraceful pleasure.

Since there is also a sort of man who takes *less* delight than he should
in bodily things, and does not abide by reason, he who is intermediate
between him and the incontinent man is the continent man; for the   25
incontinent man fails to abide by reason because he delights too much
in them, and this man because he delights in them too little; while the
continent man abides by reason and does not change on either account.
Now if continence is good, both the contrary states must be bad, as
they actually appear to be; but because the other extreme is seen in few   30
people and seldom, as temperance is thought to be contrary only to
self-indulgence, so is continence to incontinence.*

Since many names are applied analogically, it is by analogy
that we have come to speak of the 'continence' of the temperate

man; for both the continent man and the temperate man are such
35 as to do nothing contrary to reason for the sake of the bodily pleas-
1152a ures, but the former has and the latter has not bad appetites, and
the latter is such as not to feel pleasure contrary to reason, while the
former is such as to feel pleasure but not to be led by it. And the
incontinent and the self-indulgent man are also like one another;
5 they are different, but both pursue bodily pleasures—the latter,
however, also thinking that he should do so, while the former does
not think this.

*Practical wisdom is not compatible with incontinence, but
cleverness is*

10. Nor can the same man have practical wisdom and be incontinent; for it has been shown[1] that a man is at the same time practically wise, and good in respect of character. Further, a man has
practical wisdom not by knowing only but by being able to act; but
the incontinent man is unable to act—there is, however, nothing
10 to prevent a *clever* man from being incontinent; this is why it is
sometimes actually thought that some people have practical wisdom but are incontinent, namely, because cleverness and practical
wisdom differ in the way we have described in our first discussions,[2] and are near together in respect of their reasoning, but
differ in respect of their choice*—nor yet is the incontinent man
like the man who knows and is contemplating a truth, but like the
15 man who is asleep or drunk.* And he acts voluntarily (for he acts in
a sense with knowledge both of what he does and of the end to
which he does it), but is not wicked, since his choice is good; so that
he is half-wicked. And he is not a criminal; for he does not act of
malice aforethought; of the two types of incontinent man the one
does not abide by the conclusions of his deliberation, while the
excitable man does not deliberate at all.* And thus the incontinent
20 man is like a city which passes all the right decrees and has good
laws, but makes no use of them, as in Anaxandrides' jesting
remark,

The city willed it, that cares nought for laws;

but the wicked man is like a city that uses its laws, but has wicked
laws to use.

---

[1] 1144a11–b32.   [2] 1144a23–b4.

Now incontinence and continence are concerned with that which 25
is in excess of the state characteristic of most men; for the continent
man abides by his resolutions more and the incontinent man less
than most men can.

Of the forms of incontinence, that of excitable people is more
curable than that of those who deliberate but do not abide by their
deliberations, and those who are incontinent through habituation
are more curable than those in whom incontinence is innate; for it 30
is easier to change a habit than to change one's nature; even habit is
hard to change just because it is like nature, as Evenus says:

> I say that habit's but long practice, friend,
> And this becomes men's nature in the end.*

We have now stated what continence, incontinence, endurance, 35
and softness are, and how these states are related to each other.

PLEASURE

Three views hostile to pleasure and the arguments for them

11. The study of pleasure and pain belongs to the province of the 1152b
political philosopher; for he is the architect of the end, with a view
to which we call one thing bad and another good without qualification.* Further, it is one of our necessary tasks to consider them; for
not only did we lay it down that moral virtue and vice are con- 5
cerned with pains and pleasures,[1] but most people say that happiness involves pleasure; this is why the blessed man is called by a
name derived from a word meaning enjoyment.*

Now (1) some people think that no pleasure is a good, either in
itself or incidentally, since the good and pleasure are not the same;
(2) others think that some pleasures are good but that most are bad. 10
(3) Again there is a third view, that even if all pleasures are goods,
yet the best thing in the world cannot be pleasure. (1) The reasons
given for the view that pleasure is not a good at all are (*a*) that every
pleasure is a perceptible process to a natural state, and that no process is of the same kind as its end,* e.g. no process of building of the
same kind as a house. (*b*) A temperate man avoids pleasures. (*c*) A
man of practical wisdom pursues what is free from pain, not what 15
is pleasant. (*d*) The pleasures are a hindrance to thought, and the

[1] 1104b8–1105a13.

more so the more one delights in them, e.g. in sexual pleasure; for
no one could think of anything while absorbed in this. (*e*) There
is no art of pleasure; but every good is the product of some art.
(*f*) Children and the brutes pursue pleasures. (2) The reasons for
20 the view that not all pleasures are good are that (*a*) there are pleasures that are actually base and objects of reproach, and (*b*) there are
harmful pleasures; for some pleasant things are unhealthy. (3) The
reason for the view that the best thing in the world is not pleasure
is that pleasure is not an end but a process.

Discussion of the view that pleasure is not a good

25 **12.** These are pretty much the things that are said. That it does
not follow from these grounds that pleasure is not a good, or even
the chief good, is plain from the following considerations. (A) (*a*)
First, since that which is good may be so in either of two senses
(one thing good simply and another good for a particular person),
natural constitutions and states of being, and therefore also the
corresponding movements and processes, will be correspondingly
divisible. Of those which are thought to be bad some will be bad if
taken without qualification but not bad for a particular person, but
30 worthy of his choice, and some will not be worthy of choice even
for a particular person, but only at a particular time and for a short
period, though not without qualification; while others are not even
pleasures, but seem to be so, namely, all those which involve pain
and whose end is curative, e.g. the processes that go on in sick
persons.*

(*b*) Further, one kind of good being activity and another being
state, the processes that restore us to our natural state are only inci-
35 dentally pleasant; for that matter the activity at work in the appetites for them is the activity of so much of our state and nature as
has remained unimpaired;* for there are actually pleasures that
1153a involve *no* pain or appetite (e.g. those of contemplation), the nature
in such a case not being defective at all. That the others are incidental is indicated by the fact that men do not enjoy the same pleasant
objects when their nature is in its settled state as they do when it is
being replenished, but in the former case they enjoy the things
that are pleasant without qualification, in the latter the contraries
5 of these as well; for then they enjoy even sharp and bitter things,
none of which is pleasant either by nature or without qualification.

And so it is the same with the pleasures; for as pleasant things differ, so do the pleasures arising from them.

(c) Again, it is not necessary that there should be something else better than pleasure, as some say the end is better than the process; for pleasures are not processes nor do they all involve process—they are activities and ends; nor do they arise when we are acquiring some faculty, but when we are exercising it; and not all pleasures have an end different from themselves, but only the pleasures of persons who are being led to the perfecting of their nature.* This is why it is not right to say that pleasure is perceptible process, but it should rather be called activity of the natural state, and instead of 'perceptible' 'unimpeded'.* It is thought by *some* people to be process just because they think it is in the strict sense *good*; for they think that activity is process, which it is not.

(B) The view that pleasures are bad because some pleasant things are unhealthy is like saying that healthy things are bad because some healthy things are bad for moneymaking; both are bad in the respect mentioned, but they are not *bad* for *that* reason—indeed, thinking itself is sometimes injurious to health.

Neither practical wisdom nor any state of being is impeded by the pleasure arising from it; it is foreign pleasures that impede, for the pleasures arising from thinking and learning will make us think and learn all the more.

(C) The fact that no pleasure is the product of any art arises naturally enough; there is no art of any other activity either, but only of the corresponding faculty; though for that matter the arts of the perfumer and the cook *are* thought to be arts of pleasure.

(D) The arguments based on the grounds that the temperate man avoids pleasure and that the man of practical wisdom pursues the painless life, and that children and the brutes pursue pleasure, are all refuted by the same consideration. We have pointed out[1] in what sense pleasures are good without qualification and in what sense some are not good; now both the brutes and children pursue pleasures of the latter kind (and the man of practical wisdom pursues tranquil freedom from that kind), namely, those which imply appetite and pain, i.e. the bodily pleasures (for it is these that are of this nature) and the excesses of them, in respect of which the self-indulgent man is self-indulgent. This is why the

[1] 1152b26–1153a7.

35   temperate man avoids these pleasures; for even he *has* pleasures of
his own.

Discussion of the view that pleasure is not the chief good

1153b   **13.** But further (E) it is agreed that pain is bad and to be avoided;
for some pain is without qualification bad, and other pain is bad
because it is in some respect an impediment to us. Now the contrary
of that which is to be avoided, *qua* something to be avoided and bad,
is good. Pleasure, then, is necessarily a good. For the solution of
5   Speusippus, that it's like the way that the greater is contrary both
to the less and to the equal, is not successful; since he would not say
that pleasure is essentially just a species of evil.*

And (F) if certain pleasures are bad, that does not prevent the
chief good from being some pleasure, just as the chief good may be
some form of knowledge though certain kinds of knowledge are bad.
Perhaps it is even necessary, if each disposition has unimpeded
10   activities, that, whether the activity (if unimpeded) of all our dispositions or that of some one of them is happiness, this should be the thing
most worthy of our choice; and this activity is pleasure. Thus the chief
good would be some pleasure, though most pleasures might perhaps
be bad without qualification.* And for this reason all men think that
15   the happy life is pleasant and weave pleasure into their ideal of happiness—and reasonably too; for no activity is perfect when it is impeded,
and happiness is a perfect thing; this is why the happy man needs the
goods of the body and external goods, i.e. those of fortune, namely, in
order that he may not be impeded in these ways. Those who say that
the victim on the rack or the man who falls into great misfortunes is
20   happy if he is good are, whether they mean to or not, talking nonsense.* Now because we need fortune as well as other things, some
people think good fortune the same thing as happiness; but it is not
that, for even good fortune itself when in excess is an impediment, and
perhaps should then be no longer called good fortune; for its limit is
fixed by reference to happiness.

25   And indeed the fact that all things, both brutes and men, pursue
pleasure is an indication of its being somehow the chief good:

No voice is wholly lost that many peoples . . .*

But since no one nature or state either is or is thought the best for
30   all, neither do all pursue the same pleasure; yet all pursue pleasure.

And perhaps they actually pursue not the pleasure they think they pursue nor that which they would say they pursue, but the same pleasure; for all things have by nature something divine in them. But the bodily pleasures have appropriated the name both because we oftenest steer our course for them and because all men share in them; thus, because they alone are familiar, men think there are no others. 35

It is evident also that if pleasure, i.e. the activity of our faculties, 1154a is not a good, it will not be the case that the happy man lives a pleasant life; for to what end should he need pleasure, if it is not good but the happy man may even live a painful life?* For pain is neither an evil nor a good, if pleasure is not; why then should he avoid it? 5 Therefore, too, the life of the good man will not be pleasanter than that of anyone else, if his activities are not more pleasant.

Discussion of the view that most pleasures are bad, and of the tendency to identify bodily pleasures with pleasure in general

14. (G) With regard to the bodily pleasures, those who say that *some* pleasures are very much to be chosen, namely, the noble pleasures, but not the bodily pleasures, i.e. those with which the self- 10 indulgent man is concerned, must consider why, then, the contrary pains are bad. For the contrary of bad is good. Are the necessary pleasures good in the sense in which even that which is not bad is good? Or are they good up to a point?* Is it that where you have states and processes of which there cannot be too much, there cannot be too much of the corresponding pleasure, and that where there can be too much of the one there can be too much of the other also? Now there can be too much of bodily goods, and the bad man 15 is bad by virtue of pursuing the excess, not by virtue of pursuing the necessary pleasures (for *all* men enjoy in some way or other both dainty foods and wines and sexual intercourse, but not all men do so as they ought). The contrary is the case with pain; for he does not avoid the excess of it, he avoids it altogether; and this is peculiar to him, for the alternative to excess of pleasure is not pain, except 20 to the man who pursues this excess.

Since we should state not only the truth, but also the cause of error—for this contributes towards producing conviction, since when a reasonable explanation is given of why the false view appears true, this tends to produce belief in the true view—therefore we 25

must state why the bodily pleasures appear the more worthy of
choice. (*a*) Firstly, then, it is because they expel pain; owing to the
excesses of pain that men experience, they pursue excessive and in
general bodily pleasure as being a cure for the pain. Now curative
30 agencies produce intense feeling—which is the reason why they are
pursued—because they show up against the contrary pain. (Indeed
pleasure is thought not to be good for these two reasons, as has been
said,[1] namely, that (α) some of them are activities belonging to a
bad nature—either congenital, as in the case of a brute, or due to
habit, i.e. those of bad men; while (β) others are meant to cure a
defective nature, and it is better to be in a healthy state than to be
1154b getting into it, but these arise during the process of being made
perfect and are therefore only incidentally good.) (*b*) Further, they
are pursued because of their intensity by those who cannot enjoy
other pleasures. (At all events they go out of their way to manufac-
ture thirsts somehow for themselves. When these are harmless, the
5 practice is irreproachable; when they are hurtful, it is bad.) For
they have nothing else to enjoy and, besides, a neutral state is painful to many people because of their nature. For the animal nature
is always in travail, as the students of natural science also testify,
saying that sight and hearing are painful; but we have become used
to this, as they maintain.* Similarly, while, in youth, people are,
10 owing to the growth that is going on, in a situation like that of
drunken men, and youth is pleasant, on the other hand people of
excitable nature always need relief; for even their body is ever in
torment owing to its special composition, and they are always under
the influence of intense desire; but pain is driven out both by the
contrary pleasure, and by any chance pleasure if it be strong; and for
15 these reasons they become self-indulgent and bad. But the pleasures that do not involve pains do not admit of excess; and these are
among the things pleasant by nature and not incidentally. By things
pleasant incidentally I mean those that act as cures (for because as
a result people are cured, through some action of the part that
remains healthy,* for this reason the process seems to be pleasant);
20 by things naturally pleasant I mean those that stimulate the action
of the healthy nature.

There is no one thing that is always pleasant, because our nature
is not simple but there is another element in us as well, inasmuch

[1] 1152b26–33.

as we are perishable creatures, so that if the one element does something, this is unnatural to the other nature, and when the two elements are evenly balanced, what is done seems neither painful nor pleasant; for if the nature of anything were simple, the same action 25 would always be most pleasant to it. This is why god always enjoys a single and simple pleasure; for there is not only an activity of movement but an activity of immobility,* and pleasure is found more in rest than in movement. But 'change in all things is sweet', as the poet says,* because of some vice; for as it is the vicious man that is changeable, so the nature that needs change is vicious; for it 30 is not simple nor good.

We have now discussed continence and incontinence, and pleasure and pain, both what each is and in what sense some of them are good and others bad; it remains to speak of friendship.

BOOK VIII · FRIENDSHIP

KINDS OF FRIENDSHIP

Friendship both necessary and noble: main questions about it

1155a 1. AFTER what we have said, a discussion of friendship would
naturally follow, since it is a virtue or implies virtue, and is besides
5 most necessary with a view to living.* For without friends no one
would choose to live, though he had all other goods; even rich men
and those in possession of office and of dominating power are
thought to need friends most of all; for what is the use of such
prosperity without the opportunity of beneficence, which is exercised chiefly and in its most laudable form towards friends? Or how
10 can prosperity be guarded and preserved without friends? The
greater it is, the more exposed is it to risk. And in poverty and in
other misfortunes men think friends are the only refuge. It helps
the young, too, to keep from error; it aids older people by minister-
ing to their needs and supplementing the activities that are failing
from weakness; those in the prime of life it stimulates to noble
15 actions—'two going together'[1]—for with friends men are more
able both to think and to act. Again, parent seems by nature to feel
it for offspring and offspring for parent, not only among men but
among birds and among most animals; it is felt mutually by mem-
20 bers of the same race, and especially by men, whence we praise
lovers of their fellow men. We may see even in our travels how near
and dear every man is to every other. Friendship seems too to hold
states together, and lawgivers to care more for it than for justice; for
25 concord seems to be something like friendship, and this they aim at
most of all, and expel faction as their worst enemy; and when men
are friends they have no need of justice, while when they are just
they need friendship as well, and the truest form of justice is
thought to be a friendly quality.*

But it is not only necessary but also noble;* for we praise those
30 who love their friends, and it is thought to be a fine thing to have
many friends; and again we think it is the same people that are good
men and are friends.

[1] *Iliad* x.224.

Not a few things about friendship are matters of debate. Some define it as a kind of likeness and say like people are friends, whence come the sayings 'like to like', 'Birds of a feather flock together,' 35 and so on; others on the contrary say 'Two of a trade never agree.' On this very question they inquire for deeper and more physical 1155b causes, Euripides saying that 'Parched earth loves the rain, and stately heaven when filled with rain loves to fall to earth,' and Heraclitus that 'It is what opposes that helps' and 'From different tones comes the fairest tune' and 'all things are produced through 5 strife'; while Empedocles, as well as others, expresses the opposite view that like aims at like.* The physical problems we may leave alone (for they do not belong to the present inquiry); let us examine those which are human and involve character and feeling, e.g. 10 whether friendship can arise between any two people or people cannot be friends if they are wicked, and whether there is one species of friendship or more than one. Those who think there is only one because it admits of degrees have relied on an inadequate indication; for even things different in species admit of degree. We have 15 discussed this matter previously.[1]

Three objects of love: implications of friendship

2. The kinds of friendship may perhaps be cleared up if we first come to know the object of love.* For not everything seems to be loved but only the lovable, and this is good, pleasant, or useful; but it would seem to be that by which some good or pleasure is pro- 20 duced that is useful, so that it is the good and the pleasant that are lovable as ends. Do men love, then, *the* good, or what is good *for them?** These sometimes clash. So too with regard to the pleasant. Now it is thought that each loves what is good for himself, and that the good is without qualification lovable, and what *is* good for each man is lovable for him; but each man loves not what is good for him 25 but what seems good. This however will make no difference; we shall just have to say that this is 'that which seems lovable'. Now there are three grounds on which people love:* of the love of lifeless objects we do not use the word 'friendship', for it is not mutual love, nor is there a wishing of good to the other (for it would surely be ridiculous to wish wine well; if one wishes anything for it, it is 30 that it may keep, so that one may have it oneself); but to a friend

---

[1] Place unknown.

we say we ought to wish what is good for his sake. But to those who thus wish good we ascribe only goodwill, if the wish is not recipro-cated; goodwill when it *is* reciprocal being friendship. Or must we 35 add 'when it is recognized'? For many people have goodwill to those whom they have not seen but judge to be good or useful; and 1156a one of these might return this feeling. These people seem to bear goodwill to each other; but how could one call them friends when they do not know their mutual feelings? To be friends, then, they must be mutually recognized as bearing goodwill and wishing well 5 to each other for one of the aforesaid reasons.*

Three corresponding kinds of friendship

3. Now these reasons differ from each other in kind; so, therefore, do the corresponding forms of love and friendship. There are therefore three kinds of friendship, equal in number to the things that are lovable; for with respect to each there is a mutual and rec-ognized love, and those who love each other wish well to each other 10 in that respect in which they love one another. Now those who love each other because of utility do not love each other for themselves but in virtue of some good which they get from each other.* So too with those who love because of pleasure; it is not for their character that men love ready-witted people, but because they find them pleasant. Therefore those who love because of utility love because of what is good *for themselves*, and those who love because of pleas-15 ure do so because of what is pleasant *to themselves*, and not because of who the loved person is but in so far as he is useful or pleasant. And thus these friendships are only incidental; for it is not as being the man he is that the loved person is loved, but as providing some good or pleasure.* Such friendships, then, are easily dissolved, if the parties do not remain like themselves; for if the one party is no 20 longer pleasant or useful the other ceases to love him.

Now the useful is not permanent but is always changing. Thus when the reason for the friendship is done away, the friendship is dissolved, inasmuch as it existed only for the ends in question. This kind of friendship seems to exist chiefly between old people (for at 25 that age people pursue not the pleasant but the useful) and, of those who are in their prime or young, between those who pursue utility. And such people do not live much with each other either; for some-times they do not even find each other pleasant; therefore they do not need such companionship unless they are useful to each other; for they are pleasant to each other only in so far as they rouse in each other hopes of something good to come. Among such friend- 30 ships people also class the friendship of host and guest.* On the other hand the friendship of young people seems to aim at pleasure; for they live under the guidance of emotion, and pursue above all what is pleasant to themselves and what is immediately before them; but with increasing age their pleasures become different. This is why they quickly become friends and quickly cease to be so; their friendship changes with the object that is found pleasant, and such 35 pleasure alters quickly. Young people are amorous too; for the 1156b greater part of the friendship of love depends on emotion and pleas- ure; this is why they fall in love and quickly fall out of love, changing often within a single day. But these people do wish to spend their days and lives together; for it is thus that they attain the purpose of 5 their friendship.

Perfect friendship is the friendship of men who are good, and alike in virtue; for these wish well alike to each other *qua* good, and they are good in themselves. Now those who wish well to their friends for their sake are most truly friends; for they do this by 10 reason of their own nature and not incidentally; therefore their friendship lasts as long as they are good—and goodness is an enduring thing.* And each is good without qualification and to his friend, for the good are both good without qualification and useful to each other. So too they are pleasant; for the good are pleasant 15 both without qualification and to each other,* since to each his own activities and others like them are pleasurable, and the actions of the good *are* the same or like. And such a friendship is, as might be expected, permanent, since there meet in it all the qualities that friends should have. For all friendship is because of good or of pleasure—good or pleasure either in the abstract or such as will be 20 enjoyed by him who has the friendly feeling—and is based on a certain resemblance; and to a friendship of good men all the qual- ities we have named belong in virtue of the nature of the friends themselves; for in the case of this kind of friendship the other qualities also are alike in both friends, and that which is good with- out qualification is also without qualification pleasant, and these are the most lovable qualities. Love and friendship therefore are found most and in their best form between such men.

But it is natural that such friendships should be infrequent; for
25 such men are rare. Further, such friendship requires time and
familiarity; as the proverb says, men cannot know each other till
they have 'eaten salt together'; nor can they admit each other to
friendship or be friends till each has been found lovable and been
trusted by each. Those who quickly show the marks of friendship
30 to each other wish to be friends, but are not friends unless they both
are lovable and know the fact; for a wish for friendship may arise
quickly, but friendship does not.

Contrast between the best and inferior kinds

4. This kind of friendship, then, is perfect both in respect of dur-
ation and in all other respects, and in it each gets from each in all
respects the same as, or something like what, he gives; which is what
35 ought to happen between friends. Friendship because of pleasure
1157a bears a resemblance to this kind; for good people too *are* pleasant to
each other. So too does friendship because of utility; for the good
are also useful to each other. Among men of these inferior sorts too,
friendships are most permanent when the friends get the same thing
from each other (e.g. pleasure), and not only that but also from the
5 same source, as happens between ready-witted people, not as happens between lover and beloved.* For these do not take pleasure in
the same things, but the one in seeing the beloved and the other in
receiving attentions from his lover; and when the bloom of youth is
passing the friendship sometimes passes too (for the one finds no
pleasure in the sight of the other, and the other gets no attentions
10 from the first); but many lovers on the other hand are constant,
if familiarity has led them to love each other's characters, these
being alike. But those who exchange not pleasure but utility in their
amour are both less truly friends and less constant. Those who are
friends because of utility part when the advantage is at an end; for
15 they were lovers not of each other but of profit.

Because of pleasure or utility, then, even bad men may be friends
of each other, or good men of bad, or one who is neither good nor
bad may be a friend to any sort of person, but clearly only good men
can be friends because of themselves; for bad men do not delight in
20 each other unless some advantage come of the relation.

The friendship of the good too, and this alone, is proof against
slander; for it is not easy to trust anyone's talk about a man who has

long been tested by oneself; and it is among good men that trust and the feeling that 'he would never wrong me' and all the other things that are demanded in true friendship are found. In the other kinds of friendship, however, there is nothing to prevent these evils arising.   25

For men apply the name of friends even to those whose motive is utility, in which sense states are said to be friendly (for the alliances of states seem to aim at advantage), and to those who love each other for the sake of pleasure, in which sense children are called friends. Therefore we too ought perhaps to call such people friends, and say that there are several kinds of friendship—firstly   30 and in the proper sense that of good men *qua* good, and by resemblance the other kinds;* for it is in virtue of something good and something akin to what is found in true friendship that they are friends, since even the pleasant is good for the lovers of pleasure. But these two kinds of friendship are not often united, nor do the same people become friends because of utility and of pleasure; for things that are only incidentally connected are not often coupled together.

Friendship being divided into these kinds, bad men will be   1157b friends for the sake of pleasure or of utility, being in this respect like each other, but good men will be friends because of themselves, i.e. in virtue of their goodness.* These, then, are friends without qualification; the others are friends incidentally and through a resemblance to these.

The state of friendship distinguished from the activity of friendship and from the feeling of friendliness

5. As in regard to the virtues some men are called good in respect   5 of a state of character, others in respect of an activity, so too in the case of friendship; for those who live together delight in each other and confer benefits on each other, but those who are asleep or locally separated are not performing, but are disposed to perform, the activities of friendship; distance does not break off the friend-   10 ship absolutely, but only the activity of it. But if the absence is lasting, it seems actually to make men forget their friendship; hence the saying 'Many a friendship has lack of conversation broken.' Neither old people nor sour people seem to make friends easily; for there is little that is pleasant in them, and no one can spend his days   15 with one whose company is painful, or not pleasant, since nature

seems above all to avoid the painful and to aim at the pleasant. Those, however, who approve of each other but do not live together seem to be well disposed rather than actual friends. For there is nothing so characteristic of friends as living together (since while it
20 is people who are in need that desire benefits, even those who are supremely happy desire to spend their days together; for solitude suits such people least of all); but people cannot live together if they are not pleasant and do not enjoy the same things, as friends who are companions seem to do.*

25   The truest friendship, then, is that of the good, as we have frequently said;[1] for that which is without qualification good or pleasant seems to be lovable and desirable, and for each person that which is good or pleasant to him; and the good man is lovable and desirable to the good man for both these reasons. Now it looks as if loving were a feeling, friendship a state of character; for loving may
30 be felt just as much towards lifeless things, but mutual love involves choice and choice springs from a state of character; and men wish well to those whom they love, for their sake, not as a result of feeling but as a result of a state of character. And in loving a friend men love what is good for themselves; for the good man in becoming a friend becomes a good to his friend. Each, then, both loves what is
35 good for himself, and makes an equal return in goodwill and in pleasantness; for friendship is said to be equality, and both of these are found most in the friendship of the good.

Various relations between the three kinds

1158a 6. Between sour and elderly people friendship arises less readily, inasmuch as they are less good-tempered and enjoy companionship less; for these are thought to be the greatest marks of friendship and most productive of it. This is why, while young men become
5 friends quickly, old men do not; it is because men do not become friends with those in whom they do not delight; and similarly sour people do not quickly make friends either. But such men may bear goodwill to each other; for they wish one another well and aid one another in need; but they are hardly *friends*, because they do not spend their days together or delight in each other, and these are thought the greatest marks of friendship.

---

[1] 1156b7, 23, 33, 1157a30, b4.

One cannot be a friend to many people in the sense of having friendship of the perfect type with them, just as one cannot be in love with many people at once (for being in love is a sort of excess of feeling, and it is the nature of such only to be felt towards one person); and it is not easy for many people at the same time to please the same person very greatly, or perhaps even to be good in his eyes. One must, too, acquire some experience of the other person and become familiar with him, and that is very hard. But with a view to utility or pleasure it is possible that many people should please one; for many people are useful or pleasant, and these services take little time.

Of these two kinds that which is because of pleasure is the more like friendship, when both parties get the same things from each other and delight in each other or in the same things, as in the friendships of the young; for generosity is more found in such friendships. Friendship based on utility is for the commercially minded. People who are supremely happy, too, have no need of useful friends, but do need pleasant friends;* for they wish to live with *someone* and, though they can endure for a short time what is painful, no one could put up with it continuously, nor even with the Good itself if it were painful to him;* this is why they look out for friends who are pleasant. Perhaps they should look out for friends who, being pleasant, are also good, and good for them too; for so they will have all the characteristics that friends should have.

People in positions of authority seem to have friends who fall into distinct classes; some people are useful to them and others are pleasant, but the same people are rarely both; for they seek neither those whose pleasantness is accompanied by virtue nor those whose utility is with a view to noble objects, but in their desire for pleasure they seek for ready-witted people, and their other friends they choose as being clever at doing what they are told, and these characteristics are rarely combined. Now we have said that the *good* man *is* at the same time pleasant and useful;[1] but such a man does not become the friend of one who surpasses him in station, unless he is surpassed also in virtue; if this is not so, he does not establish equality, by being proportionally exceeded in both respects. But people who surpass him in both respects are not so easy to find.*

---

[1] 1156b13–15, 1157a1–3.

1158b   However that may be, the aforesaid friendships involve equality;
for the friends get the same things from one another and wish the
same things for one another, or exchange one thing for another, e.g.
pleasure for utility; we have said,[1] however, that they are both less
5 truly friendships and less permanent. But it is from their likeness
and their unlikeness to the same thing that they are thought both to
be and not to be friendships. It is by their likeness to the friendship
of virtue that they seem to be friendships (for one of them involves
pleasure and the other utility, and these characteristics belong to
the friendship of virtue as well); while it is because the friendship
of virtue is proof against slander and permanent, while these
quickly change (besides differing from the former in many other
10 respects), that they appear *not* to be friendships; i.e. it is because of
their unlikeness to the friendship of virtue.

RECIPROCITY OF FRIENDSHIP

In unequal friendships a proportion must be maintained

7. But there is another kind of friendship, namely, that which
involves an inequality between the parties, e.g. that of father to son
and in general of elder to younger, that of man to wife and in general that of ruler to subject. And these friendships differ also from
15 each other; for it is not the same that exists between parents and
children and between rulers and subjects, nor is even that of father
to son the same as that of son to father, nor that of husband to wife
the same as that of wife to husband. For the virtue and the function
of each of these is different, and so are the reasons for which they
love; the love and the friendship are therefore different also. Each
20 party, then, neither gets the same from the other, nor ought to seek
it; but when children render to parents what they ought to render
to those who brought them into the world, and parents render what
they should to their children, the friendship of such persons will be
abiding and excellent. In all friendships implying inequality the love
25 also should be proportional, i.e. the better should be more loved
than he loves, and so should the more useful, and similarly in each
of the other cases; for when the love is in proportion to the merit of
the parties, then in a sense arises equality, which is certainly held to
be characteristic of friendship.*

[1] 1156a16–24, 1157a20–33.

But equality does not seem to take the same form in acts of justice and in friendship; for in acts of justice what is equal in the 30 primary sense is that which is in proportion to merit, while quantitative equality is secondary, but in friendship quantitative equality is primary and proportion to merit secondary.* This becomes clear if there is a great interval in respect of virtue or vice or wealth or anything else between the parties; for then they are no longer friends, and do not even expect to be so. And this is most manifest 35 in the case of the gods; for they surpass us most decisively in all good things. But it is clear also in the case of kings; for with them, 1159a too, men who are much their inferiors do not expect to be friends; nor do men of no account expect to be friends with the best or wisest men. In such cases it is not possible to define exactly up to what point friends can remain friends; for much can be taken away and friendship remain, but when one party is removed to a great distance, as god is, the possibility of friendship ceases. This is in fact 5 the origin of the question whether friends really wish for their friends the greatest goods, e.g. that of being gods; since in that case their friends will no longer be friends to them, and therefore will not be good things for them (for friends *are* good things).* The answer is that if we were right in saying that friend wishes good to 10 friend for his sake,[1] his friend must remain the sort of being he is, whatever that may be; therefore it is for him only so long as he remains a man that he will wish the greatest goods. But perhaps not *all* the greatest goods; for it is for himself most of all that each man wishes what is good.

Loving is more of the essence of friendship than being loved

8. Most people seem, owing to love of honour, to wish to be loved rather than to love; which is why most men love flattery; for the flatterer is a friend in an inferior position, or pretends to be such 15 and to love more than he is loved; and being loved seems to be akin to being honoured, and this is what most people aim at. But it seems to be not for its own sake that people choose honour, but incidentally. For most people enjoy being honoured by those in positions of authority because of their hopes (for they think that if 20 they want anything they will get it from them; and therefore they delight in honour as a token of favour to come); while those who

---
[1] 1155b31.

desire honour from good men, and men who know, are aiming at
confirming their own opinion of themselves; they delight in honour, therefore, because they believe in their own goodness on the
strength of the judgement of those who speak about them.* In being
25 loved, on the other hand, people delight for its own sake; whence it
would seem to be better than being honoured, and friendship to be
desirable in itself. But it seems to lie in loving rather than in being
loved, as is indicated by the delight mothers take in loving; for some
mothers hand over their children to be brought up, and so long as
they know their fate they love them and do not seek to be loved in
30 return (if they cannot have both), but seem to be satisfied if they see
them prospering; and they themselves love their children even if
these owing to their ignorance give them nothing of a mother's
due.* Now since friendship depends more on loving, and it is those
who love their friends that are praised, loving seems to be the characteristic virtue of friends, so that it is only those in whom this is
35 found in due measure that are lasting friends, and only their friend-
1159b ship that endures.

It is in this way more than any other that even unequals can be
friends; they can be equalized. Now equality and likeness are friendship, and especially the likeness of those who are like in virtue;
for being steadfast in themselves they hold fast to each other, and
5 neither ask nor give base services, but (one may say) even prevent
them; for it is characteristic of good men neither to go wrong themselves nor to let their friends do so. But wicked men have no stead-
fastness (for they do not remain even like to themselves), but become
friends for a short time because they delight in each other's wicked-
10 ness. Friends who are useful or pleasant last longer; i.e. as long as
they provide each other with enjoyments or advantages. Friendship
for utility's sake seems to be that which most easily exists between
contraries, e.g. between poor and rich, between ignorant and learned;
for what a man actually lacks he aims at, and one gives something
15 else in return. But under this head, too, one might bring lover and
beloved, beautiful and ugly. This is why lovers sometimes seem
ridiculous, when they demand to be loved as they love; if they are
equally lovable their claim can perhaps be justified, but when they
have nothing lovable about them it is ridiculous. Perhaps, however,
20 contrary does not even aim at contrary by its own nature, but only
incidentally, the desire being for what is intermediate; for that is

what is good, e.g. it is good for the dry not to become wet but to come to the intermediate state, and similarly with the hot and in all other cases. These subjects we may dismiss; for they are indeed somewhat foreign to our inquiry.*

RELATION OF RECIPROCITY IN FRIENDSHIP TO THAT INVOLVED IN OTHER FORMS OF COMMUNITY

Parallelism of friendship and justice: the state comprehends all lesser communities

9. Friendship and justice seem, as we have said at the outset of our 25 discussion,[1] to be concerned with the same objects and exhibited between the same persons. For in every community there is thought to be some form of justice, and friendship too; at least men address as friends their fellow voyagers and fellow soldiers, and so too those associated with them in any other kind of community. And the extent of their association is the extent of their friendship, as it is 30 the extent to which justice exists between them. And the proverb 'What friends have is common property' expresses the truth; for friendship depends on community. Now brothers and comrades have all things in common, but the others to whom we have referred have definite things in common—some more things, others fewer; for of friendships, too, some are more and others less truly friend-ships. And the claims of justice differ too; the duties of parents to 35 children and those of brothers to each other are not the same, 1160a nor those of comrades and those of fellow citizens, and so, too, with the other kinds of friendship. There is a difference, therefore, also between the acts that are unjust towards each of these classes of associates, and the injustice increases by being exhibited towards those who are friends in a fuller sense; e.g. it is a more terrible thing to defraud a comrade than a fellow citizen, more terrible not 5 to help a brother than a stranger, and more terrible to wound a father than anyone else. And the demands of justice also seem to increase with the intensity of the friendship, which implies that friendship and justice exist between the same persons and have an equal extension.

[1] 1155a22–8.

Now all forms of community are like parts of the political com-
10 munity; for men journey together with a view to some particular
advantage, and to provide something that they need for the purposes of life; and it is for the sake of advantage that the political
community too seems both to have come together originally and to
endure, for this is what legislators aim at, and they call just that
which is to the common advantage. Now the other communities
15 aim at advantage bit by bit, e.g. sailors at what is advantageous on a
voyage with a view to making money or something of the kind,
fellow soldiers at what is advantageous in war, whether it is wealth
or victory or the taking of a city that they seek, and members of
tribes and demes act similarly [Some communities seem to arise for
the sake of pleasure, namely, religious guilds and social clubs; for
20 these exist respectively for the sake of offering sacrifice and of companionship. But all these seem to fall under the political community; for it aims not at present advantage but at what is advantageous
for life as a whole],* offering sacrifices and arranging gatherings for
the purpose, and assigning honours to the gods, and providing
25 pleasant relaxations for themselves. For the ancient sacrifices and
gatherings seem to take place after the harvest as a sort of first
fruits, because it was at these seasons that people had most leisure.
All the communities, then, seem to be parts of the political community; and the particular kinds of friendship will correspond to
30 the particular kinds of community.

Classification of constitutions: analogies with family relations

10. There are three kinds of constitution, and an equal number of
deviation forms—perversions, as it were, of them. The constitutions are monarchy, aristocracy, and thirdly that which is based on
a property qualification, which it seems appropriate to call timo-
35 cratic, though most people are wont to call it polity.* The best of
these is monarchy, the worst timocracy. The deviation from mon-
1160b archy is tyranny; for both are forms of one-man rule, but there is
the greatest difference between them: the tyrant looks to his own
advantage, the king to that of his subjects. For a man is not a king
unless he is sufficient to himself and excels his subjects in all good
5 things; and such a man needs nothing further; therefore he will not
look to his own interests but to those of his subjects; for a king who
is not like that would be a mere titular king. Now tyranny is the

very contrary of this; the tyrant pursues his own good. And it is clearer in the case of tyranny that it is the worst deviation-form; but it is the contrary of the best that is worst.* Monarchy passes over into tyranny; for tyranny is the evil form of one-man rule and the bad king becomes a tyrant. Aristocracy passes over into oligarchy by the badness of the rulers, who distribute contrary to equity what belongs to the city—all or most of the good things to themselves, and office always to the same people, paying most regard to wealth; thus the rulers are few and are bad men instead of the most worthy. Timocracy passes over into democracy; for these are coterminous, since it is the ideal even of timocracy to be the rule of the majority, and all who have the property qualification count as equal. Democracy is the least bad of the deviations;* for in its case the form of constitution is but a slight deviation. These then are the changes to which constitutions are most subject; for these are the smallest and easiest transitions.

One may find resemblances to the constitutions and, as it were, patterns of them even in households. For the association of a father with his sons bears the form of monarchy, since the father cares for his children; and this is why Homer calls Zeus 'father';[1] it is the ideal of monarchy to be paternal rule. But among the Persians the rule of the father is tyrannical; they use their sons as slaves. Tyrannical too is the rule of a master over slaves;* for it is the advantage of the master that is brought about in it. Now this seems to be a correct form of government, but the Persian type is perverted; for the modes of rule appropriate to different relations are diverse. The association of man and wife seems to be aristocratic; for the man rules in accordance with his worth, and in those matters in which a man should rule, but the matters that befit a woman he hands over to her. If the man rules in everything the relation passes over into oligarchy; for in doing so he is not acting in accordance with their respective worth, and not ruling in virtue of his superiority. Sometimes, however, women rule, because they are heiresses; so their rule is not in virtue of excellence but due to wealth and power, as in oligarchies. The association of brothers is like timocracy; for they are equal, except in so far as they differ in age; hence if they differ *much* in age, the friendship is no longer of the fraternal type. Democracy is found chiefly in masterless dwellings (for here everyone

10

15

20

25

30

35

1161a

5

---

[1] e.g. *Iliad* i.503.

is on an equality), and in those in which the ruler is weak and every one has licence to do as he pleases.

Corresponding forms of friendship, and of justice

10 11. Each of the constitutions may be seen to involve friendship just in so far as it involves justice. The friendship between a king and his subjects depends on an excess of benefits conferred; for he confers benefits on his subjects if being a good man he cares for them with a view to their well-being, as a shepherd does for his sheep (whence Homer called Agamemnon 'shepherd of the peoples').[1]
15 Such too is the friendship of a father, though this exceeds the other in the greatness of the benefits conferred; for he is responsible for the existence of his children, which is thought the greatest good, and for their nurture and upbringing. These things are ascribed to ancestors as well. Further, by nature a father tends to rule over his sons, ancestors over descendants, a king over his subjects. These
20 friendships imply superiority of one party over the other, which is why ancestors are honoured. The justice therefore that exists between persons so related is not the same on both sides but is in every case proportioned to merit; for that is true of the friendship as well. The friendship of man and wife, again, is the same that is found in an aristocracy; for it is in accordance with virtue—the better gets more of what is good, and each gets what befits him; and
25 so, too, with the justice in these relations. The friendship of brothers is like that of comrades; for they are equal and of like age, and such persons are for the most part like in their feelings and their character. Like this, too, is the friendship appropriate to timocratic government; for in such a constitution the ideal is for the citizens to be equal and fair; therefore rule is taken in turn, and on equal terms;* and the friendship appropriate here will correspond.
30   But in the deviation-forms, as justice hardly exists, so too does friendship. It exists least in the worst form: in tyranny there is little or no friendship. For where there is nothing common to ruler and ruled, there is not friendship either, since there is not justice; e.g.
35 between craftsman and tool, soul and body, master and slave; the
1161b latter in each case is benefited by that which uses it, but there is no friendship or justice towards lifeless things. But neither is there friendship towards a horse or an ox, nor to a slave *qua* slave.

[1] e.g. *Iliad* ii.243.

For there is nothing common to the two parties; the slave is a living tool and the tool a lifeless slave. *Qua* slave, then, one cannot be 5 friends with him. But *qua* man one can; for there seems to be some justice between any man and any other who can share in a system of law or be a party to an agreement; therefore there can also be friendship with him in so far as he is a man.* Therefore while in tyrannies friendship and justice hardly exist, in democracies they exist more fully; for where the citizens are equal they have much in 10 common.

Various forms of friendship between relations

12. Every form of friendship, then, involves association, as has been said.[1] One might, however, mark off from the rest both the friendship of kindred and that of comrades. Those of fellow citizens, fellow tribesmen, fellow voyagers, and the like are more like mere friendships of association; for they seem to rest on a sort of compact. With 15 them we might class the friendship of host and guest.

The friendship of kinsmen itself, while it seems to be of many kinds, appears to depend in every case on parental friendship; for parents love their children as being a part of themselves, and children their parents as having themselves originated from them. Now (1) parents know their offspring better than their children know 20 that they are their children, and (2) the originator feels his offspring to be his own more than the offspring do their begetter; for the product belongs to the producer (e.g. a tooth or hair or anything else to him whose it is), but the producer does not belong to the product, or belongs in a less degree. And (3) the length of time produces the same result; parents love their children as soon as 25 these are born, but children love their parents only after time has elapsed and they have acquired understanding or the power of discrimination by the senses. From these considerations it is also plain why mothers love more than fathers do. Parents, then, love their children as themselves (for their issue are by virtue of their separate existence a sort of other selves), while children love their parents as being born of them, and brothers love each other as being born of 30 the same parents; for their identity with them makes them identical with each other (which is the reason why people talk of 'the same blood', 'the same stock', and so on). They are, therefore, in a sense

[1] 1159b29–32.

the same thing, though in separate individuals. Two things that contribute greatly to friendship are a common upbringing and similarity of age; for 'two of an age take to each other', and people
35 brought up together tend to be comrades; whence the friendship of
1162a brothers is akin to that of comrades. And cousins and other kinsmen are bound up together by derivation from brothers, i.e. by being derived from the same parents. They come to be closer together or farther apart by virtue of the nearness or distance of the original ancestor.

The friendship of children to parents, and of men to gods, is a rela-
5 tion to them as to something good and superior; for they have conferred the greatest benefits, since they are the causes of their being and of their nourishment, and of their education from their birth; and this kind of friendship possesses pleasantness and utility also, more than that of strangers, inasmuch as their life is lived more in common. The
10 friendship of brothers has the characteristics found in that of comrades (and especially when these are good), and in general between people who are like each other, inasmuch as they belong more to each other and start with a love for each other from their very birth, and inasmuch as those born of the same parents and brought up together and similarly educated are more akin in character; and the test of time has been applied most fully and convincingly in their case.

15   Between other kinsmen friendly relations are found in due proportion. Between man and wife friendship seems to exist by nature; for man is naturally inclined to form couples—even more than to form cities, inasmuch as the household is earlier and more necessary than the city, and reproduction is more common to man with
20 the animals. With the other animals the union extends only to this point, but human beings live together not only for the sake of reproduction but also for the various purposes of life; for from the start the functions are divided, and those of man and woman are different; so they help each other by throwing their peculiar gifts into the common stock. It is for these reasons that both utility and
25 pleasure seem to be found in this kind of friendship. But this friendship may be based also on virtue, if the parties are good; for each has its own virtue and they will delight in the fact. And children seem to be a bond of union (which is the reason why childless people part more easily); for children are a good common to both and what is common holds them together.

How man and wife and in general friend and friend ought mutu- 30
ally to behave seems to be the same question as how it is just for
them to behave; for a man does not seem to have the same duties to
a friend, a stranger, a comrade, and a schoolfellow.

CASUISTRY OF FRIENDSHIP

Principles to be observed (a) in friendship between equals

13. There are three kinds of friendship, as we said at the outset of
our inquiry,[1] and in respect of each some are friends on an equality 35
and others by virtue of a superiority (for not only can equally good
men become friends but a better man can make friends with a
worse, and similarly in friendships of pleasure or utility the friends 1162b
may be equal or unequal in the benefits they confer). This being so,
equals must effect the required equalization on a basis of equality in
love and in all other respects, while unequals must render what is
in proportion to their superiority or inferiority.

Complaints and reproaches arise either only or chiefly in the 5
friendship of utility, and this is only to be expected. For those who
are friends on the ground of virtue are anxious to do well by each
other (since that is a mark of virtue and of friendship), and between
men who are emulating each other in this there cannot be complaints or quarrels; no one is offended by a man who loves him and 10
does well by him—if he is a person of nice feeling he takes his
revenge by doing well by the other. And the man who excels the
other in the services he renders will not complain of his friend,
since he gets what he aims at; for each man desires what is good.*
Nor do complaints arise much even in friendships of pleasure; for
both get at the same time what they desire, if they enjoy spending
their time together; and a man who complained of another for *not* 15
affording him pleasure would seem ridiculous, since it is in his
power not to spend his days with him.

But the friendship of utility is full of complaints; for as they use
each other for their own interests they always want to get the better
of the bargain, and think they have got less than they should, and
blame their partners because they do not get all they 'want and
deserve'; and those who do well by others cannot help them as 20
much as those whom they benefit want.

[1] 1113a22–33.

Now it seems that, as justice is of two kinds, one unwritten and the other legal, one kind of friendship of utility is moral and the other legal.* And so complaints arise most of all when men do not dissolve the relation in the spirit of the same type of friendship in
25 which they contracted it. The *legal* type is that which is on fixed terms; its purely commercial variety is on the basis of immediate payment, while the more liberal variety allows time but stipulates for a definite *quid pro quo*. In this variety the debt is clear and not ambiguous, but in the postponement it contains an element of friendliness; and so some states do not allow suits arising out of such
30 agreements, but think men who have bargained on a basis of credit ought to accept the consequences. The *moral* type is not on fixed terms; it makes a gift, or does whatever it does, as to a friend; but one expects to receive as much or more, as having not given but lent; and if a man is worse off when the relation is dissolved than he was when it was contracted he will complain. This happens
35 because all or most men, while they wish for what is noble, choose what is advantageous; now it is noble to do well by another without
1163a a view to repayment, but it is the receiving of benefits that is advantageous.

Therefore if we can we should return the equivalent of what we have received (for we must not make a man our friend against his will; we must recognize that we were mistaken at the first and took a benefit from a person we should not have taken it from—since it was not from a friend, nor from one who did it just for the sake of
5 acting so—and we must settle up just as if we had been benefited on fixed terms). Indeed, one would agree to repay if one could (if one could not, even the giver would not have expected one to do so); therefore if it is possible we must repay. But at the outset we must consider the man by whom we are being benefited and on what terms he is acting, in order that we may accept the benefit on these terms, or else decline it.

10 It is disputable whether we ought to measure a service by its utility to the receiver and make the return with a view to that, or by the beneficence of the giver. For those who have received say they have received from their benefactors what meant little to the latter and what they might have got from others—minimizing the service; while the givers, on the contrary, say it was the biggest thing they
15 had, and what could not have been got from others, and that it was

given in times of danger or similar need. Now if the friendship is because of *utility*, surely the advantage to the receiver is the measure. For it is he that asks for the service, and the other man helps him on the assumption that he will receive the equivalent; so the assistance has been precisely as great as the advantage to the receiver, and therefore he must return as much as he has received,   20 or even more (for that would be nobler). In friendships based on *virtue*, on the other hand, complaints do not arise, but the purpose of the doer is a sort of measure;* for in purpose lies the essential element of virtue and character.

Principles to be observed (b) in friendship between unequals

14. Differences arise also in friendships based on superiority; for each expects to get more out of them, but when this happens the   25 friendship is dissolved. Not only does the better man think he ought to get more, since more should be assigned to a good man, but the more useful similarly expects this; they say a useless man should not get as much as they should, since it becomes an act of public service and not a friendship if the proceeds of the friendship do not answer to the worth of the benefits conferred. For they think   30 that, as in a commercial partnership those who put more in get more out, so it should be in friendship. But the man who is in a state of need and inferiority makes the opposite claim; such men think it is the part of a good friend to help those who are in need; what, they say, is the use of being the friend of a good man or a   35 powerful man, if one is to get nothing out of it?

At all events it seems that each party is justified in his claim, and   1163b that each should get more out of the friendship than the other—not more of the same thing, however, but the superior more honour and the inferior more gain; for honour is the prize of virtue and of beneficence, while gain is the assistance required by inferiority.

It seems to be so in constitutional arrangements also; the man   5 who contributes nothing good to the common stock is not honoured; for what belongs to the public is given to the man who benefits the public, and honour does belong to the public. It is not possible to get wealth from the common stock and at the same time honour. For no one puts up with the smaller share in *all* things; therefore to the man who loses in wealth they assign honour and to   10 the man who is willing to be paid, wealth, since the proportion to merit equalizes the parties and preserves the friendship, as we have said.[1]

This then is also the way in which we should associate with unequals; the man who is benefited in respect of wealth or virtue must give honour in return, repaying what he can. For friendship
15 asks a man to do what he can, not what is proportional to the merits of the case; since that cannot always be done, e.g. in honours paid to the gods or to parents; for no one could ever return to them the equivalent of what he gets, but the man who serves them to the utmost of his power is thought to be a good man.

This is why it would not seem open to a man to disown his father (though a father may disown his son); being in debt, he should
20 repay, but there is nothing by doing which a son will have done the equivalent of what he has received, so that he is always in debt. But creditors can remit a debt; and a father can therefore do so too. At the same time it is thought that presumably no one would repudiate a son who was not far gone in wickedness; for apart from the natural friendship of father and son it is human nature not to reject a
25 son's assistance. But the son, if he *is* wicked, will naturally avoid aiding his father, or not be zealous about it; for most people wish to get benefits, but avoid doing them, as a thing unprofitable. So much for these questions.

---

[1] 1162a34–b4, cf. 1158b27, 1159a35–b3.

BOOK IX · FRIENDSHIP (*cont.*)

*Principles to be observed (c) where the motives on the two sides
are different*

1. In all friendships between dissimilars it is, as we have said,[1]
proportion that equalizes the parties and preserves the friendship;
e.g. in the political form of friendship the shoemaker gets a return
for his shoes in proportion to his worth, and the weaver and all
other craftsmen do the same. Now here a common measure has   1164a
been provided in the form of money, and therefore everything is
referred to this and measured by this; but in the friendship of lovers
sometimes the lover complains that his excess of love is not met by
love in return (though perhaps there is nothing lovable about him),
while often the beloved complains that the lover who formerly   5
promised everything now performs nothing. Such incidents happen
when the lover loves the beloved for the sake of pleasure while the
beloved loves the lover for the sake of utility, and they do not both
possess the qualities expected of them. If these be the objects of the
friendship it is dissolved when they do not get the things that formed
the motives of their love; for each did not love the other person   10
himself but the qualities he had, and these were not enduring; that
is why the friendships also are transient. But the love of character,
as has been said, endures because it is self-dependent.[2] Differences
arise when what they get is something different and not what they
desire; for it is like getting nothing at all when we do not get what
we aim at; compare the story of the person who made promises to   15
a lyre-player, promising him the more, the better he sang, but in
the morning, when the other demanded the fulfilment of his promises, said that he had given pleasure for pleasure.* Now if this had
been what each wanted, all would have been well; but if the one
wanted enjoyment but the other gain, and the one has what he
wants while the other has not, the terms of the association will not   20
have been properly fulfilled; for what each in fact wants is what he
attends to, and it is for the sake of that that he will give what he has.

---

[1] This has not been said precisely of friendship between dissimilars, but cf. 1132b31–3,
1158b27, 1159a35–b3, 1162a34–b4, 1163b11.

[2] 1156b9–12.

But who is to fix the worth of the service; he who makes the sacrifice or he who has got the advantage? At any rate the other seems to leave it to him. This is what they say Protagoras used to
25 do:* whenever he taught anything whatsoever, he bade the learner assess the value of the knowledge, and accepted the amount so fixed. But in such matters some men approve of the saying 'Let a man have his fixed reward.'*

Those who get the money first and then do none of the things they said they would, owing to the extravagance of their promises, naturally find themselves the objects of complaint; for they do not
30 fulfil what they agreed to. The sophists are perhaps compelled to do this because no one would give money for the things they *do* know.* These people, then, if they do not do what they have been paid for, are naturally made the objects of complaint.

But where there is *no* contract of service, those who give up something for the sake of the other party cannot (as we have said)[1]
35 be complained of (for that is the nature of the friendship of virtue),
1164b and the return to them must be made on the basis of their purpose (for it is purpose that is the characteristic thing in a friend and in virtue). And so too, it seems, should one make a return to those with whom one has studied philosophy; for their worth cannot be measured against money, and they can get no honour which will balance their services, but still it is perhaps enough, as it is with the
5 gods and with one's parents, to give them what one can.

If the gift was not of this sort, but was made with a view to a return, it is no doubt preferable that the return made should be one that seems fair to both parties, but if this cannot be achieved, it would seem not only necessary that the person who gets the first
10 service should fix the reward, but also just; for if the other gets in return the equivalent of the advantage the beneficiary has received, or the price he would have paid for the pleasure, he will have got what is fair as from the other.

We see this happening too with things put up for sale, and in some places there are laws providing that no actions shall arise out of voluntary contracts, on the assumption that one should settle with a person to whom one has given credit, in the spirit in which
15 one bargained with him. The law holds that it is more just that the person to whom credit was given should fix the terms than that the

---

[1] 1162b6–13.

person who gave credit should do so. For most things are not assessed at the same value by those who have them and those who want them; each class values highly what is its own and what it is offering; yet the return is made on the terms fixed by the receiver. But no doubt the receiver should assess a thing not at what it seems worth when 20 he has it, but at what he assessed it at before he had it.

Conflict of obligations

2. A further problem is set by such questions as whether one should in all things give the preference to one's father and obey him, or whether when one is ill one should trust a doctor, and when one has to elect a general should elect a man of military skill; and similarly whether one should render a service by preference to a 25 friend or to a good man, and should show gratitude to a benefactor or oblige a friend, if one cannot do both.

All such questions are hard, are they not, to decide with precision? For they admit of many variations of all sorts in respect both of the magnitude of the service and of its nobility and necessity. But that we should not give the preference in all things to the same 30 person is plain enough; and we must for the most part return benefits rather than oblige friends, as we must pay back a loan to a creditor rather than make one to a friend. But perhaps even this is not always true; e.g. should a man who has been ransomed out of the hands of brigands ransom his ransomer in return, whoever he may 35 be (or pay him if he has not been captured but demands payment), or should he ransom his father? It would seem that he should ran- 1165a som his father in preference even to himself. As we have said,[1] then, generally the debt should be paid, but if the gift is exceedingly noble or exceedingly necessary, one should defer to these consid- erations.* For sometimes it is not even fair to return the equivalent 5 of what one has received, when the one man has done a service to one whom he knows to be good, while the other makes a return to one whom he believes to be bad. For that matter, one should some- times not lend in return to one who has lent to oneself; for the one person lent to a good man, expecting to recover his loan, while the other has no hope of recovering from one who is believed to be bad. Therefore if the facts really are so, the demand is not fair; and if 10 they are not, but people think they are, they would be held to be

---

[1] 1164b31–1165a2.

doing nothing strange in refusing. As we have often pointed out,[1]
then, discussions about feelings and actions have only as much
definiteness as their subject-matter.*

That we should not make the same return to everyone, nor give
15 a father the preference in everything, as one does not sacrifice
everything to Zeus, is plain enough; but since we ought to render
different things to parents, brothers, comrades, and benefactors, we
ought to render to each class what is appropriate and becoming.
And this is what people seem in fact to do: to marriages they invite
their kinsfolk, for these have a part in the family and therefore in
20 the doings that affect the family; and at funerals also they think that
kinsfolk, before all others, should meet, for the same reason. And it
would be thought that in the matter of food we should help our
parents before all others, since we owe our own nourishment to
them, and it is more honourable to help in this respect the authors
of our being even before ourselves; and honour too one should give
to one's parents as one does to the gods, but not any and every
honour; for that matter one should not give the same honour to
25 one's father and to one's mother, nor again should one give them
the honour due to a philosopher or to a general, but the honour due
to a father, or again to a mother. To all older persons, too, one
should give honour appropriate to their age, by rising to receive
them and finding seats for them and so on; while to comrades and
brothers one should allow freedom of speech and common use of all
30 things. To kinsmen, too, and fellow tribesmen and fellow citizens
and to every other class one should always try to assign what is
appropriate, and to compare the claims of each class with respect to
nearness of relation and to virtue or usefulness. The comparison is
easier when the persons belong to the same class, and more laborious when they are different. Yet we must not on *that* account shrink
35 from the task, but decide the question as best we can.

Occasions of breaking off friendship

3. Another question that arises is whether friendships should or
should not be broken off when the other party does not remain the
1165b same. Perhaps we may say that there is nothing strange in breaking
off a friendship based on utility or pleasantness, when our friends

---

[1] 1094b11–27, 1098a26–9, 1103b34–1104a5.

no longer have these attributes. For it was of these attributes that we were the friends; and when these have failed it is reasonable to love no longer. But one might complain of another if, when he loved us for our usefulness or pleasantness, he pretended to love us for our character. For, as we said at the outset,[1] most differences arise between friends when they are not friends in the spirit in which they think they are. So when a man has deceived himself and has thought he was being loved for his character, when the other person was doing nothing of the kind, he must blame himself; but when he has been deceived by the pretences of the other person, it is just that he should complain against his deceiver; he will complain with more justice than one does against people who counterfeit the currency, inasmuch as the wrongdoing is concerned with something more valuable.

But if one accepts another man as good, and he turns out badly and is seen to do so, must one still love him? Surely it is impossible, since not everything can be loved, but only what is good. What is evil neither can nor should be loved; for it is not one's duty to be a lover of evil, or to become like what is bad; and we have said[2] that like is dear to like. Must the friendship, then, be forthwith broken off? Or is this not so in all cases, but only when one's friends are incurable in their wickedness? If they are capable of being reformed one should rather come to the assistance of their character or their property, inasmuch as this is better and more characteristic of friendship. But a man who breaks off such a friendship would seem to be doing nothing strange; for it was not to a man of this sort that he was a friend; when his friend has changed, therefore, and he is unable to save him, he gives him up.

But if one friend remained the same while the other became better and far outstripped him in virtue, should the latter treat the former as a friend? Surely he cannot. When the interval is great this becomes most plain, e.g. in the case of childish friendships; if one friend remained a child in intellect while the other became a fully developed man, how could they be friends when they neither approved of the same things nor delighted in and were pained by the same things? For not even with regard to each other will their tastes agree, and without this (as we saw)[3] they cannot be

_____
[1] 1162b23–5.   [2] 1156b19–21, 1159b1.   [3] 1157b22–4.

friends; for they cannot live together. But we have discussed these matters.[1]

Should he, then, behave no otherwise towards him than he would if he had never been his friend? Surely he should keep a remembrance of their former intimacy, and as we think we ought to oblige
35 friends rather than strangers, so to those who have been our friends we ought to make some allowance for our former friendship, when the breach has not been due to excess of wickedness.*

INTERNAL NATURE OF FRIENDSHIP

Friendship is based on self-love

1166a 4. Friendly relations with one's neighbours, and the marks by which friendships are defined, seem to have proceeded from a man's relations to himself.* For (1) we define a friend as one who wishes and does what is good, or seems so, for the sake of his friend, or (2) as one who wishes his friend to exist and live, for his sake; which
5 mothers do to their children, and friends do who have come into conflict.* And (3) others define him as one who lives with and (4) has the same tastes as another, or (5) one who grieves and rejoices with his friend; and this too is found in mothers most of all. It is by some one of these characteristics that friendship too is defined.

10 Now each of these is true of the good man's relation to himself (and of all other men in so far as they think themselves good; virtue and the good man seem, as has been said,[2] to be the measure of every class of things). For his opinions are harmonious, and he desires the same things with all his soul; and therefore he wishes for
15 himself what is good and what seems so, and does it (for it is characteristic of the good man to work at the good), and does so for his own sake (for he does it for the sake of the intellectual element in him, which is thought to be the man himself); and he wishes himself to live and be preserved, and especially the element by virtue of which he thinks. For existence is good to the virtuous man, and
20 each man wishes himself what is good, while no one chooses to possess the whole world if he has first to become someone else (for that matter, even now god possesses the good);* he wishes for this only on condition of being whatever he is; and the element that thinks

---

[1] 1157b17–24, 1158b33–5.   [2] 1113a22–33, cf. 1099a13.

would seem to be the individual man, or to be so more than any other element in him.* And such a man wishes to live with himself; for he does so with pleasure, since the memories of his past acts are 25 delightful and his hopes for the future are good, and therefore pleasant. His mind is well stored too with subjects of contemplation. And he grieves and rejoices, more than any other, with himself; for the same thing is always painful, and the same thing always pleasant, and not one thing at one time and another at another; he has, so to speak, nothing to regret.

Therefore, since each of these characteristics belongs to the good 30 man in relation to himself, and he is related to his friend as to himself (for his friend is another self*), friendship too is thought to be one of these attributes, and those who have these attributes to be friends. Whether there is or is not friendship between a man and himself is a question we may dismiss for the present; there would seem to be friendship in so far as he is two or more,* to judge from 35 the aforementioned attributes of friendship, and from the fact that 1166b the extreme of friendship is likened to one's love for oneself.

But the attributes named seem to belong even to the majority of men, poor creatures though they may be. Are we to say then that in so far as they are satisfied with themselves and think they are good, they share in these attributes? Certainly no one who is thoroughly bad and impious has these attributes,* or even seems to do so. They 5 hardly belong even to inferior people; for *they* are at variance with themselves, and have appetites for some things and rational desires for others. This is true, for instance, of incontinent people; for, instead of the things they themselves think good, they go for things that are pleasant but hurtful; while others again, through cowardice 10 and laziness, shrink from doing what they think best for themselves. And those who have done many terrible deeds and are hated for their wickedness even shrink from life and destroy themselves. Besides, wicked men seek for people with whom to spend their days, and shun themselves; for they remember many a grievous 15 deed, and anticipate others like them, when they are by themselves, but when they are with others they forget. And having nothing lovable in them they have no feeling of love to themselves. Therefore also such men do not rejoice or grieve with themselves; for their soul is rent by faction, and one element in it by reason of its wickedness grieves when it abstains from certain acts, while the other part 20

is pleased, and one draws them this way and the other that, as if
they were pulling them in pieces. If a man cannot at the same time
be pained and pleased, at all events after a short time he is pained
because he was pleased, and he could have wished that these things
had not been pleasant to him; for bad men are full of regrets.*

25   Therefore the bad man does not seem to be amicably disposed
even to himself, because there is nothing in him to love; so that if
to be thus is the height of wretchedness, we should strain every nerve
to avoid wickedness and should endeavour to be good; for so and
only so can one be either friendly to oneself or a friend to another.

Relation of friendship to goodwill

30 **5.** Goodwill is characteristic of friendship, but is not *identical* with
friendship; for one may have goodwill both towards people whom
one does not know, and without their knowing it, but not friendship.
This has indeed been said already.[1] But goodwill is not even friendly
feeling. For it does not involve intensity or desire, whereas these
accompany friendly feeling; and friendly feeling implies intimacy
35 while goodwill may arise of a sudden, as it does towards competi-
1167a tors in a contest; we come to feel goodwill for them and to share in
their wishes, but we would not *do* anything with them; for, as we
said, we feel goodwill suddenly and love them only superficially.

Goodwill seems, then, to be a beginning of friendship, as the
pleasure of the eye is the beginning of love. For no one loves if he
5 has not first been delighted by the form of the beloved, but he who
delights in the form of another does not, for all that, love him, but
only does so when he also longs for him when absent and craves for
his presence; so too it is not possible for people to be friends if they
have not come to feel goodwill for each other, but those who feel
goodwill are not for all that friends; for they only *wish* well to those
for whom they feel goodwill, and would not do anything with them
10 or take trouble for them. And so one might by an extension of the
term 'friendship' say that goodwill is inactive friendship, though
when it is prolonged and reaches the point of intimacy it becomes
friendship—not the friendship based on utility nor that based on
pleasure; for goodwill too does not arise on those terms.* The man
who has received a benefit bestows goodwill in return for what has
15 been done to him, but in doing so is only doing what is just; while

[1] 1155b32–1156a5.

he who wishes someone to prosper because he hopes for enrichment through him seems to have goodwill not to him but rather to himself, just as a man is not a friend to another if he cherishes him for the sake of some use to be made of him. In general, goodwill arises on account of some excellence and worth, when one man seems to another beautiful or brave or something of the sort, as we 20 pointed out in the case of competitors in a contest.

Relation of friendship to concord

6. Concord also seems to be characteristic of friendship.* For this reason it is not identity of opinion; for that might occur even with people who do not know each other; nor do we say that people who have the same views on any and every subject are in accord, e.g. those who agree about the heavenly bodies (for concord about these 25 is not a characteristic of friendship), but we do say that a city is in accord when men have the same opinion about what is to their interest, and choose the same actions, and do what they have resolved in common. It is about things to be done, therefore, that people are said to be in accord, and, among these, about matters of consequence and in which it is possible for both or all parties to get what they want; e.g. a city is in accord when all its citizens think 30 that the offices in it should be elective, or that they should form an alliance with Sparta, or that Pittacus should be their ruler*—at a time when he himself was also willing to rule. But when each of two people wishes himself to have the thing in question, like the captains in the *Phoenissae*,* they are in a state of faction; for it is not concord when each of two parties thinks of the same thing, whatever that may be, but only when they think of the same thing in the same 35 hands, e.g. when both the common people and those of the better class wish the best men to rule; for thus and thus alone do all get 1167b what they aim at. Concord seems, then, to be political friendship, as indeed it is commonly said to be; for it is concerned with things that are to our interest and have an influence on our life.

Now such concord is found among good men; for they are in accord both in themselves and with one another, being, so to say, of 5 one mind (for the wishes of such men are constant and not at the mercy of opposing currents like a strait of the sea), and they wish for what is just and what is advantageous, and these are the objects of their common endeavour as well. But bad men cannot be in

10 accord except to a small extent, any more than they can be friends,
since they aim at getting more than their share of advantages, while
in labour and public service they fall short of their share; and each
man wishing for advantage to himself criticizes his neighbour and
stands in his way; for if people do not watch it carefully the common weal is soon destroyed. The result is that they are in a state of
15 faction, putting compulsion on each other but unwilling themselves
to do what is just.

The pleasure of beneficence

7. Benefactors are thought to love those they have benefited, more
than those who have been well treated love those that have treated
them well, and this is discussed as though it were paradoxical. Most
20 people think it is because the latter are in the position of debtors
and the former of creditors; and therefore as, in the case of loans,
debtors wish their creditors did not exist, while creditors actually
take care of the safety of their debtors, so it is thought that benefactors wish the objects of their action to exist since they will then get
their gratitude, while the beneficiaries take no interest in making
25 this return. Epicharmus would perhaps declare that they say this
because they 'look at things on their bad side', but it is quite like
human nature; for most people are forgetful, and are more anxious
to be well treated than to treat others well. But the cause would
seem to be more deeply rooted in the nature of things; the case of
those who have lent money is not even analogous.* For they have
30 no friendly feeling to their debtors, but only a wish that they may
be kept safe with a view to what is to be got from them; while those
who have done a service to others feel friendship and love for those
they have served, even if these are not of any use to them and never
will be. This is what happens with craftsmen too; every man loves
35 his own handiwork better than he would be loved by it if it came
1168a alive; and this happens perhaps most of all with poets; for they have
an excessive love for their own poems, doting on them as if they
were their children. This is what the position of benefactors is like;
for that which they have treated well is their handiwork, and therefore they love this more than the handiwork does its maker. The
5 cause of this is that existence is to all men a thing to be chosen and
loved, and that we exist by virtue of activity (i.e. by living and acting),
and that the handiwork *is*, in a sense, the producer in actuality; he

loves his handiwork, therefore, because he loves existence. And this is rooted in the nature of things; for what he is in potentiality, his handiwork manifests in actuality.*

At the same time, to the benefactor that is noble which depends on his action, so that he delights in the object of his action, whereas to the patient there is nothing noble in the agent, but at most something advantageous, and this is less pleasant and lovable. What *is* pleasant is the activity of the present, the hope of the future, the memory of the past; but most pleasant is that which depends on activity, and similarly this is most lovable. Now for a man who has made something his work remains (for the noble is lasting), but for the person acted on the utility passes away. And the memory of noble things is pleasant, but that of useful things is not likely to be pleasant, or is less so; though the reverse seems true of expectation.

Further, love is like activity, being loved like passivity; and loving and its concomitants are attributes of those who are the more active.

Again, all men love more what they have won by labour; e.g. those who have made their money love it more than those who have inherited it; and to be well treated seems to involve no labour, while to treat others well is a laborious task. These are the reasons, too, why mothers are fonder of their children than fathers; bringing them into the world costs them more pains, and they know better that the children are their own. This last point, too, would seem to apply to benefactors.

The nature of true self-love

8. The question is also debated, whether a man should love himself most, or someone else.* People criticize those who love themselves most, and call them self-lovers, using this as an epithet of disgrace, and a bad man seems to do everything for his own sake, and the more so the more wicked he is—and so men reproach him, for instance, with doing nothing apart from his own interest—while the good man acts for the sake of the noble, and the more so the better he is, and acts for his friend's sake, and sacrifices his own interest.

But the facts clash with these arguments, and this is not surprising.* For men say that one ought to love best one's best friend, and a man's best friend is one who wishes well to the object of his wish for his sake, even if no one is to know of it; and these attributes are found most of all in a man's attitude towards himself, and so are all

the other attributes by which a friend is defined; for, as we have
5 said,[1] it is from this relation that all the characteristics of friendship
have extended to our neighbours. All the proverbs, too, agree with
this, e.g. 'A single soul', and 'What friends have is common property,' and 'Friendship is equality,' and 'The knee is closer than the
shin'; for all these marks will be found most in a man's relation to
10 himself; he is his own best friend and therefore ought to love
himself best. It is therefore a reasonable question, which of the two
views we should follow; for both are plausible.

Perhaps we ought to mark off such arguments from each other
and determine how far and in what respects each view is right. Now
if we grasp the sense in which each school uses the phrase 'lover of
self', the truth may become evident. Those who use the term as one
15 of reproach ascribe self-love to people who assign to themselves the
greater share of wealth, honours, and bodily pleasures; for these are
what most people desire, and busy themselves about as though they
were the best of all things, which is the reason, too, why they become
objects of competition. So those who are grasping with regard to
20 these things gratify their appetites and in general their feelings and
the irrational element of the soul; and most men are of this nature
(which is the reason why the epithet has come to be used as it is—it
takes its meaning from the prevailing type of self-love, which is a
bad one); justly, therefore, are men who are lovers of self in this way
reproached for being so. That it is those who give themselves the
preference in regard to objects of this sort that most people usually
25 call lovers of self is plain; for if a man were always anxious that
he himself, above all things, should act justly, temperately, or in
accordance with any other of the virtues, and in general were always
to try to secure for himself what is noble, no one would call such a
man a lover of self or blame him.*

But such a man would seem more than the other a lover of self;
at all events he assigns to himself the things that are noblest and
30 best, and gratifies the most authoritative element in himself and in
all things obeys this; and just as a city or any other systematic whole
is most properly identified with the most authoritative element in
it, so is a man; and therefore the man who loves this and gratifies it
is most of all a lover of self. Besides, a man is said to have or not to
35 have self-control according as his reason has or has not the control,

[1] Ch. 4.

on the assumption that this is the man himself; and the things men
have done on a rational principle are thought most properly their   1169a
own acts and voluntary acts. That this is the man himself, then, or
is so more than anything else, is plain, and also that the good man
loves most this part of him.* Whence it follows that he is most truly
a lover of self, of another type than that which is a matter of
reproach, and as different from that as living according to a rational   5
principle is from living as passion dictates, and desiring what is
noble from desiring what seems advantageous. Those, then, who
busy themselves in an exceptional degree with noble actions all men
approve and praise; and if *all* were to strive towards what is noble
and strain every nerve to do the noblest deeds, everything would be
as it should be for the common weal, and everyone would secure for   10
himself the goods that are greatest, since virtue is the greatest of
goods.

Therefore the good man should be a lover of self (for he will both
himself profit by doing noble acts, and will benefit his fellows),* but
the wicked man should not; for he will hurt both himself and his
neighbours, following as he does evil passions. For the wicked man,   15
what he does clashes with what he ought to do, but what the good
man ought to do he does; for reason in each of its possessors
chooses what is best for itself, and the good man obeys his reason.
It is true of the good man too that he does many acts for the sake of
his friends and his country, and if necessary dies for them; for he   20
will throw away both wealth and honours and in general the goods
that are objects of competition, gaining for himself nobility; since
he would prefer a short period of intense pleasure to a long one of
mild enjoyment, a twelvemonth of noble life to many years of hum-
drum existence, and one great and noble action to many trivial
ones. Now those who die for others doubtless attain this result; it is   25
therefore a great prize that they choose for themselves. They will
throw away wealth too on condition that their friends will gain
more; for while a man's friend gains wealth he himself achieves
nobility; he is therefore assigning the greater good to himself.* The
same too is true of honour and office; all these things he will sacri-   30
fice to his friend; for this is noble and laudable for himself. Rightly
then is he thought to be good, since he chooses nobility before all
else. But he may even give up actions to his friend; it may be nobler
to become the cause of his friend's acting than to act himself.* In all

35 the actions, therefore, that men are praised for, the good man is
1169b seen to assign to himself the greater share in what is noble. In this
sense, then, as has been said, a man should be a lover of self; but in
the sense in which most men are so, he ought not.

THE NEED OF FRIENDSHIP

Why does the happy man need friends?

9. It is also disputed whether the happy man will need friends or not.
It is said that those who are supremely happy and self-sufficient
5 have no need of friends; for they have the things that are good, and
therefore being self-sufficient they need nothing further, while a
friend, being another self, furnishes what a man cannot provide by
his own effort; whence the saying 'When fortune is kind, what need
of friends?' But it seems strange, when one assigns all good things
to the happy man, not to assign friends, who are thought the great-
10 est of external goods.* And if it is more characteristic of a friend to
do well by another than to be well done by, and to confer benefits
is characteristic of the good man and of virtue, and it is nobler to do
well by friends than by strangers, the good man will need people to
do well by. This is why the question is asked whether we need
friends more in prosperity or in adversity, on the assumption that
15 not only does a man in adversity need people to confer benefits on
him, but also those who are prospering need people to do well by.
Surely it is strange, too, to make the supremely happy man a solitary;
for no one would choose the whole world on condition of being
alone, since man is a political creature and one whose nature is to
live with others.* Therefore even the happy man lives with others;
20 for he has the things that are by nature good. And plainly it is better
to spend his days with friends and good men than with strangers or
any chance persons. Therefore the happy man needs friends.

What then do holders of the first view mean, and in what respect
are they right? Is it that most men identify friends with useful
people? Of such friends indeed the supremely happy man will have
25 no need, since he already has the things that are good; nor will he
need those whom one makes one's friends because of their pleasantness, or he will need them only to a small extent (for his life, being
pleasant, has no need of adventitious pleasure); and because he does
not need *such* friends he is thought not to need friends.

But that is surely not true. For we have said at the outset[1] that happiness is an activity; and activity plainly comes into being and is not present at the start like a piece of property. If happiness lies 30 in living and being active, and the good man's activity is virtuous and pleasant in itself, as we have said at the outset,[2] and a thing's being one's own is one of the attributes that make it pleasant, and we can contemplate our neighbours better than ourselves and their actions better than our own, and if the actions of virtuous men 35 who are their friends are pleasant to good men (since these have 1170a both the attributes that are naturally pleasant)—if this be so, the supremely happy man will need friends of this sort, since his purpose is to contemplate worthy actions and actions that are his own, and the actions of a good man who is his friend have both these qualities.*

Further, men think that the happy man ought to live pleasantly. Now if he were a solitary, life would be hard for him; for by oneself 5 it is not easy to be continuously active; but with others and towards others it is easier.* With others therefore his activity will be more continuous, and it is in itself pleasant, as it ought to be for the man who is supremely happy; for a good man *qua* good delights in virtuous actions and is vexed at vicious ones, as a musical man enjoys 10 beautiful tunes but is pained at bad ones. A certain training in virtue arises also from the company of the good, as Theognis has said before us.

If we look deeper into the nature of things, a virtuous friend seems to be naturally desirable for a virtuous man. For that which is good by nature, we have said,[3] is for the virtuous man good and 15 pleasant in itself. Now life is defined in the case of animals by the power of perception, in that of man by the power of perception or thought; and a power is defined by reference to the corresponding activity, which is the essential thing; therefore life seems to be essentially the act of perceiving or thinking. And life is among the things that are good and pleasant in themselves, since it is deter- 20 minate and the determinate is of the nature of the good; and that which is good by nature is also good for the virtuous man (which is the reason why life seems pleasant to all men); but we must not apply this to a wicked and corrupt life or to a life spent in pain; for

---

[1] 1098a16, b31–1099a7.   [2] 1099a14, 21.   [3] 1099a7–11, 1113a25–33.

such a life is indeterminate, as are its attributes. The nature of pain
25 will become plainer in what follows.[1] But if life itself is good and
pleasant (which it seems to be, from the very fact that all men desire
it, and particularly those who are good and supremely happy; for to
such men life is most desirable, and their existence is the most
supremely happy); and if he who sees perceives that he sees, and he
30 who hears, that he hears, and he who walks, that he walks, and in
the case of all other activities similarly there is something which
perceives that we are active, so that if we perceive, we perceive that
we perceive, and if we think, that we think; and if to perceive that
we perceive or think is to perceive that we exist (for existence was
1170b defined as perceiving or thinking); and if perceiving that one lives
is in itself one of the things that are pleasant (for life is by nature
good, and to perceive what is good present in oneself is pleasant);
and if life is desirable, and particularly so for good men, because to
them existence is good and pleasant (for they are pleased at the
consciousness of the presence in them of what is in itself good); and
5 if as the virtuous man is to himself, he is to his friend also (for his
friend is another self)—if all this be true, as his own being is desirable for each man, so, or almost so, is that of his friend.* Now his
being was seen to be desirable because he perceived his own goodness, and such perception is pleasant in itself. He must, therefore,
10 perceive the existence of his friend together with his own, and this
will be realized in their living together and sharing in discussion
and thought; for this is what living together would seem to mean in
the case of man, and not, as in the case of cattle, feeding in the same
place.*

If, then, being is in itself desirable for the supremely happy man
15 (since it is by its nature good and pleasant), and that of his friend is
very much the same, a friend will be one of the things that are desirable. Now that which is desirable for him he must have, or he will
be deficient in this respect. The man who is to be happy will therefore need virtuous friends.

The limit to the number of friends

20 **10.** Should we, then, make as many friends as possible, or—as
in the case of hospitality it is thought to be suitable advice, that
one should be 'neither a man of many guests nor a man with

[1] X.1–5.

none'*—will that apply to friendship as well; should a man neither be friendless nor have an excessive number of friends?

To friends made with a view to *utility* this saying would seem thoroughly applicable; for to do services to many people in return is a laborious task and life is not long enough for its performance. 25 Therefore friends in excess of those who are sufficient for our own life are superfluous, and hindrances to the noble life; so that we have no need of them. Of friends made with a view to *pleasure*, also, few are enough, as a little seasoning in food is enough.

But as regards *good* friends, should we have as many as possible, or is there a limit to the number of one's friends, as there is to the 30 size of a city? You cannot make a city of ten men, and if there are a hundred thousand it is a city no longer.* But the proper number is presumably not a single number, but anything that falls between certain fixed points. So for friends too there is a fixed number— perhaps the largest number with whom one can live together (for 1171a that, we found,[1] is thought to be very characteristic of friendship); and that one cannot live with many people and divide oneself up among them is plain. Further, they too must be friends of one another, if they are all to spend their days together; and it is a hard business for this condition to be fulfilled with a large number. It is 5 found difficult, too, to rejoice and to grieve in an intimate way with many people, for it may likely happen that one has at once to be happy with one friend and to mourn with another. Presumably, then, it is well not to seek to have as many friends as possible, but as many as are enough for the purpose of living together; for it would seem actually impossible to be a great friend to many people. 10 This is why one cannot love several people; love is ideally a sort of excess of friendship, and that can only be felt towards one person; therefore great friendship too can only be felt towards a few people. This seems to be confirmed in practice; for we do not find many people who are friends in the comradely way of friendship, and the famous friendships of this sort are always between two people. 15 Those who have many friends and mix intimately with them all are thought to be no one's friend, except in the way proper to fellow citizens, and such people are also called obsequious.* In the way proper to fellow citizens, indeed, it is possible to be the friend of many and yet not be obsequious but a genuinely good man; but one

[1] 1157b19, 1158a3, 10.

cannot have with many people the friendship based on virtue and
on the character of our friends themselves, and we must be content
20 if we find even a few such.

Are friends more needed in good or in bad fortune?

11. Do we need friends more in good fortune or in bad? They are
sought after in both; for while men in adversity need help, in prosperity they need people to live with and to make the objects of their
beneficence; for they wish to do well by others. Friendship, then, is
more necessary in bad fortune, and so it is useful friends that one
25 wants in this case; but it is more noble in good fortune, and so we
also seek for good men as our friends, since it is more desirable to
confer benefits on these and to live with these. For the very presence of friends is pleasant both in good fortune and also in bad,
since grief is lightened when friends sorrow with us. Hence one
30 might ask whether they share as it were our burden, or—without
that happening—their presence by its pleasantness, and the thought
of their grieving with us, make our pain less. Whether it is for these
reasons or for some other that our grief is lightened, is a question
that may be dismissed; at all events what we have described appears
to take place.

35   But their presence seems to contain a mixture of various factors.
1171b The very seeing of one's friends is pleasant (especially if one is in
adversity), and becomes a safeguard against grief (for a friend tends
to comfort us both by the sight of him and by his words, if he is
tactful, since he knows our character and the things that please or
pain us); but to see him pained at our misfortunes is painful; for
5 every one shuns being a cause of pain to his friends. For this reason
people of a manly nature guard against making their friends grieve
with them, and, unless he be exceptionally insensible to pain, such
a man cannot stand the pain that ensues for his friends, and in
general does not admit fellow mourners because he is not himself
10 given to mourning; but women and womanly men enjoy sympa-
thizers in their grief, and love them as friends and companions in
sorrow. But in all things one obviously ought to imitate the better
type of person.*

On the other hand, the presence of friends in our *prosperity*
implies both a pleasant passing of our time and the pleasant thought
of their pleasure at our own good fortune. For this cause it would

seem that we ought to summon our friends readily to share our 15
good fortunes (for the beneficent character is a noble one), but summon them to our bad fortunes with hesitation; for we ought to give
them as little a share as possible in our evils—whence the saying
'Enough is *my* misfortune.' We should summon friends to us most
of all when they are likely by suffering a few inconveniences to do
us a great service.

Conversely, it is fitting to go unasked and readily to the aid of 20
those in adversity (for it is characteristic of a friend to render services, and especially to those who are in need and have not demanded
them; such action is nobler and pleasanter for both persons); but
when our friends are prosperous we should join readily in their
activities (for they need friends for these too), but be tardy in coming forward to be the objects of their kindness; for it is not noble to 25
be keen to receive benefits. Still, we must no doubt avoid getting
the reputation of kill-joys by repulsing them; for that sometimes
happens.*

The presence of friends, then, seems desirable in all circumstances.

The essence of friendship is living together

12. Does it not follow, then, that, as for lovers the sight of the
beloved is the thing they love most, and they prefer this sense to the 30
others because on it love depends most for its being and for its
origin, so for friends the most desirable thing is living together? For
friendship is a partnership, and as a man is to himself, so is he to
his friend; now in his own case perceiving his being is desirable, and
so therefore is perceiving his friend's being, and perceiving is active 35
when they live together,* so that it is natural that they aim at this. 1172a
And whatever existence means for each class of men, whatever it is
for whose sake they value life, in *that* they wish to occupy themselves with their friends; and so some drink together, others dice
together, others join in athletic exercises and hunting, or in the study
of philosophy, each class spending their days together in whatever 5
they love most in life; for since they wish to live with their friends,
they do and share in those things which give them the sense of
living together. Thus the friendship of bad men turns out an evil
thing (for because of their instability they unite in bad pursuits, and
besides they become evil by becoming like each other), while the 10

friendship of good men is good, being augmented by their companionship; and they are thought to become better too by their activities and by improving each other; for from each other they take the
mould of the characteristics they approve—whence the saying
'Noble deeds from noble men.'—So much, then, for friendship;
15 our next task must be to discuss pleasure.

BOOK X · PLEASURE, HAPPINESS

PLEASURE

Two opposed views about pleasure

1. AFTER these matters we ought perhaps next to discuss pleasure.*
For it is thought to be most intimately connected with our human 20
nature, which is the reason why in educating the young we steer them
by the rudders of pleasure and pain; it is thought, too, that to enjoy
the things we ought and to hate the things we ought has the greatest
bearing on virtue of character. For these things extend right through
life, with a weight and power of their own in respect both to virtue
and to the happy life, since men choose what is pleasant and avoid 25
what is painful; and such things, it will be thought, we should least
of all omit to discuss, especially since they admit of much dispute.
For some say pleasure is the good,* while others, on the contrary, say
it is thoroughly bad*—some no doubt being persuaded that the facts
are so, and others thinking it has a better effect on our life to exhibit 30
pleasure as a bad thing even if it is not; for most people (they think)
incline towards it and are the slaves of their pleasures, for which
reason they ought to lead them in the opposite direction, since thus
they will reach the middle state. But surely this is not correct. For
arguments about matters concerned with feelings and actions are less 35
reliable than facts: and so when they clash with the facts of perception they are despised, and discredit the truth as well; if a man who 1172b
runs down pleasure is once seen to be aiming at it, his inclining
towards it is thought to imply that it is all worthy of being aimed at;
for most people are not good at drawing distinctions. True arguments seem, then, most useful, not only with a view to knowledge but
with a view to life also; for since they harmonize with the facts they 5
are believed, and so they stimulate those who understand them to live
according to them.—Enough of such questions; let us proceed to
review the opinions that have been expressed about pleasure.

Discussion of the view that pleasure is the good

2. Eudoxus thought pleasure was the good because he saw all things,
both rational and irrational, aiming at it, and because in all things 10

that which is the object of choice is what is excellent, and that which is most the object of choice the greatest good; thus the fact that all things moved towards the same object indicated that this was for all things the chief good (for each thing, he argued, finds its own good, as it finds its own nourishment); and that which is good for all things and at which all aim was *the* good.* His arguments

15 were credited more because of the excellence of his character than for their own sake; he was thought to be remarkably temperate, and therefore it was thought that he was not saying what he did say as a friend of pleasure, but that the facts really were so. He believed that the same conclusion followed no less plainly from a study of the contrary of pleasure: pain was in itself an object of aversion to all things, and therefore its contrary must be similarly an object of

20 choice.* And again, that is most an object of choice which we choose not because or for the sake of something else, and pleasure is admittedly of this nature; for no one asks anyone to what end he is pleased, thus implying that pleasure is in itself an object of choice.* Further, he argued that pleasure when added to any good, e.g. to just or temperate action, makes it more worthy of choice, and

25 that it is only by itself that the good can be increased.

This argument seems to show it to be one of the goods, and no more a good than any other; for every good is more worthy of choice along with another good than taken alone. And so it is by an argument of this kind that Plato proves the good *not* to be pleasure; he argues that the pleasant life is more desirable with wisdom than

30 without, and that if the mixture is better, pleasure is not the good; for the good cannot become more desirable by the addition of anything to it. Now it is clear that nothing else, any more than pleasure, can be the good if it is made more desirable by the addition of any of the things that are good in themselves.* What, then, is there that satisfies this criterion, which at the same time we can participate in? It is something of this sort that we are looking for.

35   Those who object that that at which all things aim is not necessarily good are, we may surmise, talking nonsense. For we say that that which

1173a everyone thinks really is so; and the man who attacks this conviction will hardly have anything more convincing to maintain instead. If it were irrational creatures that desired the things in question, there might be something in what is said; but if intelligent creatures do so as well, how can there be anything in it? But perhaps even in

inferior creatures there is some natural good stronger than them- 5
selves which aims at their proper good.

Nor does the argument about the contrary of pleasure seem to be
correct. They say that if pain is an evil it does not follow that pleasure is a good; for evil is opposed to evil and at the same time both
are opposed to the neutral state—which is correct enough but does
not apply to the things in question. For if both pleasure and pain
belonged to the class of evils they ought both to be objects of aver- 10
sion, while if they belonged to the class of neutrals neither should be
an object of aversion or they should both be equally so; but in fact
people evidently avoid the one as evil and choose the other as good;
that then must be the nature of the opposition between them.*

Discussion of the view that pleasure is wholly bad

3. Nor again, if pleasure is not a quality, does it follow that it is not
a good; for the activities of virtue are not qualities either, nor is 15
happiness.*

They say, however, that the good is determinate, while pleasure
is indeterminate, because it admits of degrees. Now if it is from the
feeling of pleasure that they judge thus, the same will be true of
justice and the other virtues, in respect of which we plainly say that
people of a certain character are so more or less, and act more or less
in accordance with these virtues; for people may be more or less 20
just or brave, and it is possible also to act justly or temperately more
or less. But if their judgement is based on the various pleasures,
surely they are not stating the real cause, if in fact some pleasures
are unmixed and others mixed. Again, just as health admits of
degrees without being indeterminate, why should not pleasure? 25
The same proportion is not found in all things, nor a single proportion always in the same thing, but it may be relaxed and yet persist
up to a point, and it may differ in degree. The case of pleasure also
may therefore be of this kind.*

Again, they assume that the good is complete, while movements
and comings into being are incomplete, and try to exhibit pleasure 30
as being a movement and a coming into being. But they do not seem
to be right even in saying that it is a movement. For speed and
slowness are thought to be proper to every movement, and if a
movement, e.g. that of the heavens, has not speed or slowness in
itself, it has it in relation to something else; but of pleasure neither

of these things is true. For while we may *become* pleased quickly, as
1173b we may become angry quickly, we cannot *be* pleased quickly, not
even in relation to someone else, while we *can* walk, or grow, or the
like, quickly. While, then, we can change quickly or slowly into a
state of pleasure, we cannot quickly exhibit the activity of pleasure,
i.e. be pleased.* Again, how can it be a coming into being? It is not
thought that any chance thing can come out of any chance thing,
5 but that a thing is dissolved into that out of which it comes into
being; and pain would be the destruction of that of which pleasure
is the coming into being.

They say, too, that pain is the lack of that which is according to
nature, and pleasure is replenishment. But these experiences are
bodily. If then pleasure is replenishment with that which is accord-
10 ing to nature, that which feels pleasure will be that in which the
replenishment takes place, i.e. the body;* but that is not thought to
be the case; therefore the replenishment is not pleasure, though one
would be pleased when replenishment was taking place, just as one
would be pained if one was being operated on.* This opinion seems
to be based on the pains and pleasures connected with nutrition: on
the fact that when people have been short of food and have felt pain
15 beforehand they are pleased by the replenishment. But this does
not happen with all pleasures; for the pleasures of learning and,
among the sensuous pleasures, those of smell, and also many
sounds and sights, and memories and hopes, do not presuppose
pain. Of what then will these be the coming into being? There has
20 not been lack of anything of which they could be the supplying
anew.*

In reply to those who bring forward the disgraceful pleasures
one may say that these are not pleasant; if things are pleasant to
people of vicious constitution, we must not suppose that they are
also pleasant to others than these, just as we do not reason so about
the things that are wholesome or sweet or bitter to sick people, or
25 ascribe whiteness to the things that seem white to those suffering
from a disease of the eye. Or one might answer thus—that the pleasures are desirable, but not from *these* sources, as wealth is desirable,
but not as the reward of betrayal, and health, but not at the cost of
eating anything and everything. Or perhaps pleasures differ in
kind; for those derived from noble sources are different from those
derived from base sources, and one cannot get the pleasure of the

just man without being just, nor that of the musical man without 30
being musical, and so on.*

The fact, too, that a friend is different from a flatterer seems to
make it plain that pleasure is not a good, or that pleasures are different in kind; for the one is thought to consort with us with a view to
the good, the other with a view to our pleasure, and the one is
reproached for his conduct while the other is praised on the ground
that he consorts with us for different ends. And no one would choose 1174a
to live with the intellect of a child throughout his life, however
much he were to be pleased at the things that children are pleased
at, nor to get enjoyment by doing some most disgraceful deed, though
he were never to feel any pain in consequence.* And there are many
things we should be keen about even if they brought no pleasure, 5
e.g. seeing, remembering, knowing, possessing the virtues. If pleasures necessarily do accompany these, that makes no odds; we should
choose these even if no pleasure resulted. It seems to be clear, then,
that neither is pleasure the good nor is all pleasure desirable, and
that some pleasures *are* desirable in themselves, differing in kind or 10
in their sources from the others. So much for the things that are
said about pleasure and pain.

Definition of pleasure

4. What pleasure is, or what kind of thing it is, will become plainer
if we take up the question again from the beginning. Seeing seems
to be at any moment complete, for it does not lack anything whose 15
coming into being later will complete its form; and pleasure also
seems to be of this nature.* For it is a whole, and at no time can one
find a pleasure whose form will be completed if the pleasure lasts
longer. For this reason, too, it is not a movement. For every movement (e.g. that of building) takes time and is for the sake of an end, 20
and is complete when it has made what it aims at. It is complete,
therefore, only in the whole time or at that final moment. In their
parts and during the time they occupy, all movements are incomplete, and are different in kind from the whole movement and from
each other. For the fitting together of the stones is different from
the fluting of the column, and these are both different from the
making of the temple; and the making of the temple is complete (for 25
it lacks nothing with a view to the end proposed), but the making
of the base or of the triglyph is incomplete; for each is the making

of only a part. They differ in kind, then, and it is not possible to find
at any and every time a movement complete in form, but if at all,
only in the whole time. So, too, in the case of walking and all other
30 movements. For if locomotion is a movement from here to there, it,
too, has differences in kind—flying, walking, leaping, and so on.
And not only so, but in walking itself there are such differences; for
the whence and whither are not the same in the whole racecourse
and in a part of it, nor in one part and in another, nor is it the same
1174b thing to traverse this line and that; for one traverses not only a line
but one which is in a place, and this one is in a different place from
that. We have discussed movement with precision in another
work,[1] but it seems that it is not complete at any and every time, but
that the many movements are incomplete and different in kind,
5 since the whence and whither give them their form. But of pleasure
the form is complete at any and every time. Plainly, then, pleasure
and movement must be different from each other, and pleasure
must be one of the things that are whole and complete. This would
seem to be the case, too, from the fact that it is not possible to move
otherwise than in time, but it *is* possible to be pleased; for that
which takes place in an instant is a whole.*

From these considerations it is clear, too, that these thinkers are
10 not right in saying there is a movement or a coming into being *of*
pleasure.* For these cannot be ascribed to all things, but only to
those that are divisible and not wholes; there is no coming into
being of seeing* nor of a point nor of a unit, nor is any of these a
movement or coming into being; therefore there is no movement or
coming into being of pleasure either; for it is a whole.

Since every sense is active in relation to its object, and a sense
15 which is in good condition acts perfectly in relation to the most
beautiful of its objects (for perfect activity seems to be ideally of
this nature; whether we say that *it* is active, or the organ in which
it resides, may be assumed to be immaterial), it follows that in the
case of each sense the best activity is that of the best-conditioned
organ in relation to the finest of its objects. And this activity will be
20 the most complete and pleasant. For, while there is pleasure in
respect of any sense, and in respect of thought and contemplation no
less, the most complete is pleasant, and that of a well-conditioned
organ in relation to the worthiest of its objects is the most complete;

[1] *Phys.* vi–viii.

and the pleasure completes the activity.* But the pleasure does not complete it in the same way as the combination of object and sense, 25 both good, just as health and the doctor are not in the same way the cause of a man's being healthy.* (That pleasure is produced in respect to each sense is plain; for we speak of sights and sounds as pleasant. It is also plain that it arises most of all when both the sense is at its best and it is active in reference to an object which corresponds; when both object and perceiver are of the best there will 30 always be pleasure, since the requisite agent and patient are both present.) Pleasure completes the activity not as the corresponding permanent state does, by its immanence, but as an end which supervenes as the bloom of youth does on those in the flower of their age.* So long, then, as both the intelligible or sensible object and the discriminating or contemplative faculty are as they should be, the pleasure will be involved in the activity; for when both the 1175a passive and the active factor are unchanged and are related to each other in the same way, the same result naturally follows.

How, then, is it that no one is continuously pleased? Is it that we grow weary? Certainly all human things are incapable of continuous activity. Therefore pleasure also is not continuous; for it accompan- 5 ies activity. Some things delight us when they are new, but later do so less, for the same reason; for at first the mind is in a state of stimulation and intensely active about them, as people are with respect to their vision when they look hard at a thing, but afterwards our activity is not of this kind, but has grown relaxed; for which reason the pleasure also is dulled. 10

One might think that all men desire pleasure because they all aim at life; life is an activity,* and each man is active about those things and with those faculties that he loves most; e.g. the musician is active with his hearing in reference to tunes, the student with his mind in reference to theoretical questions, and so on in each case; now pleasure completes the activities, and therefore life, which they desire. It is with good reason, then, that they aim at pleasure too, since for everyone it completes life, which is desirable. But 15 whether we choose life for the sake of pleasure or pleasure for the sake of life is a question we may dismiss for the present. For they seem to be bound up together and not to admit of separation, since without activity pleasure does not arise, and every activity is com- 20 pleted by the attendant pleasure.

Pleasures differ with the activities which they accompany and
complete: criterion of the value of pleasures

5. For this reason pleasures seem, too, to differ in kind. For things
different in kind are, we think, completed by different things (we
see this to be true both of natural objects and of things produced by
25 art, e.g. animals, trees, a painting, a sculpture, a house, an imple-
ment); and, similarly, we think that activities differing in kind are
completed by things differing in kind. Now the activities of thought
differ from those of the senses, and both differ among themselves,
in kind; so, therefore, do the pleasures that complete them.

This may be seen, too, from the fact that each of the pleasures
30 is bound up with the activity it completes. For an activity is inten-
sified by its proper pleasure, since each class of things is better
judged of and brought to precision by those who engage in the
activity with pleasure; e.g. it is those who enjoy geometrical thinking that become geometers and grasp the various propositions better, and, similarly, those who are fond of music or of building, and
35 so on, make progress in their proper function by enjoying it; so the
pleasures intensify the activities, and what intensifies a thing is
1175b proper to it, but things different in kind have properties different in
kind.

This will be even more apparent from the fact that activities are
hindered by pleasures arising from other sources. For people who
are fond of playing the flute are incapable of attending to arguments
if they overhear someone playing the flute, since they enjoy flute-
5 playing more than the activity in hand; so the pleasure connected
with flute-playing destroys the activity concerned with argument.
This happens, similarly, in all other cases, when one is active about
two things at once; the more pleasant activity drives out the other,
and if it is much more pleasant does so all the more, so that one
10 even ceases from the other. This is why when we enjoy anything
very much we do not throw ourselves into anything else, and do one
thing only when we are not much pleased by another; e.g. in the
theatre the people who eat sweets do so most when the actors are
poor. Now since activities are made precise and more enduring and
15 better by their proper pleasure, and injured by alien pleasures,
evidently the two kinds of pleasure are far apart. For alien pleasures
do pretty much what proper pains do, since activities are destroyed

by their proper pains; e.g. if a man finds writing or doing sums
unpleasant and painful, he does not write, or does not do sums,
because the activity is painful. So an activity suffers contrary effects 20
from its proper pleasures and pains, i.e. from those that supervene
on it in virtue of its own nature. And alien pleasures have been
stated to do much the same as pain; they destroy the activity, only
not to the same degree.

Now since activities differ in respect of goodness and badness,
and some are worthy to be chosen, others to be avoided, and others 25
neutral, so, too, are the pleasures; for to each activity there is a
proper pleasure. The pleasure proper to a worthy activity is good
and that proper to an unworthy activity bad; just as the appetites
for noble objects are laudable, those for base objects culpable. But
the pleasures involved in activities are more proper to them than 30
the desires; for the latter are separated both in time and in nature,
while the former are close to the activities, and so hard to distinguish from them that it admits of dispute whether the activity is not
the same as the pleasure. (Still, pleasure does not seem to *be* thought
or perception—that would be strange; but because they are not
found apart they appear to some people the same.*) As activities are 35
different, then, so are the corresponding pleasures. Now sight is
superior to touch in purity, and hearing and smell to taste; the 1176a
pleasures, therefore, are similarly superior, and those of thought superior to these,* and within each of the two kinds some are superior
to others.

Each animal is thought to have a proper pleasure, as it has a
proper function; namely, that which corresponds to its activity. If
we survey then species by species, too, this will be evident; horse, 5
dog, and man have different pleasures, as Heraclitus says 'asses
would prefer sweepings to gold'; for food is pleasanter than gold to
asses. So the pleasures of creatures different in kind differ in kind,
and it is plausible to suppose that those of a single species do not
differ. But they vary to no small extent, in the case of men at least; 10
the same things delight some people and pain others, and are painful
and odious to some, and pleasant to and liked by others. This happens, too, in the case of sweet things; the same things do not seem
sweet to a man in a fever and a healthy man—nor hot to a weak man
and one in good condition. The same happens in other cases. But 15
in all such matters that which appears to the good man is thought

to be really so. If this is correct, as it seems to be, and virtue and the good man as such are the measure of each thing,* those also will be pleasures which appear so to him, and those things pleasant which
20 he enjoys. If the things he finds tiresome seem pleasant to someone, that is nothing surprising; for men may be ruined and spoilt in many ways; but the things are not pleasant, but only pleasant to these people and to people in this condition.* Those which are admittedly disgraceful plainly should not be said to be pleasures, except to a perverted taste; but of those that are thought to be good what kind of pleasure or what pleasure should be said to be that proper to man?
25 Is it not plain from the corresponding activities? The pleasures follow these. Whether, then, the perfect and supremely happy man has one or more activities, the pleasures that perfect these will be said in the strict sense to be pleasures proper to man, and the rest will be so in a secondary or even more remote way, as are the activities.

HAPPINESS

Happiness is good activity, not amusement

30 6. Now that we have spoken of the virtues, the forms of friendship, and the varieties of pleasure, what remains is to discuss in outline the nature of happiness, since this is what we state the end of human affairs to be. Our discussion will be the more concise if we first sum up what we have said already. We said,[1] then, that it is not a state; for if it were it might belong to someone who was asleep throughout his life, living the life of a plant, or, again, to someone who was suffering
35 the greatest misfortunes. If these implications are unacceptable, and
1176b we must rather class happiness as an activity, as we have said before,[2] and if some activities are necessary, and desirable for the sake of something else, while others are so in themselves, evidently happiness must be placed among those desirable in themselves, not among those desirable for the sake of something else; for happiness does
5 not lack anything, but is self-sufficient.* Now those activities are desirable in themselves from which nothing is sought beyond the activity. And of this nature virtuous actions are thought to be; for to do noble and good deeds is a thing desirable for its own sake.

Pleasant amusements also are thought to be of this nature: we
10 choose them not for the sake of other things; for we are injured

---

[1] 1095b31–1096a2, 1098b31–1099a7.   [2] 1098a5–7.

rather than benefited by them, since we are led to neglect our bodies and our property. But most of the people who are deemed happy take refuge in such pastimes, which is the reason why those who are ready-witted at them are highly esteemed at the courts of tyrants; they make themselves pleasant companions in the tyrants' favourite pursuits, and that is the sort of man they want. Now these things 15 are thought to be of the nature of happiness because people in despotic positions spend their leisure in them, but perhaps such people prove nothing; for virtue and reason, from which good activities flow, do not depend on despotic position; nor, if these people, who have never tasted pure and generous pleasure, take refuge in the 20 bodily pleasures, should these for that reason be thought more desirable; for boys, too, think the things that are valued among themselves are the best. It is to be expected, then, that, as different things seem valuable to boys and to men, so they should to bad men and to good. Now, as we have often maintained,[1] those things are both valuable and pleasant which are such to the good man; and to 25 each man the activity in accordance with his own state is most desirable, and therefore to the good man that which is in accordance with virtue. Happiness, therefore, does not lie in amusement; it would, indeed, be strange if the end were amusement, and one were to take trouble and suffer hardship all one's life in order to amuse oneself. For, in a word, everything that we choose we choose 30 for the sake of something else—except happiness, which is an end. Now to exert oneself and work for the sake of amusement seems silly and utterly childish. But to amuse oneself in order that one may exert oneself, as Anacharsis puts it, seems right; for amusement is a sort of relaxation, and we need relaxation because we 35 cannot work continuously. Relaxation, then, is not an end; for it is taken for the sake of activity.*

The happy life is thought to be virtuous; now a virtuous life 1177a requires exertion, and does not consist in amusement. And we say that serious things are better than laughable things and those connected with amusement, and that the activity of the better of any two things—whether it be two elements of our being or two men—is 5 the more serious;* but the activity of the better is *ipso facto* superior and more of the nature of happiness. And any chance person—even a slave—can enjoy the bodily pleasures no less than the best man;

[1] 1099a13, 1113a22–33, 1166a12, 1170a14–16, 1176a15–22.

but no one assigns to a slave a share in happiness—unless he assigns to him also a share in human life.* For happiness does not
10 lie in such occupations, but, as we have said before,[1] in virtuous activities.

The contemplative life is the happiest

7. If happiness is activity in accordance with virtue, it is reasonable that it should be in accordance with the highest virtue; and this will be that of the best thing in us. Whether it be reason or something else that is this element which is thought to be our natural ruler and
15 guide and to take thought of things noble and divine, whether it be itself also divine or only the most divine element in us, the activity of this in accordance with its proper virtue will be perfect happiness. That this activity is contemplative we have already said.*

Now this would seem to be in agreement both with what we said before[2] and with the truth. For, firstly, this activity is the best (since
20 not only is reason the best thing in us, but the objects of reason are the best of knowable objects*); and, secondly, it is the most continuous, since we can contemplate truth more continuously than we can *do* anything. And we think happiness ought to have pleasure mingled with it, but the activity of philosophic wisdom is admittedly the pleasantest of virtuous activities; at all events the pursuit
25 of it is thought to offer pleasures marvellous for their purity and their enduringness, and it is to be expected that those who know will pass their time more pleasantly than those who inquire.* And the self-sufficiency that is spoken of must belong most to the contemplative activity. For while a philosopher, as well as a just man or one possessing any other virtue, needs the necessaries of life, when they are sufficiently equipped with things of that sort the just
30 man needs people towards whom and with whom he shall act justly, and the temperate man, the brave man, and each of the others is in the same case, but the philosopher, even when by himself, can contemplate truth, and the better the wiser he is; he can perhaps do so better if he has fellow workers, but still he is the most self-sufficient.*
1177b And this activity alone would seem to be loved for its own sake; for nothing arises from it apart from the contemplating, while from practical activities we gain more or less apart from the action. And

[1] 1098a16, 1176a35–b9.
[2] 1097a25–b21, 1099a7–21, 1173b15–19, 1174b20–3, 1175b36–1176a3.

happiness is thought to depend on leisure; for we are busy that we may have leisure, and make war that we may live in peace. Now the 5 activity of the practical virtues is exhibited in political or military affairs, but the actions concerned with these seem to be unleisurely. Warlike actions are completely so (for no one chooses to be at war, or provokes war, for the sake of being at war; anyone would seem absolutely murderous if he were to make enemies of his friends in 10 order to bring about battle and slaughter); but the action of the statesman also is unleisurely, and aims—beyond the political action itself—at despotic power and honours, or at all events happiness, for him and his fellow citizens—a happiness different from political 15 action, and evidently sought as being different. So if among virtuous actions political and military actions are distinguished by nobility and greatness, and these are unleisurely and aim at an end and are not desirable for their own sake,* but the activity of reason, which is contemplative, seems both to be superior in serious worth and to aim at no end beyond itself, and to have its pleasure proper 20 to itself (and this augments the activity), and the self-sufficiency, leisureliness, unweariedness (so far as this is possible for man), and all the other attributes ascribed to the supremely happy man are evidently those connected with this activity, it follows that this will be the complete happiness of man, if it be allowed a complete term 25 of life (for none of the attributes of happiness is incomplete).

But such a life would be too high for man; for it is not in so far as he is man that he will live so, but in so far as something divine is present in him; and by so much as this is superior to our composite nature* is its activity superior to that which is the exercise of the other kind of virtue. If reason is divine, then, in comparison with 30 man, the life according to it is divine in comparison with human life. But we must not follow those who advise us, being men, to think of human things, and, being mortal, of mortal things, but must, so far as we can, make ourselves immortal, and strain every nerve to live in accordance with the best thing in us; for even if it be small in bulk, much more does it in power and worth surpass 1178a everything. And this would seem actually to *be* each man, since it is the authoritative and better part of him.* It would be strange, then, if he were to choose not the life of himself but that of something else. And what we said before[1] will apply now: that which is proper 5

[1] 1169b33, 1176b26.

to each thing is by nature best and most pleasant for each thing; for
man, therefore, the life according to reason is best and pleasantest,
since reason more than anything else *is* man. This life therefore is
also the happiest.

Superiority of the contemplative life further considered

8. But in a secondary degree the life in accordance with the other
10 kind of virtue is happy;* for the activities in accordance with this
befit our human estate. Just and brave acts, and other virtuous acts,
we do in relation to each other, observing what's appropriate to
each person with regard to contracts and services and all manner of
actions and with regard to passions; and all of these seem to be
typically human. Some of them seem even to arise from the body,
15 and virtue of character to be in many ways bound up with the passions. Practical wisdom, too, is linked to virtue of character, and
this to practical wisdom, since the principles of practical wisdom
are in accordance with the moral virtues and rightness in morals
is in accordance with practical wisdom. Being connected with the
passions also, the moral virtues must belong to our composite
20 nature; and the virtues of our composite nature are human;* so,
therefore, are the life and the happiness which correspond to these.
The excellence of the reason is a thing apart:* we must be content
to say this much about it, for to describe it precisely is a task greater
than our purpose requires. It would seem, however, also to need
external equipment but little, or less than moral virtue does. Grant
25 that both need the necessaries, and do so equally, even if the statesman's work is the more concerned with the body and things of that
sort; for there will be little difference there; but in what they need
for the exercise of their activities there will be much difference. The
liberal man will need money for the doing of his liberal deeds, and
30 the just man too will need it for the returning of services (for wishes
are hard to discern, and even people who are not just *pretend* to wish
to act justly); and the brave man will need power if he is to accom-
plish any of the acts that correspond to his virtue, and the temperate man will need opportunity;* for how else is either he or any of
the others to be recognized? It is debated, too, whether the will or
35 the deed is more essential to virtue, which is assumed to involve
1178b both; it is surely clear that its perfection involves both; but for
deeds many things are needed, and more, the greater and nobler the

deeds are. But the man who is contemplating the truth needs no
such thing, at least with a view to the exercise of his activity; indeed
they are, one may say, even hindrances, at all events to his contemplation; but in so far as he is a man and lives with a number of 5
people, he chooses to do virtuous acts; he will therefore need such
aids to living a human life.*

But that perfect happiness is a contemplative activity will appear
from the following consideration as well. We assume the gods to be
above all other beings blessed and happy; but what sort of actions 10
must we assign to them? Acts of justice? Will not the gods seem
absurd if they make contracts and return deposits, and so on? Acts
of a brave man, then, confronting dangers and running risks because
it is noble to do so? Or liberal acts? To whom will they give? It will
be strange if they are really to have money or anything of the kind. 15
And what would their temperate acts be? Is not such praise tasteless, since they have no bad appetites? If we were to run through
them all, the circumstances of action would be found trivial and
unworthy of gods.* Still, everyone supposes that they *live* and
therefore that they are active; we cannot suppose them to sleep like
Endymion. Now if you take away from a living being action, and 20
still more production, what is left but contemplation? Therefore
the activity of god, which surpasses all others in blessedness, must
be contemplative;* and of human activities, therefore, that which is
most akin to this must be most of the nature of happiness.

This is indicated, too, by the fact that the other animals have no
share in happiness, being completely deprived of such activity. For 25
while the whole life of the gods is blessed, and that of men too in so
far as some likeness of such activity belongs to them, none of the
other animals is happy, since they in no way share in contemplation.* Happiness extends, then, just so far as contemplation does,
and those to whom contemplation more fully belongs are more
truly happy, not as a mere concomitant but in virtue of the contem- 30
plation; for this is in itself precious. Happiness, therefore, must be
some form of contemplation.

But, being a man, one will also need external prosperity; for our
nature is not self-sufficient for the purpose of contemplation, but
our body also must be healthy and must have food and other atten- 35
tion. Still, we must not think that the man who is to be happy will 1179a
need many things or great things, merely because he cannot be

supremely happy without external goods; for self-sufficiency and
action do not involve excess, and we can do noble acts without
5 ruling earth and sea; for even with moderate advantages one can act
virtuously (this is manifest enough; for private persons are thought
to do worthy acts no less than despots—indeed even more); and it
is enough that we should have so much as that; for the life of the
man who is active in accordance with virtue will be happy. Solon,
10 too, was perhaps sketching well the happy man when he described
him as moderately furnished with externals but as having done (as
Solon thought) the noblest acts, and lived temperately; for one can
with but moderate possessions do what one ought.* Anaxagoras
also seems to have supposed the happy man not to be rich nor a
15 despot, when he said that he would not be surprised if the happy
man were to seem to most people a strange person; for they judge
by externals, since these are all they perceive. The opinions of the
wise seem, then, to harmonize with our arguments. But while even
such things carry some conviction, the truth in practical matters is
discerned from the facts of life; for these are the decisive factor. We
20 must therefore survey what we have already said, bringing it to the
test of the facts of life, and if it harmonizes with the facts we must
accept it, but if it clashes with them we must suppose it to be mere
theory. Now he who exercises his reason and cultivates it seems to
be both in the best state of mind and most dear to the gods. For if
25 the gods have any care for human affairs, as they are thought to
have, it would be reasonable both that they should delight in that
which was best and most akin to them (i.e. reason) and that they
should reward those who love and honour this most,* as caring for
the things that are dear to them and acting both rightly and nobly.
30 And that all these attributes belong most of all to the wise man is
manifest. He, therefore, is the dearest to the gods. And he who is
that will presumably be also the happiest; so that in this way too the
wise man will more than any other be happy.*

*Legislation is needed if the end is to be attained: transition to the
   Politics*

9. If these matters and the virtues, and also friendship and pleasure, have been dealt with sufficiently in outline, are we to suppose
35 that our programme has reached its end? Surely, as the saying goes,
where there are things to be done the end is not to survey and

recognize the various things, but rather to do them; with regard 1179b
to virtue, then, it is not enough to know, but we must try to have
and use it, or try any other way there may be of becoming good.
Now if arguments were in themselves enough to make men good, 5
they would justly, as Theognis says, have won very great rewards,
and such rewards should have been provided; but as things are,
while they seem to have power to encourage and stimulate the
generous-minded among our youth, and to make a character which
is gently born, and a true lover of what is noble, ready to be possessed by virtue, they are not able to encourage the *many* to nobility 10
and goodness. For these do not by nature obey the sense of shame,
but only fear, and do not abstain from bad acts because of their
baseness but through fear of punishment; living by passion they
pursue their own pleasures and the means to them, and avoid the
opposite pains, and have not even a conception of what is noble and
truly pleasant, since they have never tasted it. What argument 15
would remould such people? It is hard, if not impossible, to remove
by argument the traits that have long since been incorporated in the
character; and perhaps we must be content if, when all the influences by which we are thought to become good are present, we get
some tincture of virtue.

Now some think that we are made good by nature, others by 20
habituation, others by teaching.* Nature's part evidently does not
depend on us, but as a result of some divine causes is present in
those who are truly fortunate; while argument and teaching, we
may suspect, are not powerful with all men, but the soul of the
student must first have been cultivated by means of habits for noble 25
joy and noble hatred, like earth which is to nourish the seed. For he
who lives as passion directs will not hear argument that dissuades
him, nor understand it if he does; and how can we persuade one in
such a state to change his ways? And in general passion seems to
yield not to argument but to force. The character, then, must somehow be there already with a kinship to virtue, loving what is noble 30
and hating what is base.

But it is difficult to get from youth up a right training for virtue
if one has not been brought up under right laws; for to live temperately and hardily is not pleasant to most people, especially when
they are young. For this reason their nurture and occupations
should be fixed by law; for they will not be painful when they have 35

1180a become customary. But it is surely not enough that when they are
young they should get the right nurture and attention: since they
must, even when they are grown up, practise and be habituated
to them, we shall need laws for this as well, and generally speaking
to cover the whole of life; for most people obey necessity rather
5 than argument, and punishments rather than the sense of what is
noble.

This is why some think that legislators ought to stimulate men to
virtue and urge them forward by the motive of the noble, on the
assumption that those who have been well advanced by the forma-
tion of habits will attend to such influences; and that punishments
and penalties should be imposed on those who disobey and are of
inferior nature, while the incurably bad should be completely ban-
10 ished. A good man (they think), since he lives with his mind fixed
on what is noble, will submit to argument, while a bad man, whose
desire is for pleasure, is corrected by pain like a beast of burden.
This is, too, why they say the pains inflicted should be those that
are most opposed to the pleasures such men love.

However that may be, if (as we have said)[1] the man who is to be
15 good must be well trained and habituated, and go on to spend his
time in worthy occupations and neither willingly nor unwillingly
do bad actions, and if this can be brought about if men live in accordance with a sort of reason and right order, provided this has force—
if this be so, the paternal command indeed has not the required
force or compulsive power (nor in general has the command of one
20 man, unless he be a king or something similar*), but the law *has* compulsive power, while it is at the same time a rule proceeding from a
sort of practical wisdom and reason. And while people hate *men*
who oppose their impulses, even if they oppose them rightly, the
law in its ordaining of what is good is not burdensome.

25   In the Spartan state alone, or almost alone, the legislator seems
to have paid attention to questions of nurture and occupation; in
most states such matters have been neglected, and each man lives
as he pleases, Cyclops-fashion, 'to his own wife and children dealing
30 law'.[2] Now it is best that there should be a public and proper care
for such matters; but if they are neglected by the community it would
seem right for each man to help his children and friends towards

---

[1] 1179b31–1180a5.   [2] *Odyssey* ix.114–15.

virtue, and that they should have the power, or at least the will, to
do this.

It would seem from what has been said that he can do this better
if he makes himself capable of legislating. For public control is
plainly effected by laws, and good control by good laws; whether 35
written or unwritten would seem to make no difference, nor whether 1180b
they are laws providing for the education of individuals or of
groups—any more than it does in the case of music or gymnastics
and other such pursuits. For as in cities laws and prevailing types
of character have force, so in households do the injunctions and the
habits of the father, and these have even more because of the tie of 5
blood and the benefits he confers; for the children start with a
natural affection and disposition to obey. Further, individual education has an advantage over communal, as individual medical treatment has; for while in general rest and abstinence from food are
good for a man in a fever, for a particular man they may not be; and
a boxer presumably does not prescribe the same style of fighting to 10
all his pupils. It would seem, then, that the detail is worked out
with more precision if the oversight is on an individual basis; for
each person is more likely to get what suits his case.*

But the details can be best looked after, one by one, by a doctor
or gymnastic instructor or anyone else who has the general knowledge of what is good for everyone or for people of a certain kind (for
the sciences both are said to be, and are, concerned with what is 15
universal); not but what some particular detail may perhaps be well
looked after by an unscientific person, if he has studied accurately
in the light of experience what happens in each case, just as some
people seem to be their own best doctors, though they could give
no help to anyone else. None the less, it will perhaps be agreed that 20
if a man does wish to become master of an art or science he must go
to the universal, and come to know it as well as possible; for, as we
have said, it is with this that the sciences are concerned.*

And surely he who wants to make men, whether many or few,
better by his care must try to become capable of legislating, if it is
through laws that we can become good. For to get anyone what- 25
ever—anyone who is put before us—into the right condition is not
for the first chance comer; if anyone can do it, it is the man who
knows, just as in medicine and all other matters which give scope
for care and prudence.

Must we not, then, next examine whence or how one can learn
30 how to legislate? Is it, as in all other cases, from statesmen? Certainly
it was thought to be a part of statesmanship.[1] Or is a difference
apparent between statesmanship and the other sciences and arts? In
the others the same people are found offering to teach the arts and
35 practising them, e.g. doctors or painters; but while the sophists
1181a profess to teach politics, it is practised not by any of them but by
the politicians, who would seem to do so by dint of a certain skill
and experience rather than of thought; for they are not found either
writing or speaking about such matters (though it were a nobler
occupation perhaps than composing speeches for the law-courts
5 and the assembly), nor again are they found to have made statesmen
of their own sons or any other of their friends. But it was to be
expected that they should if they could; for there is nothing better
than such a skill that they could have left to their cities, or could
prefer to have for themselves, or, therefore, for those dearest to
10 them. Still, experience seems to contribute not a little; else they
could not have become politicians by familiarity with politics; and
so it seems that those who aim at knowing about the art of politics
need experience as well.*

But those of the sophists who profess the art seem to be very far
from teaching it. For, to put the matter generally, they do not even
know what kind of thing it is nor what kinds of things it is about;
15 otherwise they would not have classed it as identical with rhetoric
or even inferior to it, nor have thought it easy to legislate by collecting the laws that are thought well of;* they say it is possible to select
the best laws, as though even the selection did not demand intelligence and as though right judgement were not the greatest thing,
as in matters of music. For while people experienced in any department judge rightly the works produced in it, and understand by
20 what means or how they are achieved, and what harmonizes with
what, the inexperienced must be content if they do not fail to see
whether the work has been well or ill made—as in the case of painting. Now laws are as it were the 'works' of the political art; how
1181b then can one learn from them to be a legislator, or judge which are
best? Even medical men do not seem to be made by a study of text-
books. Yet people try, at any rate, to state not only the treatments,
but also how particular classes of people can be cured and should

---

[1] 1141b24.

be treated—distinguishing the various habits of body; but while this seems useful to experienced people, to the inexperienced it is 5 valueless. Surely, then, while collections of laws, and of constitutions also, may be serviceable to those who can study them and judge what is good or bad and what enactments suit what circumstances, those who go through such collections without a practised faculty will not have right judgement (unless it be as a spontaneous 10 gift of nature), though they may perhaps become more intelligent in such matters.*

Now our predecessors have left the subject of legislation to us unexamined; it is perhaps best, therefore, that we should ourselves study it, and in general study the question of the constitution, in order to complete to the best of our ability the philosophy of human 15 nature. First, then, if anything has been said well in detail by earlier thinkers, let us try to review it; then in the light of the constitutions we have collected let us study what sorts of influence preserve and destroy states, and what sorts preserve or destroy the particular kinds of constitution, and to what causes it is due that some are well and others ill administered. When these matters have been studied 20 we shall perhaps be more likely to see with a comprehensive view which constitution is best, and how each must be ordered, and what laws and customs it must use, if it is to be at its best.* Let us make a beginning of our discussion.

EXPLANATORY NOTES

BOOK I

CHAPTER 1

1094a *at which all things aim*: in X.2 Aristotle reports that Eudoxus argued that pleasure is the good, from the fact that everything pursues it. Aristotle agrees that something sought by all things must be good (even if not necessarily *the* good). Neither thinker was offering a *definition* of good as 'what everything aims at'.

BOOK I, CHAPTER 2

this must be the good and the chief good: in ch. 1 Aristotle introduced the idea that good is related to choices, ends and aims, and the idea of a hierarchy of ends. Here he moves to the idea of a single end for the sake of which all else is chosen, and seems to use a fallacious argument. If desires are not to be 'empty and vain' then at least some things must be desired for themselves, but it does not follow that all chains of desires must terminate in a single end.

And politics appears to be of this nature: by politics is meant political science. As X.9 makes clear, Aristotle regards Ethics as a branch of Politics, which is superior to Ethics, in so far as it studies the good of human beings on a larger canvas, that is, in their political setting, the Greek city-state or polis.

BOOK I, CHAPTER 3

1094b *only by convention, and not by nature*: the variety he has in mind is probably the importance of circumstance. For example, paying a debt is usually but not invariably the just thing to do. Aristotle does not endorse the suggestion that what's noble and just exists only by convention and not by nature. Rather, he points out that it is common (though erroneous, as V.7 shows) to infer from the truth that they exhibit variety to their being merely a matter of convention, *nomos*. See Introduction, p. xxii–xxiii.

1095a *a young man is not a proper hearer of lectures on political science*: Aristotle makes clear that his work is intended for those who have been well schooled in proper conduct. Without that, they will lack the crucial starting-points for ethical understanding (I.4).

BOOK I, CHAPTER 4

happiness: see Introduction, p. x for discussion of the notion of *eudaimonia*, translated 'happiness'. It was evidently something of a truism in Greek that *eudaimonia* is the highest good for human beings.

We see how different *eudaimonia* is from happiness (as commonly understood) when Aristotle immediately equates it with living well and faring well.

Now some thought . . . good in itself: I.6 will discuss and reject this view of Plato and his followers, the theory that there is a Form of the good.

1095b *For the fact is a starting-point*: *archē*, literally 'beginning', can mean both starting-point and first principle. In this difficult passage Aristotle is reinforcing the need for a student of ethics to be well brought up so that he will have some 'facts' to start from, i.e. will be aware that that act was cowardly, that this is generous, and so on. A grasp of such facts is enough for proper behaviour, but a student of ethics can use them to understand more deeply the ethical underpinnings of the 'facts' in question, i.e. can proceed to reasons, or to a higher-level knowledge.

BOOK I, CHAPTER 5

three prominent types of life—that just mentioned, the political, and thirdly the contemplative life: by 'the life of enjoyment', Aristotle means sensual enjoyment, which he dismisses as suitable only for beasts (who are incapable of more elevated activities). He does not oppose enjoyment as such. Indeed, he often argues that happiness, the best life, must be accompanied by enjoyment. By 'the political' he means the life of someone active in their community, displaying the 'moral virtues'. In X.6–8 he will conclude that the contemplative life is best, despite lengthy discussion of the moral virtues (II–V) and practical wisdom (much of VI).

Sardanapallus: also known as Asshur-bani-pal, ruler of Assyria in the seventh century BC and legendary for his life of luxury.

even this [i.e. virtue] appears somewhat incomplete: honour, considered in the previous lines, cannot be the supreme good, for it depends not on oneself but on others to bestow it, and they do so in recognition of one's virtue. But virtue is 'incomplete' in so far as it is not the mere *possession* of virtue—which one can have even when asleep—but *its exercise* or *actualization*, which Aristotle will identify with happiness (cf. I.8). Despite here claiming virtue is compatible with lifelong inactivity, Aristotle will later show (II.1–4) that people acquire virtue only by practising the relevant activities.

BOOK I, CHAPTER 6

1096a *the Forms have been introduced by friends of our own*: Aristotle was a pupil at Plato's Academy for many years. His works contain several critiques of Plato's Theory of Forms (also known as the Theory of Ideas), and he wrote a work devoted to a critique of the Theory, called *On Ideas*, fragments of which survive. Plato's *Phaedo* is the best source for the theory, which postulates non-sensible, unchanging entities, known only by the intellect and not by the senses. Thus the Form of the beautiful is said to be the reason why all the many sensible beautiful things are beautiful. In *Republic*, especially Books VI–VII, Plato introduced the Form of the Good, claiming that all other Forms have their being on account of it. In this chapter Aristotle mainly attacks the special claim that there is a Form of the Good, but adds some more general arguments against Forms later in the chapter. We might agree with Aristotle that there is not a single meaning of good, especially since it has at least two uses, one as an attributive adjective—a good F—and one in which we speak of health or knowledge as good.

since 'good' has as many senses as 'being': Aristotle uses his own doctrine of categories (see his *Categories*) to dismiss the possibility of a Form of Good as conceived by Plato. He claims that, since (1) good (like being) is predicated in all the categories, it follows that (2) it cannot be something universally present in all cases. Exactly what he means by (1) is uncertain; for discussion see Ackrill (*Essays on Plato and Aristotle*, ch. 12). The categories are the most basic, and different ways of being; therefore, since good is said of items in all categories, there are fundamentally different ways of being good.

1096b *it will not be good any the more for being eternal . . . perishes in a day*: here Aristotle uses a rather cheap argument against Platonic Forms, supposing that Plato is committed to holding that the unchanging Form of F is more F than changing F things. A more sympathetic account of Plato reads his theory as holding that the Form is F in a different way from the way in which particular Fs are F, since the latter are F by having some relation to the F itself.

Speusippus . . . followed: Speusippus, Plato's nephew, succeeded him as head of the Academy. For the reference to the Pythagorean column of goods, see *Metaphysics* I.5, but the exact point on which Aristotle prefers the Pythagorean account is unclear.

But of honour, wisdom, and pleasure . . . the accounts are distinct and diverse: even if we confine our attention to the meaning of good as said of things good in themselves (and set aside what is instrumentally good) there is still no single meaning of good, claims Aristotle. This may seem to beg the question, but his argument is presumably that any account of the goodness of, say, wisdom, must refer to the nature of wisdom, so it will differ from the account of the goodness of pleasure.

not like the things that only chance to have the same name: Aristotle recognizes that there must be something unifying all meanings of 'good'; he suggests either 'focal meaning' or an analogical account. All good things might be so called because derived from a single focus, in the way that all the various things called healthy are so called by their various connections to health.

something attainable: the question of a transcendent good (which Aristotle has argued against) is dismissed as irrelevant, since (*contra* Plato) it could not help in the discovery of the specific good of human beings, the object of the inquiry in the *Ethics*.

BOOK I, CHAPTER 7

1097a *something final*: final, or 'endlike' (*teleion*), picks up the idea of the good as what is aimed at for itself. Happiness is 'most final' since never pursued for the sake of anything else, while all other things, even those pursued for their own sake, such as pleasure or virtue, may be pursued for the sake of happiness. Elsewhere the term is sometimes translated 'complete'.

1097b *born for citizenship*: can also be translated as 'is a political creature'. Humans by nature flourish only in a *polis*.

and such we think happiness to be: as the previous sentence suggests, self-sufficiency, in its everyday sense, was the ideal of a life or a person who needed no support from others, but rather was able to support a network of family and friends. Homeric heroes displayed this kind of self-sufficiency. But here Aristotle subtly changes its meaning to describe a life lacking in nothing, by which he presumably means, lacking none of the intrinsically valuable goods.

not a thing counted as one good thing among others: an important remark, but variously interpreted. On the likeliest interpretation (cf. Ackrill, 'Aristotle on *Eudaimonia*', in *Essays on Plato and Aristotle*, ch. 11), Aristotle is giving an *inclusive* account of happiness, as, in effect, the sum of intrinsic goods. As such it can't be counted in with first-order goods, and can't be improved by the addition of further goods. Compare X.2, 1172b26. An alternative reading understands Aristotle to be claiming that happiness, identified exclusively with the highest of the intrinsic goods, contemplation, is the most choiceworthy of goods, until other goods are added to it. The earlier account of self-sufficiency tells against the latter interpretation, even if Book X does seem to favour the exclusive reading.

a function apart from all these?: connecting the human good with the human function is a key element, albeit controversial, in Aristotle's inquiry into happiness or the best life. His approach can seem flawed by the analogies he uses of items with functions: craftsmen, and parts of the body. The function of a bodily part such as the eye must be explained by reference to its role in the whole organism of which it is a part, but Aristotle does not locate the human function in the role a person plays in their *polis*, or in any larger whole. Again, Aristotle does not assume that an item with a function has been designed for a purpose, and certainly does not assume this of natural species. The key notion of 'the function of Xs' is 'what Xs ought to do or how they ought to be', as oak trees ought to be sturdy and bear acorns and leaves in summer. Compare P. Foot, *Natural Goodness*.

1098a *possessing reason and exercising thought*: see I.13 for further discussion of the division of the rational part of the soul into that which is obedient to reason (the desiring part) and the part which possesses reason, i.e. reason proper.

'life of the rational element' also has two meanings: Aristotle refers to his important distinction (cf. next chapter) between capacity (*dunamis*) and activity or actuality. A person's knowledge of, say, mathematics may or may not be actualized at a given moment; and the best condition is that in which one actualizes one's various capacities. This prepares us for the (perhaps surprising) identification of happiness with activities (as opposed to mere states or capacities).

human good turns out to be activity of soul exhibiting virtue: it may seem that Aristotle has illicitly imported the idea that to be happy one must be virtuous, that is, that a happy person must have and display the traditional moral virtues. However, though he does hold that, and does not fully justify it (but see IX.4), it is not imported by this definition. Rather, he takes it as a truism that the best human life involves human activities exhibiting virtue (i.e. done in an excellent manner), just as the best canine life will be one of canine activities exhibiting canine virtue, i.e. excellence.

in accordance with the best and most complete: *most complete*, from *teleios*, can also mean 'most final', i.e. an end more than the others are. This is best read as a hint that one activity—that of contemplation—will eventually be singled out as the best (as in Book X). An alternative, suggested by Ackrill (*Essays on Plato and Aristotle*, ch. 11), is that 'most complete' means the virtue that *includes* all the others, in line with the inclusive interpretation of happiness.

BOOK I, CHAPTER 8

1098b *into three classes*: this distinction goes back to Plato's *Euthydemus* 279ab, cf. his *Philebus* 48e, *Laws* 743e.

our account is in harmony: as Aristotle goes on to explain, such a view is near the mark but not correct, since virtues are states, and it is activities manifesting good states, rather than the states themselves, that are best. Compare I.5.

1099a *no one would call a man just who did not enjoy acting justly . . . in all other cases*: one of the most striking features of Aristotle's ethical thinking is this insistence that to count as possessing and manifesting a virtue one must enjoy doing the associated actions (cf. II.3). This is often contrasted with the more dour approach of some versions of Christian morality, and with the views of Kant in the *Groundwork of the Metaphysic of Morals*. By singling out the enjoyment intrinsic to virtuous activity, he can make room, in his account of the highest good, for pleasure as well as virtue. He thus incorporates what is correct in the popular identification of happiness with pleasure, but discards the association with bodily pleasures (which, since they conflict, cannot be true pleasures, as shown a few lines earlier).

1099b *good birth, goodly children, beauty*: while modern readers might not agree with this list of 'external goods' without which a person cannot be happy, most would accept the contention that happiness requires at least some external goods, not under one's control. Later schools of thought, especially Stoicism, held that the virtuous life was sufficient for happiness, thus denying any importance to 'external goods'.

BOOK I, CHAPTER 9

happiness should be god-given: the etymology of Greek term *eudaimonia* (happiness) is, roughly, 'having a good *daimon*', or heavenly protector. But Aristotle's theology (see *Metaphysics* Book XII) does not include gods who bestow good and evil on men, so he will content himself with the designation 'godlike' for happiness, not 'god-given'.

the definition of happiness: since happiness is virtuous activity (notwithstanding some external goods are necessary, though not part of happiness) then it is acquired by whatever means the capacity for virtuous activity is acquired. As II.1 will argue, moral virtues are acquired by habituation, intellectual ones by learning; hence the first two candidates at the beginning of the chapter provide the correct answer.

1100a *Priam in the Trojan Cycle*: Homer's *Iliad* tells of the sack of Troy, of which Priam had been the revered king. Priam became proverbial for one who suffered a great reversal of fortune.

BOOK I, CHAPTER 10

Solon: the Athenian Solon was one of the seven sages; his meeting with King Croesus of Lydia is described by Herodotus. Croesus duly suffered the reversal of fortune of which Solon warned him.

for a dead man, as much as for one who is alive but not aware of them: here Aristotle gives a common view, with an argument for it: if (as generally agreed) *awareness of* evil is not, in one's life, needed for evil to befall one, can evil not also befall a dead person (who is unaware of it)? His exploratory discussion of this issue is resumed in ch. 11.

our first difficulty: that is, the one with which the chapter opened, about the effect of a man's own (mis)fortune on his happiness. Aristotle resumes in ch. 11 the question of whether the fortunes of loved ones after one's death can affect one's happiness.

1101a *he will not reach blessedness, if he meet with fortunes like those of Priam*: Aristotle is not drawing a distinction between 'happy' and 'blessed'. His point is that misfortune may remove happiness from a happy or blessed person (so he is no longer happy), but—if his life is one of virtuous activities—cannot make him miserable (i.e. *un*happy).

Or must we add 'and who is destined to live thus and die as befits his life'?: Aristotle leaves his answer to this crucial question unclear. The chapter as a whole may seem to suggest that he does not think this proviso need be added.

BOOK I, CHAPTER 11

are presupposed in a tragedy or done on the stage: it is a little surprising that Aristotle compares (1) the difference between misfortunes of one's

loved ones affecting one when alive and when dead, with (2) the difference between witnessing terrible events on stage and them being narrated
(perhaps in a messenger speech). Tragic writers tended overwhelm-
ingly to use the device of a character reporting dreadful events, rather
than having them enacted on stage. Alternatively (Irwin) the second
contrast is between events happening during the play, and ones forming
the background to the plot. At all events, we can agree that the misfortunes that befall loved ones affect the happiness of a living person more
than that of a dead person.

1101b *it must be something weak and negligible*: this compromise answer allows
Aristotle to accept a modicum of the popular view that post-mortem
events can affect a person's happiness, while insisting on his own view
that any such influence stops short of allowing a post-mortem change
from happy to not happy, or vice versa. The role of post-mortem misfortune, like that of misfortune in one's life (ch. 10), is neither totally
denied nor given more than minimal scope.

BOOK I, CHAPTER 12

among the things that are praised or rather among the things that are prized:
alternatives to 'prized' are 'honoured' or 'revered'. By distinguishing
the things we praise (chiefly virtues) from the things we prize or revere
(chiefly happiness, but also the gods—see below—and pleasure)
Aristotle again underlines the supremacy of happiness as an end.

it seems absurd that the gods should be measured by our standard: compare
X.8, where Aristotle says it is absurd to ascribe morally virtuous acts to
the gods. In contrast to devotional practices of praising god, Aristotle
holds that such practice is absurd, since it wrongly compares gods to
human beings in respect of virtue.

Eudoxus: an important mathematical thinker, born around 390 BC. See X.2
for Aristotle's discussion of his view on pleasure. Though Aristotle will
disagree with the view that pleasure is *the* good, he here accepts Eudoxus'
argument that the best things are above praise (but instead are prized).

1102a *for it is for the sake of this [i.e. happiness] that we all do everything else*: an
important and surprising claim. Important in that it shows that, in a
sense, Aristotle holds that there is—in name at least—a single end of
everything that we do (cf. beginning of I.2). Surprising, since he accepts
that when acting incontinently one does a different action from what
one thinks is the best action available; hence the incontinent at least are
not, at those moments, acting for the sake of happiness. Perhaps this
claim should be taken to cover only actions done as choices (see III.2–3),
not all voluntary actions. Then incontinent actions will not be a counter-
example (for they are voluntary but not chosen).

BOOK I, CHAPTER 13

Since happiness . . . we must consider the nature of virtue: this important
chapter lays the foundation for the division of the virtues into moral

and intellectual, corresponding to different parts of the soul. The two kinds of virtue will then be discussed (moral virtues, II–V; virtues of intellect, VI).

the Cretans and the Spartans: Crete and Sparta were famous for educational systems featuring centralized, communal practices.

political science . . . original plan: see I.2 for the claim that politics (i.e. political science) is the study of the highest good of human beings. Greek political philosophy took it for granted that a statesman's aim, and the aim of the laws (cf. V.1) was to make the citizens virtuous.

and one has reason: the reference to *discussions outside our school* may be to one of his more popular writings. Aristotle's fullest account of the soul is in his *de Anima*, On the Soul. He leaves open the manner of the 'division' of the soul into parts or elements. Indeed the Greek avoids a noun corresponding to 'element', simply using an adjectival periphrasis, 'the irrational', and so on.

nutrition and growth: since for Aristotle all living things have souls (i.e. have capacities typical of living things), even the capacity to take nourishment and grow is a capacity of soul, but one swiftly dismissed as irrelevant to the discussion of specifically human virtue (cf. I.6).

1102b *There seems to be also another irrational element . . . shares in reason*: below, this will be identified as 'the appetitive and in general desiring element', which, though irrational ('non-rational' is perhaps better), shares in reason by obeying it. This element of the soul, the capacity for appetites and emotions, is of huge importance as the locus of the moral virtues. Before identifying the part in question, Aristotle argues for its existence by a somewhat puzzling appeal to the phenomena of continence and incontinence. See discussion in VII.1–7, and Introduction, pp. xiv–xv and xxvii–xxviii.

at any rate in the continent man it obeys reason: continent persons have unruly appetites and are thus not temperate (and hence not fully virtuous), but they stick to doing what they hold is best: hence their appetites 'obey reason'.

appetitive and in general the desiring element: see the previous two notes. There is a problem with the addition of 'in general desiring', since 'desire' is Aristotle's term for a genus that usually includes as its species not only appetites and anger (which are non-rational) but also 'wish' or rational desire.

'taking account' of one's father or one's friends . . . mathematical property: the Greek *logos*, mostly translated 'reason', can also mean 'account' as well as 'proof'. The 'appetitive part', despite being labelled 'irrational', shares in reason in that it can listen to or obey it (as the continent person shows), as we can be said to obey or 'take account of' a father or friends.

1103a *Virtue too is distinguished . . . this difference*: Aristotle leaves it implicit that the moral virtues correspond to (and are excellent states of) the appetitive part of the soul, since they are concerned with appetites, feelings, and emotions, while the intellectual virtues are excellent states of the part of the soul that 'has reason in the strict sense'. But even though moral virtue is the virtue of the non-rational, appetitive part of the soul, its perfection requires an intellectual virtue, practical wisdom, as will become clear in Book VI.

a man's character: the Greek for 'moral virtues' is *ēthikai aretai*, literally 'virtues of character'.

BOOK II

CHAPTER I

we are adapted by nature to receive them, and are made perfect by habit: whether a person had virtue by nature was a much debated question; see especially Plato's *Meno*. Aristotle's compromise view, expressed here, is attractive. At VI.13 he allows a kind of 'natural virtue', such as a naturally brave child might possess, but distinguishes it from virtue proper. Habit is not to be thought of as unthinking, but rather as intentional habituation, which then becomes second nature.

this is plain in the case of the senses: Aristotle likes to contrast capacities such as sight, which, he holds, we possess before we exercise, with arts and virtues, where exercise—i.e. doing the appropriate actions—is needed for them to develop. Concerning the senses (perceptual capacities), modern physiologists would probably dissent and insist that infants must use their rudimentary capacities to develop them into senses proper.

1103b *brave or cowardly*: though developing a virtue, like an art or expertise, depends on what one regularly does, it also depends—as shown here—on how one feels: an aspect absent from the realm of expertise.

BOOK II, CHAPTER 2

but in order to become good: a puzzling remark. Even if Aristotle wishes to emphasize the practical import of his *Ethics*, it is surely one of his aims that the reader or hearer learns what virtue is. And he is certainly not offering a recipe for becoming good; part of his thesis is that, once you know what virtue is, you will see why no such recipe can exist.

1104a *have no fixity, any more than matters of health*: cf. I.3, 1094b14–16. Fixed rules or formulae cannot answer questions of what is right in the given circumstances, or what is healthy for a given individual. See also Introduction, p. xxiii.

in the art of medicine or of navigation: two branches of skill or expertise that offer a neat parallel for moral virtue, since each *is* an expertise, not a matter of chance, but to be an expert does not consist in knowing and being able to apply a set of rules.

as boors do, becomes in a way insensible: Aristotle invents the term 'insensible' to describe someone who is deficient in the enjoyment of bodily pleasures, cf. ch. 7, 1107b7–8.

and preserved by the mean: the term 'mean', *mesotēs*, is the noun cognate with *meson*, 'intermediate'. Chapter II.6 will expand on the 'doctrine of the mean', cf. notes *ad loc*. As the preceding lines show, the mean is closely connected with what is appropriate (1104a8), and what is proportionate (1104a18).

by abstaining from pleasures we become temperate: Aristotle does not recommend total abstention from pleasures—that is a deficiency—but abstaining from *inappropriate* indulgence in (bodily) pleasures.

BOOK II, CHAPTER 3

1104b *pained is a coward*: 'pain' covers any kind of distress, annoyance, displeasure, etc. Cf. I.8, 1099a19 ff. for this striking claim that enjoying one's good acts is a prerequisite for possessing a virtue, and finding them irksome disqualifies someone from the title of possessing virtue. This chapter emphasizes, with a series of arguments, the intimate connection between virtue and vice, and pleasure and pain.

virtues are concerned with actions and passions: Aristotle seems to intend that each virtue has both an associated range of actions and an associated passion (i.e. feeling or emotion) such as fear (courage), desire for bodily pleasures (temperance), anger (good temper).

it is the nature of cures to be effected by contraries: like Plato in his *Gorgias*, Aristotle here likens punishment to medical treatment (a highly painful matter in Greek times). His argument does not rely on this, however, but rather highlights the role of pain and pleasure in punishment and reward, i.e. in actions whose purpose is to discourage or encourage certain kinds of behaviour.

certain states of impassivity and tranquillity: Aristotle mentions but disputes a rival account of virtue (perhaps held by Speusippus, cf. VII.13), in terms of impassivity, i.e. not being affected *at all* by emotions such as fear, anger, and so on.

1105a *Heraclitus' phrase*: Heraclitus was a sixth-century philosopher from Ephesus, renowned for his cryptic sayings. 'Anger' translates *thumos*, also 'spirit'. The whole quotation is otherwise unattested, whereas Aristotle elsewhere (e.g. at *Eudemian Ethics* 1223b22–4) quotes a rather different saying of Heraclitus: 'For it's a hard thing', he says, 'to fight against spirit; for it buys victory at the price of life.'

BOOK II, CHAPTER 4

Or is this not true even of the arts?: Aristotle started with an objection to his view that (1) people become just by doing just acts. The objector says (2) people who do just acts are already just, as (3) people who do grammatical acts are already grammarians. Here in reply Aristotle denies (3), pointing out that one can spell a word correctly by chance or with a teacher's help. This helps him to deny (2).

it does not follow that they are done justly or temperately: it is crucial to recognize that Aristotle allows that an act can be just without 'being done justly' (in the same way that you can spell a word right without doing it in a 'good-spellerly way', i.e. without being a good speller). Someone might pay a debt (do a just act) but only to avoid a lawsuit. He goes on to explain that for both virtues and arts (i.e. kinds of expertise) you need extra conditions over and above just doing the correct act, but the extra conditions are *different* for virtues and for arts. See next note.

knowledge has little or no weight: Aristotle here plays down the import- ance of knowledge as a condition for possessing a virtue, perhaps for two reasons: (1) to counter the well-known Socratic claim that virtue is nothing but knowledge (see VI.13, 1144b18), and (2) to stress the importance of the *other* conditions. To possess a virtue V, one must choose one's V actions, choose them for their own sake, and do so from a firm and unchangeable character. Note that these are conditions that must be fulfilled if the agent of the acts in question is to be credited with possessing a virtue.

when they are such as the just or the temperate man would do: this import- ant point gives the reply to the objector (see beginning of chapter). Acts may be called just even though not *in fact* done by a just person; rather, they are what a just person *would* do. Hence Aristotle can pre- serve his claim that young persons must first get used *to doing just acts* in order to become just. See also Introduction, p. xx–xxi.

BOOK II, CHAPTER 5

Since things that are found in the soul . . . virtue must be one of these: in I.13 (see 1103a3 with note) Aristotle suggested that moral virtue relates to the division of the non-rational soul he labels 'appetitive'. Hence, the three alternatives he offers here are the relevant ones relating to that part or aspect of the soul. He will eliminate passions and capacities (i.e. that in virtue of which a person is *able* to feel fear, anger, envy, and so on), leaving states of character as the genus of a moral virtue (see end of this chapter). Chapter 6 will then say what kind of state of character counts as a moral virtue.

and well if we feel it in an intermediate way: as ch. 6 will explain, the phrase *in an intermediate way* roughly equates to 'appropriately', invok- ing the second way of being 'intermediate'. It means: in a way that is between (doing and/or feeling) too much and too little.

1106a *modes of choice or involve choice*: choice, *prohairesis*, is a key concept, already introduced at II.4, 1105a31–2, and further discussed in III.2–4. He will conclude that virtue is a state of character concerned with choice, i.e. one that issues in choices.

all that remains is that they should be states of character: despite appearances, this is more than a lame argument by elimination, for many of the points made earlier positively support the claim that virtues are states of character.

BOOK II, CHAPTER 6

virtue or excellence: the single term *aretē* is used in this paragraph, translated 'excellence' where it refers to excellence in general and 'virtue' where specifically human excellence is concerned. See Introduction, p. xii–xiii.

neither too much nor too little: Aristotle first tries to clarify matters by distinguishing two senses of 'intermediate'. In the first sense—the 'intermediate in terms of the thing itself'—the intermediate is simply the mid-point, between more (than half) and less (than half). But it is the second (evaluative) sense that is relevant to moral virtue, which he labels 'the intermediate relative to us'. This is between *too much* and *too little*, and, as was evident in II.2, is equivalent to the *appropriate* or the *proportionate*. So the second intermediate is an evaluative notion; it is what lies between excess and deficiency (also evaluative notions). 'Relative to us' probably means relative to us as human beings, that is, relative to human needs and purposes, rather than relative to individual agents. See next note but one, and for a fuller discussion see L. Brown, 'What is the "Mean Relative to Us" in Aristotle's Ethics?', *Phronesis* 1997.

nor the same for all: this probably means, not the same in all cases. See next note.

1106b *it does not follow that the trainer will order six pounds . . . too much for the beginner in athletic exercises*: the point is often misunderstood. Note that the person to whom Aristotle will liken the moral agent is the trainer, who chooses the 'relative-to-us' intermediate in every circumstance. To fit the diet to the recipient, *the trainer* will choose a hefty diet for a seasoned athlete such as the famous wrestler Milo, a more meagre one for a beginner. For the expert, to choose the 'intermediate relative to us' is to choose what is appropriate to the circumstances; the same goes for the moral agent. Aristotle is *not* claiming that the ethical intermediate, i.e. the appropriate action-cum-feeling, is different for different moral agents (except where their differences amount to a difference in circumstances, such as the greater wealth of one person, cf. IV.1).

a master of any art avoids excess and defect . . . relatively to us: once again the qualification 'relatively to us' is used to emphasize that the intermediate in question is not to be arrived at by calculation, but by the skilled judgement of experts such as trainers, doctors, etc.

the mean preserves it: 'the mean' translates *mesotēs*, the abstract noun cognate with *meson*, which is translated 'intermediate'. So it is an 'intermediate' state. As with 'intermediate', Aristotle intends an *evaluative* use of *mesotēs* or 'mean'.

to feel them at the right times . . . is what is both intermediate and best, and this is characteristic of virtue: this way of spelling out what is meant by 'intermediate' is of crucial importance. First, it explicitly equates 'intermediate' with 'best'. Second, it supplements the simple contrast of *too little—the right amount—too much*, with a range of further parameters, which takes the account beyond a purely quantitative notion of the intermediate.

1107a *Virtue then is a state of character . . . determine it*: the reference to 'the man of practical wisdom' (the *phronimos*) is taken up in VI.1, 5, and 8–13. Aristotle will conclude that a person cannot be virtuous without practical wisdom, nor the converse. By *a state of character concerned with choice* he means: a state disposing one to choose in certain ways, cf. II.4.

imply by their names that they are themselves bad: the point is not that the items listed are exceptions to the theory of the mean. Rather, if you choose a certain designation, such as *spite*, or *murder*, you already locate the item as a vice. Envy is by its very name *inappropriate* distress at another's good fortune (whereas distress at undeserved good fortune is a virtue: righteous indignation or *nemesis*, II.8, 1108b1). The same is true of *murder* (always wrong) as opposed to killing, of which there may be a mean, i.e. appropriate occasions of killing, for example of a condemned criminal.

there is no excess and deficiency of temperance and courage: describing a characteristic as temperance already implies it is a virtue. As he goes on to say, the *intermediate is in a sense an extreme*—i.e. at the top! Self-indulgence is an excess of what temperance is the mean of, i.e. enjoyment of bodily pleasures. It is not an excess (or deficiency) of temperance.

BOOK II, CHAPTER 7

from our table: we may assume Aristotle displayed a chart or table, with four columns, the first giving the sphere (e.g. *feelings of fear and confidence*, or, further on, *giving and taking of money*). The next three columns will name in turn each of the triad: virtue, excess, deficiency, related to the named sphere.

such persons also have received no name . . . 'insensible': Aristotle is prepared to invent a name where common usage has not marked off a given vice (or virtue, cf. 1107b30 on ambition, 1108a5 on 'good-temper'). In this he is going beyond the mere codifying of current moral views.

1108a *With regard to truth . . . mock-modest*: the virtue of 'truthfulness' has a narrow sphere: it is a matter of neither exaggerating nor underplaying one's own merits. Truthfulness in the wider sense does not get a mention, though traditionally it was regarded as a part of justice, i.e. of giving others what they are due. Justice is discussed in Book V.

1108b *Righteous indignation . . . that he even rejoices*: Ross's note on this passage may be repeated: 'Aristotle must mean that while the envious man is pained at the good fortune of others, whether deserved or not, the spiteful man is pleased at the *bad* fortune of others, whether deserved or not. But if he had stated this in full, he would have seen that there is no real opposition.'

BOOK II, CHAPTER 8

in some cases the deficiency, in some the excess is more opposed: Aristotle here tries to accommodate a common view that to each virtue there is just one opposed vice: courage/cowardice; temperance/self-indulgence, without giving up his own triadic structure of excess–mean–deficiency.

BOOK II, CHAPTER 9

beyond that surf and spray: Aristotle misremembers Homer and attributes to Calypso advice that Circe gave, reported by Odysseus at *Odyssey* xii.219.

1109b *some to another*: this good advice should not be taken to imply that Aristotle considers that if A is bolder than B, bravery for A is different from bravery for B. Rather, it will be a different, and harder, task for B to become brave.

the decision rests with perception: an important point about moral episte-mology. Such matters—e.g. what counts as an appropriate display of anger in a given set of circumstances—cannot be reasoned out from principles, but require a kind of judgement that is more akin to percep-tion. See further VI.8 and 11.

BOOK III

CHAPTER 1

and of punishments: two reasons for the investigation of the voluntary are given here: first, the importance of virtue in the work, and second, its importance for legislators. Voluntary acts extend beyond chosen ones (see next chapter), and it is choice, rather than the voluntary as such, which is connected to virtue. This chapter seems to reflect the second concern more; its aim is to delimit and account for those cases where the law regards a person as having acted involuntarily, and therefore as appropriately escaping blame and punishment.

by reason of ignorance: the criterion 'by force' is discussed first and 'by reason of ignorance' in the second half of the chapter, from 1110b18.

1110a *it may be debated whether . . . or voluntary*: Aristotle recognizes a ten-dency to say 'I was forced to do it' (or 'I was compelled to do it') in certain cases. But his analysis distinguishes these cases from the above examples of 'by force' such as being manhandled, or blown off course.

mixed . . . relative to the occasion: the initial label 'mixed' reflects the fact that an act such as throwing cargo overboard is one no one chooses for itself. As he has just said: 'in the abstract no one throws away goods voluntarily'. But his final verdict (1110b5–7) will be that such acts are voluntary, since chosen by the agent in the circumstances as the price of saving lives. The word here translated 'chosen' is *haireta*: it is a weaker notion than the choice (*prohairesis*) discussed in the following chapter, where choices (in the later, stronger sense) form only a sub-class of voluntary actions.

voluntary . . . choose any such act in itself: see previous note.

endure something base . . . inferior person: despite the terminology of '*endure* something base or painful', it seems clear that Aristotle is think-ing of an action, as in the earlier phrase: if a tyrant were to order one to do something shameful or base. Someone opting for what in normal circumstances is a shameful or base action may merit praise if the end secured is sufficiently worthy, but if not, not.

cannot be compelled to do . . . seem absurd: probably *cannot be compelled to do* means cannot justifiably claim to be compelled to do. Alcmaeon, apparently, made such a claim in the lost play of Euripides. He was ordered by his father Amphiareus to kill his mother, since she had inveigled Amphiareus into taking part in a battle in which he died. Aristotle judged the claim in this case absurd, but whether he held that *no* circumstances would justify the killing of a mother is not clear.

1110b *but now and in return for these gains voluntary*: Aristotle rightly insists on his initial, narrow definition of forced actions. Actions that are thought of as forced or compelled, but which really are chosen to avoid a worse alternative, must be considered in their actual circumstances, hence they are voluntary. The cases discussed in the previous lines make it clear that declaring them voluntary does not in itself imply the agent should be blamed: depending on the circumstances praise or pity or blame may be the appropriate response.

not voluntary; it is only what produces pain and regret that is involuntary: Aristotle now turns to the second kind of case, where ignorance is involved. In the remaining discussion, it helps to think of the involun-tary as the unintentional, the voluntary as the intentional. What is the rationale for this distinction (among actions done *by reason of ignorance*) between the *not voluntary* and a subset, of that, the *involuntary*? (The notion of *by reason of ignorance* is explained in the next paragraph.) The simplest explanation is that the Greek term translated 'involuntary' could connote 'with a heavy heart' as well as denying voluntariness or intention; hence it would be odd to label 'involuntary' an action that the doer does not regret, even when it satisfied the conditions for being not voluntary. Alternatively Aristotle may reason thus: if you don't regret the unintentional action, once you discover the mistake, that shows you would have done it intentionally if you *had* known, hence it cannot be called *in*voluntary, since that equates to *contrary to one's intention* (and not merely *unintentional*).

ignorance of particulars . . . with which it is concerned: Aristotle's first attempt to explain the difference between actions done *by reason of ignorance* (for which the doer is not blamed) and *in ignorance* (for which the doer may be blamed) is confusing. He aligns the first with ignorance of particulars, and the second (blameworthy kind) with ignorance of universals. But, as he will recognize in ch. 5, the key issue is whether the ignorance is the doer's own fault or not. Here Aristotle writes as if all and only cases where one fails to know a particular circumstance are cases of acting *by reason of ignorance*, but it is obvious that in some such cases the agent should have known (e.g. that the gun was loaded). Later (ch. 5) he recognizes that such cases should not be labelled 'by reason of ignorance' but are such for which one can be blamed. He assumes that all cases of 'ignorance of the universal'—i.e. where one fails to know right from wrong—are one's fault, hence such ignorance does not exculpate the agent, and the acts are done merely *in ignorance*, hence voluntary.

1111a *moving principle is in the agent . . . of the action*: Aristotle leaves unexplained what it is for the moving principle to be in the agent himself, but he later excludes growing old from something we do voluntarily (1135b2). To be able to exclude an act due e.g. to an epileptic fit from being voluntary, he must mean that the moving principle is in the person's appetitive or rational faculties.

1111b *odd, then, to treat them as involuntary*: the opponent may not find convincing the argument about children and animals, since it assumes both act voluntarily. The next argument (that there are things we ought to get angry about or want) rests on the principle that 'ought' implies 'can', and scarcely proves that no action done in anger or desire is involuntary. But Aristotle is aiming for an account of involuntariness suitable for a law court, and no judge will accept anger or desire as an excusing circumstance.

BOOK III, CHAPTER 2

voluntary, but not as chosen: choice (*prohairesis*) entails voluntariness but not vice versa. The category of 'voluntary-but-not-chosen' acts includes (1) those of children and animals (neither of which is capable of choice) and (2) acts done in anger or on the spur of the moment, or when incontinent. They are voluntary, and merit praise or blame, but it is the narrower class of chosen acts that reflects a virtuous or vicious character. This chapter and the next explore *choice* further.

continent . . . but not with appetite: a key tenet in the theory of continence and incontinence; see VII.1-9. So incontinent actions are voluntary (and blameworthy) but not chosen.

only the things . . . by his own efforts: Aristotle correctly notes that while you can wish for the impossible, you cannot choose what you know is impossible.

choice seems to relate . . . in our own power: the statement that choice relates to the means, wish to the end, may seem incompatible with the earlier insistence (II.4) that a virtuous person chooses his acts for their own sake. But it is not. One can choose to do something (and for its own sake) but one can't *choose* (but only wish for) an end such as being happy or healthy.

1112a *choice is praised for being right . . . opinion for being true*: see further VI.2.

name seems to suggest that it is what is chosen before other things: the prefix *pro* in the word *prohairesis* can mean both 'before' and 'in preference to'. Probably both meanings are salient here: choice is of one course of action rather than another, but it also (see previous sentence) is *what has been decided by earlier deliberation* (i.e. before action).

BOOK III, CHAPTER 3

incommensurability . . . side of a square: that the square's diagonal is incommensurable with its side is a favourite example of a mathematical truth, hence something eternally true.

1112b *We deliberate not about ends but about means*: this surprising claim can be made more plausible by two considerations. First, deliberation presupposes an end to be achieved; hence the doctor at the patient's bedside deliberates how to, but not whether to, cure her. Second, the term translated 'means' is literally 'the things that promote the ends'. They may be instrumental means (medicine, a speech, etc.) but the term can include what contributes to an end (as, for instance, a person's virtue contributes to his happiness) without being an instrument towards achieving it.

in the order of becoming: a comparison between deliberation—where one works back from the assumed goal, via the intermediate steps, to the thing to be done here and now—and solving a mathematical problem. Cf. Ross's note: 'the problem being to construct a figure of a certain kind, we suppose it constructed and then analyse it to see if there is some figure by constructing which we can construct the required figure, and so on until we come to a figure which our existing knowledge enables us to construct'.

1113a *the kings announced their choices to the people*: Aristotle somewhat fancifully compares the Homeric kings (as they stand to their subjects) with the 'leading part', i.e. the practical intellect of an individual person—as the origin of choices.

BOOK III, CHAPTER 4

to each man: this confusing chapter raises, then tries to solve, a problem about the 'object of wish'. Is it (1) the good or (2) the apparent good? Answer (1) prompts the objection that the target of one who doesn't choose aright can't, then, be an object of wish. Answer (2) faces the problem that *there is no natural object of wish*; apparently an *unpleasing consequence*.

and in each the truth appears to him?: Aristotle finds some truth in each answer, and distinguishes two ways of being the 'object of wish'.

Answer (1), the good, gives what is 'absolutely and in truth the object of wish', while answer (2), the apparent good, gives what is the object of wish for each person. He then aligns the good with what the good man judges good, and draws comparisons with judgements about (*a*) what is wholesome and (*b*) what is bitter, sweet or hot, and (*c*) what is noble or pleasant. He ignores differences between these kinds of case. Does he want the good man's wished-for object to be *constitutive of what is good*, as case (*b*) might suggest—since the judgements of healthy people on sweet and bitter establish what is sweet or bitter? Or, more likely, to be a reliable indicator of what's really good, as case (*a*) would suggest? For a healthy person's appetites are a reliable indicator of what is really wholesome.

being as it were the norm and measure of them: the language recalls Protagoras' 'man is the measure' dictum (Plato, *Theaetetus* 152a), but Aristotle corrects Plato by making the *good* man the measure. See previous note for ways of understanding this.

BOOK III, CHAPTER 5

1113b *then it is in our power to be virtuous or vicious*: the chapter is devoted to showing that virtue and vice are in our power, but this first argument is hardly conclusive, since it equates being good with doing noble acts (and being bad with doing bad ones). But it was a key point (see II.2–4) that being good is more than merely doing good acts. The later arguments are more persuasive.

acts whose moving principles are in us . . . be in our power and voluntary: this has been thought to suggest that Aristotle denies determinism, as incompatible with responsibility. More probably he is simply pointing—in the phrase 'the moving principles are in ourselves'—to the fact that, in voluntary actions, the causes that count are the agent's own desires and choices.

ignorance for which they are not themselves responsible: an important addition to the discussion of ignorance in ch. 1; see 1110b25 and note. The key issue, for questions of culpability, is whether or not the agent could have avoided the error or ignorance.

penalties are doubled in the case of drunkenness: at *Politics* 1274b19 Aristotle reports that Pittacus of Mytilene enjoined such double punishment (once for the crime, once for the drunkenness).

1114a *since they have the power of taking care*: cf. P. F. Strawson's famous essay 'Freedom and Resentment'. Both authors argue from the practice of blaming and punishing in some cases but not others, to the conclusion that some actions and states are ones we are responsible for.

irrational to suppose . . . does not wish . . . to be self-indulgent: a surprising claim. You can knowingly do bad acts without wishing to be a bad person, even if you know that being a bad person will result. But it *is* correct that you can be held to account for becoming e.g. self-indulgent, even if incorrect to say that you wished to be so.

not possible for them not to be so: seemingly a strong claim that character, once formed, cannot be altered. We might prefer a weaker claim that *some* character traits—like *some* bodily states voluntarily acquired, notably blindness—are irreversible. Blindness is mentioned a few lines below.

1114b *whatever they do*: it is somewhat feeble to reply that, if the objector's view is correct, we are no more responsible for our virtues than for our vices, for this is exactly what the powerful objection Aristotle has just outlined was arguing.

we are ourselves somehow part-causes of our states of character: with the expression *somehow part-causes* Aristotle seems to concede something to the opponent's denial of responsibility for virtues and vices, while still insisting on his own position.

BOOK III, CHAPTER 6

1115a *fear and confidence . . . already been made evident*: see II.6, 1107a33–b4. Fear is treated both as an emotion (cf. confidence) and as a motive. This chapter focuses on fear; in the next, confidence complicates the account of courage.

expectation of evil: the definition of fear found in Plato, notably *Laches* 198b and *Protagoras* 358d. It omits the 'emotional disturbance' aspect of fear.

is a fearless person: despite this 'popular' account of a brave person, Aristotle's own view will be that the brave person is not wholly fearless, but feels the *appropriate* fear for a given circumstance; see ch. 7.

e.g. at sea or in disease: it strikes a modern reader as bizarre to exclude danger at sea, disease, or financial ruin as situations in which courage can be displayed. Socrates, in Plato's *Laches*, disagrees with Aristotle, and allows for courage at sea and in illness.

BOOK III, CHAPTER 7

1115b *while he will fear . . . he will face them . . . for the sake of the noble*: that a virtuous person acts for the sake of the noble is a key part of Aristotle's account. He regards it as self-evident and not in need of further explanation.

and in whatever way reason directs: cf. II.6. As elsewhere, Aristotle stresses that many parameters must be correct ('from the right motive, in the right way and at the right time', etc.). On reason, see II.6 and VI.1.

the Celts: inhabiting areas from Spain to Asia Minor, the Celts were a byword for fearlessness and savagery.

BOOK III, CHAPTER 8

1116a *fled from my face*: the first quotation is from *Iliad* xxii. 100, the second from *Iliad* viii.148–9.

avoidance of disgrace, which is ignoble: how does the (lesser) courage of the citizen-soldier, here described, differ from true courage as described earlier, in chs. 6 and 7? The prime motive here is to gain public honour—a noble thing—and avoid disgrace, while the truly brave person acts for the sake of the noble (ch. 7).

escape from the dogs: i.e. from death and exposure of their bodies. The Homeric commander Aristotle quotes here is in fact Agamemnon (*Iliad* ii.391–3) not Hector.

1116b *Socrates thought courage was knowledge*: in Plato's *Laches* 199 and *Protagoras* 360d. But, in the former, Socrates explicitly distinguishes the knowledge he identifies with courage from experience.

at the temple of Hermes: at Coronea in 353 BC, when the mercenaries abandoned the citizen forces, whom the Phocians defeated.

'his blood boiled': thumos, here translated 'passion', can also mean anger; it is etymologically related to English 'fume'. While the first three phrases are, roughly, found in Homer, the last is not.

1117a *if choice and motive be added*: if, that is, the right choice and goals are added. There is further discussion of the difference between a so-called 'natural virtue' and full virtue at VI.13.

state of character: there is a prima facie conflict between the plausible claim here and some earlier claims. Here Aristotle claims (1) it is the mark of a braver man to be fearless in sudden dangers, where there is no time to deliberate. But (2) at II.4 he argued that a virtuous person is one who *chooses* his acts, and (3) at III.2 choice was identified with what is selected after *deliberation*. The best solution is to allow Aristotle to maintain both (1) and (2) and to regard (3) as typifying most (but not all) choices. Thus the spur-of-the-moment brave actions flow from a brave character that was formed with the help of reflection and deliberation; but they need not be the product of deliberation at the time, to count as acts betokening true courage.

took them for Sicyonians: an event reported by Xenophon, *Hellenica* iv.4.10, which took place at the Long Walls of Corinth.

BOOK III, CHAPTER 9

1117b *pleasant, except in so far as it attains its end*: a welcome refinement of the claim about enjoying virtuous acts in II.3, 1104b3–8. Here Aristotle acknowledges that brave persons will be distressed at facing death and wounds. But they recognize the nobility of doing so, and to that extent do so gladly, and they are pleased by the noble outcome.

BOOK III, CHAPTER 10

1118a *these remind them of the objects of their appetite*: having excluded the pleasures of sight and hearing, in his search for which pleasures form the sphere of temperance, Aristotle gives a more nuanced account of smell. Though strictly a person can't be deemed intemperate for their love of smells, a predilection for perfumes or savouries betrays an excessive love for the pleasures of sex or food.

meal of it: for the lion quotation see *Iliad* iii.24. That animals—as Aristotle claims—don't enjoy smells as such is taken to confirm that temperance and self-indulgence are not concerned with the pleasures of smell.

1118b *only certain parts*: presumably the sexual organs and, in the case of greed, the organs of eating and drinking (the mouth and throat). The whole chapter shows how very narrowly Aristotle restricts the sphere of temperance: the pleasures of eating and drinking are treated as pleasures of touch, since the greedy person enjoys, not the taste, but the contact of the food with his throat!

BOOK III, CHAPTER 12

1119a–b *childish faults . . . the later is called after the earlier*: a somewhat obscure remark. The point seems to be that the word translated 'self-indulgent', *akolastos* (literally, 'unrebuked' or 'unpunished'), is used also of spoilt children, and this reference to the 'earlier' state is the primary one.

1119b *according to the direction of his tutor*: the tutor was a slave, a *paidagōgos*, who took the child to school. His role, controlling the child, is compared to that of reason controlling appetite.

BOOK IV

CHAPTER I

liberality: an alternative translation is 'generosity', but 'liberality' reflects the connection of the Greek noun with *eleutheros*, free.

1120a *ruined by his own fault*: one meaning of *asōtos*, here translated 'prodigal', is 'not saved', i.e. ruined. Aristotle links this to the relevant meaning here, 'unsparing' or 'spendthrift'.

1121a *the saying of Simonides*: at *Rhetoric* II.16 Aristotle reports Simonides as saying that it is better to be rich than clever, since clever men dine at the tables of the rich.

BOOK IV, CHAPTER 2

1122a *in great things*: magnificence is marked off from, and is a special case of, liberality (discussed in previous chapter), since it is concerned only with large-scale giving. The quotation is from *Odyssey* xvii.420.

chorus . . . trireme . . . entertain the city, in a brilliant way: a list of some typical 'liturgies', i.e. large-scale public expenditure expected of rich citizens; 'equip a chorus', i.e. for one of the drama festivals.

BOOK IV, CHAPTER 3

1123a *Pride . . . try to answer*: pride translates *megalopsychia*, literally great-souledness. Some translations prefer 'magnanimity' to retain the connection with greatness, but that word now has quite different connotations. Ross's choice of 'pride' lacks the connection with greatness, but is in other respects appropriate, so long as it is borne in mind that Aristotle is describing a *virtue*: proper pride is what is meant. A useful discussion of pride can be found in R. Crisp, 'Aristotle on Greatness of Soul', in R. Kraut, *Blackwell Guide to Aristotle's Nicomachean Ethics*.

1123b *he will be concerned with one thing in particular*: i.e. honour. Concerned, not in the sense that he thinks about it a lot, but in the sense that honour is the sphere of pride. The proud person thinks himself, and is, worthy of great honour.

1124a *crown of the virtues*: 'crown' translates *cosmos*, taken in the sense of an added adornment. How does pride make the virtues greater? Perhaps by spurring on the proud person to greater achievement, as suggested by Crisp, 'Aristotle on Greatness of Soul', 167 (see above).

to whom even honour is a little thing the others must be so too: is this inconsistent with the characterization of pride as correctly thinking of oneself as worthy of great honours? Not if we recall that it is not honour, but what merits it, i.e. virtue, that the good person cares about (see I.5 1095b26–30). However honour, if deserved, is one of the external goods that is most worth having, hence the role for pride.

1124b *Thetis . . . Spartans . . . they had received*: Thetis was the mother of Achilles. In fact she did remind Zeus of her services, *Iliad* i.503. What event occasioned the reference to Spartan tact is uncertain.

in irony to the vulgar: just as a proud person is unassuming towards ordinary people (see above b19–20) so he will play down his merits (so-called 'irony') in their company. But in IV.7 this is labelled a failing.

1125a *both commoner and worse*: much of Aristotle's account of pride is repugnant to modern sensibilities, and the closing ranking of vanity above humility compounds this.

BOOK IV, CHAPTER 4

1125b *loves it more than is right*: both the Greek *philotimia*, literally 'love of honour', and English 'ambition' can be used either to praise or to censure, and this—as Aristotle remarks—is typical of words beginning 'fond of' or 'lover of'. For a similar case, see Aristotle's discussion in IX.10 of the term 'lover of self'.

BOOK IV, CHAPTER 5

1126b *the decision depends on the particular facts and on perception*: for this key point in Aristotle's ethical theory compare II.9 1109b23, and VI.8, 11.

BOOK IV, CHAPTER 6

no name . . . most resembles friendship: for a lengthy discussion of *philia*, 'friendship', see VIII and IX, where it is called 'a virtue, or involves virtue'. The good state here discussed—officially nameless—is a propensity to be civil in dealings with others.

BOOK IV, CHAPTER 7

1127a *this also is without a name*: as (officially) were the virtues described in the previous three chapters. But here, as in those cases, Aristotle proceeds to name the person in the virtuous state, here labelling him 'truthful'. As the contrast with boastfulness and mock-modesty shows, the virtue concerns being truthful only about one's own qualities and achievements, not being truthful in general.

We are not speaking . . . in his agreements: here being true to one's word is explicitly excluded from what it is to be truthful in the current sense. Honesty and keeping of contracts belong to justice, discussed in Book V.

as Socrates used to do: mock-modesty translates *eironeia* (irony) for which Socrates became a byword, since he regularly professed ignorance. Whether Aristotle took this profession to be insincere is unclear; whether Plato intended his readers to take the Socratic disavowal of knowledge as sincere or not is a matter of intense scholarly dispute.

Spartan dress: typically austere; for a non-Spartan to sport it was pretentious.

BOOK IV, CHAPTER 8

1128a *boorish and unpolished*: *agroikos*, translated 'boorish', has 'rustic' as its literal meaning. Cf. 'urbane' meaning witty. The boor has no interest in being pleasant company, hence falls short of the appropriate willingness to enjoy and dispense humour.

the old and the new comedies: old comedies are probably those of Aristophanes (died *c.*386), at least his earlier ones, which abound in obscene and abusive language. What Aristotle means by new comedies is uncertain; he cannot mean those by Menander, whose first play was performed in 321, the year after Aristotle's death.

being as it were a law to himself: the phrase, which St Paul made famous, is here used to underline that an external law regulating abusive humour is unnecessary for a good man.

1128b *three in number*: i.e. friendliness (ch. 6), 'truthfulness' (about one's merits, ch. 7), and here ready wit.

BOOK IV, CHAPTER 9

fear of dishonour: here shame is a feeling restraining people, especially the young, from bad actions. As such it played an important role in Greek culture; see D. Cairns, *Aidōs: The Psychology and Ethics of Honour and Shame in Greek Literature* (1993). The chapter's focus shifts to shame as felt *after the deed*, cf. below 'sense of disgrace'.

as to do any disgraceful action: see previous note. As shame is now characterized as something felt after a bad action, it isn't good, or rather, as Aristotle goes on to explain, it is not *unconditionally* good.

BOOK V

CHAPTER 1

1129a *as the preceding discussions*: the discussion of justice in this book is in fact rather different from those of the other virtues in the preceding three books. There are many signs that this is a work in progress, or perhaps a provisional compilation, rather than a polished discussion. For example, the first lines of ch. 6 do not fit their context, and the discussion that begins in ch. 8 is interrupted by a digression in ch. 10 before resuming in ch. 11. The nature of the subject matter means that a preliminary chapter is needed. It distinguishes a more general notion— justice as 'complete virtue in relation to another' (1129b)—from the specific kinds of justice Aristotle will be mainly concerned with in the subsequent chapters. In contrast to the other virtues, the focus is more on justice as property of actions or enactments than on justice as a character trait. The reason for this is connected to the reason why justice is a mean in a different way from the other virtues; see ch. 5, 1133b29 ff., with notes.

wish for what is unjust: but there is an asymmetry here. A just person desires just acts because they are just, while to be unjust it suffices that a person is insufficiently concerned for justice. An unjust person doesn't necessarily wish for what is unjust *as such*.

a state . . . does not produce the contrary results . . . as a healthy man would: Aristotle illustrates the point with the example of health (from which only healthy things result). But his interest lies in *states of character*, which are dispositions *to choose* only one kind of action (good ones, if the state is a virtue).

the unjust the unlawful and the unfair: as explained soon (1130a22–4) these are related as whole to part: 'All that is unfair is unlawful but not all that is unlawful is unfair.' Unlike in the case of the word for key, used both of collarbones and door-keys, the ambiguity of *unjust* and *just* escapes notice, and it is Aristotle who first delineates this distinction.

1129b *thought to be grasping*: Greek *pleonektēs*, literally, 'trying to get more'. Chapter 2 will identify graspingness, *pleonexia*, as the major motive for injustice: it is wanting more than one's fair share of goods, or less than one's share of burdens.

are lawful . . . and each of these, we say, is just: but Aristotle is not here espousing legalism; he is not *equating* the just with the legal, as lines 24–5 below make clear.

complete virtue . . . in relation to another: the kind of justice later called 'the whole of virtue' (1130a8) is here demarcated. Aristotle probably has in mind Plato's *Republic* (e.g. 442d–443e), where justice is the virtue motivating the whole range of actions in which a person does the right thing by another.

in justice is every virtue comprehended: a verse from Theognis, a further source (cf. previous note) for the wide conception of justice as 'the whole of virtue in relation to another'.

1130a *is thought to be 'another's good'*: the phrase used by Thrasymachus in *Republic* I.343c. This phrase was part of a critique of justice, as benefiting *only others*, and hence not worth cultivating. Though Aristotle disagrees, he accepts the point that the hallmark of justice is that it is other-regarding.

as a certain kind of state without qualification, virtue: a favourite piece of terminology to show that a single state has two definitions: virtue, when considered in itself, justice, when considered in its essentially other-regarding aspect.

BOOK V, CHAPTER 2

to no form of wickedness but injustice: to demarcate the narrow kind of justice, Aristotle notes a subset of acts that are blamed as unjust on the grounds that the agent *makes gain* by his act. These acts, which can be attributed to *graspingness*, betoken a different vice to those ascribed, for example, to cowardice, even if they involve the same act-type such as desertion on the battlefield. Desertion for gain might be exploiting your comrades' willingness to stay at their posts to gain your own safety. Adultery for gain might be seducing someone's wife so she will exert her influence on your behalf (rather than out of desire for her).

1130b *honour or money or safety*: on safety see previous note. All these are thought of as goods in limited supply, such that if I am grasping and get more than my fair share, someone else loses out. Grabbing a plank from a fellow survivor of a shipwreck would be a case in point.

man and man: having argued at length for a distinct kind of justice, 'particular justice', Aristotle now turns to *its* subdivisions. 'Distributive' is discussed in ch. 3, rectificatory, which is further subdivided, in ch. 4.

1131a *origin of these actions is voluntary*: the two branches of rectificatory justice correspond to two categories of offence to be rectified. (Compare the later distinction between torts and crimes.) The distinction between voluntary and involuntary refers to the type of transaction. The involuntary ones, such as theft, presuppose no initial collaboration between victim and offender; the voluntary ones, such as fraud, do, though the victim is not defrauded voluntarily.

BOOK V, CHAPTER 3

unfair or unequal: the single word *anison* means both *unfair* and *unequal*; *ison*, likewise, means both *fair* and *equal*. In what follows *unequal* is generally used, but the point is often clearer when the dual use is borne in mind.

also what is equal: as well as that indicated in the previous note, there is a further ambiguity that English cannot convey. *More* and *less* can also mean *too much* and *too little*. Hence the fair is between too much and too little, while the equal is between more and less.

greater and less: cf. previous note. The just share is between too great a share and too small a share.

if they are not equal, they will not have what is equal: a just distribution will not give equal shares to people who are unequal in some relevant respect, as explained shortly.

with virtue: two crucial points here. First, a just distribution is proportional to some quality—the catchphrase is *according to merit*. But second, it is a controversial matter what quality or merit is relevant. Aristotle illustrates the point using familiar controversies over distributing political rights (e.g. the right to hold office, or have a say in the city's affairs) where each group claims its favoured criterion to be the relevant 'merit'. Though he here leaves open the question of the correct political distribution, in *Politics* IV.7–8 he makes clear his preference for an aristocratic system where possession of virtue is the qualifying characteristic.

1131b *the just, too, involves at least four terms . . . between the persons and between the things*: in the simplest case of distributive justice there are two persons A and B, and some good to be divided between them 'in proportion to merit' (see previous note). For example, if A has worked twice as many hours as his co-worker B, then A's pay—C—should be twice as much as B's pay, D.

in the same ratio to the whole: person A + thing C to person B + thing D.

for the proportional is intermediate, and the just is proportional: intermediate, *meson*, has an evaluative overtone, equating to 'appropriate'; cf. II.7. A just share is (intermediate) between too large a share and too small a one.

call this kind of proportion geometrical: in contrast to so-called arithmetical proportion, associated with rectificatory justice in ch. 4. Geometrical proportion is that used in distributing according to merit, as opposed to strictly *equal* distribution.

has too much . . . too little, of what is good: Aristotle here assumes that if a party to a distribution ends up with more than their fair share, then that party did the distributing, and was unjust. Thus he overlooks the case where the distributor is not also a recipient, but see 1135a1–3.

the lesser evil is rather to be chosen than the greater: so the account can cover also unjust distribution of burdens such as taxation or military service.

BOOK V, CHAPTER 4

rectificatory: though it deals with offences, this branch of 'particular justice' is not regarded as punitive, but as putting things right for the victim. One may compare the recent interest in 'restorative justice'.

violates the proportion: a recapitulation—with a new example drawn from a joint business venture—of the account of distributive justice; *the kind of proportion mentioned above* is geometric proportion.

1132a　*the judge tries to equalize things . . . gain of the assailant*: the account treats all offences as cases where the offender makes an unfair *gain* at the expense of the victim. But it immediately goes on to acknowledge that *gain* and *loss* are not entirely appropriate in the case of, say, a wounding. It is striking that 'equalizing' is seen merely as restoring both parties to equality—i.e. restoring the *status quo* before the offence, as made clear at the end of the chapter.

the just in rectification will be the intermediate between loss and gain: if the just penalty is imposed on the offender, neither party ends up with more, or less, than before the offence.

they say they have 'their own'—i.e. when they have got what is equal: i.e. what is fair, what they are entitled to. Cf. *Republic* IV.433e for a popular characterization of justice as where each has his own.

1132b　*subtract from the greatest that by which it exceeds the intermediate*: up to this point a fairly simple idea is conveyed by the idea of a single line initially divided into equal parts. It signifies the status quo between the two parties before the offence. The offender by his action 'gains' a portion of the victim's 'half'; the judge's act of imposing the penalty restores the status quo ante. It is likened to taking away that amount by which the (now) greater segment exceeds half and adding to the (now) smaller segment.

by the segment CD: it is not clear why a new illustration, involving three lines, has been introduced, since the point being made seems to be the same as above.

It is simplest to assume that AE (what was taken from the victim) = DC (what the offender initially gained), although this is not made explicit.

an equal amount before and after the transaction: here it is made crystal clear that the judge's task in 'equalizing' is to make the position of each party equal to what it was before the offence. He does not make them equal to each other. It is also made explicit that, in the sphere of what rectificatory justice rectifies, any 'loss' on the part of the victim is involuntary, even where the original transaction was a voluntary one. For instance, if the other party failed to pay the amount promised.

BOOK V, CHAPTER 5

'reciprocity' fits neither distributive nor rectificatory justice: in ch. 2 only two kinds of 'particular justice' were mentioned: distributive and rectificatory. Here a third is introduced and said to be different from those two. The initial discussion treats 'reciprocity' as a kind of retaliation or

requital, but it emerges that it is a kind of justice in 'associations for exchange'.

right justice would be done: Rhadamanthus was one of the supposed judges in the afterlife, cf. Plato, *Gorgias* 523.

punished in addition: if Aristotle is here discussing rectificatory justice, as he seems to be, then this aside adds an important qualification to the account in ch. 4. There rectificatory justice consisted simply in 'equalizing', i.e. in imposing a penalty or damages equal to the harm done. Here Aristotle not only rejects a simple account—*inflict the very same harm*—but adds, in effect, that the wrongness of the act should also be reflected in the rectification. If the officer was within his rights to wound, he did no wrong, while the private person's wrongdoing went beyond the wound he inflicted.

1133a *in showing it*: Aristotle has moved on to discuss justice in exchange and proportional requital, claiming that they hold the city together. Here his focus is on the general notion of returning good for good—an act of *charis* or grace—and evil for evil. He soon narrows his focus to the exchange of (material) goods.

by cross-conjunction . . . C a house, D a shoe: the discussion that begins here and ends at 1133b28 is puzzling and its interpretation is much disputed. Does Aristotle promise an account of *just* exchange, or merely an account of how exchanges (e.g. a house for *n* pairs of shoes) come about? We expect an account of just or fair exchange, and the reference to proportionate equality (1133a10) confirms this. But it is unclear what the account is. *Secured by cross-conjunction*: i.e. by linking diagonally in this square:

A builder	B shoemaker
C house	D shoes.

Below we have further illustrations: farmer and shoemaker and their products; houses and beds.

the result we mention will be effected: i.e. proportionate return. The point seems to be this: a fair rate of exchange is established, then an actual exchange of goods (*reciprocal action*).

they must therefore be equated: but it is not yet explained how. Some critics (Ross, Hardie) assume that the measure is the time taken to produce the object—be it a house or a pair of shoes. But this is nowhere said. Below *need* is said to be the measure; see next note.

money has become by convention a sort of representative of need: *need* translates *chreia*, often rendered by 'demand'. Need holds things together by being the impetus for mutual dealings, and for communities based on division of labour. To translate 'demand' would make this an early foray into free market economic theory. Judson ('Aristotle on Fair Exchange') rejects this on the ground that need is an objective notion, while demand is a subjective one, and as such unsuitable as a basis for a theory of *just* exchange. However, need is hardly more suitable.

Though the term means *need*, Aristotle is clearly thinking of something like demand as the basis for the actual fixing of the rate of exchange, either in barter or with money.

is to that of the farmer's work for which it exchanges: this makes the misleading suggestion that the farmer and shoemaker can be compared in worth, as well as their products. But there is no other basis for this, and the theory is better off without that assumption.

1133b *but when they still have their own goods*: cf. IX.1. In a commercial dealing, prices should be fixed before the exchange takes place.

the money value of five beds: though the account has explained well how money facilitates exchange, and is a kind of surety for the future purchase of what we later need, it has left obscure the basis of a *fair* or *just* exchange.

we have now defined the unjust and the just: the remainder of the chapter is only loosely connected with what precedes. The second question in ch. 1, what sort of a mean is justice? is now discussed.

a kind of mean, but not in the same way as the other virtues: i.e. it is not a mean between two vices, because *being unjustly treated* is a bad state of affairs but not, of course, a vice. That seems to be the point of the next remark that justice *relates to an intermediate amount*. In a just distribution or other transaction, the *outcome*—the amount distributed, for example—is neither too much nor too little but an intermediate, i.e. fair, amount.

1134a *to have too much is to act unjustly*: here Aristotle overlooks something he noted a few lines earlier: the person who distributes may not be one of the recipients. If A distributes to B and C *not* according to their 'merits', and gives too much to B, then B 'has too much', but it is A who has acted unjustly.

BOOK V, CHAPTER 6

in all other cases: this first paragraph is unconnected with the main theme of ch. 6. The discussion is continued in ch. 8.

either proportionately or arithmetically equal: cf. chs. 3 and 4. In a democracy male citizens are strictly, i.e. arithmetically, equal; in an oligarchy or aristocracy they are proportionately equal, i.e. have roles in proportion to their 'merit'.

Injustice . . . unjust action: to be explained in ch. 8; cf. II.4.

1134b *man's chattel*: i.e. his slave.

an equal share in ruling and being ruled: this is Aristotle's ideal in *Politics* 1283b.

BOOK V, CHAPTER 7

part legal: the distinction between what is by nature and what is merely by law or convention played an important role in the intellectual debates of the fifth century. Callicles in Plato's *Gorgias* distinguished between the just by nature—the strong suppressing the weak—and the just by convention or law. Protagoras in Plato's *Theaetetus* argues that what is just for a given city is simply what is enjoined by law or convention, and denies that anything is just in itself, independently of people's holding it to be so. Aristotle rejects both the denial of the 'just by nature', and the Calliclean version of what it is.

while they see change in the things recognized as just: Aristotle gives, and will go on to rebut, the argument that no justice is 'by nature' which derives from the observation that there is *change* in what is just. He may have two kinds of variation in mind; (1) variation across cities, or over time, in what is *held to be* just, and (2) the existence of exceptions to any principle holding that to do such and such is just. *Brasidas*: Thucydides, *Peloponnesian War* V.11, tells how games were instituted in honour of this Spartan general. *Decrees* introduced specific ordinances, rather than laws. The examples of what is just merely by law—the amount to sacrifice, for instance—are designed to invoke recognition that most things ordained by law, such as the prohibition of murder or the enjoining of debt-paying, are not *merely* just by law, but also by nature.

by nature, yet all of it is changeable: see previous note. Variability does not indicate non-naturalness; (1) even if one state forbids x-ing while another allows it, x-ing may still be unjust by nature, and (2) even if in some circumstances it is right, say, to withhold payment of a debt, that does not undermine the general principle that it is just (by nature) to repay one's debts. See Introduction, pp. xxii–xxiii.

1135a *one which is everywhere by nature the best*: Aristotle's view in *Politics* IV.7–8 is that rule by those possessing virtue is best.

since it is universal: a seemingly unrelated point recalling that actions are particulars (cf. III.1) not universals, while a rule—whether of natural or merely legal justice—mentions a *type* of action, such as 'it is right to repay your debts'.

BOOK V, CHAPTER 8

just or unjust: this chapter draws on, and elaborates, the account of the voluntary and involuntary at III.1 and 5. There is a rather different discussion in *EE* II.6–10.

not in his own power: for the criterion of being in one's power see 1110a17. The cases of acting *in ignorance* supplement those at 1110b24–33. The example of an involuntary-because-forced action used here—where my hand strikes another person but only because a third person forces it—supplements the earlier cases of 'carried away by the wind' and 'by men who have you in their power' (1110a3–4).

the whole action: a clarification: it is not enough to characterize an act simply as done with or without knowledge, since I may know that I'm hitting a man but not know he is my father. Aristotle is thinking of the murder of Laius by Oedipus. By 'the end' he means the outcome (not one's purpose, since one could not be unaware of that).

1135b *growing old or dying*: a further clarification of the account at III.1. Though growing old is an *internal* process—its cause is in the agent—it is not thereby voluntary, nor is it involuntary.

without previous deliberation: for the distinction between choice and the (merely) voluntary see III.2, end, where choice was defined with reference to deliberation.

three kinds of injury in transactions between man and man: the discussion is somewhat confusing because Aristotle uses *mistake* both in a general sense (in the next clause) and in a more specific sense at b17–19 below. Mistakes, as a genus, are all injuries involving ignorance; these will be subdivided into those involving non-culpable ignorance (labelled *misadventure*) and culpable ignorance (labelled *mistake*). Together they form the first category of injury. The second kind is *an act of injustice*, where there is knowledge but not deliberate choice, and the third (and worst) where there is choice, implying that the doer himself is unjust.

victim of misfortune when the origin lies outside him: it is not said explicitly that *mistakes* are voluntary and blameworthy, while *misfortunes* are neither, but it is said that the fault originates in the doer in the case of a mistake. This is because, although he was ignorant, it was not *contrary to reasonable expectation*. So it is his fault that he is ignorant.

injury is not due to vice: for this category of bad and blameworthy act, which does not stem from a bad character, see 1111a22–b3: acts done in anger or from desire (including those of children, who don't possess bad characters) are voluntary and blameworthy.

from choice . . . vicious man: in II.4 acting from choice was a necessary but not a sufficient condition of the possession of a vicious character. To be vicious required *regularly* choosing bad acts: perhaps Aristotle takes this for granted here.

1136a *are not excusable*: for the distinction between acting (merely) *in ignorance*—when one can and should be blamed—and acting *by reason of ignorance* see III.1, 1110b24–7 with note. It's not clear what kind of case Aristotle has in mind, in referring to acts stemming from passions that are *neither natural nor such as man is liable to*, which induce ignorance, and which are *not excusable*. A further problem is that these are a subset of *involuntary* acts, and hitherto involuntary acts have been excusable. One suggestion is that he has in mind drunken actions, but that hardly fits the description of the relevant passion as neither natural nor human. See VII.5 and 6 on human and non-human pleasures.

BOOK V, CHAPTER 9

as all unjust action is voluntary?: the discussion of the issues raised in this chapter continues in ch. 11, after a digression in ch. 10 on the equitable. For the (negative) answer to the first question: *can someone willingly be unjustly treated?* see 1136b21-9. The quotation is from the lost *Alcmaeon* of Euripides.

for some are unwillingly treated justly: presumably those who receive just punishment. So being treated justly is sometimes voluntary, sometimes involuntary, while being unjustly treated is—he will argue—always involuntary.

1136b   add '*contrary to the wish of the person acted on*'?: i.e. we *should* make this addition. The point is a fair one: voluntarily suffering what is unjust does not yet amount to being unjustly treated voluntarily. But the argument from incontinence that follows is hardly compelling.

the price of a hundred oxen for nine: At *Iliad* vi.236 Homer relates how Glaucus made an unfavourable exchange, swapping his gold suit of armour for the bronze one of Diomede. Since Diomede did not treat him unjustly, Glaucus has not been unjustly treated.

gets more than his share . . . of intrinsic nobility: it is somewhat paradoxical to suggest that the man who takes *less than* his fair share of money gets *more than his share of* the noble. In any case, to do so is not to act unjustly, Aristotle rightly concludes. Nor is it *any* kind of vice, it seems. As Aristotle noted (at the end of ch. 5), justice is not intermediate between two vices.

1137a   *either of gratitude or of revenge*: a rather desperate move to preserve the association between acting unjustly and graspingness, i.e. aiming at more than one's fair share, cf. V.1, 1129b1-10. A judge who makes an unfair distribution between two others *may* do so from one of these bad motives, but equally he may simply be careless or in a hurry.

nor in our power: to become unjust is in my power, but if I'm not now an unjust person, I can't now act from an unjust state of character. Cf. III.5.

turn to flight in this direction or in that: because the just person knows what just and unjust acts are, men think he *can* easily do unjust ones. But as II.4 has stressed (against the Socratic idea that virtue is simply knowledge) to be just involves not simply knowledge but a fixed disposition to choose just actions.

essentially something human: this paves the way for the surprising claim in X.8 that justice is not a quality the gods possess or act from.

BOOK V, CHAPTER 10

the equitable . . . the just: 'equitable' (*epieikēs*) in ordinary speech was used of someone who does not insist on their full due; a decent person. Aristotle enlarges on this to develop an important theme: equity is the tendency to discern where adjustments have to be made to what a strict application of justice would prescribe (and act accordingly).

1137b   *a correction of legal justice*: as explained, this does not make the equitable superior to what is really just.

and is not rigid: this seems to refer to a method, originating on the island of Lesbos, for measuring stone with a malleable leaden rule, perhaps to carve another that fits it.

is no stickler for his rights in a bad sense: this picks up the popular use of *equitable*; see first note on this chapter.

BOOK V, CHAPTER II

1138a *is evident from what has been said*: ch. 9, 1136a10–1137b4, argued that a man cannot treat himself unjustly.

what it does not expressly permit it forbids: this is a highly puzzling statement, which some editors have dealt with by emendation of the text. One suggestion is that Aristotle means that the law forbids any *killing* it does not expressly permit or command. He can hardly mean the law forbids *any* action it does not command or expressly permit.

treating the state unjustly: this paragraph is concerned with injustice in the wide sense (see ch. 1) and argues that, in that kind of justice as well, a person cannot treat himself unjustly. The suicide *harms himself*, and (perhaps) treats the state—not himself—unjustly.

he could be voluntarily treated unjustly: this was ruled out in ch. 9.

1138b *Incidentally . . . theory cares nothing for this*: ethical theory holds that doing injustice is worse than suffering it, as medical theory holds that pleurisy is worse than a fall, albeit a fall may happen to leave you much worse off.

BOOK VI

CHAPTER I

the intermediate is determined by reason, let us discuss this: see II.3 and 6, especially 1107a1, where a key part of the definition of moral virtue refers to it being determined by reason.

what correct reason is and what is the standard that fixes it: these seem to be two questions. To the first—what is correct reason?—the answer will be practical wisdom, *phronēsis*. It is not clear that Aristotle does, or can, give a different answer to the second question, although the analogy with the medical art would lead us to expect a standard, as health is the standard by which the medical art is judged.

1139a *with their objects . . . the knowledge they have*: Aristotle finds it natural to align different subdivisions of the rational part of the soul with different objects of knowledge: the *scientific* part is that which grasps the *invariable*, i.e. necessary truths and objects, and the *calculative* part that which grasps *variable* things. The virtue or excellence of the first will turn out to be wisdom, a combination of scientific knowledge and intuitive reason; that of the second will turn out to be practical wisdom, *phronēsis*.

BOOK VI, CHAPTER 2

no share in action: Aristotle here uses action in a narrow sense, confining it to what is chosen. Perception originates animal movement, but not action. The originator of action in this narrow sense will turn out to be choice, a combination of reason and desire.

truth in agreement with right desire: we might have expected the claim that as truth is what contemplative thought aims at, so the good is what practical thinking aims at. Instead Aristotle makes truth the goal or proper work (*ergon*) of each kind of thinking, adding the qualification 'in agreement with right desire' to practical thinking's goal. Perhaps we should understand as follows: the goal of practical thinking is to reach a true conclusion about what is to be done *and* to have a correct desire, i.e. a desire for the action specified.

its efficient, not its final cause: Aristotle's doctrine of 'four causes' is in *Physics* II.3. The other two are matter and form. Choice is the efficient cause, i.e. the origin of movement. The final cause is the end aimed at.

aims at an end and is practical: in saying 'intellect alone moves nothing' Aristotle may seem to be adopting a Hume-type approach to reason. But the concession that *practical* intellect can move a person immediately mitigates that impression.

1139b *that which is made is not an end in the unqualified sense . . . only that which is done is that*: for the important distinction between making and doing see chs. 4 and 5. *Making* is desired for the end or product, not for itself. *Doing*, in this technical sense, is desired for its own sake.

and desire aims at this: good action, i.e. acting well, is the true and proper end of a person. Aristotle does not mean to deny that we can desire to make something.

that have once been done: Agathon, a tragic poet, features in Plato's *Symposium*, celebrating the victory of one of his plays.

BOOK VI, CHAPTER 3

we may be mistaken: the five truth-attaining states are discussed one by one in chs. 3–7, after which issues concerning practical wisdom dominate the remainder of Book VI.

is of necessity: when he uses the term strictly, Aristotle insists that scientific knowledge, *epistēmē*, is of what cannot be otherwise, i.e. necessary and eternal truths. Aristotle does not explain why 'we all suppose this', as it is not part of everyday thinking about knowledge (the standard meaning of *epistēmē*) that only necessary truths can be known. Probably 'we' are fellow philosophers, especially from the Academy.

in the Analytics also: *Posterior Analytics* I.1.

by induction that they are acquired: since scientific knowledge is knowledge arrived at by syllogism, i.e. by demonstrative reasoning from known premisses, the premisses or starting-points themselves cannot be the objects of such knowledge. In ch. 6 this role—grasp of the starting-points—is ascribed to intuitive reason, *nous*.

which we specify in the Analytics: *Posterior Analytics* I.3: we have scientific knowledge of p when we have demonstrated p—a necessary truth—from starting-points that are themselves known, and better known, than the conclusions derived from them.

BOOK VI, CHAPTER 4

1140a *capacity to make*: art—i.e. technical expertise—and practical wisdom are both concerned with 'the variable', i.e. things that can be otherwise. This chapter analyses art.

to make, involving true reasoning: architecture (including actual building) is chosen as an example to illustrate the general thesis that equates art with reasoned capacity to make.

chance loves art': on Agathon see note on VI.2, 1139b9. Chance, necessity, nature, and art were listed at III.3 as types of cause, but the point of the quotation is obscure.

BOOK VI, CHAPTER 5

to the good life in general: an important claim, one that counteracts some later descriptions that seem to give a more confined role to practical wisdom. He now contrasts this with having practical wisdom in some particular sphere (e.g. one's business life) as well as with being good at some form of making (an art).

1140b *are different kinds of thing*: as argued in ch. 4.

good or bad for man: i.e. for a human being, as *passim*. 'State of capacity to act' means a disposition manifested in *actions*, in contrast to art, manifested in *making* something. So to be practically wise a person must act, and not merely deliberate.

cause of action: the whole parenthetical section elaborates on Aristotle's improbable etymological derivation of temperance, *sōphrosunē*, as meaning 'saving *phronēsis* (practical wisdom)'. Over time intemperance will destroy judgements about 'what is to be done', i.e. about right and wrong.

in practical wisdom, as in the virtues, he is the reverse: see II.4. Practical wisdom resembles moral virtue in that, with both, we prefer an unintentional mistake to a deliberate one. In art, and in general expertise, the reverse is true: the more skilled practitioner is the one who, for example, plays a wrong note *intentionally*.

practical wisdom cannot: another point in which practical wisdom is closer to the moral virtues (cf. I.10, 1100b15–16) than it is to arts or indeed other kinds of knowledge that one does readily forget.

BOOK VI, CHAPTER 6

scientific knowledge involves demonstration: as shown in ch. 3, scientific knowledge involves demonstration, i.e. proof, from better known starting-points. In this chapter Aristotle assigns to intuitive reason, *nous*, the grasp of these starting-points or first principles. An example of such a starting-point in the natural sciences is the principle that every element has its natural place.

1141a *intuitive reason that grasps the first principles*: in ch. 11 Aristotle will recognize a second kind of intuitive reason connected with practical wisdom, whose object is particulars.

BOOK VI, CHAPTER 7

nor wise in anything else: the quotation (from *Margites*, not in fact by Homer) is here used to underline the point that Aristotle's focus is on an *unqualified* wisdom, and not being wise at, for instance, ploughing.

combined with scientific knowledge: here Aristotle reveals that the last of his five initial states to be discussed, wisdom, is not an independent state but the combination of two already discussed: scientific knowledge (ch. 3) and intuitive reason (ch. 6).

1141b *the bodies of which the heavens are framed*: being *invariable* objects, whose movements, according to Aristotle, are invariable, the heavenly bodies are superior to and *more divine in their nature* than human beings, who are merely the best of animals.

but useless: Anaxagoras (5th cent.) and Thales (6th cent.) were bywords for unworldly philosophers. Plato relates a story of Thales falling into a well while stargazing.

practice is concerned with particulars: doing is always doing some particular action. Reasoning which remains at the level of universals cannot result in action, a further ground for distinguishing practical wisdom from philosophic wisdom. However, in what follows, Aristotle seems to use *particular* to pick out the more specific (e.g. chicken) in contrast to the more general—light meat.

is more likely to produce health: despite not *knowing* in the strict sense (see ch. 3), a person of experience—if they are aware that chicken is wholesome, but not that light meat is—is more likely to end up healthy than one who knows only the latter.

both forms of it, or the latter in preference to the former: this contains the interesting suggestion—perhaps mitigated by the following sentence—that knowledge of *particular truths only* may suffice for practical wisdom, though ideally a practically wise person will know both kinds of truth.

a controlling kind: *sc.* of practical wisdom, as explained in the next chapter. Aristotle returns to emphasizing the importance of an overarching grasp of the good (as well as of particulars).

BOOK VI, CHAPTER 8

legislative wisdom . . . 'do things': both political wisdom and practical wisdom have two aspects, an overarching or controlling one (legislative wisdom, and concern for the general good, respectively), and a narrower one. For political wisdom, the narrower one is politics in the everyday sense: doing things. For practical wisdom, the narrower aspect is concerned with the agent's own good, as the next paragraph explains.

1142a *busybodies; hence the words of Euripides*: see previous note for the misconception that practical wisdom is exclusively concern with one's own good. In what follows Aristotle counters the view that exercising practical wisdom on a grand scale is being a busybody. The quotation is from the lost *Philoctetes* of Euripides, Odysseus speaking.

weighs heavy: while this amplifies remarks in ch. 7, the precise train of thought is unclear.

opposed, then, to intuitive reason: practical wisdom, being a grasp of 'the ultimate particular fact', lies at the opposite pole from intuitive reason, which grasps very general principles, here called *limiting premisses*: see ch. 6. Particulars are labelled *ultimate* since they come last in a piece of practical reasoning.

peculiar to each sense: practical wisdom involves a kind of perception, here distinguished from (1) the perception exercised by the five senses and (2) the perception that a given figure is a triangle. But it resembles (2) more than (1). For more on practical wisdom as a kind of perception, see ch. 11.

BOOK VI, CHAPTER 9

excellence in deliberation: (*euboulia*); it needs investigating since ch. 7 laid down that it is a mark of the man of practical wisdom to deliberate well.

1142b *an object of opinion is already determined*: opinion, being a kind of inner assertion, cannot be what excellence in deliberation is, since the latter is a kind of inquiry.

to attain what is good: an important clarification. Merely to deliberate successfully and achieve your end does not count as excellence in deliberation, if your end is bad, like that of the incontinent person. See further VII.6, 1149b14 ff.

apprehends truly: the Greek leaves it open whether Aristotle is saying that practical wisdom apprehends truly (*a*) the end or (*b*) what conduces to the end. (*a*) is the more likely construal, though it may seem to conflict with what was said in ch. 5. If that reading is correct, we have the puzzle that different objects ((*a*) and (*b*)) seem to be assigned to practical wisdom, and to excellence in deliberation, and yet the latter was discussed since it is what practical wisdom is, in large part.

BOOK VI, CHAPTER 10

1143a *practical wisdom issues commands . . . but understanding only judges*: having narrowed down practical wisdom to the sphere of the practical—see ch. 8 with which this chapter fits best—Aristotle now contrasts it with understanding. An exercise of understanding might lie in judging a practical proposal—see later in this chapter—while that of practical wisdom involves making a recommendation (to oneself or another).

when it means . . . knowledge: the Greek word *manthanein*, 'to learn', also means 'to understand'. This was a source of eristic puzzles, see Plato's *Euthydemus* 275–8, and Aristotle's *Soph. El.* ch. 4.

BOOK VI, CHAPTER 11

judgement . . . '. . . sympathetic judges' . . . the equitable: For a discussion of the equitable, see V.10. The first part of this chapter discusses the further intellectual virtues of judgement (*gnōmē*) and sympathetic judgement (*sungnōmē*). Like understanding (ch. 10) they are close to practical wisdom, but they judge, rather than 'issue commands'.

and understanding: the list of qualities said to converge now includes intuitive reason (*nous*) though earlier (chs. 3 and 6) that was confined to invariables, and was the grasp of the first principles of scientific knowledge.

1143a–b *intuitive reason is concerned with the ultimates in both directions . . . i.e. the minor premiss*: see previous note about the addition of intuitive reason to the list of qualities dealing with particulars. The *ultimates in both directions* are (1) the very general first principles of science and (2) the last and variable facts in practical reasoning. Aristotle assigns great weight to the grasp of (2), so we may assume it includes key judgements such as 'eating that cake would be greedy' or 'to repay this debt now would be just'. What (1) and (2) have in common is that no *rational account* (*logos*), i.e. no proof, of them can be given. But this still allows that reason, in a broad sense, is involved in grasping such truths.

this perception is intuitive reason: cf. the end of ch. 8, where Aristotle likened to perception the cognitive grasp exercised by a man of practical wisdom. Here he chooses to label it *intuitive reason*, though 'intuition' would better capture the quasi-perceptual aspect he is emphasizing.

experience has given them an eye they see aright: experience—in a well brought up person—has shaped the ability to 'see' the appropriate response, i.e. the ultimate or particular (moral) facts. Compare end of ch. 8.

a different part of the soul: cf. ends of chs. 1 and 2.

BOOK VI, CHAPTER 12

Difficulties . . . qualities of mind: this chapter and the next, which conclude the discussion of philosophic and practical wisdom, discuss puzzles concerning the two virtues, and in so doing introduce important new claims about the relation of moral virtue to practical wisdom, and the inseparability of the moral virtues. Replies to the first two difficulties occupy this entire chapter and most of ch. 13, while the end of ch. 13 replies briefly to the third difficulty.

none the more able to act for having the art of medicine or of gymnastics: this first objection—questioning the value of both philosophic and practical wisdom—relies on an alleged analogy with medical knowledge. Merely knowing what manifests health, such as a healthy complexion, doesn't enable one to achieve health, says the objector.

but again it is of no use to those who have not virtue: this overstates the case, which is more accurately put in what follows—you *can* get by with the help of someone else's practical wisdom.

strange if practical wisdom ... is to be put in authority over it ... issues commands about that thing: for the reply to this third objection see ch. 13, 1145a6-11.

1144a *virtues of the two parts of the soul respectively*: i.e. the subdivisions of the rational part of the soul. See VI.1, 1139a6-8.

health produces health: as health is the 'formal cause' of health—in contrast to the art of medicine, its efficient cause—so philosophic wisdom, *a part of virtue entire*, is a formal cause of happiness. This second reply in effect restates the first: both virtues benefit us simply by being virtues, i.e. parts of happiness.

virtue makes the goal correct, and practical wisdom makes what leads to it correct: this is a highly problematic statement, in so far as it *suggests* a division of labour between virtue (i.e. moral virtue) and practical wisdom analogous to Hume's division of labour between goal-setting—the province of desire—and means-finding, the sole province of reason, according to Hume. But such a division of labour cannot be Aristotle's overall view. He does not confine practical wisdom to the finding of means; he allows it a role, together with moral virtue, in making the goal correct. But as a reply to the objection, he needs stress only its other role, making *what leads to (the goal) correct*. This may include both (1) choosing the correct route to a determinate goal, or (2) further specifying an indeterminate goal.

and for the sake of the acts themselves: cf. II.4. To reply to the second objection above—taking advice from a practically wise person can make you good—Aristotle distinguishes yet again merely doing good acts from being a good person, i.e. choosing the good acts, and for their own sakes.

clever or smart: smart (*panourgos*) is the label used for a clever but wicked person. A different textual reading would yield: 'hence we call both men of practical wisdom and smart men clever'. 'Clever' is a neutral term, but 'practically wise' can be used only of a good person.

the syllogisms ... is not evident except to the good man: this is a new point, the claim that all pieces of practical reasoning start from general principles, which only a good man can grasp. Earlier, in chs. 8 and 9, the emphasis was on knowledge of particular truths.

impossible to be practically wise without being good: this somewhat surprising conclusion is drawn from the claim that wickedness perverts the starting-points, but it goes far beyond that. It is easy to see why a wicked person cannot be practically wise, but why cannot a continent person? In I.13 Aristotle claimed that we praise the rational principle of the continent person. Perhaps the restrictions on good deliberation in ch. 9 explain this exclusion (so Irwin *ad loc*.). At any rate, it is an important claim, that only the good person can be practically wise.

BOOK VI, CHAPTER 13

1144b *natural virtue to virtue in the strict sense*: virtue in this chapter means moral virtue. Aristotle has not referred so far to natural virtue, though in II.1 he wrote that we are adapted by nature to receive the (moral) virtues. Just as cleverness is not practical wisdom, for the latter needs virtue, so natural virtue is not virtue in the strict sense, for the latter needs practical wisdom.

children and brutes have the natural dispositions . . . without reason these are evidently hurtful: the reference to children suggests (contrary to the earlier 'from the moment of birth') that Aristotle relies on the observation that some small children are naturally braver, or more fair-minded than others. That is, their feelings and tendencies to act resemble those of the possessors of those virtues, but they lack the rational appreciation and goals that are needed for full virtue. *Reason* here translates *nous* (elsewhere 'intuitive reason'). Aristotle evidently means it to be roughly equivalent to practical wisdom, as in ch. 11.

Socrates . . . he was right: Aristotle seems to refer to the historical Socrates and not merely to the character in Plato's dialogues. In *Protagoras* and *Laches* Plato's Socrates defends the claim that all the virtues are forms of knowledge: knowledge of good and bad. Aristotle represents this as the claim that the virtues are 'forms of practical wisdom', and, a few lines later, that they are 'instances of reason': a view that has some truth in it but needs refining.

and practical wisdom is correct reason about such matters: Aristotle refines the commonplace that virtue must be 'in accordance with right reason' to insist, as elsewhere, that the virtuous person must himself possess correct reason, i.e. practical wisdom. (A different interpretation of the distinction between 'in accordance with' and 'implies the presence of' is defended by J. A. Smith in *Classical Quarterly*, 1920.)

involve reason: again Aristotle makes the required correction to Socrates' view. It is uncertain whether in saying that virtue *involves reason* (literally, 'is with reason') Aristotle means that practical wisdom is a necessary condition of virtue or—a stronger claim—that it is a necessary part or facet of moral virtue. The latter harmonizes better with the overall tenor of chs. 12 and 13.

the natural virtues, but not . . . without qualification good: to have virtue in the strict sense, you must have all the virtues (because to have any of them you must have practical wisdom, which is inseparable from all the virtues). What the objectors urged, that one can possess one virtue without the rest, is true only of the natural virtues. Even though this claim stops short of proclaiming the *unity* of the virtues (as Socrates does in Plato's *Protagoras*), it is still surprising to find the argument that the virtues are *inseparable*, on the ground that each entails possession of practical wisdom which in turn entails possession of all the virtues. The last point is hard to square with the fact that to possess some virtues (e.g. magnificence, IV.2) one needs (for instance) great wealth.

1145a *it is not supreme over philosophic wisdom . . . affairs of the state*: the reply to point (3) in ch. 12 relies on an analogy. In regulating religious practice, a politician does not thereby 'rule the gods'; just so, even if practical wisdom is exercised by, say, setting up a research programme, it is not for that reason superior to the virtue it is promoting, philosophic wisdom.

BOOK VII

CHAPTER 1

1145b *incontinence and softness . . . continence and endurance . . . nor as a different genus*: an important plank in Aristotle's overall account is the distinction he draws between, on the one hand, vice proper and the lesser faults of incontinence and softness, and, on the other, between virtue proper and the good states which fall short of it, continence and endurance. He now devotes several chapters to a fuller account of these, which have already been discussed at many points, especially I.13 and II.3.

set the apparent facts before us . . . resolve the difficulties . . . we shall have proved the case sufficiently: approaching a subject by setting out *apparent facts* (i.e. common opinions, as the sequel shows) and the difficulties they entail is a favourite ploy of Aristotle, found also in *de Anima* I and *Physics* I.

BOOK VII, CHAPTER 2

what kind of right judgement has the man who behaves incontinently: the second common opinion in ch. 1 was that the incontinent knows what he does is bad; it will be the main focus of chs. 2 and 3. In this formulation (*right opinion*) it is left open whether an incontinent can have *knowledge* that what he is doing is bad.

Socrates . . . people act so only by reason of ignorance: this is a summary of the position of Socrates in Plato's *Protagoras*; the phrase *drag it about like a slave* is an echo of *Prot.* 352b. In *Prot.* Socrates does not deny that people can succumb to temptation, but gives a different account of the phenomenon from the one 'the many' give. His view is that as long as you know or believe that x is better than y you will not do y; only a change in your evaluation of the two can allow a choice of y. Hence, at the time of choosing y, you are ignorant that x is the better option, on the view voiced in Plato's dialogue by Socrates.

what is the manner of his ignorance?: Here Aristotle hypothesizes some kind of ignorance; earlier he spoke of some kind of right judgement. His (not very clear) verdict on the cognitive state of the incontinent comes at the end of ch. 3.

they say that the incontinent man has not knowledge . . . but opinion: this was not the line Socrates took in *Protagoras* (see note above), nor is it a solution Aristotle adopts. To the reasons he gives in this chapter for rejecting it, he adds another in ch. 3 1146b24–31.

1146a *the man of practical wisdom . . . has the other virtues*: see VI chs. 5, 7, and 13. Whatever good cognitive state is compatible with incontinence—the question under discussion—it cannot be practical wisdom, given the intrinsic connection between that and virtue, and hence good action.

pained at telling a lie: in Sophocles' *Philoctetes* the young Neoptolemos reneges on a previous agreement to trick Philoctetes. Hence he is an example of 'good incontinence' if such exists. Chapter 9 resolves the puzzle.

and not what is evil: see ch. 9 for the solution to this puzzle.

1146b *something quite different*: ch. 8 will argue for the contrary (and less paradoxical thesis) that to be incontinent is *less* bad than to be self-indulgent—i.e. than to pursue disreputable pleasures out of conviction.

BOOK VII, CHAPTER 3

as is shown by the case of Heraclitus: here we have a further argument against the suggestion in ch. 2 that an incontinent person can act against opinion—here, right opinion—but not against knowledge. Aristotle rejects the suggestion, drawing on the strength of opinion manifested in the dogmatic pronouncements of the sixth-century philosopher Heraclitus.

or is exercising it: apparently the terms 'using' and 'exercising' pick out the same contrast with merely 'having' knowledge. In the case of theoretical knowledge the point is clear: I may 'have' lots of knowledge—e.g. of historical dates—that I'm not 'exercising', i.e. I'm not currently aware of them. It is less clear what the distinction amounts to in the practical sphere: is using/exercising knowledge (1) being aware of it or (2) acting on it? See next but one note.

1147a *or is not exercising the knowledge*: to quote Ross: i.e., if I am to be able to deduce from (*a*) 'dry food is good for all men' that 'this food is good for me', I must have (*b*) the premiss 'I am a man' and (*c*) the premisses (i) '*x* food is dry', (ii) 'this food is *x*'. I cannot fail to know (*b*), and I may know (*c* i); but if I do not know (*c* ii), or know it only 'at the back of my mind', I shall not draw the conclusion.

would be extraordinary: commentators differ sharply on whether Aristotle is here describing a case of incontinence, or just drawing distinctions relevant to incontinence. The 'extraordinary' case would have to be where a person has full knowledge of all the above, and is 'using' his knowledge, but does not choose the dry food. This passage seems to show that 'using' cannot simply mean acting on, for then the case would be (not extraordinary but) logically impossible.

asleep, mad, or drunk: an important but problematic comparison. What these states share with each other and with incontinence, according to the comparison, is that they count as 'having knowledge and yet not having it'. When awake, I may have but not 'use' bits of knowledge; when asleep, I *cannot* use them until first awakened. Likewise a drunk person must first become sober, a mad person sane, before they can 'use' the knowledge they 'have'. The strong desires of the incontinent— so Aristotle suggests—place the knowledge he has temporarily 'out of reach', like the knowledge of the drunkard.

no more than its utterance by actors on the stage: Aristotle here answers the objector who protests that incontinent people 'use the language that flows from knowledge'. (For example, the incontinent person may say 'I shouldn't be doing this.') Their saying this doesn't prove they know it, any more than the words of a drunk, or, he now adds, of an actor. Empedocles (5th-cent. Sicilian) wrote natural philosophy in verse.

a student of nature would: cf. Aristotle's *On the Movement of Animals*, ch. 7 where, as here, he explains human actions (i.e the movement special to humans) by reference to practical reasoning. This paragraph, which promises to explain incontinence as a student of nature would, is difficult and its interpretation is contested. These notes adopt a 'traditional' interpretation whose elements include: (1) Aristotle here further describes the kind of case described in the previous paragraph, whereby some kind of ignorance or failure of reasoning (akin to that of the drunk) explains incontinence. (2) He distinguishes theoretical from practical reasoning. (3) He describes incontinence as involving a failure either to be fully aware of a key premiss or to draw the conclusion 'I shouldn't be doing this'. (1) is denied by Charles and Irwin, (2) by Charles, and (3) by Broadie as well as Charles and Irwin.

it must immediately act: probably Aristotle here contrasts theoretical with practical reasoning (despite using the term 'productive'). At *On the Movement of Animals*, ch. 7, he writes that the conclusion of a piece of practical reasoning *is* an action. But here he writes only that 'when a single opinion results'—i.e. when a conclusion is reached—one must act. ('The soul must act' means no more than 'the person must act'.)

the one opinion bids us avoid this, but appetite leads us towards it (for it can move each of our bodily parts): the first clause here is the chief piece of evidence that (contrary to the traditional interpretation) Aristotle allows for what the popular account of incontinence assumes, i.e. for the agent to do the wrong thing in spite of forming the judgement that he should 'avoid this'. 'Avoid this' certainly seems to be the *conclusion* of the 'good' reasoning of the incontinent person, which, the next clause tells us, is disregarded in favour of the bidding of appetite. However, it is hard to square this with all the other indications that Aristotle believes that some kind of cognitive failure is involved in incontinence, e.g. the previous section likening the incontinent to someone asleep, mad, or drunk, and the claim a few lines earlier that one who reaches a practical conclusion 'must immediately act'. So we should perhaps understand 'the one opinion bids us avoid this' in terms of premiss bidding the agent avoid *this type* of action. See also next note.

1147b *the position that Socrates sought to establish . . . perceptual knowledge*: clearly Aristotle makes some concession to the position of Socrates he had earlier labelled counter-intuitive. The concession is that the 'knowledge' that he (Aristotle) holds is somehow affected or diminished when a person acts incontinently is not universal knowledge (e.g. that no sweet things should be tasted) but 'perceptual knowledge' or that of the 'last premiss'. Thus 'true knowledge' (universal knowledge) is untouched, on this view, and the effect appetite has is only on 'perceptual knowledge'. But there are difficulties in working out the detail of his explanation. (1) Above—see previous note—he spoke of an opinion bidding us 'avoid this', which could be the conclusion of a piece of reasoning as follows: Universal premiss: avoid all sweet things; Particular premiss: this is sweet; Conclusion: avoid this. But now he speaks of the 'last premiss'—which must be either the particular premiss or the conclusion—as something the person either *doesn't have* or has only in the attenuated way of the drunk. So he seems *both* to say (to account for incontinence) that there is a crucial bit of ignorance, *and* (in the previous paragraph) to say something inconsistent with that. (2) And if the incontinent person is—as the example suggests—to act on his appetite for sweet things, he must indeed be aware that 'this is sweet'. One solution to these problems is to think of a pairing between a universal and a particular premiss: the incontinent pairs the premiss 'this is sweet' not with his universal knowledge that sweet things are to be avoided, but with the opinion (prompted by appetite) that 'everything sweet is pleasant'. Hence the particular premiss 'this is sweet' is *active* in connection with the opinion that sweet things are pleasant—hence he grabs the sweet thing—but *overlooked* in its connection with the Universal premiss 'Avoid all sweet things'. The effect of the strong appetite for the sweet thing in question is this crucial and selective 'overlooking'. (3) The phrase *it's not in the presence of knowledge proper that the passion occurs* is puzzling, since Aristotle in the next phrase insists that knowledge proper is not affected. Hence some accept a conjecture by Stewart (*dokousēs periginetai*), yielding the sense 'it is not what seems to be knowledge in the proper sense that the passion overcomes . . . but perceptual knowledge'.

BOOK VII, CHAPTER 4

not simply incontinent . . . by reason of a resemblance: in III.10 the sphere of temperance and self-indulgence was restricted to the pleasures of taste and touch. The same restriction is now applied to simple or unqualified incontinence and continence. This approach is in contrast with a modern one (made famous in D. Davidson's essay 'How is Weakness of the Will Possible?') whereby incontinence, or acting against one's better judgement, is treated as a single phenomenon, regardless of what emotion or other motivation prompts it.

Anthropos: the Greek for 'Man' (i.e. human being); it was the name of an Olympic victor in 456 BC.

1148a *some of them make a deliberate choice while the others do not*: the ones who don't *choose* the course of action they pursue are the incontinent, who a few lines earlier were said to act 'contrary to choice and judgement'. Cf. VII.3, 1146b23.

some pleasant things are by nature worthy of choice . . . to adopt our previous distinction: Aristotle presumably refers to the discussion earlier in this chapter, at 1147b23–31, though he phrases the distinctions here rather differently.

Niobe . . . Satyrus: in myth, excessive pride in her children was Niobe's downfall. The reference to Satyrus is uncertain but he seems to have been a king who deified his father.

1148b *by nature a thing worthy of choice . . . excesses . . . are . . . to be avoided*: cf. 1148a3 for the distinction between vice and a state that is not a vice (since it deals with an object worthy of choice, such as respect for parents or children) but whose excess is to be avoided.

BOOK VII, CHAPTER 5

the brutish states . . . story told of Phalaris: 'brutishness' is due to *originally bad natures*. Phalaris, tyrant of Acragas, roasted his victims alive in a bronze bull; perhaps *the story* added that Phalaris ate the roasted flesh. Cf. 1149a15 below.

1149a *in respect of fits of anger . . . but not incontinent simply*: ch. 6 discusses incontinence in respect of anger.

BOOK VII, CHAPTER 6

appetite . . . springs to the enjoyment of it: anger is a more specifically human emotion than appetite, as shown by its ability to reason with universal principles.

1149b *dragged his father only as far as that*: angry disputes between father and son were a stock theme of comedies.

more given to plotting . . . more criminal: this third argument seems at first sight inconsistent with the first, which held incontinence due to anger to be less disgraceful *precisely because* it uses a sort of reasoning. But the difference is that the object of anger—revenge—is intrinsically reasonable (Aristotle holds) while the object of sexual desire is not. *Plotting* to obtain the latter enhances the disgrace.

both incontinence without qualification and in a sense vice: but this (worse) kind of incontinence is still not strictly speaking a vice, as has often been emphasized, especially in ch. 1 1145a35 ff.

commits wanton outrage: Greek *hubris*, typically committed by drunken young men.

As, among men, madmen are: it is odd to compare madmen, who are a departure from the norm for their species, with an entire animal species that gets labelled self-indulgent, if only by metaphor. Presumably such a species is a departure from animal nature generally.

1150a *as a brute*: i.e. a beast or non-human animal. Brutishness in this paragraph names the condition of beasts, in contrast to chs. 1 and 5 where it is used for a condition of naturally depraved human beings.

BOOK VII, CHAPTER 7

cannot be cured: 'self-indulgent' translates *akolastos*, literally 'uncorrected' or 'incorrigible'.

a kind of softness: not softness proper, which is the counterpart of incontinence, avoiding pains but not on principle (not 'by choice'). Here the vice labelled *a kind of softness* is the one described before the parenthetical sentence: avoiding pains by choice and without regrets.

1150b *Xenophantus*: reference uncertain. The two playwrights mentioned are contemporaries of Aristotle whose plays do not survive.

impetuosity . . . weakness . . . led by their emotion: who are these incontinent people who *have not deliberated*? They cannot be persons who have not formed any choices on the matter, since it is part of the definition of incontinent action that it is 'contrary to choice' (e.g. 1148a9). In the light of the illustration that follows, he probably means those who are taken off their guard when a temptation is presented. Each part of this twofold division into *weak* and *impetuous* incontinence is puzzling, and hard—though not impossible—to make consistent with what is said elsewhere (esp. in ch. 3) about incontinence. The *weak*, who *fail to stand by the conclusions of their deliberation*, are hard to reconcile with those parts of ch. 3 that suggest that the incontinent does not reach or does not fully appreciate the conclusion of a deliberation resulting in the judgement that this action should not be done.

BOOK VII, CHAPTER 8

in the formulation of the problem: i.e. at 1146a31–b2, where the puzzle proposed that it is the self-indulgent person who is easier to cure. This chapter argues for the contrary thesis.

incontinence is not <unconscious of itself>: unlike a bad man, an incontinent person recognizes his own condition.

1151a *while the latter is not*: for the incontinent to be persuaded to change his mind is for him to be brought to act well, in accordance with the good convictions he already has.

virtue either natural or produced by habituation . . . about the first principle: to strengthen his argument that the self-indulgent person is worse and less curable than the incontinent, Aristotle stresses the role of good character (as against reason) in grasping the correct first principle. By 'virtue produced by habituation' he probably means full virtue. For the contrast between this and 'natural virtue' see VI.13. Only habituated virtue can consistently produce the right first principle, though natural virtue may do so by chance.

for the best thing in him, the first principle, is preserved: this is inconsistent with the claim in VI.12 that the right starting-point is evident only to the good person (hence, apparently, not to the incontinent, or even the continent). This reflects a tension in two ways of thinking about the incontinent and the continent. (1) Their grasp of good and bad is faultless—as this passage suggests; their flaws are excessive desires. (2) VI.12 and 13 suggest that, because of these character flaws, the incontinent and the continent have a faulty grasp of good and bad.

BOOK VII, CHAPTER 9

1151b *by Odysseus to tell a lie*: cf. ch. 2, 1146a20 with note.

is seen in few people and seldom . . . so is continence to incontinence: the alleged (rare) fault is one in which a person has a correct belief about the appropriate pleasures to enjoy, but falls short in such enjoyment through a failing opposed to incontinence.

BOOK VII, CHAPTER 10

1152a *cleverness and practical wisdom . . . near together in respect of their reasoning, but differ in respect of their choice*: see VI, 1144a23–b4 on the relation between cleverness and practical reason. A clever person's choice, but not that of a practically wise person, may be bad. Irwin offers a different translation 'near in their definition', to avoid the suggestion that reasoning belongs to both the practically wise and the clever person.

who is asleep or drunk: cf. ch. 3, 1147a11–17 and 1147b6–9 for the comparison between the incontinent and a person asleep or drunk. In that respect the incontinent is not like one who 'knows and is contemplating truth', but in what follows Aristotle will say the incontinent acts *in a sense* with knowledge.

while the excitable man does not deliberate at all: cf. ch. 7, 1150b19–28.

this becomes man's nature in the end: Evenus was a fifth-century sophist. The distinction between incontinent by nature and by habit is new. Here habit (despite the quotation) does not mean practice, since one does not practise being incontinent.

BOOK VII, CHAPTER 11

1152b *the architect of the end . . . good without qualification*: for political philosophy as having an overarching remit, cf. I.2, 1094a6–8. The end with a view to which we call things good or bad is *eudaimonia*. Hence the question about pleasure is its place in the best life. This is the first treatment of pleasure in *NE*; the second is at X.1–8. On the relation between them see the first note on X.1.

blessed . . . from a word meaning enjoyment: 'blessed' renders *makarios*, which by a fanciful etymology Aristotle connects with *chairein*, to enjoy.

no process is of the same kind as its end: Aristotle will deny that pleasure is a process (*genesis*: sometimes translated 'coming-to-be'), something that had been argued in Plato's *Philebus*, 53–4. He agrees that if it were a process, it could not be as good as the end (*telos*) of the process. While Book VII discusses views asserting that some or all pleasures are not good, Book X will consider the view (of Eudoxus) that pleasure is *the* good.

BOOK VII, CHAPTER 12

are not even pleasures, but seem to be so . . . the processes that go on in sick persons: what does the claim that some processes are not even pleasures amount to? If a sick person relishes sharp-tasting foods, are we to say he only thinks he is enjoying it, but isn't really? The formulation suggests a less extreme claim: the sick person may really be enjoying the food, but eating such food isn't (truly) a pleasure.

the activity of so much of our state and nature as has remained unimpaired: determined to deny processes a role in pleasure, Aristotle here claims that what a recuperating patient really enjoys is not the recovery *process* but the *activity* of some unimpaired part of his make-up. But the argument that follows—that some pleasures do not involve (the processes of) pain or appetite—is insufficient to show that no pleasure is a process.

1153a *to the perfecting of their nature*: for further elaboration of Aristotle's rejection of the view that pleasure is a process see X.3 and 4.

instead of 'perceptible' 'unimpeded': the proponents of the view that pleasure is a process added the qualification 'perceptible', presumably because not all processes are pleasurable. For analogous reasons Aristotle adds 'unimpeded' to his characterization of pleasure as an activity. But the rival view, in stressing that pleasure must be something of which a person is aware, made an important point, which is missing from Aristotle's alternative characterization 'unimpeded activity'.

BOOK VII, CHAPTER 13

1153b *Speusippus . . . just a species of evil*: Speusippus was Plato's nephew and successor. It is uncertain just what his view was and to what extent he is Aristotle's main target in the accounts of pleasure. See Gosling and Taylor, *The Greeks on Pleasure*, ch. 12. The solution mentioned seems to be this: pain can have two contraries in the same way that greater has two—less and equal. So it is the intermediate—neither pleasure nor pain—that is the good state. Aristotle seems to object that this commits Speusippus to making pleasure essentially bad. For a similar but not identical argument from contraries see X.2, 1173a6–13.

the chief good would be some pleasure . . . bad without qualification: a remarkable conclusion, which in effect equates pleasure, as well as happiness, with unimpeded activity of the best kind.

the victim on the rack . . . is happy . . . talking nonsense: cf. I.5, 1096a1–2 for a similar dismissal of the possibility. Plato in *Republic* (particularly Books II–IV) may be the target of Aristotle's criticism here, for maintaining that a just person, despite enduring torture and other hardships, is happier than an unjust person, however many pleasures and other goods the latter enjoys.

that many peoples: Hesiod, *Works and Days* 763–4.

1154a *if it is not good but the happy man may even live a painful life?*: Aristotle takes this to be obviously false, and in conflict with what all men think, cf. 1153b15 above.

BOOK VII, CHAPTER 14

or are they good up to a point?: this is Aristotle's own view. He rejects the views (1) that all bodily pleasures are bad, and (2) that they are merely 'not bad' and in that sense only good.

1154b *the students of natural science . . . as they maintain*: Aristotle apparently accepts the theory that sight and hearing involve pain that we have mostly got used to and hence don't notice. Its source is unknown.

through some action of the part that remains healthy: for this odd theory, cf. ch. 12, 1152b35–6 and note.

but an activity of immobility: for Aristotle's views on god's nature see *Met.* XII. 7. Though unchanging, god—according to Aristotle—enjoys the unending activity of thinking. Mortals can think only for shorter periods.

as the poet says: Euripides, *Orestes* 234.

BOOK VIII

CHAPTER 1

1155a *friendship . . . with a view to living*: friendship translates *philia*, which covers more than the English term would suggest. One's *philoi*— 'friends'— include family, business-partners, and fellow-citizens as well as those more naturally labelled 'friends'.

the truest form of justice . . . a friendly quality: Aristotle probably means equity, discussed in V.10. It involves not demanding everything one is strictly entitled to.

not only necessary but also noble: hence friendship is not just a sine qua non of happiness, as the earlier paragraphs may have suggested, but a virtue, and hence a component of happiness.

1155b *like aims at like*: the writings of the pre-Socratic philosophers Aristotle mentions, Heraclitus and Empedocles, featured *philia*—friendship or love—and strife as two cosmological principles.

BOOK VIII, CHAPTER 2

object of love: Greek *philēton*. The Greek term has a variety of meanings that the English cannot capture. *Philēton* is cognate with *philia* (here translated friendship) and can mean any of the following: 'worthy of love', 'what is loved', and 'lovable'. Below 'lovable' is used.

or what is good for them?: cf. III.4, where the same problem arises.

three grounds on which people love: i.e. as mentioned above under 'objects of love': the good, the pleasant, and the useful. They form the basis of the three kinds of friendship discussed in the next chapters.

1156a *for one of the aforesaid reasons*: this probably means, for any one of them. If so, the account of friendship is that it requires reciprocal well-wishing, and mutual awareness thereof, based on one of the three 'lovable' qualities—the good, the pleasant, and the useful. But Aristotle will go on (in ch. 3) to privilege only one ground: the good, i.e. virtue.

BOOK VIII, CHAPTER 3

because of utility . . . some good which they get from each other: the phrases 'because of utility' and 'because of pleasure' refer sometimes to the cause of the friendship and sometimes to the ground or motive. The translation 'because of' allows all these. Loving on one of these grounds contrasts with loving a person *for himself* and *for his character*, which Aristotle equates with each other and with 'for who he is'—see next note.

not as being the man he is . . . but as providing some good or pleasure: see previous note—a third way of characterizing the best ground of friendship. The other friendships are *only incidental* since based on features of the person—his being pleasant or useful to one—that are not essential to him.

friendship of host and guest: traditional host–guest ties between families from different city-states gave rise to long-standing relationships and obligations of hospitality to visitors.

1156b *Perfect friendship . . . and goodness is an enduring thing*: these lines introduce an important refinement on loving someone *for their sake* or *for themselves*. These are now—surprisingly—equated with loving someone for their good qualities. The linking idea is that of loving someone for their essential qualities (cf. *by reason of their own nature and not incidentally*) which—Aristotle assumes—one does only when the other is a virtuous person.

pleasant both without qualification and to each other: to be pleasant without qualification is to be pleasant to the good person. It follows that virtue friendship will be both pleasant without qualification and to each of the parties. Other types of friendship will be, at best, pleasant *only* to the parties concerned.

BOOK VIII, CHAPTER 4

1157a *between lover and beloved*: a typical homoerotic relationship was between a younger beloved and a (slightly) older lover, who plied the beloved with gifts and attention in return for sexual favours. As Aristotle goes on to point out, while many of these relationships were transient, lasting only as long as the beloved was of a certain age, others were longer-lasting. See K. J. Dover, *Greek Homosexuality*, and J. Davidson *The Greeks and Greek Love*.

in the proper sense . . . and by resemblance to the other kinds: Aristotle does not here take exactly the line he does in *EE* 1236a15 ff. There he says the three kinds of friendship are so-called by the special kind of homonymy he labels 'focal meaning'. Here he allows a similarity, and hence they are all entitled to the name 'friendship'.

1157b *because of themselves, . . . i.e. in virtue of their goodness*: as noted above, Aristotle equates loving someone for himself with loving him for his good qualities.

BOOK VIII, CHAPTER 5

live together . . . companions seem to do: the focus is on spending time with one's companions (i.e. chosen friends), not living under the same roof. Even when he goes on to praise the contemplative life as one capable of being lived by a solitary person (X.7) Aristotle still acknowledges that it is better shared with friends.

BOOK VIII, CHAPTER 6

1158a *but do need pleasant friends*: cf. IX.9, which returns to the question why the happy man, being self-sufficient, needs friends.

the Good itself if it were painful to him: probably a joking reference to Plato's Form of the Good, on which see I.6.

who surpass him in both respects are not so easy to find: a good person will rarely find a superior who also exceeds him in virtue, and hence will rarely be friends with one *who surpasses him in station*.

BOOK VIII, CHAPTER 7

1158b *equality . . . characteristic of friendship*: where the parties are unequal (as in a parent–child relationship) the kind of equality present in the friendship will be proportionate equality, cf. V.3.

and proportion to merit secondary: in the case of friendship proportionate equality—found in unequal friendships, is only second-best, since strict equality—here labelled *quantitative equality*, is best in friendships. Where (distributive) justice is concerned, the priority is reversed, and proportionality to merit is best.

1159a *e.g. that of being gods . . . (for friends are good things)*: on the usual interpretation, which the translation assumes, the puzzle Aristotle notices is this. Commonly friends are said to wish the best for their friends, but X does not wish his friend Y to become a god, since, though that might be best for Y, it would deprive X of Y's friendship. Others interpret the passage differently, such that it is out of consideration for Y's good that X would not wish him to become a god, since, being a god, Y would lack friends. The end of the chapter favours the first interpretation; X.8 further discusses whether a good person loves his friend the most, or himself.

BOOK VIII, CHAPTER 8

they delight in honour . . . judgement of those who speak about them: see I.5 for the claim that what we desire for itself is not honour but the virtue which is—or should be—the ground of being honoured.

nothing of a mother's due: the altruistic love of a mother for her child is often remarked on by Aristotle. See also 1161b26, 1166a5, 1168a25. On the one hand it is the most striking instance of loving another for that other's sake, even to the extent of being prepared to part with the child for its benefit. But this very willingness comes at the cost of mutual love, which is another hallmark of friendship.

1159b *foreign to our inquiry*: cf. ch. 1, 1155b9, where Aristotle declines to pursue friendship as a cosmological or physical principle.

BOOK VIII, CHAPTER 9

1160a *for life as a whole]*: Ross brackets these lines, noting that 'It seems best to treat ll 19–23 as an insertion from an alternative version.' In this he goes beyond the Oxford Classical Text, which brackets—i.e. deletes— ll. 19–20 but retains line 21. Some words are missing in line 23.

BOOK VIII, CHAPTER 10

timocratic . . . are wont to call polity: Greek *politeia*—literally constitution, as in the first line of the chapter—is also used by Aristotle as his label for what he regards as the best kind of constitution, a limited democracy based on a property qualification (Greek *timēma*). This must not be confused with Plato's use of the word timocracy in *Republic* for the rule of those who love honour (*timē*). For the six constitutions, see next note.

1160b *but it is the contrary of the best that is worst*: since tyranny is evidently the worst regime, monarchy must be the best, though this is less obvious. Here monarchy is the rule of one who is good, wise, and benevolent. The overall ranking is thus

Constitution type		Deviation-form	
(best)	monarchy	(worst)	tyranny
(second)	aristocracy	(fifth)	oligarchy
(third)	timocracy	(fourth)	democracy

Democracy is the least bad of the deviations: perhaps because in tyranny and oligarchy bad men are in power, while the fault of democracy is that all (adult male) citizens have a share in power however poor and lowly. At *Politics* III. 7 the common fault of all three 'deviations' is that they aim exclusively at the good of whoever holds power.

master over slaves: in *Politics*, especially I.3–7, Aristotle defends slavery but with certain limitations. It is surprising to find him here both approving of the master–slave relationship and labelling it tyranny. His claim that Persians treated their sons as slaves betokens a typical Greek belief.

BOOK VIII, CHAPTER 11

1161a *rule is taken in turn, and on equal terms*: see *Politics* III.6 for this as Aristotle's ideal constitutional arrangement, one where suitably qualified persons rule and are ruled in turn. To suggest this is characteristic of fraternal relations is perhaps stretching too far the analogies between political and familial relationships.

1161b *party to an agreement; therefore . . . friendship with him in so far as he is a man*: cf. ch. 10, 1160b29 with note. Aristotle does not resolve the conflict between the claims that one cannot be friends with a slave *qua* slave, but with one *qua* man one can. His notorious doctrine in *Politics* I.5 that some men are natural slaves is hard to reconcile with his appreciation here that justice and hence friendship can exist between all—including slaves—who can *share in a system of law and be party to an agreement*.

BOOK VIII, CHAPTER 13

1162b *since he gets what he aims at; for each man desires what is good*: a rather contrived explanation for the obvious fact that in true friendship a person does not complain if he does more favours than he receives. For further discussion of the explanation offered—that in doing more favours one is getting what one desires—the good, i.e. good actions—see IX.8.

and the other legal: contractual relations are here regarded as a kind of utility friendship. They are further subdivided into those requiring immediate fulfilment and those allowing a delay. Natural and legal justice were discussed at V.7, but the distinction is rather different from that between legal, i.e written, and unwritten agreements.

1163a *the purpose of the doer is a sort of measure*: purpose translates *prohairesis*, elsewhere choice. This distinction, whereby the measure of benefit in utility friendship is what one party *gains*, while in virtue friendship it is the benefit the giver *intended*, is typical of Aristotle's insightful discussion of these cases in VIII.13–IX.3.

BOOK IX

CHAPTER 1

1164a *pleasure for pleasure*: in return for the pleasure the listener gained, the player had enjoyed a night of anticipating his fee.

Protagoras used to do: his self-confident policy of fee-collection is related by the fifth-century sophist Protagoras in Plato, *Protagoras* 328bc: 'When someone's taught by me, if they want to, they pay the sum of money that I charge; but if they don't want to do that, they can go to a temple, state under oath how much they think the teaching was worth and leave an offering of that amount.'

'Let a man have his fixed reward': Hesiod's advice at *Works and Days* 368.

no one would give money for the things they do know: despite the reference to Protagoras' reliance on payment in arrears a few lines earlier, Aristotle here displays his poor opinion—shared with Plato—of the sophists' claim to knowledge.

BOOK IX, CHAPTER 2

1165a *generally the debt should be paid . . . defer to these considerations*: as is typical, Aristotle qualifies a general rule—that one should pay a debt before benefiting a friend—and notes exceptions, here the memorable example of ransoming your father rather than repaying the debt owed to the man who ransomed you. Piracy was a perennial hazard. The deed would be both *noble* and *necessary*, presumably.

have only as much definiteness as their subject-matter: by *discussions about feelings and actions* Aristotle means discussions of ethical matters. See Introduction, pp. xxii–xxiii. All universal rules (unless they are stated in morally loaded terms) have exceptions.

BOOK IX, CHAPTER 3

1165b *the breach . . . excess of wickedness*: in stressing the relevance of past ties between two persons, even where there is now a marked disparity of virtue, Aristotle shows greater allegiance to a common-sense account of friendship than his 'official' account perhaps warrants.

BOOK IX, CHAPTER 4

1166a *seem to have proceeded from a man's relations to himself*: this claim, that the marks of friendship *derive* from a man's relations to himself, is bold and scarcely plausible. The argument shows at most that the marks of friendship set out in the first paragraph apply equally to the good man's relations to himself.

mothers do to their children, and friends do who have come into conflict: see VIII.8, 1159a31 for mothers who wish well to the children they have given up. Estranged friends will still wish each other well despite the parting.

someone else (for that matter even now god possesses the good): to help show that no one wishes to possess great goods at the price of becoming someone else, Aristotle points out that god's possessing the good is no good to me, hence becoming a person in possession of goods who is no longer me would also be no good to me. Hence I can't rationally wish it.

the element that thinks . . . to be so more than any other element in him: for the identification of a person with his thinking part, see ch. 8 and X.7, 1178a2–7.

his friend is another self: it is perhaps telling that Aristotle derives this from the proportion: X is to his friend as X is to X. He is less certain whether the reverse transference applies, i.e. whether to conclude that X is a friend of himself, given that he has the relation to himself that he has to his friend. See next note.

In so far as he is two or more: though dismissing the question whether a man can be a friend to himself, Aristotle hazards that it *is* possible if a man is two or more. He probably has in mind the distinction into the thinking and the non-rational part of a human being, for which see I.13, and 1166a22-3 above.

1166b *no one who is thoroughly bad and impious has these attributes*: *sc.* of being satisfied with themselves and having a good opinion of themselves. This seems inconsistent with earlier claims (e.g. at 1152a4-6) that the vicious person, in the form of the self-indulgent, is comfortable with his actions, which he chooses and thinks he should be doing. However, Aristotle still maintains a difference between the vicious and the incontinent, as the next lines show.

bad men are full of regrets: see previous note. In VII it was the incontinent, not the bad, who were characterized as prone to regret. But the incontinent regret their actions at the time; perhaps the point about the bad is that they regret *past* actions.

BOOK IX, CHAPTER 5

1167a *for goodwill too does not arise on those terms*: this passage is subject to contrary interpretations. If Aristotle is claiming that good will does not exist at all in friendships based on usefulness or pleasure, this seems inconsistent with the most natural interpretation of VIII.2, 1155b31 ff. One solution (John M. Cooper, 'Aristotle on Friendship', in Rorty 1980) is to confine the point Aristotle is making to the narrow one that good will—if it was initially present without full friendship—cannot *develop into* these other kinds of friendship, but only into a character friendship. However, the points in the following lines seem to show he is making the more general claim (so Irwin, Pakaluk).

BOOK IX, CHAPTER 6

Concord also . . . characteristic of friendship: Concord, *homonoia*, was an important concept in political discourse. Aristotle confines it to agreement over policy, excluding shared *beliefs*.

or that Pittacus should be their ruler: Pittacus was the elected supreme ruler of Mytilene who relinquished office after ten years; see Aristotle, *Politics* 1285a.

captains in the Phoenissae: Euripides' play depicts the struggle for power between the brothers Polynices and Eteocles. Faction or civil strife, *stasis*, was the scourge of Greek city-states.

BOOK IX, CHAPTER 7

1167b *the case of those who have lent money is not even analogous*: Aristotle rejects the cynical explanation of the paradoxical thesis that forms the theme of this chapter: benefactors love those they have benefited more than the converse. Cynics liken benefactors to debtors who have an interest in the debtor's survival.

1168a *for what he is in potentiality, his handiwork manifests in actuality*: Aristotle has replaced the creditor–debtor model with a craftsman–handiwork model to explain the phenomenon that is the subject of the chapter. The fantasy of an artefact coming alive is not strictly essential to the argument. The argument draws on many themes from his theoretical philosophy and its key idea is that active beneficence is good activity akin to the activity of making exemplified by a craftsman. Both are choice-worthy precisely because existing is choice-worthy and this, for a human being, is 'living and acting'. To say that the handiwork manifests in actuality what the craftsman is in potentiality is a fancy way of saying that the product shows that the craftsman's potential (his craft) has been actualized—put into practice. It is supposed to explain why the craftsman loves his product—anyone prefers actuality to mere potentiality.

BOOK IX, CHAPTER 8

whether a man should love himself most, or someone else: it is unfortunate that Aristotle puts the issue this way, since he could make the points he will make below about good self-love without suggesting there is a contest of the above kind.

facts clash . . . not surprising: the points in favour of self-love are labelled facts, but they consist (like the points against it already rehearsed) in appeals to common opinions including proverbs. Aristotle has no hesitation in calling some well-established beliefs facts.

1168b *no one would call such a man a lover of self or blame him*: though this is true of common parlance—which would not call striving after noble deeds self-love, Aristotle will argue that it should properly be so-called.

1169a *the good man loves most this part of him*: cf. ch. 4 and X.7, 1178a2–7, for the claim that a man properly is his rational part—here identified as the origin of noble actions.

for he will both himself profit by doing noble acts, and will benefit his fellows): this formulation shows a way of avoiding the opening question of the chapter: should a man love himself most or someone else? There is no competition between the two kinds of benefit—doing noble deeds, and benefiting others. But in the remainder of the chapter Aristotle returns to formulating the issue as if there is a competition.

he is therefore assigning the greater good to himself: this exemplifies the point made in the previous note.

it may be nobler to become the cause of his friend's acting than to act himself: a nice paradox. If I try to pass to my friend the opportunity for greater nobility, I'm bound to fail, since to do so is nobler!

BOOK IX, CHAPTER 9

1169b *greatest of external goods*: on the happy life as self-sufficient, see I.7, 1097b6 ff. The debate about the compatibility of self-sufficiency and friendship goes back to Plato's *Lysis* (e.g. at 215A6) and *Symposium*. On external goods, see I.8. Friends, like other external goods, are a necessary condition of happiness—chiefly, as Aristotle will argue, as persons to treat well and to spend time with in rational activities. He must show they are not merely useful to virtuous activity—as wealth, for instance, is.

a political creature and one whose nature is to live with others: cf. 1097b11.

1170a *have both these qualities*: my friend's actions, if he is good, are both worthy and 'my own'. But a few lines earlier Aristotle said that I can contemplate my friend's actions better than I can my own. So the argument needs two different senses in which actions can be 'one's own', (1) the ones I do and (2) ones my friend does which are 'my own' (*oikeia*) in the sense of being familiar, congenial.

continuously active; but with others and towards others it is easier: this stretch of argument relies on the definition of happiness as activity or actuality. He here claims—plausibly—that when solitary it is hard to be active continuously. But in X.7 he will praise contemplation as the activity a man can carry on longest on his own—though better still with others.

1170b *if all this be true, as his own being is desirable for each man, so, or almost so, is that of his friend*: this is the interim conclusion of a long and convoluted argument that proceeds from claims about human nature, i.e. that what's good by nature is good and pleasant to the good person, and the claim that (for men) to live is to perceive and think. The role of the curious claims about the reflexive nature of perceiving is unclear, though if the point is that reflecting on our own thinking and perceiving, when these are good, is extra pleasant, it is doubtless correct. Recapitulating the point (from IX.4) that the good person is to his friend as he is to himself, he reaches the interim conclusion that my friend's being is (almost) as desirable to me as my own.

sharing in discussion and thought . . . and not, as in the case of cattle, feeding in the same place: the overall conclusion of this long argument is now drawn. The happy man must perceive the existence of his friend together with his own (*sunaisthanesthai*: see below), and that means sharing his activities, specifically, discussions. *Perceiving together* seems to bridge both the reflexive perception mentioned above, and the perception of shared activities which this final conclusion invokes. The lengthy argument seems more of a philosophical *tour de force* than a convincing argument for the thesis that a good man needs friends, though its conclusion, that good activity shared with congenial friends is essential to a happy life, is indisputable.

BOOK IX, CHAPTER 10

of many guests nor a man with none': Hesiod, *Works and Days* 715. On host–guest relations see VIII.3, 1156a31 and note.

it is a city no longer: see *Politics* VII.4, 1326a5 ff. for Aristotle's strictures on the proper upper (and lower) population limits for a city to remain a viable political entity.

1171a *obsequious*: see IV.4.

BOOK IX, CHAPTER 11

1171b *better type of person*: better both because more manly and more careful to avoid burdening others with one's grief.

kill-joys by repulsing them; for that sometimes happens: the common-sense arguments and advice of this chapter contrast sharply with the abstract reasoning of ch. 9.

BOOK IX, CHAPTER 12

perceiving is active when they live together: since living together involves undertaking joint activities, we actively perceive these, and actual perceiving is preferable to merely having the capacity to perceive.

BOOK X

CHAPTER 1

next to discuss pleasure: we can infer that the two treatments of pleasure (here, and in VII.11–14) originally belonged to different works, since no indication is given that this is a second treatment. The Book X discussion is longer, and contains novel discussion of the pro-hedonist arguments of Eudoxus as well as fuller treatment of the claim that pleasure is not a movement (*kinēsis*) or a coming-to-be or process (*genesis*). In VII, esp. ch. 12, Aristotle characterizes pleasure as 'unimpeded activity'; the account in X is more nuanced and complex. A major issue is the relation between pleasure and the activity in which a person takes pleasure.

pleasure is the good: Eudoxus, whose views are discussed in ch. 2.

others . . . say it is thoroughly bad: perhaps Speusippus, whose anti-hedonist views were discussed in VII. But VII.13 suggests he did not go so far as to call pleasure thoroughly bad.

BOOK X, CHAPTER 2

at which all aim was the good: cf. I.1 for the linkage between the good and that at which everything aims. But Aristotle does not endorse the conclusion that pleasure is the good; perhaps he rejects the assumption that pleasure is a single thing, while accepting that all (living) things aim at pleasure.

its contrary must be similarly an object of choice: Aristotle accepts the badness of pain, but will conclude that it shows pleasure is *a* good, not the good.

implying that pleasure is in itself an object of choice: this third argument starts from an important point: pleasure or enjoyment is reason-giving.

Again, Aristotle can agree that pleasure is 'chosen not for the sake of something else' but resist concluding that it is *the* good; cf. I.7, 1097b1–5.

by the addition of any of the things that are good in themselves: Aristotle endorses this argument, drawn from Plato's *Philebus*, esp. 21–2 and 60–1. The principle that *the* good cannot be made better by the addition of other goods played a key role in his argument that happiness is the chief good (for human beings), in I.7, 1097b14–20.

1173a *opposition between them*: Aristotle here rebuts objections to Eudoxus' hedonist thesis, criticizing two counter-arguments. He accepts the underlying principle that a thing may have more than one contrary, cf. 1153b1–7. But he denies the opponents' application of this principle to pleasure and pain.

BOOK X, CHAPTER 3

nor is happiness: the objection 'pleasure is not a quality' may have been used in the Academy. Since happiness is not a quality (but is evidently good), the argument fails.

of this kind: another Academic argument, based on Plato, *Philebus* 24–5, 31a.

1173b *we can change quickly or slowly . . . we cannot quickly exhibit the activity of pleasure, i.e. be pleased*: as in VII.12–13, Aristotle denies the Platonic view that pleasure is a movement (*kinēsis*) or coming-to-be (*genesis*), and thus can deny that pleasure is *incomplete*, i.e. imperfect or not end-like. This new argument, that quick and slow apply to movements but not to pleasure/ being pleased, is a subtle one, and relies on a distinction between quickly becoming pleased (which is possible) and quickly being pleased (which is impossible). It is disputed whether this is an argument from ways of speaking, or from the supposed metaphysics of pleasure as a natural phenomenon.

takes place, i.e. the body: Plato's *Republic* and *Philebus* both contain the view of pleasure as a replenishment, i.e. a movement towards a natural state of satiety. It took as paradigms the pleasures of eating and drinking. Aristotle's objection—that on that view it would be the body which feels pleasure, but it is not—is noteworthy in opposing a common view that the bodily pleasures are experienced by the body.

if one was being operated on: this translates the manuscripts' text *temnomenos*. But the text may be corrupt, for the argument needs a word for being depleted—the opposite of being replenished.

supplying anew: like Plato, Aristotle insists that not all pleasures follow a perceived lack. Both give as their counter-example the pleasures of learning. But one might reasonably claim that the pleasure of proving a theorem, for example, is enhanced if one has previously suffered frustration at lacking such a proof and has had an intense desire to prove it.

without being musical, and so on: that pleasures differ in kind, reflecting the differences in what is enjoyed, is a profound point, and one that helps Aristotle resist the Eudoxan thesis, which assumes pleasure is of a single kind. See first note on ch. 2 above.

1174a *though he were never to feel any pain in consequence*: compare, with this point that there are some pleasures—childish, or wicked ones—that no right-minded adult would choose, J. S. Mill's 'competent judges test' for superior quality pleasures in *Utilitarianism—*, ch. 2.

BOOK X, CHAPTER 4

pleasure also seems to be of this nature: this chapter contains the fullest defence of the claim that pleasure is not a movement—i.e. something incomplete until it is over—but is like seeing which is *at any moment complete*. Even if what I'm seeing takes time—e.g. a horse race—my seeing it does not take time to complete. Likewise enjoyment or pleasure, Aristotle suggests. Most of his examples are of enjoying activities, such as looking at beautiful sights or listening to music, but he does allow (1175a34–5) that one can enjoy building—a paradigm of a movement.

1174b *that which takes place in an instant is a whole*: literally 'in the now', cf. *Physics* IV.10–14. The contrast is with a period of time, which a movement needs, since it has a beginning, middle, and end.

a coming into being of pleasure: the text here has been emended to read *tēs hēdonēs*.

there is no coming into being of seeing: Aristotle does not deny that a person can see at a later time what he did not see at an earlier time. Rather, the transition from not seeing to seeing is not a coming to be, a process.

pleasure completes the activity: having earlier *compared* pleasure to seeing, Aristotle now attempts to explain the relation between the pleasure one takes in an activity and the activity itself. He focuses on what he regards as paradigm human pleasures, enjoying the activities of our sense-faculties and intellect. In seeing a beautiful sunset, for example, the sense *acts perfectly in relation to its object*. It is unclear just what he means by saying pleasure completes the activity. Perhaps he simply means that enjoying seeing a sunset makes perfect the activity/actualization involved when I see the sunset. But see next note but one.

not in the same way the cause of a man's being healthy: in the example, the doctor is the efficient cause and health is the formal cause. But it is not clear that the distinction applies to the case in point, where *the combination of object and sense* and *the pleasure* are causes in different ways of the 'completion' involved when one enjoys seeing a beautiful object.

but as an end which supervenes as the bloom of youth does on those in the flower of their age: though memorable, this phrase does not fully clarify Aristotle's answer to the question: what is the relation between the pleasure of seeing and the seeing? On one interpretation, Aristotle is remarking that while actual seeing of a fine object is something perfect (cf. being in the flower of youth), enjoying it is an added perfection (cf. 'bloom'—a facial beauty—added to the flower of youth). Evidently he wishes to avoid two errors; first, that of equating seeing a sunset with enjoying doing so, but second, that of making the enjoyment something quite distinct from the seeing itself. See the further discussion in ch. 5, 1175b34–5.

1175a *life is an activity*: *life* is more than just being alive. Here, as elsewhere (e.g. IX.9, 1170a13–19) living is equated principally with the activities of human perception and intellect.

BOOK X, CHAPTER 5

1175b *appear to some people the same*: Aristotle has (1) *compared* pleasure to seeing and other activities, and has denied pleasure is a movement (ch. 4), and (2) has now pointed out that pleasures differ in kind as their corresponding activities do (this chapter). So it is not surprising that *to some people pleasure and the activity enjoyed appear the same*. This belief, which he here insists is wrong, could easily have been prompted also by his own statement in VII.12, 1153a12–15, that pleasure is unimpeded activity.

1176a *sight is superior to touch in purity . . . and those of thought superior to these*: sight and hearing are *purer* than taste and touch since they are less dependent on a physical medium. For the same reason, thought—which does not even require a sense-organ—is superior to any sense perception, and its pleasures are correspondingly purer.

are the measure of each thing: on the good person as the measure, see III.4, 1113a31–3 with note. There the good man's discernment was the measure of what is *really good* or *desirable*; here, what the good man/healthy person enjoys is the mark of what is *really pleasant*.

only pleasant to these people and to people in this condition: presumably Aristotle does not deny that the wicked and sick actually enjoy their (abnormal) pleasures. Rather, they are wrong if they judge that those things are really pleasant. See previous note.

BOOK X, CHAPTER 6

happiness does not lack anything, but is self-sufficient: Aristotle recaps the essential characteristics of happiness, as outlined in I: it is an activity, lacking in nothing, desirable for its own sake, and self-sufficient (I.7). He will proceed to argue that contemplation (*theōria*) best satisfies these criteria, while a life of (morally) virtuous activity comes second (ch. 8).

for the sake of activity: amusement is ruled out as a candidate for happiness, even though it appears to satisfy one key criterion: being chosen for its own sake. Anacharsis was a Scythian prince who came to typify the wise barbarian. His aphorism demotes amusement to a *means*, a form of relaxation whose end is activity.

1177a *is the more serious*: Aristotle here prepares the ground for the next chapter, where he will allow supreme value to serious *leisure* activities, not to be confused with unserious amusement, which this chapter dismisses.

no one assigns to a slave a share in happiness —unless . . . human life: on slaves see VIII.11, 1161b2–8. Since slaves don't enjoy a life of the activities that constitute happiness, they cannot be held to be happy. A more obvious reason might be that they don't have autonomous choice, but that happiness requires this remains unstated. At *Politics* 1280a31–4 *natural* slaves are said to be *incapable* of happiness, but that is not the point he is making here.

BOOK X, CHAPTER 7

That this activity is contemplative we have already said: contemplative activity occurs when the intellect studies the highest truths and objects, as distinct from the use of the intellect in practical matters. For the distinction see Book VI, esp. ch. 1, 1139a15–17. In VI wisdom was the virtue of the contemplative intellect, practical wisdom that of the practical intellect. Despite the claim that *we have already said* this, he has not explicitly identified contemplative activity as the best. But Book I hinted that one excellent activity is best, at chs. 7, 1098a16–18, and 8, 1099a29–39. The focus on contemplative activity is somewhat unexpected, both in the light of the overall tenor of the work and of the remark in this very paragraph about reason as the *natural ruler and guide*, suggesting that practical thought is included in reason.

the objects of reason are the best of knowable objects: unchanging objects, such as numbers, and invariable truths, e.g. about the movements of the heavens, are, *qua* unchanging, the best objects of knowledge, cf. VI.7, 1141b1–3. This argument, from superiority of object to superiority of cognitive state, is brief but important to Aristotle's enterprise.

pass their time more pleasantly than those who inquire: to rank the pleasures of inquiring below those of knowing is highly counter-intuitive. But Aristotle is committed to this ranking, since it is required by his ranking things that are for the sake of an end (such as inquiring) below things that are chosen only for themselves (such as contemplation, here labelled knowing). Another reason may have been the thought that god only contemplates, and has no need ever to inquire. Nonetheless the reader is likely to surmise that Aristotle himself spent more time (and had more enjoyment) inquiring than knowing.

is the most self-sufficient: see I.7, 1097b6–21 for the insistence that the best life must be self-sufficient. Here Aristotle concedes that a contemplative life is not fully self-sufficient but more nearly so than a life requiring just and temperate actions. The argument, repeated and developed in the next chapter, relies on a new, and rather unconvincing, notion of self-sufficiency, such that to need people to behave justly towards is to lack self-sufficiency.

1177b *are not desirable for their own sake*: A puzzling claim. It is used as a further reason for ranking the life of political activity (i.e. the exercise of moral virtue in the political sphere) lower than that of contemplative. Aristotle relies on the point from the previous sentence that it aims at ends other than itself. But that does not prevent the activities also being aimed at for their own sake, which he stipulated of acts manifesting moral virtue at II.4. Irwin, to remove this puzzle, favours an alternative translation: 'and are desirable for something other than themselves'.

something divine is present in him . . . composite nature: in an abrupt shift from the recent claim that the contemplative life will be the *complete happiness of man*, Aristotle now labels it divine, in contrast to the activity of our *composite nature*. By *composite* he may mean soul plus body, or—more appropriate in this context—rational plus non-rational parts of the soul (see I.13). The nature of human beings is composite in both ways. God is incomposite, being nothing but contemplative intellect. Hence our contemplative intellect is the most godlike part of us.

1178a *This would seem actually to be each man . . . better part of him*: correcting the remark above, Aristotle now claims that reason, as the best and most divine part of a man, *is* what a man is. So man is not, after all, something of a composite nature.

BOOK X, CHAPTER 8

in a secondary degree the life in accordance with the other kind of virtue is happy: since the word *happy* has to be supplied, some have argued that instead we should supply *happiest*, from the last sentence of the previous chapter. Either way, the life of moral virtue (whether in the political or private sphere) is what is intended by *the other kind of virtue*, and it is being ranked second to the contemplative life. There is a dispute over whether Aristotle is comparing and ranking whole lives, or (as some claim) the relevant aspects of the life of a single person. His language— harking back to the traditional comparison of lives—certainly suggests the former, but this leaves it puzzling that, having lavished considerable attention on delineating the moral virtues, he ranks only second a life manifesting these. Later in this chapter he notes that the contemplative person will choose to do virtuous acts *in so far as he is a man and lives with* others.

virtues of our composite nature are human: cf. note on ch. 7, 1177b28, for *composite nature*.

is a thing apart: i.e. from our composite nature. The contemplative intellect can be defined without reference to the non-rational soul-parts or to the body. Whether it can exist independently of these is a matter debated in *De Anima* III.4–5.

temperate man will need opportunity: further arguments (cf. ch. 7) to show that the life practising moral virtue is less self-sufficient than that practising contemplation.

1178b *need such aids to living a human life*: though his life is more self-sufficient, and is hindered by *too many* possessions, the man living the contemplative life will *qua* man choose morally good acts, for which some externals are required.

trivial and unworthy of gods: Aristotle here rejects traditional Greek ideas of the gods as subject to passions, and as capable of, e.g., just acts.

activity of god . . . must be contemplative: given that god is a living being, and that his nature does not allow acting (i.e. making a difference to the world) or producing anything, only contemplative activity is left. *Endymion*: a young man beloved of the Moon who was endowed with eternal sleep.

other animals . . . they in no way share in contemplation: but they also lack the capacity of rational choice, so this point hardly justifies placing contemplation above practical activity.

1179a   *Solon . . . do what one ought*: cf. I.10, 1100a10, on Solon. Aristotle can accept the views of Solon and Anaxagoras only up to a point, i.e. as endorsing the claims (to constitute happiness) of the life of moral virtue, albeit only in second place.

should reward those who love and honour this most: it is controversial to what extent Aristotle endorses this last argument, to the effect that gods will reward mortals whose activities are most godlike. Against a serious endorsement one may cite (1) the tentative phrasing *if the gods have any care for human affairs, as they are thought to have*, (2) *Metaphysics* XII.7–9: the gods do not know or care about mortals, and (3) earlier in this chapter he denied moral virtues to the gods, but here he suggests they reward contemplation among mortals. But he certainly endorses the conclusion that the wise person—i.e. the person with the virtue of the contemplative intellect—is dearest to the gods.

wise man . . . happy: as in VI, the wise man is the possessor of philosophic wisdom, wisdom about the unchanging truths and objects.

BOOK X, CHAPTER 9

1179b   *others by teaching*: cf. II.1. The debate is featured in Plato's *Meno*. Aristotle's answer invokes the need for good laws and hence the ability to design them. Since *nomos* means custom as well as written law, he is not thinking of *written* legislation at every point. See 1180a35–b2 below.

1180a   *unless he be a king, or something similar*: as in VII.10, a king is any ruler who is acknowledged as wise and benevolent.

1180b   *to get what suits his case*: education, like medical treatment, must focus on the requirements of the individual—child or patient. But such treatment is, as he will point out, typically best given by one with universal knowledge.

with this that the sciences are concerned: cf. VII.6 and *Metaphysics* I.1 on how universal knowledge develops from experience.

1181a   *need experience as well*: the line of thought in this paragraph owes much to Plato's discussion in *Meno* and *Protagoras* of the question: who teaches virtue, or political excellence? Strictly Aristotle's question is a different one: who teaches the art of legislation?—but the issues are similar. Sophists are ruled out on the grounds they do not practise the art they profess to teach, while politicians are ruled out since unable to teach their own sons (echoing *Protag.* 319e–320a, *Meno* 93c–94e). However, at least they have the requisite experience.

easy to legislate by collecting the laws that are thought well of: a critical reference to the *Antidosis* of Isocrates, a fourth-century writer and orator, who wrote the work to defend his own profession and beliefs.

1181b *in such matters*: the mere assembly of good sets of laws will not make a person a good legislator; experience is a key ingredient, though reading sets of good laws will improve one's understanding.

what laws and customs it must use, if it is to be at its best: here Aristotle announces the programme for his *Politics*, a programme that he largely follows in that work. Already at I.2 he had announced that the current inquiry belonged to politics, the most authoritative art.

GLOSSARY OF KEY TERMS

action, conduct	*praxis*	
activity, actuality, actualization	*energeia*	
appetite	*epithumia*	non-rational desire
art	*technē*	i.e. expertise, craft
capacity	*dunamis*	sometimes 'faculty'
choice	*prohairesis*	also sometimes 'purpose'
compulsory, compelled	*anagkaion*	
continence	*enkrateia*	i.e. self-control or self-mastery
desire	*orexis*	the generic term, covering 'appetite' and 'wish'
equity, equitable	*epieikeia, epieikēs*	
final, complete, perfect	*teleion*	literally 'end-like'
force, forced	*bia, biaion*	
function	*ergon*	also 'product', 'work'
happiness, happy	*eudaimonia, eudaimon*	
incontinence	*akrasia*	i.e. lack of self-control or self-mastery
intermediate (cf. mean)	*meson*	often this has an evaluative connotation, and means 'appropriate'
intuitive reason	*nous*	sometimes just 'reason'
involuntary	*akousion*	at some points 'unintentional' would convey the meaning better
making	*poiēsis*	contrasted with action, VI.4–5; cf. 'art'
mean (cf. intermediate)	*mesotēs*	literally 'intermediate state'
movement	*kinēsis*	also means 'change'
noble	*kalon*	sometimes 'beautiful'
pain	*lupē*	the general term for distress
passion, emotion, feeling	*pathos*	
perception	*aisthēsis*	sometimes, 'sensation' or 'sense'
pleasure	*hēdonē*	
practical wisdom	*phronēsis*	
pride	*megalopsuchia*	literally 'greatness of soul'
process, coming-into-being	*genesis*	literally 'becoming'
reason / right reason	*logos / orthos logos*	most often used for something grasped by a rational faculty; sometimes for the faculty itself

scientific knowledge	*epistēmē*	sometimes just 'knowledge'
state of character	*hexis*	sometimes just 'state', 'state of capacity'
virtue	*aretē*	occasionally 'excellence'
voluntary	*hekousion*	at some points 'intentional' would convey the meaning better
wisdom	*sophia*	restricted to philosophic wisdom by Aristotle
wish	*boulēsis*	used to denote rational desire

INDEX

The Oxford World's Classics Website

www.worldsclassics.co.uk

- Browse the full range of Oxford World's Classics online

- Sign up for our monthly e-alert to receive information on new titles

- Read extracts from the Introductions

- Listen to our editors and translators talk about the world's greatest literature with our Oxford World's Classics audio guides

- Join the conversation, follow us on Twitter at OWC_Oxford

- Teachers and lecturers can order inspection copies quickly and simply via our website

www.worldsclassics.co.uk

American Literature

British and Irish Literature

Children's Literature

Classics and Ancient Literature

Colonial Literature

Eastern Literature

European Literature

Gothic Literature

History

Medieval Literature

Oxford English Drama

Poetry

Philosophy

Politics

Religion

The Oxford Shakespeare

A complete list of Oxford World's Classics, including Authors in Context, Oxford English Drama, and the Oxford Shakespeare, is available in the UK from the Marketing Services Department, Oxford University Press, Great Clarendon Street, Oxford OX2 6DP, or visit the website at www.oup.com/uk/worldsclassics.

In the USA, visit www.oup.com/us/owc for a complete title list.

Oxford World's Classics are available from all good bookshops. In case of difficulty, customers in the UK should contact Oxford University Press Bookshop, 116 High Street, Oxford OX1 4BR.

Bhagavad Gita

The Bible Authorized King James Version
With Apocrypha

Dhammapada

Dharmasūtras

The Koran

The Pañcatantra

**The Sauptikaparvan (from the
Mahabharata)**

**The Tale of Sinuhe and Other Ancient
Egyptian Poems**

The Qur'an

Upaniṣads

ANSELM OF CANTERBURY   **The Major Works**

THOMAS AQUINAS   **Selected Philosophical Writings**

AUGUSTINE   **The Confessions
On Christian Teaching**

BEDE   **The Ecclesiastical History**

HEMACANDRA   **The Lives of the Jain Elders**

KĀLIDĀSA   **The Recognition of Śakuntalā**

MANJHAN   **Madhumalati**

ŚĀNTIDEVA   **The Bodhicaryāvatāra**

	Late Victorian Gothic Tales
JANE AUSTEN	**Emma**
	Mansfield Park
	Persuasion
	Pride and Prejudice
	Selected Letters
	Sense and Sensibility
MRS BEETON	**Book of Household Management**
MARY ELIZABETH BRADDON	**Lady Audley's Secret**
ANNE BRONTË	**The Tenant of Wildfell Hall**
CHARLOTTE BRONTË	**Jane Eyre**
	Shirley
	Villette
EMILY BRONTË	**Wuthering Heights**
ROBERT BROWNING	**The Major Works**
JOHN CLARE	**The Major Works**
SAMUEL TAYLOR COLERIDGE	**The Major Works**
WILKIE COLLINS	**The Moonstone**
	No Name
	The Woman in White
CHARLES DARWIN	**The Origin of Species**
THOMAS DE QUINCEY	**The Confessions of an English Opium-Eater**
	On Murder
CHARLES DICKENS	**The Adventures of Oliver Twist**
	Barnaby Rudge
	Bleak House
	David Copperfield
	Great Expectations
	Nicholas Nickleby
	The Old Curiosity Shop
	Our Mutual Friend
	The Pickwick Papers